Hugh Brune lives in London. He is the author of one previous novel, *Your House is Mine*

Also by Hugh Brune

Your House is Mine

Daytrippers

HUGH BRUNE

SCEPTRE

Copyright © 1999 Hugh Brune
First published in 1999 by Hodder and Stoughton
A division of Hodder Headline
A Sceptre Paperback

The right of Hugh Brune to be identified as the Author of
the Work has been asserted by him in accordance with the
Copyright, Designs and Patents Act 1988.

10 9 8 7 6 5 4 3 2 1

A CIP catalogue record for this title is available from
the British Library

ISBN 0 340 71875 7

Printed and bound in Great Britain by
Mackays of Chatham PLC, Chatham, Kent.

Hodder and Stoughton
A division of Hodder Headline
338 Euston Road
London NW1 3BH

For my parents

'*C'est l'histoire d'un mec qui tombe d'un immeuble de cinquante étages.*
A chaque étage, au fur et à mesure de sa chute, le mec n'arrête pas de
se répéter:

Jusqu'ici tout va bien
Jusqu'ici tout va bien
Jusqu'ici tout va bien

Tout ça c'est pour dire que l'important, c'est pas la chute ... c'est
l'atterrissage.'

from *La Haine*, written and directed by Matthieu Kassovitz,
produced by Christophe Rossignon

'And it's been my luck to live to tell
The only tale I can
It don't hurt you when you fall
Only when you land'

from 'Over the Waterfall' by Michelle Shocked

00.01

Riley was dreaming . . . His usual dream. In a plane, the door wide open, everyone shouting at him that he's the next to go. But he hasn't got a chute, his back feels empty and weightless where the chute should be, *he hasn't got a chute!* He imagines himself, as he often does at this point, as a cartoon character running over the edge of a cliff, running off a cliff and keeping going, running and running and running on thin air, running until his legs stop moving and he looks down . . .

He focuses on the light: red for ready. He feels sick in his stomach; the low-flying Hercules always makes him feel this way. Lieutenant Stuart steps up to him and shouts in his face: You're next, Riley! But, sir, I haven't . . . *You're next!*

He takes a step forward, into thin air, and begins the fall . . .

00.01

Meanwhile, as the clocks all over London slipped past midnight, Candy stood shaking and terrified in George Johnson's office with a gun pressed against her head. Not just any gun either. This, as Johnson was at pains to point out, was a French gun. A bloody good-for-nothing frog gun, he kept calling it. A bloody froggy rivet-rivet Monsieur je ne sais pas cordon bleu useless bloody frog gun. He was quite clear on the point.

Candy peered at the weapon out of the corner of her eye. It was fuzzy and distorted at the extremity of her vision, but as far as she could tell it was an ordinary gun: black, hard, metallic. It felt cold against her cheek the way a gun should. Not that Candy was an expert on guns.

'Don't know why you're so bleeding scared,' Johnson said. 'Bet this thing don't even work. Bet if I was to pull the trigger nothing would happen. Bloody useless piece of frog shit . . .'

He pulled the gun away slightly from Candy's face and his chubby trigger finger tensed. Candy clamped her eyes shut and focused all her attention on maintaining control of herself. She was aware that in the grand scheme of things, if you were just about to get your head blown off at close range it didn't much matter whether you'd pissed yourself first or not, but this gave her something to concentrate on. Something other than that gun. She pressed her legs tightly together, gripped her blouse with both hands, held her breath.

But the shot never came. Instead Johnson withdrew the gun altogether and let out a huge, belching roar of laughter.

'I'm not going to shoot you, old girl! If I wanted to do that I'd have got the boys to do it outside that nightclub of yours, I wouldn't have brought you all the way here to do it. Would I?'

Candy reopened her eyes and stared directly ahead. Of course, put like that it made perfect logical sense, but somehow her sense of logic seemed to have deserted her for the moment. Johnson was moving over to his desk in the corner of his spacious, spartan, entirely book-free office, waving the gun around matter-of-factly as he spoke.

'Anyway, why should I want to shoot you, old girl? What harm have you ever done me? Apart from the obvious . . .'

It was clear from the silence that followed this last remark that it was meant to be some kind of joke. Behind her, Candy heard one of Johnson's men sniggering obediently.

'Come over here and sit down and let's you and me have an old chinwag.' Johnson beckoned her over to the plastic orange primary-school chair facing his desk. 'How was the show tonight?'

A chinwag, thought Candy, how delightful. She sat down gin-gerly. The chair was too small for her and the crisp edges cut into her backside, which was still aching from the kicking. She tried to think back to this evening's show – or at least the first set of this evening's show; she'd been prevented from completing her performance. It could only have been an hour or so since she had left the stage at BabyCakes, but already it seemed like a lifetime ago. A different world altogether. She had, she supposed, been amazing: most nights she was amazing. She had curtsied to thunderous applause, teasingly declined any further encores, graciously deflected some of the ovation towards Simone, her accompanist, received as always two hideously large (and just plain hideous) bouquets from Mr Potts, her number-one fan, and then retired breathlessly to the dressing room to be beastly to Johnny, the stage manager. Oh yes, and *then* she had starrishly refused to sign autographs or speak to anyone waiting outside for her. It had struck her at the time that now she must truly be a star, now she was refusing to meet and greet her audience, now they were nothing more than a burden to her. It had seemed a satisfying revelation. How simple that world seemed to her now, how quaint almost.

'It was fine, I guess,' she said quietly. 'Actually I still had another set to do.'

'Fine?' Johnson said jokingly. 'Only fine?' He looked over at his shaven-headed thugs, still standing sentry-like at the back of the room. 'Les, Bill, how was it really?'

There was no answer immediately and Candy could sense Les and Bill shuffling uneasily on their feet. Candy's show consisted almost entirely of theatrically performed Jacques Brel numbers sung in her own unique brand of Leicestershire French. Something about Les's and Bill's general demeanour – the tattoos, the grade-one haircuts, the turned-up Levis – made you suspect they weren't *huge* Jacques Brel fans.

'How was it really?' Johnson repeated, standing up behind his desk.

'Well, you know guv,' said one of the boys nervously. 'It was bollocks, wasn't it. Bunch of fucking queens singing songs in French.'

3

Johnson marched across the room and whacked the philistine across the face with the handle of his pistol. The boy went down, clutching his nose, which began to spill blood.

'You know your problem, Billy boy?' Johnson said, towering over his crumpled employee, raising his voice only slightly. 'You don't know Art when you see it, do you. You don't know nothing of the finer things in life. Music. Wine. Art. Literature.'

He paused to pull a handkerchief out of his jacket pocket and toss it down for Billy to hold against his nose, so he might stop bleeding all over the carpet.

'Now, I'm willing to bet it was fantastic,' Johnson went on, speaking to the room in general. 'And do you know why I say that, even though obviously I wasn't there myself? I say that because, gentlemen, this lady is an Artiste. We are in the presence of a fucking Ar*tiste* here.' He flung his arms out flamboyantly to indicate Candy, who had discovered that the only way to make the chair bearable was to sit on her hands, and was rocking back and forth, gently trying to shoo her pain and fear away. 'And a true Artiste will never ever give less than one hundred and ten per cent. That's what makes the difference between people like her and people like you.'

He went up to Les, the other monkey boy, and prodded him hard in the chest to emphasise the word *you*.

'To be honest, guv,' Les began bravely, 'we didn't really catch much of the show. We got there just as it was finishing and, you know, we had work to do so we were concentrating on thinking about that rather than anything else, like what was going on on stage. If you see what I mean.'

Johnson shook his head with exaggerated weariness, but refrained from further violence. 'I don't know, I just don't know,' he tut-tutted, walking back over to Candy. 'What do you make of these two? Bet you wonder why you bother, don't you?'

Candy attempted a smile.

'I hope they didn't hurt you bringing you in. This was supposed to be in the nature of an invitation rather than a kidnapping,' said the new, caring, sharing, art- and music-loving George Johnson.

Candy took her hands out from under her backside and rubbed her left arm where it had been twisted and bruised. She fingered the collar of her yellow satin blouse where the blood from the gash across her chin had thickened into a deep stain. She started to say: 'Well, actually . . .'

But Johnson held up a hand to stop her. 'Forget it. I don't give a toss really whether they hurt you or not, and obviously it's not a bloody invitation. I just like saying things I've heard gangsters saying in films. Now . . . down to business, eh?' He exhaled noisily and pulled a cigar out of the box on his desk.

And then, having promised to get down to business, he said nothing at all for ages. He fiddled about with his cigar, twirling it in his fingers, pulling the end off, finally lighting it, leaning back and puffing out satisfying billows of smoke. Saying nothing.

Candy shoved her hands back under her thighs and did her best to ignore the only sound in the room, Billy-boy's moans as he tried to work out whether or not his nose was broken. She looked around the empty, musty office, taking in her surroundings properly for the first time since she had been thrown, whimpering, on the floor on her arrival. It didn't look much like a Nazi's office. Where was the portrait of Hitler? Where were the shelves groaning with semi-legal right-wing literature? Where were the swastikas? The flag of St George draped across the back wall? This was nothing more than a room above an East End sex shop, swept and tidied and transformed into a nondescript office that wouldn't have looked out of place in a City bank. She would have assumed George Johnson's place of work would have reflected a little more of his personality – his viciousness, his insane, half-formed ideology, his desperate emphasis on his own dubious Englishness.

For George Johnson was not George Johnson's real name, a fact which he tried violently to suppress and which almost everybody knew. His real name was Yiorgos Something-or-other-opoulos. Not even George could remember his original surname these days. His parents were Greek Cypriots who had come to London in the fifties, just as the war against the Brits in Cyprus was gathering speed.

5

His father opened a chip shop near Camden tube station and his mother took in sewing. They both worked staggeringly long hours and practically wrecked the relationship within their marriage in order to feed, clothe and educate their son; whereupon Yiorgos passed a couple of O-levels and went off to a sixth-form college to fill his head with fascism. He returned home, aged nineteen, to inform his parents that as far as he was concerned they were lazy bubble immigrant scrounging wankers, little better than the bloody niggers, and he was joining the National Front in order to drive people like them out of his homeland.

But it wasn't just ideology with Johnson. He quickly found that, applied in the right way, nationalist politics could be a nice little moneyspinner. It took you to the edges of the law, brought you into contact with all sorts of people who didn't mind hurting other people to get what they wanted, gave you a purpose and commanded a good deal of fear and respect – well, fear mainly, but there was very little to choose between the two in George's mind. Soon it was hard to tell where the politics ended and the criminal empire began: it was all business of one kind or another. By the end of the seventies he had left the National Front, which had become far too mainstream and respectable for his liking, and started his own splinter organisation, the Bulldog League. He stood for council elections, acquired local businesses (that was the word he preferred to use: *acquired*), put himself about a bit, generally got his name known. And when he was bored of his little patch of London, he looked further afield. Persuading himself that this was all for the greater good of England, he forged links with like-minded businessmen abroad.

One of whom was Jean-Pierre le Blanc. Johnson had been profitably doing business with him for several years. Le Blanc, a former leading light in the *Front National* in Marseille, had relocated to Orléans to make money and be brutal to people. Over the course of six or seven years he had become a highly successful old-school gangster, his fingers deeply immersed in a number of nefarious pies: drug-trafficking, gambling rings, prostitution, protection rackets, the occasional bit of arms-smuggling, the regular portfolio of criminal interests. Le Blanc also of course maintained his links with the far-right community (and these days it really was a community: a continent-wide network of Eurofascists, united against European unity) which is what brought him into contact with George Johnson. They became trading partners, exchanged information, organised football riots, laundered money and hid weapons for each other. Le Blanc's reputation rested on widely spread rumours that he had once tortured his own nephew in order to glean information about a political rival. He was one of the few genuinely awe-inspiring men that George Johnson, who was not much prone to awe, had ever met. It was le Blanc's gun, the useless piece of frog shit, sitting, gleaming on the desk, tantalisingly out of Candy's reach – not that she'd have had the guts to do anything about it anyhow.

'Got a job for you, old girl,' Johnson said finally.

Candy looked up. Maybe, after all, there was going to be a point to this, other than just beating her up because it passed the time.

'A little bird tells me you're going to France tomorrow.'

Candy shook her head. 'No, not me. Some of the others . . .' she began to say.

Johnson interrupted her. 'I said you're going to France tomorrow, it's not a fucking question.' He paused for Candy to nod. 'Those little God-botherers who run that dirty, horrible hostel you live in are organising a daytrip for you all tomorrow. Now, normally hearing about this sort of thing would drive me up the bloody wall, throwing away good, honest taxpayers' money on taking a bunch of fucking scroungers on a booze cruise, but it just so happens I can put this one to some use.'

Candy was struck by this heartfelt complaint on behalf of good, honest taxpayers from a man who was neither good nor honest nor, she strongly suspected, in any meaningful way a taxpayer.

'So you're going on this trip,' he went on. 'Frankly I think it would be rude of you not to go, after all the effort that's been put in. And you're going to take this gun with you, which happens to belong to my colleague and business partner, Monsieur Jean-Pierre le Blanc.' He exaggerated the vowel sounds in the name. 'You speak French, old girl?'

Candy shook her head.

'Then what are you doing singing all those froggy songs in your show?'

Belgian songs actually, but Candy felt it might not be wise to correct him. Probably Belgians counted as honorary froggies anyway.

Johnson picked up the gun again. 'What's the matter, don't you like English songs or something?' he said, absent-mindedly pointing it at Candy. She gripped the chair again.

'It's not that . . .'

'What about The Who? You like The Who?'

Candy wasn't sure how to answer. 'Uh-huh,' she nodded nervously.

'And The Jam. You must like The Jam.'

What was Candy supposed to say? She'd never discussed pop music at gunpoint before.

'You know what song you should do . . . ? "English Rose"! That's a beautiful song, that is.' He launched into a verse of it.

'Well, actually,' Candy said, more to shut him up than anything, 'I've been thinking of incorporating some English songs into the set . . . you know, mixing *chansons* with English pop ballads . . . I think it might work.'

Johnson smiled. 'Anyway, back to this trip of yours. You're going to go and you're going to take Monsieur le Blanc's gun back to him. You deliver it to this address.'

He pushed a piece of paper across the desk to Candy. It had the name and address of a bar scrawled on it. Le Chat Noir, Avenue de Paris, Orléans. She picked it up and read it.

'This is in Orléans.'

'Well spotted, old girl. I knew you'd be right for this job.'

'But we're going to Calais. I don't even know where Orléans is.'

Johnson sounded exasperated. 'Look at a fucking map before you go. What you do is this: you go as far as Calais with your mates, then slip away and go down to Orléans. It's just a little bit south of Paris, OK? And Avenue de Paris is right by the train station, I think I'm right in saying, so it should be easy enough to find. Just ask for the station. Jean-Pierre'll no doubt slip you a few quid for giving him his gun back, so you'll be able to get home no problem. And Bob's your uncle. Easy.'

'But how do I get there?'

'Look, you're going to have a fucking gun on you, you'll find you can go pretty much where you want.' He flicked open the gun and showed it to Candy. 'Look at this, right? It's a PA15, the magazine holds fifteen rounds, that means you can shoot up to fifteen people in order to get a ride to Orléans. OK? Piece of fucking piss, even for someone like you.'

Candy still looked unsure. It was a horrible situation. On the one hand she was comprehensively terrified of George Johnson, and especially his monkey boys (there again, she suspected she was going to get another kicking before she left whether she agreed to this insane plan or not); on the other hand, she really, absolutely, didn't want any part of this.

'It won't work,' she said, shaking her head. 'I'll never get it through customs, they always stop people like me because of the way I look.'

Johnson looked her up and down; he'd almost forgotten while they were talking just how repulsive she was. The sight of her sickened him all over again. George Johnson had room enough in his heart to hate a lot of people: he hated, personally and without prejudice, frogs, krauts, I-ties, niggers, spics, wops, dagos, commies, Pakis, bubbles (especially the fucking bubbles), yids, towelheads, dykes, social workers, Christians, charity workers and coppers. But most of all, more than any of these, he hated people like Candy. He fucking *hated* poofs.

For Candy wasn't Candy's real name either. Nor was she strictly speaking a she, not in the usual, biological, *genital* sense of the word. Candy Skinn was simply a stage name; but, as she liked to point out, the whole world was Candy's stage. Her real name, the one on her passport, was Stephen Hall. Her mother still called her Stephen; no one else did.

Johnson felt his stomach heave just looking at her. He stood up and instructed his boys to hold her down. They obliged, pulling her arms out from underneath her and pinning them roughly behind the chair.

'No, please, I'll do it . . . !' she managed to splutter before the blow across the face.

There were three more blows and then Johnson crouched down so his face was very close to Candy's. 'The subject's not up for fucking discussion,' he said. 'You're going to France and you're taking this gun and that's that. Now, if you don't feel you can make it through customs yourself, get one of the others to do it for you. Someone who looks a bit more fucking normal. There must be someone in that shit-hole of yours who owes you a favour, someone you've got something on – get them to do it for you. I don't care how the bloody thing gets there, just as long as it does.'

Candy mumbled OK. She could feel her eye swelling up.

'Right, boys, let him go,' Johnson ordered. 'Billy, give him the hanky.'

Billy handed Candy the handkerchief, which was soaked through with his own blood. She mopped gently at the fresh cut beneath her left eye.

'You know what, old girl?' Johnson said as he retook his seat. 'As much as I want to keep up good relations with Jean-Pierre, part of me really hopes you fuck this up so I can come and find you and sort you out. Just remember that.'

He pushed the gun across the desk.

Candy picked the weapon up nervously and examined it. Her finger found the trigger. This was her chance. The gun was fully loaded, she'd been shown. All she had to do was point it at this bastard across the desk and pull the trigger. She might have to take out the other two as well, but in all probability not. She reckoned they'd be glad to see their bullying governor with his brains on the floor.

Johnson grinned broadly. 'You wouldn't fucking dare,' he said. And of course she wouldn't. They all knew that.

'Anyway,' he went on, 'bet you nothing would happen even if you tried. Fucking useless piece of rivet-rivet frog shite.'

He roared with laughter again.

Candy

BabyCakes. The first time I ever went there, I knew I'd come home. The stage, the glitterball, the tables with candles, the menus in French, the men with cigars, the spangly dressed boy waitresses, the lights, the music, the whole big bundle of sophistication and glamour. Yes, that's it, more than anything else it was the glamour. It was the kind of glamour that sends shivers down your spine (if you're prone to that sort of thing), makes you all goose-pimply. I was just a small-town queen from the Midlands. Before then I'd only ever seen wasted glamour or faded glamour or ironic, postmodern, make-believe glamour or tragic, not-quite-there glamour: this, though, this is *glamorous* glamour. Know what I mean?

I'm sitting at one of the tables at the back with a middle-aged punter in an expensive-looking Italian suit. He's going to be one of the good guys, I can tell. After you've been doing the job a while, you can tell. This one's been a sweetie right from the word go. He's pulled up in his polished green MG, driven slowly past the line of boys, all pouting and cooing at him because they know he's one of the good guys, then he's picked me out and beckoned me over. I can't believe my luck: he's not fat, he's not stubbly, he doesn't appear to smell (or rather he does smell: he smells of some *divinely* expensive aftershave). He's not handsome exactly, his chin is crooked and his eyes just slightly too far apart, but he's immaculately groomed, which counts for more in my book. It's not often you get job satisfaction in my line of work, but when you do get it, boy do you get it. You get well and truly *satisfied*. He's just been to see this really interesting play at the National Theatre, he tells me,

11

and now he's looking for a date to take in a club with him, have a few drinks and maybe something to eat. So I've climbed in next to him, felt that leather upholstery squirming against my thighs, waved grandly at the other boys and I'm having to remind myself that this guy's a punter and I must get some money from him at the end of the evening and not fall madly and disastrously in love with him. Then he's driven me very quickly into the West End and brought me to this place. And now: now he's only gone and ordered bloody champagne! Champagne! Just the word makes me giggly.

The waitress smiles sweetly at him and says that the cheapest bottle they have is fifty-five pounds; to which he snorts and says, well in that case we'll have the most expensive then. And then he turns to me and winks. He *winks* at me – I nearly die.

Once the waitress is gone, he takes my hand across the table. So you been here before? he asks. No never. Like it? Oh God yes. It's ... it's marvellous, I tell him breathlessly, actually meaning what I say for once. Feels peculiar to be talking straight with a punter. Yes I like it, he says, they're very uh discreet in here. And they usually put on a good show. He falls silent, stroking my hand and gazing at my face as if he's trying to work out where he's seen me before. I pull out a ciggie and light it, finding my hand shaking slightly as I do so. He declines to join me, just carries on gazing. After a while I realise he's probably waiting for me to say something. I rack my brains for something to talk about, something that's not too tacky or too boring, and eventually ask him about the play he's been to see. Oh it was all right, he goes, quite good actually. It was about these four people, two men and two women, who fall in and out of love with each other over a number of years. Good story, funny dialogue and lots and lots of swearing – he leans forward, bringing us closer together – call me old fashioned but I *like* a lot of swearing, he says. Honestly it was fuck this and fuck that and fuck the other. Of course it was all wildly heterosexual. The guys didn't fall in love with each *other* needless to say, that would have been just too interesting ...

I nod my head to try and show interest, but once he's finished telling me about it I've nothing to add, so we fall back into silence and then he starts staring at me again. How long have you been dressing like that? he asks me. Like what? I say although obviously I know what he means. You know . . . the leggings, the blouse, the make-up . . . Like a woman you mean? Yeah. I sigh a deep one. I don't know, I reply, I suppose I started experimenting with my mother's clothes when I was in my early teens, you know, when my parents were out and stuff; they never really accepted it. But now . . . now I live away from home I pretty much wear what I want. And I think this stuff suits me . . . I look over to the punter for signs of encouragement. Don't you? He just looks off into the distance, staring at the empty stage.

But you're still a boy right? Underneath? he goes eventually.

I know what he's getting at. I feel soiled and abused by the question. Yeah, I tell him, I'm still a boy.

Not for long, though, I think to myself – and I start entertaining wild fantasies about this guy falling hopelessly in love with me and insisting on paying for my operation, selling his MG to finance it. Then we're married and living in a tumbledown cottage in the country with a garden and a stream at the bottom of the garden and we've got dogs and we've adopted children and the children have swings and slides in the garden which they're playing on . . . This make-believe world takes on a momentum of its own, galloping away in my imagination, adding detail after detail.

The waitress arrives with the champagne. She sets down two tall, thin glasses on our table, pops open the bottle, and fills them brimful with bubbles, all the while smiling a sweet, sweet smile. That OK gentlemen? she says. Fine thanks. Yeah lovely. We're sitting in awkward silence and I realise our conceit is broken. Up to now she might have taken us for lovers on a date, the way he's been holding my hand and looking at me, but this silence, the very uncomfortableness of it, lets the whole world know who we are: trade and punter doing business, turning a trick. Nothing more. So what do you do? I ask him in another clumsy attempt at small talk. I work in banking, he replies without expanding. We fall back into silence and are still sitting in silence when the lights go down and the show begins. An impossibly tall MC in a pink tuxedo takes to the stage. I've no idea what to expect; I'm just relieved we don't have to try and talk any more. He tells a couple of exceptionally lame jokes (not even I laugh, and I'll laugh at pretty much anything, especially when I've been drinking champagne), says hello to his special friends in the audience and then asks us to please put our hands together and give a warm BabyCakes welcome for . . . Nigella!

And the crowd goes wild.

Nigella *glides* on to the stage. She is the loveliest, most imposing thing I have ever seen. Eight foot six, at *least* eight foot six, wearing a deep blue ribboned dress that Shirley Bassey would die for. Or more likely kill for. She makes the impossibly tall MC look like Kylie Minogue in high heels. Bouquets and confetti are thrown, balloons cascade from the ceiling, the audience claps and stamps and whoops and hollers. When it eventually dies down the small band strike up a few chords and Nigella launches into 'I Am A Woman In Love', the Barbra Streisand song. And I realise, joltingly, that right here, right now, I have discovered my calling in life. I want to be this woman. I want to *be* this woman. Just listen to her! Her voice is rough and raspy from too many cigarettes, but she has a set of lungs that could power a jet plane. She belts this song out. And this is a song that can take some belting. I AM A WOMAN IN LOVE! she belts. I lean over and grab the punter by the arm. I've got to let him know, I've got to make him understand how I feel. At last I have something *real* to tell him. This is what I want to do! I yell at him feverishly above the music, pointing over to the stage. I want to be like her! He smiles kindly. Well you've got to follow your dream, he says. My dream . . . I sit and watch Nigella, enraptured, hardly touching my champagne. I imagine myself floating across the crowded tables, down on to the stage and into her head. Through Nigella's eyes I can see the microphone stand silhouetted against the tumbling dry ice and beyond that the dusky shapes that I know to be my audience, and perhaps the occasional twinkle of a lit cigarette. I can hear myself singing, I can hear the band playing and most of all, above it all, I can hear the applause. The applause sounds like strawberries taste. It sends shivers all the way through me, the very glamour of it turning me on.

So you do much singing? says the punter as a song finishes and I'm lapping up the adulation. Snapping me right out of it. Uh a little. Mostly in the bath. You know. He smiles again, just a little less kindly this time. You got to practise a lot to get as good as her, he tells me – like he's my dad or something. It's a long way from walking the streets to working a class joint like this.

What's he trying to say?

He can see the disappointment on my face. Hey come on I didn't mean to shatter your illusions, he says, it's just that I know how hard it can be. He looks thoughtful for a moment. I was going to be an actor when I was younger, he goes on, went to a lot of auditions, got a few small parts in plays, even did a couple of adverts . . . hey you remember those Mars bar ads, bunch of teenagers at school, then playing football and swimming and stuff, then at home watching the telly . . . ? Sure you do . . . Nope. Never heard of them, but I nod enthusiastically. Don't ever forget: you're the one up for rent, he's paying, of *course* you remember his advertisements. You *loved* his advertisements. Well I was the kid with glasses, he goes on, the swotty-looking one . . . He waits for a reaction from me and I try a few wow noises. Then his face goes all glum again. But it never got any better than that, he says sadly, I got uglier as I got older, I was in a few things that bombed, one or two lousy reviews that singled me out, my agent dropped me, it all dried up by the time I was twenty . . . and so I ended up in banking, which I guess has its own rewards . . . He fingers the sleeve of his perfectly cut jacket and once again looks over to me for a reaction. Underneath it all, of course, he *is* an actor; can't perform without an audience. I'm getting kind of tired of this though. OK sweetie-pie you fucked up your dream. Doesn't mean that I have to fuck up mine too. Look all I'm saying, he drones on, all I'm saying, right, is hold on to your dream but you know don't go to pieces if it doesn't work out for you . . . OK?

We go back to listening to Nigella, who's now moved on to 'I Will Always Love You', but I can sense the punter's still all agitated; he keeps fidgeting and smoothing back his hair and he's stopping me from concentrating. I want to get back inside Nigella's head. Finally he taps me on the shoulder. Got to go to the men's room, he says. OK, I nod. No: with you. I look over at him. It isn't an invitation. I-EE-I-EE-I, sings Nigella as we cross the crowded floor, squeezing between tables, excusing ourselves, WILL ALWAYS LOVE YOU-OU. It's not too obvious, is it, two guys at the same table get up and go off to the lavatory together. Inside the gents he kicks open one of the cubicles and manhandles me inside. He shuts the door behind him but doesn't bother to lock it and starts breathing in my ear. Say eat me, he tells me urgently. Uh . . . eat me? Say it like you mean it! Eat me. What do you want me to do? Eat me! What? EAT ME! (Actually I want him to stop licking my face like a dog and let me go back inside to catch the rest of the show, but business is business.) After a bit of fumbling he teases my meal ticket out of my leggings and drops to his knees. This has all taken me rather by surprise and I'm still flabby and unprepared. I close my eyes, grit my teeth and try to act like a professional. I've been here before (haven't we all?). I think first of all the lovers I've ever had, not punters, proper lovers, the ones I actually fancied, one by one . . . then Mr Dawson, my old English teacher . . . finally Chris Isaak in the Wicked Game video . . . bingo. It doesn't take long – practice makes perfect. I shoot a respectable load into his mouth and sit down on the toilet seat to get my head together. Then it gets ugly. He spits the load back out all over my blouse, chucks a couple of crumpled fifties in my face – twice the normal fee, not to mention all that champagne – and then he walks out muttering, loudly so he knows I can hear, fucking slut, singer my arse, cheap good-for-nothing whore . . .

I sit back on the toilet waiting for my head to clear and for the tears I know are on their way. Blubbing away, I clean myself up the best I can and practically run out of the place, crying my eyes out like a fucking baby. On the way out Nigella is singing 'I Will

Survive'. GO ON NOW, GO! she's singing. WALK OUT THE DOOR! I don't think I can bear it.

06.45

Riley woke up and farted. Or maybe it was the fart that woke him up; it usually took a violent bodily function of some description to rouse him from his catatonic slumbers these days. Moved unconsciously by the hunger in the pit of his belly and the pounding in his head, he fumbled for the small, fiddly set of keys in his trouser pocket. One of the keys – the smallest, fiddliest one – opened his bedside cabinet which contained the remnants of a can of Tennent's Extra, specially, lovingly saved from last night and locked away. Because if it hadn't been locked away and the key secreted about his person, someone else would have had it five minutes after he'd dropped off; he wouldn't even have heard them come into the room.

And the one thing Riley needed, before he'd even shaken the sleep from his eyes, was a drink.

It took Herculean will power to stop his hand shaking enough to get the key into the lock. He gripped the small, fiddly thing as tightly as he could between his thumb and forefinger, so tight the skin began to redden, and fixed his eyes on the lock. Key and lock drifted muggily in and out of focus, he banged the key clumsily a number of times against the outer casing of the lock; it made a disheartening clunk every time he did so. He held his right wrist in his left hand, willing it to stop shuddering, and kept on trying. Fortunately he was used to Herculean will power at this time in the morning, it was a regular requirement, and on maybe the eighth or ninth attempt the key finally slotted home. He reached inside the cabinet, tenderly grasped the can and brought it to his lips . . . Oh boy. The beer was warm and flat and looked like it had bits of cigarette ash floating in it. It was the best he'd ever tasted.

Slowly other things came into focus, things that weren't locks or keys or cans of lager, the shaking subsided to a manageable tremor, the pounding became a tapping. Oh yeah, *that* was better. Once again the words of Dean Martin floated into his head. I feel sorry for people who don't drink (Dean was supposed to have said) because when they wake up in the morning, that's as good as they're going to feel all day. Wise words. Riley could feel himself becoming more human, or less inhuman, with every second that passed. He took another drink.

You weren't really supposed to drink in the bedrooms. In fact you weren't supposed to drink anywhere in the hostel apart from the coyly named 'wet room' (so called, as far as Riley could see, because people seemed to go there in order to wet themselves). But what the hell. All the other men in their rooms were either asleep or also drinking. The only two members of staff would probably be downstairs feeding their faces with breakfast, or else they'd still be asleep too. Even if they came up they'd be cool about it. Most of the people who worked here understood that a man needed a drink first thing in the morning. The only one you had to watch out for was Philip, the hostel manager, the bloody jobsworth. Flipping Philip they all called him because he seemed to have learned how to swear from watching *Grange Hill*. Blimey! he'd say when something went wrong. Crikey! I say! Gosh! He'd always been a pain in the arse, both to staff and residents, but had become even more unbearable recently following a few little thefts of hostel property. Apart from the telly going walkabout, which was of course a serious matter, these thefts were mostly minor things: glasses mainly, a few plates and pieces of cutlery, just the occasional item of furniture. Nothing untoward. It was only natural really: you fill a hostel up with people who like to drink and can't afford to drink, stuff is going to go missing. Philip, however, had seen this as an excuse to introduce something approaching martial law. Break one of his precious rules and you got a written warning; break another and you got booked out. No trial, no jury. It worked like the red and yellow card system, he told everyone cheerfully. You blokes all understand the rules of flipping football, don't you? Bloody stuck-up middle-class bloody berk. Reminded Riley of some of the chinless wonders he'd known in the army. Still, Philip never got in before eight thirty. So by that time it was a good idea to have got up, had a couple of drinks and your breakfast and settled down in the wet room or preferably, if it was a nice day or you had some work on, got out of the place altogether.

Riley drained his can and walked unsteadily down the corridor to the stairs. The first few steps of the day were always the most difficult – he'd get the hang of it again pretty soon. 'Morning Riley,' called a couple of the blokes as he plodded by and he grunted a reply. The smells and the sounds of this place never changed: the smell of unbathed, drinking men, of disinfectant sprayed liberally everywhere, of stale cigarette smoke and hash, of vomit, of piss, of Belinda, the large West Indian breakfast cook frying the fuck out of anything in the kitchen that wasn't nailed down; and the sound of wheezing and coughing, of snoring and spluttering, of ringpulls cracking open. And above all, every bloody morning, the sound of people whinging.

Benny, sitting on the bed in Diesel Dave's room: 'Oh come on, Diesel, what do we have to get up now for? It's not even seven,' he was whinging.

Diesel Dave whinging back: 'Hey, Ben, give us a cig . . .'

Benny: 'We smoked them all last night.'

Dave: 'No we didn't. I kept a butt specially for this morning.'

Benny: 'Yeah, I smoked it after you fell asleep. They're all gone, Diesel.'

Dave: 'You never! You bastard!'

And so on. Every morning, whinge moan, the same thing, day after day after day.

'Anyway,' said Benny, 'you still haven't said what we're getting up this early for. This is unholy, this is.'

'It's the trip,' said Diesel. 'Got to get out of the place before seven thirty, otherwise we'll get roped into going.'

Mention of the trip stirred something in Riley. Instinctively he reached into his pocket, not for his keys this time but for a folded-up scrap of paper just as precious to him. He opened it and read the name and address scrawled in his own drunken hand. Riley had kept this name and address in his pocket for eight years. Every couple of years or so, when it looked like the ink might be fading or the edges of the paper were getting too worn and dog-eared and he was afraid it would tear, he would copy it out afresh. This particular scrap was maybe six months old. He tried yet again to memorise the words just in case by some terrible accident he lost it, but it was no use. His memory was shot to fuck. He couldn't remember what he was doing two days ago, let alone all these words making up a whole name and address, most of which were in a foreign language.

He butted in on Benny and Diesel. 'So you two faggots not coming then?'

'Fuck off Riley,' said Diesel. 'All the way to France with that shower of bleeding do-gooders? You must be joking. They'll have us handing out leaflets, going to prayer meetings, God knows what.'

Riley looked at him. 'Leave it out. It won't be nothing like that. It'll just be a laugh. You know, bit of a booze cruise . . . Benny, you're coming, aren't you?'

Benny shook his head. 'Sorry mate, it's not for me. I'm going down the park same as usual, drink some whisky, talk to the ducks.'

Riley didn't like the sound of this. While he didn't particularly want to spend the day with these two, usually he made a point of getting a long way away from them in fact, a disturbing thought had struck him. What would happen if not enough people wanted to go on the trip? Would they call the whole thing off? A lot of the bedroom doors, he noticed, were already open and the beds empty.

'Come on Diesel,' he pleaded. It stuck in the gut to have to plead. 'There won't be no God stuff. Honest, I promise you. This isn't even a church bloody hostel.'

'It isn't?'

'No.' Of course it bloody wasn't.

'Hang on.' Dave looked confused. 'Isn't this St Stephen's?'

Riley shook his head. 'No. It's Stamford Street. You're in

Stamford Street, Diesel. Nothing to do with no church. No God stuff at all.'

Diesel Dave looked at his surroundings, blinking, as though scales had just fallen biblically from his eyes. '*Stam*ford Street . . .' he murmured to himself. 'Well, bugger me . . .' Then he shrugged and pointed to Benny with his thumb. 'Sorry mate. I got to stay with him. He owes me a smoke.'

Riley turned his lip up. 'OK, fuck the both of you then.' He turned away. 'Glad you're not coming.'

Benny and Diesel gathered up their stuff. It looked like a good time to make a move. Riley walked up and down the corridor, knocking on doors, checking on who was left.

No one was left. Not one fucker at all, apart from a snoring lump in the far room, audible all the way down the corridor, which he knew to be Peter Freeman. Freeman was a thieving, conniving little bastard – which didn't exactly set him apart among the residents of Stamford Street, but there was something about the way he possessed these qualities – and Riley would almost rather have not gone at all than go with him. It was Freeman who'd stolen the colour TV out of the wet room a few weeks ago and sold it down the market for booze money and since then, not only had they had to watch their telly on a fuzzy black and white portable which was bloody useless for the football, reminded Riley of watching *Match of the Day* when he was a kid, but it was this theft particularly which had led to Flipping Philip acting like he was running a prison rather than a hostel, issuing yellow and red cards all over the shop like a foreign referee. Also Freeman was the biggest bloody moaner of the lot of them. He made you want to punch him every time he opened his mouth.

He got to the end of the corridor. No one. Peter Freeman was the *only* person left.

The bastards. The ungrateful, selfish, small-minded bastards.

He ran down the stairs, or at least got as close to running as he ever did these days. At the bottom was Dougal Fraser. Dougal was a tall, wiry man, mild mannered to the point of being annoying.

At least Riley found it annoying. The word *wuss* seemed to have been invented to describe Dougal. Private Godfrey out of *Dad's Army* could have had him in a fight. Riley went up to him and grabbed his collar. 'Dougal, you're coming on this trip to France, right? *Right?*'

'Oh yes. Yes, of course I am,' said Dougal. 'My sister wants me to get some shopping for her.'

Riley had already drawn back his fist, ready to thump some compliance into him. He managed to stop himself short. 'Oh,' he said. 'Well . . . great.'

'I'm just waiting for them now as it happens,' Dougal went on. 'Frank said seven thirty and I thought it would be best to be a few minutes early.'

Riley loosened his grip on Dougal's throat and straightened his tie for him – the man was wearing a tie for fuck's sake. 'I'll see you later then, Doogie. Now don't you go hiding yourself away anywhere. OK?'

He marched into the dining room where half a dozen burping and hungover men were munching on their breakfasts with an air of resignation.

'OK, listen up the lot of you,' he barked at them. 'You're all coming to France on the trip today. Right?'

It was a technique he'd picked up in the Paras. How to make a polite invitation extended to a group of people sound like a deep and personal threat made to each member of that group individually. It was one of the first things they looked for when selecting those with officer potential.

The man furthest from the door, Mikey Williams, raised a tentative hand. Riley went over and stood above him to convince him of the need to think extremely carefully before opening his mouth.

'What do you reckon, Riley?' Mikey said when he had finished his mouthful of toast. 'Is there a beach there?'

'Course there's a beach. It's by the sea, isn't it. Bound to be a beach.'

Mikey nodded. 'And are we going to have to pay for anything?'

Riley roared with laughter. 'Course not! None of us have got any money, have we? Eh?' He turned around to indicate the room in general, to reinforce the point that it was largely full of people who didn't have any money, and saw that Mad Freddie, the nearest to the door, was making a dash for it. 'FREDDIE!' he yelled. 'You bastard! Come back here!'

Jumping over a couple of tables with something approaching agility, he gave chase to Mad Freddie. Out of the dining room, down the corridor, through the front door. He saw Freddie disappearing left down Stamford Street and then ducking into Broadwall. He kept on going, he wasn't having this; he wasn't having people just running away from him like this. He followed Freddie through Gabriel's Wharf, past the sandwich shop and the pizza restaurant and the cluster of benches where he often sat drinking, facing the river on sunny afternoons, and halfway to the bloody South Bank before it dawned on him that while he was busy doing this, practically killing himself in the process, the others would be breezily slipping off in the other direction. Freddie was pulling away from him; almost out of sight. Riley stopped running and started coughing. Jesus, he was unfit. Who'd have believed in the army he used to run ten miles a day. With all kinds of shit on his back as well. A long time ago . . . He turned and walked quickly back to the hostel.

Of course. By the time he got back all the others had pissed off too. All except Dougal and Mikey and the poof, the young one who liked to dress himself up as a girl, who was coming out of the staff ladies toilet, which he insisted on using. This one looked in a bad way – cut on his cheek, gash across his chin, bruises all over his face. He had make-up on, but not like he usually did, slapped all over his face, just enough to cover the worst of the bruises. Queer bashers must have caught him last night.

'Hey, you OK?' Riley said, still gasping for breath.

'Yeah,' the lad replied. 'Just walked into a couple of doors . . . I'm looking forward to the trip, aren't you?' He was wearing reasonably normal – for him – clothes. Men's clothes at least:

a proper shirt, untucked and dangling down to his knees, and smartish chinos. But then he went and spoiled it all by draping a *handbag* over his shoulder. Honestly, he didn't do himself any favours.

'Yeah, *I'm* looking forward to it,' Riley said, gazing around at the meagre collection of raggedy-arsed drunkards. 'Where's everyone else, though? That's what I want to know. I don't reckon they'll bother if it's just us lot.'

The lad looked alarmed. 'Yeah, you reckon?'

'Stands to reason.'

'But they've got to take us. They promised! I've been looking forward to it . . . it wouldn't be fair.'

'Don't suppose fair comes into it,' said Riley. 'Anyway, I'm starving. I'm going to see if I can get some breakfast . . .' He paused. 'Don't suppose anyone here's got anything to drink?'

He said it just menacingly enough that Mikey produced from the inside pocket of his jacket a small bottle of Bacardi, about a quarter full.

'Cheers. You're a good bloke, Mikey. Always said so.'

Riley drank all but a drop and handed the bottle back to Mikey, who looked at it disparagingly and then finished it off.

Feeling much better, Riley marched back into the now empty dining room and rapped on the door through to the kitchen. Belinda pulled it open and he peered into the hot, smoky room behind her. On her industrial cooker, in a frying pan the size of a paddling pool, she appeared to be frying an entire loaf of bread all at once. For fun, presumably, as there was no one waiting for breakfast.

'What you want?' she said sharply. Riley was trouble.

'Uh, let me see . . . sausage, egg and beans please . . . And maybe a slice of fried bread. If you can spare any.'

'Sure thing. Coming up.'

'Oh, and another thing . . .'

'Yeah?'

'Do you fancy coming to France today, Belinda?'

07.00

Three stops further down the Northern Line, Frank and Jonquil were also having breakfast. Jonquil was having a job keeping her Alpen down this early in the morning. She'd been up since well before the crack of dawn, trying to work out what to wear, what to take with her, worrying unnecessarily about it all. She allowed herself a wry smile as she caught herself packing a book, the battered second-hand copy of *The Go-Between* she had bought for a pound on her and Frank's first ever date, and which she hadn't got around to starting yet. How much time was she going to get to *read* today? She yawned and winced. She was suffering from lack of sleep, a headache and stomach-churning period pains. And Frank was talking about churchy stuff again – something or other to do with helping run the youth club. Jonquil had warned him about bringing up churchy stuff first thing in the morning.

'Remind me again why we're leaving this early,' she interrupted him.

'To beat the rush hour,' said Frank. 'And because we want to be away before Philip shows up because he's still against the whole idea and will probably try and stop us going somehow.'

'Oh yeah . . .'

'Look, it was your idea to go this early, remember? What's the matter now?'

'I don't know . . . I'm just feeling tired and grumpy.'

Silence.

'What?' said Jonquil.

'What do you mean, what?'

'You know. That face.'

'What face?'

'That face you're making. The one you always make.'

She stood up and cleared her half-finished cereal bowl away. 'You know perfectly well,' she said on her way through to the kitchen.

It was going to be a long, long day.

'I love you,' Frank called after her hopefully.

'I love you too,' she called back.

Jonquil

An ice cream?

Yeah . . .

You don't want to come and see me any more because of an ice cream?

Yeah . . . It's not the ice cream itself, more what the ice cream, you know, symbolised.

Must have been some ice cream.

You know, I really think I'm sorted now. All the little things are just falling into place, and that's what I mean about the ice cream. It was only a tiny, tiny thing, but it went *right*, you know? Instead of going wrong.

So you took this as a sign?

Yeah, I guess. It was yesterday and I was walking home from work and it was still blazing hot. You remember how hot it was yesterday? First really hot day of the year, brings everyone out. I was walking through the park, like I always do, and the park was full of all these people sunbathing and jogging and playing football and snogging. And there's this little café in the middle of the park where they sell ice cream, and I walk past this place every day of my life and I've never been in, but yesterday I just thought I really fancy an ice cream. So I went in and got myself one of those 99s, you know, with the Flake sticking out? And I came back outside with my ice cream and before I'd even taken a lick of the ice cream I pulled the Flake out, like, really slowly, eased it out of its hole, and then I started to nibble at it from the ice-cream-covered end, and then when I'd nibbled all the way up to the clean, pure, chocolatey bit of Flake, I dipped that into the ice cream and carried on until all the chocolate was gone. So I'd eaten all of the Flake before I even started on the ice cream. See, that's the way I always used to eat 99s when I was a kid. I hadn't had a 99 for years and years but I hadn't forgotten. I hadn't forgotten the special way I always eat them. Because I think it says a lot about your character and personality, the way you eat something like a 99, don't you? You know, whether you eat the Flake first, like me, or take it bit by bit as it comes, or lick round it carefully, like I've seen some people doing, keeping all of the chocolate till the end and then shoving it with your tongue down into the wafer. You must notice stuff like this in your line of work, yeah? I mean, what my method says about me obviously is that if I see a good time I want to have it right now, you know, no hanging about. I want it all right now and fuck tomorrow – excuse me – because, you know, tomorrow may never come, right? And I think that's a really important, really positive thing to know about myself, that I'm not afraid to go for it. I may have these little doubts from time to time, but basically, deep down, I'm not afraid to go out and get what I want. Right here, right now . . . And then do you know what I did? Right after I'd eaten all of the Flake? I licked all around the hole where it had been, which was all speckled with bits of chocolate, and then, as far as I could, I pushed the ice cream down into the body of the cornet, so I could eat the ice cream and the wafer together. It's my way, it's the way I always do it. I always eat an apple the same way too. And Jaffa cakes, I always eat Jaffa cakes layer by layer. You know, I pick off the chocolate, then lick up the marmaladey stuff and then eat the biscuity bit on its own . . . Gross really . . . But, you want to know the really important thing about this ice cream?

Please . . .

The important thing is, *I went in there and I bought it*. It actually occurred to me to buy it, to treat myself. Last month, last week even, it would never have crossed my mind. Or if it had done,

I wouldn't have had the right money, or I'd have dropped it as soon as I left the shop, or it would've melted all over my hands and clothes, or it wouldn't have tasted good. And boy, let me tell you, this ice cream tasted *fantastic*. I mean, it was only vanilla ice cream, the plainest, boringest kind of ice cream in the world, but I don't know, the taste was somehow sharper, sweeter, fuller than I remember vanilla ice cream being before. And it was proper vanilla too, you know, the proper yellow stuff, not that pale white synthetic gloop they sometimes try and pass off as vanilla . . . you know?

So why this ice cream? Why yesterday?

What do you mean? Why are things looking good for me right now?

Yes.

Well . . . I met this guy.

Ah . . . So it's not just ice cream.

He's really sweet.

Sounds like he must be.

His name's Frank. He's . . . twenty-six. He's a Virgo. He's got shortish brown hair, brown eyes, big bushy eyebrows and he's . . . really sweet. Like I said. He's got a really kind smile. He's one of those people who smile with their eyes, you know? And I think he's going to be really good for me.

You mentioned his star sign. Is that important to you?

Yeah, I don't know . . . No, I guess not. Not really. It's just something to ask a bloke when you first meet him, isn't it. You know, a kind of shorthand. You can ask what he's like without asking any really deep questions straight away and scaring him off.

So you believe that people's personalities are, to some degree, governed by their star signs?

Well . . . no, not really. Not deep down. On a superficial level maybe. Look, all I'm saying is Virgos are supposed to be kind, sweet people and Frank seems like a kind, sweet guy. That's all. OK?

Where did you meet?

Couple of nights ago. I went to this benefit concert at the University of London with my friend Rhona. I've told you about Rhona, right? I'm not quite sure what it was a benefit for. Some kind of animal rights thing, I think. Anti-vivisection or something. Anyway, Rhona used to go out, about a million years ago, with the bass player in the third band on the bill, so we had to go because she wanted to see how he was getting on.

So we went along and it was a student bar with student prices, so we started getting a bit pissed on the cider. And there seemed to be about a hundred bands on and they were all *terrible*. I mean, really bad. They all sounded like they'd been formed about two hours earlier. We didn't even notice Rhona's ex's band when they came on, we'd got so bored of watching by then. And we were too drunk to care.

Anyway, we've had a few ciders and Rhona starts moaning on about how her and me are seeing way too much of each other just recently. I mean, we're best mates and everything, she goes, but the fact that we're spending so much time going out together simply means that neither of us has got a *man*, doesn't it. So I say to her, well here's your chance. Here we are, pissed and leery, in a room full of young, thrusting, inexperienced males who've just arrived at their sexual peak. If we can't score here, we may as well give up and go and live in a fucking convent – excuse me. Yeah, she goes, but take a look around you. Who here would you want to shag?

So we have a look around.

Well him for a start, I say, pointing out Frank, who I've spotted standing on his own at the back of the hall.

OK, says Rhona, without even stopping to think about it, you take him and I'll take the shy-looking blond over there and we'll meet up in the ladies in an hour's time and see if we aren't going home separately tonight.

You know Rhona, she's so competitive. I should've known better than to even get involved in this conversation. So I take a little amble over towards Frank. And this is serious stuff now because you can be pretty sure that Rhona's not going to pull any punches to get what she wants and I can't let her be the only one to score, she'll never shut up about it. So, you know, there's pressure on. So I go up to Frank and I just say to him, straight up, no introduction or warning or nothing, I say: What the hell's a gorgeous bloke like you doing standing on his own then?

I just said it, just like that. I mean, how pissed must I have been to have said something like that? God, it's so unlike me. Anyway, he looks at me kind of nonplussed, like you would if some mad, drunken woman had just come up to you and said that, and he tells me that he came with a mate but they had an argument and his mate's stormed off. Yeah? What you argue about? I ask him. Animal rights, he goes. Animal rights! In my state this just seems like a ridiculous thing to fall out over. Yeah, he goes, this is an animal rights benefit, in case you hadn't noticed. Oh yeah . . . so are you a vegetarian then? I ask him. And I should mention at this point that he was wearing this heavy, brand-new-looking leather jacket. Yeah, he goes. What about the jacket then? I say. That's made out of dead cows. And do you know what his reply was?

What?

It was really funny . . . He goes, get this, right . . . I wasn't planning to eat the jacket! Isn't that the funniest, sweetest thing you've ever heard?

Almost.

So anyway, then we got talking and it turned out he wasn't a student, in fact I don't think he's been to uni at all, he'd just come down to support the cause and I think he'd vaguely heard of one of the bands. Turns out he works at one of those Office Mate shops, you know those huge warehouse places where you can buy folders and computer disks and all the little yellow post-it notes you can handle, and they obviously pay him enough that he can buy brand-new leather jackets. So, a little past his sexual peak unfortunately, but I'm sure he'll make up for it on the experience front.

So you haven't slept with him yet? You didn't go home with him that night?

No. In the end he decided to go and look for his friend to make up with him. So I gave him my phone number and I made it very clear to him that I didn't hand out my phone number to strangers very often, that he was in a *very* privileged position and he wasn't to abuse that privilege. If he accepted my number, I took that as a definite promise that he would call me. And he'd better fucking – sorry – he'd better keep his promises to me. Of course Rhona took the piss something chronic when I met up with her. But then she took her bloke home and shagged him and they've split up already, whereas I've still got the first proper date with mine to come. So, you know, where would you rather be?

So he did call you then?

Very next day. None of this pricking about, playing it cool, making me hang around three or four days. Very next day, yesterday, he calls me up and asks me out. Like a gentleman, you know? So we've got a date on Sunday. And guess where we're going . . . ?

. . . ?

The Tate Gallery. How cool is that? None of this oh why don't we just go for a drink, or let's go to the cinema where we can't see or speak to each other. But the Tate fuck––, the Tate Gallery! We're going to go and be quiet and cultured and talk about interesting things. You know, apart from anything else I've got to show him I can be sober some of the time.

And this is it? You really feel comfortable stopping our sessions now?

Yeah.

It's early days. What if it all goes wrong?

I'm in love. I know it sounds stupid because I've only met him once and I'd had a few at the time. But I really think I'm in love with him. That's what this strange, positive feeling is. That's why I bought the ice cream.

Jonquil . . . it's important not to build your hopes up too much at this stage.

I know. But I'm in love, what can I do? It's happened. I can't decide *not* to be in love, just to try and protect myself. I'm in love and everything is going to work out, I just know it.

I'm sure it will. But I'm always here . . . just in case. You will remember that, won't you.

07.35

It was a tough morning ahead. There were any number of potential disasters as far as Frank could see, and one of Frank's particular skills was identifying potential disasters. First there was the minibus. The charity owned one minibus, a dark blue, dented old Ford with a dodgy ignition. Frank had picked it up from one of the other hostels the previous evening and parked it outside his flat overnight. Would it still be there? And if it was still there, would it start? Frank didn't know a thing about dodgy ignitions. His method for starting cars if they were giving him problems was initially to pray for spiritual guidance and if that failed to swear and hit the bonnet and storm off in a huff. And the engine had been making funny noises last night. He'd listened to it clunking and scraping away all the way from Shepherds Bush to Stockwell.

Then there was the trip itself. He really wasn't sure he'd made it clear enough that the minibus would only hold twenty people.

What if they got there and the whole hostel wanted to come? The blokes didn't get many opportunities like this after all. They'd have to choose who could come and who couldn't and there'd probably be a fight and the whole thing would be terrible. And he was still half-convinced that Flipping Philip was going to show up early and find an excuse to forbid them from going before they'd even left. He'd been so uptight recently.

And lastly there was Jonquil. What was up with her all of a sudden? OK it was, as far as he could remember these things, that time of the month again (he usually remembered because she was very regular and his rent was due around the same time) and certain allowances had to be made; but tired and grumpy didn't begin to cover it. She had gone to bed her usual, calm, pleasant, desirable self and woken up like this, like she was now. Slumped in the passenger seat, feet on the dashboard, hands stuffed into the pockets of her favourite baggy grey cardigan, straining herself to look as glum as possible. He wouldn't have minded so much, but it was her idea. The whole thing. The trip to France was her idea and leaving at the crack of dawn to beat the traffic and their increasingly unhinged boss was her idea as well. She just didn't make any sense sometimes.

So it was with some surprise and relief that Frank found himself, shortly after half past seven, turning into the hostel car park in a resolutely unstolen minibus, engine purring sweetly to find only about half a dozen people waiting outside and the Manager: Strictly Reserved parking space satisfyingly empty.

'Morning all,' he said, climbing down from the vehicle. 'Surely that isn't everyone. Are the others waiting inside?'

'No, I'm afraid this is it,' said Joyce, the other staff member accompanying them. She was waiting outside with the residents, having apparently done her weekly shop on the way into work. She was surrounded by bulging supermarket bags. Frank had actually thought they might do a spot of shopping in France; bringing stuff from Tesco's with you to Calais seemed almost perverse. But he was too concerned by the lack of residents to ask her why she'd felt the need to bring groceries with her. 'The hostel is completely empty apart from the two night-workers,' Joyce added.

'It can't be.' Frank walked past her into the building. Why was he doing this? Surely he didn't think Joyce could have overlooked a large group of residents waiting to go on a daytrip? No, it was just that he couldn't believe it. He couldn't believe that they could put so much effort into organising a day like this and only four of the ungrateful bastards could be bothered to show up. It was hardly worthwhile going as they were.

Jonquil also climbed out of the minibus. Mikey waved at her. 'Morning Jonquil!' he called with a broad grin on his face. Jonquil was his favourite member of staff: her name never ceased to amuse him. He couldn't even pronounce it without a smile. Jonquil! What were her parents thinking of? What names had they rejected in favour of this one? Mikey himself had more children than he cared to remember, by almost as many mothers, and some of them were daughters, and true, it was a bit of a struggle after you'd used up all of the obvious names – Rebecca, Louise, Diana and so on – and had to move into the realm of things like Tara or Marlene, but not even he had been reduced to Jonquil. And he was a piss-artist.

'Hi Mikey,' Jonquil replied, sounding slightly the worse for wear. 'How are you?'

'Looking forward to the trip,' Riley answered for him. 'Aren't you Mikey?'

'Oh yeah. Looking forward to the trip. Especially the beach.' Mikey liked beaches.

'Not many of you, are there?' Jonquil said.

At that moment Frank came out of the hostel again, pushing angrily at the door. 'No, you're right. There's no one there,' he said irritably. 'So what are we going to do? It hardly seems worth going with so few people. There's almost as many staff as there are residents. What do you reckon?'

He looked over to Joyce. To Joyce, Jonquil noticed, not her, even though she, despite her age, was the senior member of staff.

'Uh, I don't know . . .' said Joyce with typical decisiveness.

'We've got to go! You promised!' Candy piped up from the back, where she had been standing apart from the others, rubbing cream into her bruises.

'Yeah, I know we did,' said Frank, 'but . . . goodness, what happened to you?'

'He walked into a couple of doors apparently,' said Riley.

Frank went over to Candy to get a closer look at her injuries. 'My God, Candy. These look terrible. Are you OK? Did you see a doctor? Did you report this to the police?'

Candy shook her head and then resumed cream-rubbing. 'What's the point? I've had worse.'

'You should!' Frank insisted. 'You shouldn't let these people get away with this, otherwise they'll just carry on doing it. It's not right.'

Despite herself, Jonquil found she was touched by Frank's genuine anger and concern. Damn, and she'd decided she was going to be pissed off with him all day.

'Look, I know we promised,' Frank went on, 'but with so few people I don't know if it's really viable. I think Philip'd have a fit. You know, if there was just one other person . . .'

'I think I heard snoring inside,' Candy said quickly. 'There may be one other person.'

'You did?' said Frank.

'No you didn't,' said Riley. He didn't want to go with Freeman. Not *Freeman*.

'Yeah, I'm pretty sure I did. Why don't we go inside and check it out again?'

Candy turned round and went in. Frank and Joyce followed her. Riley considered his options. Not *Freeman* . . . On the other hand, it looked as though Freeman might be the difference between them going and them not going, and he had to go. He couldn't bear not to go. Even though he was by no means sure things were going to work out the way he wanted, he had to go and give it a *go*. He'd been carrying that address around with him for ten whole years: he'd been wanting it for too long not to go.

He followed the others inside.

There was indeed some snoring going on, but you couldn't really hear it until you got upstairs; then it was easy to follow it down the corridor to Peter Freeman's room at the end.

'How'd you manage to hear this all the way downstairs?' Frank asked.

'What? Freeman's elephantine rumblings?' said Candy. 'You can hear them halfway down the street. They keep me awake at nights.'

Smiling at Candy's choice of adjective, Frank went over to the bed and pulled back the blankets. 'Hey Peter,' he said, patting him gently about the face. 'Peter, wake up. We've got a surprise for you.'

It took some rather more severe patting and then some shaking to rouse Peter. When he did wake, he woke suddenly. He sat up, pushing Frank away.

'Get your fucking hands off me!' he said. Or at least that was what Frank assumed he was saying. It sounded more like an all-purpose snarl. GERRARROAARR!

'Come on you lazy git, get up,' said Riley. 'You're coming to France with us.' As he said the words, Riley could feel his heart sinking. A whole *day* spent listening to Peter Freeman wheezing and complaining. Freeman had a low, slow way of speaking, as though the batteries in his voice box were running down; Riley thought of it as a sort of cross between Eeyore and Marvin the Paranoid Android, only without the unbridled enthusiasm. What are we doing *now*? he would groan. What's the point of *that*? And Riley would be forced (yes forced – he took no pleasure from it whatsoever) to take the piss out of him, mimicking his rumbling voice. DOOM! GLOOM! Riley would intone when Peter was on a roll. WE´RE ALL GOING TO DIE! WE´RE ALL GOING TO DIE! And then, generally, there would be violence.

'France?' said Peter, fighting his way to lucidity. 'Yeah? What's the point of that then?'

Doom! Gloom!

'You remember. The trip. We were talking about it yesterday and you were saying how keen you were to go,' Candy lied firmly.

'Hmm . . . don't remember that. Mind you, yesterday, it's a bit of a blur already if you know what I mean . . . When are we going then?'

'Now,' said Frank.

'Now? What, without any breakfast or anything?'

'Yes. Now.'

'What's the point of that? I can't travel on an empty stomach. It's dangerous.'

'Don't worry about that,' Joyce said brightly. 'I've brought mountains of sandwiches.' Those Tesco bags: she'd brought enough to feed an army.

'Yeah, but it's not breakfast is it?'

'You can have sandwiches for your fucking breakfast!' Riley shouted at him. 'Excuse my French.'

Peter closed his eyes and willed them all to go away. But they didn't.

Downstairs Jonquil had decided that they ought to go whether or not there was anyone else still asleep. No one had asked her opinion, but she had one and this was it. And she *was* the senior member of staff, as long as they managed to get away before Philip arrived. It would be too bad to let people like Candy and Dougal down just because the others couldn't be bothered.

Eventually the rest of them reappeared, having persuaded Peter Freeman to drag himself out of bed. It had taken an age before he'd stopped shaking enough to pull some clothes on. Frank and Joyce turned a blind eye while he drained a can of lager. Then he insisted on putting on every single item of clothing strewn around his tiny room, even his heavy, beer-sodden anorak. 'What are you doing?' Frank said. 'It's going to be a lovely day. You'll boil in that.' 'Yeah, well I feel the cold sometimes,' said Peter. 'Better safe than sorry.'

So that was that then. Freeman was coming with them and there was nothing Riley could do about it. Oh well then. He resigned himself to the fact and decided not to worry about it. Life's too short to worry, he told himself: it was the favourite phrase of someone he had once known in the Paras. A long time ago.

They all climbed into the bus, the five residents in the back, the three members of staff in the front. Each of the three members of staff prided themselves on how good they were at relating to the residents on a one-to-one basis, how they spoke to the residents as equals, how they were able to blur the distinction between helper and helped. Although not, obviously, when it came to serious things like seating arrangements in the minibus. Here an important hierarchy applied. Frank, the guy on the trip, drove. Jonquil, in her position as senior member of staff, *not* just because she was Frank's girlfriend, sat next to him. And Joyce sat next to the window. To make more room, Joyce packed her shopping into the sizeable ethnic-style shoulder bag she had also brought with her. This didn't stop Jonquil tutting and sighing and making it generally clear to everyone that it was still a bit of a squash up here, and it would be a lot more comfortable for everyone if only Joyce, and her mountains of bloody sandwiches, would go and sit back with the residents. The dodgy ignition took four gos to splutter into life. As they chugged out of the car park, Frank caught himself wondering whether this was such a great idea after all.

Candy

I spent the first part of the hundred quid from the punter on a coach ticket back to Leicester. To see the old girl. I haven't seen my mum in over two years and the last time I went back I was strung out on smack and I only dropped by to score some cash off her, so she's naturally a little suspicious when I show up out of the blue like this. But what can she do? She's my mother. She's a slave to her base maternal instincts. Even though she knows deep down that I've only come to rip her off she can't help but be pleased to see me. She practically tears the chain off the door, throws it open and gives me a big mother's hug. Stephen! she says, and I wonder for a second who she's talking to.

Though I don't see too much of her these days, my dear darling mother never fails to surprise me. Surprise and depress me. There's still a good-looking woman lurking somewhere beneath the apron and the fag-ash and the *Woman's Weekly*'s. She's still got gorgeous, thin fair hair, her figure's more or less intact, she's still got a wicked sense of humour when she's not too pissed to use it. But she does nothing with all this. She wears the dowdiest clothes you can imagine, she *never* wears make-up, not even the simplest things like lipstick and eye-liner, the basics . . . honestly, for as long as I've known what make-up is, I've never, not once, seen her do anything with that tired, lived-in old face. I suppose she thinks she doesn't have to bother because she never goes out. But it's cause and effect isn't it. She never wears make-up because she doesn't go out: she doesn't go out because she looks so fucking rough the whole time. So she just stays at home every evening with her television and her magazines and her housework and her bottle of gin. And the wicked sense of humour stays locked away, out of sight of everyone.

She shows me in and the house is in the same state as it always is: hoovered to fuck. Every available surface has a knick-knack of some description on it, all beautifully polished, perfectly in place, not a speck of dust anywhere – heaven forbid. Some people use their drinking as an excuse to let their personal habits go to hell. Not the old girl – her obsessive tidiness is *fuelled* by the alcoholism. And maybe I should stop having a go; she seems happy enough with it, bless her. In the spick and span kitchen the only thing out of place is the half-empty bottle of Gordon's sitting with its top off on the table, winking slyly.

We spend most of the evening watching telly. It's only about half seven when I get there but already the old girl looks knackered. She slumps in her favourite chair, glass by her side. The midweek lottery draw comes on and we try to bond over the fact that neither of us has won. I haven't even bought a ticket, so it's not a crushing disappointment for me, but I play along. She makes me cheese on toast for tea. I've no idea if she's had anything to eat herself. She asks me loads of questions about how I'm doing down in London, what I'm getting up to and so on. And I tell her, like a dutiful son, what she wants to hear. I tell her I'm working in a record shop; that I'm applying for various college courses; that I'm sharing a flat with two very nice students; that I've got a girlfriend . . . No, she doesn't believe a word of it, but it doesn't hurt to pretend. After all, how could either of us cope with the truth? I couldn't tell her, and even if I could tell her, she couldn't bear to hear it. Actually Mum, I'm a rent boy. I walk the streets for a living. I suck cocks and I take it up the arse. I can't get a proper job because I haven't got a place to live and I can't get a place to live because I haven't got a job, so I live in a hostel for the homeless full of criminals and drunks and psychopaths. Oh and I like to dress in women's clothes so on a fairly regular basis someone comes along and kicks seven shades of shit out of me . . . Why should I be afraid to tell her this? It's just words, just the words of my life. Sticks and stones may break my bones but words . . . well it depends on the words doesn't it. Words may break my heart. Hey, at least I'm off the drugs. More or less.

By half past nine she's nodded off. I help her through to her room and then bed myself down on the couch. The following morning she's bright and breezy and you wouldn't guess for a second she had the best part of a bottle of gin last night. I'm in a worse state than her and I only had a single g and t. She asks me how long I'm planning on staying and I tell her a few days probably, and she knows I'm lying, of course she knows I'm lying. She knows I won't be here when she gets home from work and there'll be stuff missing from her house and she won't see me again for a couple of years, not until the next time I'm in some kind of unspecified trouble. I can sense her looking around, trying to work out what I'm going to take. Not the telly love, she's thinking, help yourself to anything else, but not the telly. You can be damn sure she's not left a scrap of cash anywhere in the house, or her jewellery – such as it is.

So I kiss her on the doorstep and wave goodbye and watch her up the street. See you tonight, she calls. Yeah see you tonight Mum.

And the second she's out of sight I shut the door, go back inside, straight into her bedroom where I fling open the wardrobe and start rifling through her clothes. This is what I want, Mum, not your valuables or your precious bloody television . . . *your frocks!*

But Jesus, what a miserable fucking collection of frocks it is. I knew she wasn't Princess Diana but this is like a closing-down sale at Oxfam – after all the good stuff has gone. I'd envisaged a whole morning trying various things on, working out which looked and felt the best. I'd been looking forward to it. In the end there's only one I'd consider: a long, dark red, velvety dress, which is actually rather lovely. God knows what my mum was thinking of buying it. It's not her, not at all. In fact I'm doing her a favour by removing it. She might get completely pissed one night and wear it by mistake. I feel it and rub it against my body and smell it before putting it on. It feels so right. I find it hard to explain. It's not just the way it looks, although this dress does look stupendous on me even if I say so myself. It's the feel, the whole thing. I check myself out in the mirror and this is me, this is the Real Me. This is the way I am inside my head. Do you see what I'm saying? Of course there's no bloody make-up anywhere so there'll have to be another raid on Boots when I get back to London, but I do manage to score a fetching pair of silver, dangly earrings. These are just sitting on the dresser, in plain view, and are the only items of jewellery to be found anywhere, so I persuade myself that they were left out deliberately for me to take. Tights are easy enough: there's a whole drawer stuffed full of tights. Tight City. Shoes, though, shoes are more of a problem. As far as I can see she's only got two pairs of shoes other than those she's wearing so chances are she'll notice if I take a pair. And anyway her feet are smaller than mine. I try and squeeze my feet into the more appealing pair, the black shiny ones with the slightly raised heels, and I feel like an Ugly Sister trying on the glass slipper. Clearly I'm going to have to provide my own shoes. Which is a shame: I'd had this idea that my mother would provide, unwittingly, my whole wardrobe for my audition and this would bring me luck. I would tell her later, when I was famous, how I owed it all to her, maybe dedicate an album to her, and she would be charmed and thrilled and proud. I guess maybe I'd been dreaming too hard.

I look at myself in the mirror before leaving. I look, and there is no escaping this fact, fantastic in this dress. I blow my reflection a little kiss.

08.35

The traffic was horrific. They'd been going nearly an hour and they weren't out of London yet. Sitting in a solid jam on the East India Dock Road, his foot aching from pumping the clutch, Frank continued to entertain serious doubts about the whole trip. How in God's name had he let Jonquil talk him into it? How had he let himself be whisked along by her enthusiasm?

Philip was right, it was a mad idea. For all his brusqueness and bossiness and general told-you-so-ness, it was worth remembering that Philip was the one with the most experience of this client group. If he said this was a mad idea, it was probably a mad idea. In fact he'd put it quite succinctly. You're serious? he'd said. You want to take a group of homeless drunks on a booze cruise? That's not just asking for trouble: it's saying pretty please with a cherry on top. It's like taking a group of paedophiles on a school flipping outing.

He had a point. When you thought about it, there were any number of things that could go wrong. Just the thought of the drinking was terrifying in itself. How were they going to control the men once they were all tight? Tom Riley looked pretty far gone already. His eyes were closed and he was rocking his head, singing softly to himself. He looked quite sweet actually, but it wasn't yet nine o'clock and he was already in this state.

How had Frank let Jonquil twist his arm? It would be a wonderful opportunity for the residents, she'd said. A chance to take them away from their environment for a day, to show them the possibility of an alternative life. Why not just go to the zoo or something then? Frank had asked. No, it was important to actually leave the country. It was symbolic. The channel would be the passage between their current way of life and the possibilities of the future. Oh, uh, right, Frank had said. Jonquil had been to university and he hadn't and sometimes in their conversations it showed. What if one of them went missing, though? Well, they'd have to keep a close eye on them all, obviously, Jonquil said. But if they really did lose somebody, at the end of the day it would be that person's responsibility. This wasn't a school trip, they weren't the residents' legal guardians. Anyone could make their own way home.

Right, thought Frank. They could make their own way home. With no money, no grasp of the language and a drink habit. They could just jump in a cab, couldn't they.

Riley had started singing more loudly and Frank could sense it was starting to get on other people's nerves as well as his own. It was an old American song:

> Irene goodnight, Irene goodnight,
> Goodnight Irene, goodnight Irene
> I'll see you in my dreams

Mikey started to join in. His voice was, if this was possible, even worse than Riley's.

IRENE GOODNIGHT, IRENE GOODNIGHT . . .

'Hey, shut up,' Riley shouted at him.

'Just having a little sing-song . . . you know, brighten up the journey a little,' said Mikey.

'Yeah, well this is my song. Sing your own song if you want to sing.'

Riley started up again. Once again Mikey joined in.

'I said sing your own fucking song!'

'Language,' said Frank because he felt he ought to.

Riley had that look on him, though. Frank wasn't about to argue with that look and neither was Mikey. So when Riley started up again, Mikey did sing his own song. Riley sang 'Goodnight Irene'; Mikey sang 'She'll Be Coming Round The Mountain When She Comes'. Both sang badly. It sounded terrible.

'Hey guys,' said Frank who felt he was about to lose it any second, 'give it a rest, eh?'

Riley gave him the look again. Directly, in the rear-view mirror.

'Please?' added Frank hopefully. 'At least until we get clear of this traffic.'

'Yes, it's dreadful isn't it,' said Joyce, who had dug a black and white *A to Z*, dated 1972, out of the glovebox and was pretending to look for alternative routes in order to be helpful. 'Right everyone, new rule: no singing until we get out of this jam, OK?'

Jonquil said nothing. Who was Joyce to be making new rules? *Who* was the senior member of staff?

'Yeah, what about this traffic,' said Peter, seizing on an opportunity to complain about something. 'I mean, what is the point of this. Getting up at the crack of dawn, no breakfast or nothing, just to sit in all this, probably getting poisoned by the fumes ... with no breakfast or nothing.'

Doom, gloom, thought Riley. We're all going to die.

'Of course, poor Peter, you didn't get your breakfast did you. You must be starving,' said Joyce. 'Here, have a sandwich. I've got mountains of sandwiches.' She rustled around in the bulging bag at her feet. It gave her an excuse to put the map down; she hadn't even found which page they were on yet.

'Thanks,' said Peter, reaching greedily across the others.

'Anyone else for a sandwich? Dougal? Candy?'

They all shook their heads. All except Mikey.

'Did you say you had some Coke as well?' said Mikey.

'Oh yes. Mountains of Coke.'

'Oh, that's lovely. Lovely.' As soon as he had the can, Mikey turned in his seat and opened it secretively, as if he'd smuggled his own bottle into a pub and was topping his glass up.

'So you found us a way out of this yet?' Jonquil asked Joyce, knowing that she hadn't.

'Uh, no, not yet,' said Joyce, retrieving the *A to Z* from the floor and studying it intently for a few moments – upside down.

Jonquil shook her head. 'I told you we should have gone out through south London. Would have been much quicker.'

If she said that again, Frank was going to hit her.

'Here, why don't I have a look,' she said, taking the map from Joyce before Joyce could object and turning it the right way up.

There was an atmosphere, definitely an atmosphere. To Candy it was like holiday trips when she was a kid, only now there were three parents bickering in the front instead of two. There wasn't quite silence, but no one said anything for a short while. The only sounds were Peter munching his sandwich with his mouth open, Mikey slurping, still undercover, on his drink and the bus engine chugging away stoically as it grew hotter and hotter.

'I know,' said Joyce brightly. 'Does anyone want to play a game?'

Still no one spoke. Joyce took this to be a yes.

'I spy with my little eye something beginning with W,' she said firmly.

'Wanker,' said Peter before he could stop himself, his mouth still full. Dougal was sprayed with half-chewed bits of prawn mayonnaise sandwich which he calmly picked off himself.

'Language!' barked Frank from the front.

'Yeah, watch yourself. There's ladies present,' said Riley.

'Wuss,' said Mikey, turning around from his drink, staring at Candy and Dougal in turn, trying to get a rise out of one or other of them.

'Any sensible suggestions?' said Joyce with a sigh.

'Wheel,' said Frank to be helpful.

Wet blanket, thought Jonquil to herself.

'Windscreen,' said Candy.

'Windscreen wipers,' said Mikey quickly.

'Wiper blades!' said Frank excitedly. But still Joyce shook her head.

'Water,' said Peter.

'Where can you see water, Peter?'

'Uh . . . in the engine? Isn't there water in the engine?'

'Yeah, but you can't *see* it, you bloody idiot,' Riley growled at him. 'You've got to be able to *see* it.' Christ, what kind of man needed the rules of I-Spy explaining to him.

'Watch,' said Candy.

'Wrist.'

'Wristwatch.'

'Wrinkles.'

'Worry lines.'

'No, that's two words. That would be W.L.'

'Wrinkles then.'

'No.'

'Waist.'

'Woman.'

'Weakling.'

'Wart.'

'Frank!'

'Wretch.'

'The whole world!'

'Window.'

'Yes, that's right Candy. Window.'

'What?' said Riley. 'Window? You can't have that, it's too easy.'

'Just because you lost,' said Candy, and then immediately wished she hadn't.

'Well I didn't want to make it too difficult for you all,' said Joyce.

'So you think we're *thick*, do you,' said Riley. 'You think we're all bloody clueless berks who can't cope with anything more complicated than a bloody kids' game . . .'

'That's not what I meant at all, Tom—'

'How about some lateral-thinking puzzles,' suggested Jonquil, who'd had enough of trying to make sense of the bloody *A to Z*.

'*Thinking*?' said Mikey suspiciously.

Frank smiled. There was that university education again. He made a left turn and they enjoyed a brief spell of movement, the stagnant air in the bus temporarily reshuffling itself, before they came to rest again at the back of the queue for the Blackwall Tunnel.

'Lateral thinking,' she persevered. 'They're kind of like conundrums. I give you a puzzle and you have to work out what's going on. You know? Much more challenging than I-Spy.' She looked over at Joyce, who didn't respond. 'For example, a man flies to London on Sunday afternoon, stays three nights at the Ritz and one night at the Dorchester and flies out again on Sunday afternoon. He never leaves the London area and doesn't stay anywhere except these two hotels. So – how come he arrives and leaves on Sunday afternoon?'

Jonquil smiled. This should keep them quiet for a bit.

Mikey, however, piped up immediately. 'Easy. He sleeps rough the other three nights.'

'Eh?' said Jonquil who might have guessed someone would say something like this.

'He spends four nights in these posh hotels, then three nights he sleeps in one of the parks and then he leaves again on Sunday. In fact, I don't know why he doesn't just spend the whole time in the park. It's summer; the weather's OK. And these hotels are a waste of money if you ask me.'

'Maybe he bunks in,' suggested Peter. 'Maybe he's not paying for them at all. What do you reckon, Jonquil, is he bunking in or what?'

'No . . . no, I think he's paying his bills.'

Peter shook his head in disgust.

'But, no, he doesn't sleep in the park,' Jonquil continued. 'As I said, he doesn't spend any nights anywhere other than these two hotels.'

'Why does he change hotel after three nights?' Candy asked. Surely, if you were lucky enough to be staying at the Ritz you'd just stay there, wouldn't you?

'I don't know . . . he fancies a change of scenery, I guess,' Jonquil said unconvincingly.

'Yes, but—' Candy began to argue.

But Peter talked over the top of her. 'Where's he from anyway, this geezer?'

'It's irrelevant,' said Jonquil.

'*Irrelevant?*' exclaimed Peter. Only he pronounced it irrevelant. '*Irrevelant?* What do you mean? He's got to come *from* somewhere to arrive in London, hasn't he.' That stood to reason.

'OK . . .' said Jonquil, who was beginning now to see the fatal flaw in her plan. Lateral thinking puzzles didn't keep people *quiet*, did they. They simply invited people who were already quite adept at asking awkward and pointless questions to ask really awkward and really pointless questions. In abundance. Her notion that they would all silently chew the problem over and then offer a solution in half an hour or so was, she now realised, a little far-fetched. 'He comes from Germany,' she decided.

'Germany?'

'Yes.'

'So he's German?'

'Uh . . . yes.'

Peter threw his hands in the air. 'Well there you go then. They're bloody mad, the *Germans*.'

'Yes, but that doesn't explain the mystery,' Jonquil insisted. 'How did he arrive on Sunday afternoon, leave on Sunday afternoon, yet only spend four days in London?'

'It was a leap year,' said Mikey. This sentence started high-pitched, full of eureka-ish confidence and hope, and then fell away sharply towards the end as even Mikey realised what a monumentally stupid suggestion it was. No one bothered to respond to it. Instead they fell into silence, each thinking of other, more interesting things.

After a short while, during which Jonquil first appreciated the peace and then began to suspect the truth – that no one was thinking about her stupid puzzle at all – she probed Frank. 'Any ideas?'

Frank made a show of thinking. His furry eyebrows arched in concentration above his sunglasses. 'You say he arrived *on* Sunday afternoon?'

'Yes.'

'And left *on* Sunday afternoon?'

'Yes.'

'So . . .' He turned to face her. One furry eyebrow rose higher than the other. 'Sunday Afternoon could be the name of his plane then. Am I warm?'

Jonquil was furious; it had taken her nearly an hour to get this when Katy had tried it on her. 'You knew already!' she accused him. 'You've heard this before!' She sat back in her seat with a loud humph and folded her arms as tightly and as petulantly as she could.

'I haven't heard it before,' Frank protested. 'I just worked it out . . . something about the way you said *on*.'

'I don't get it,' said Mikey. Which was, of course, the story of his life.

Frank warmed to the game now it had given him a chance to show off. 'You see Mikey, he has a private plane *called* Sunday Afternoon. So he arrives on Friday morning, say. On Sunday Afternoon. Then he leaves on Tuesday morning, on Sunday Afternoon.' He did his best to enunciate the capital letters, almost giving himself hiccups in the process.

'Oh . . .' said Mikey vaguely. 'I see.' He didn't.

'That's rubbish,' said Peter indignantly.

'No, that's the answer,' said Jonquil.

'Bollocks,' said Peter. 'No one calls an aeroplane Sunday Afternoon. What kind of a name is that?'

'It's only a game,' said Riley. 'He can call the plane what he bloody well likes.'

'Well it's a bloody stupid game if you ask me . . . don't know what we're even playing it for . . .'

'Yeah, doom, gloom, we're all going to die,' said Riley half-heartedly, and Peter kicked him.

Riley was the only one who felt a little disappointed with himself at not guessing this. They'd done puzzles like this when he was in the Paras, on long journeys. If only he could coax some gentle action from his brain he might be able to recall one or two of them. They'd still be bobbing about somewhere, anchored to the sea-bed of his memory.

Jonquil returned to the *A to Z*. When Mikey shouted brightly 'OK! Give us another!' – not because he wanted another puzzle, but because he thought that was what she wanted to hear – she ignored him.

'OK, OK,' said Joyce, turning around to face the men in the back of the bus and taking control again. 'I've got the perfect game: Call My Bluff!'

'Ah, that's more like it,' said Riley. 'That's proper intellectual, that is. Now, how does that music go again . . . di-di-d-di . . . no, that's not it . . .'

'Di di di di *di* d-di d-di . . .' Joyce began.

Jonquil stared at the map even more intently. She wasn't even going to try and compete with this.

Riley joined in. 'Di di di di *di* d-di d-di . . . di! di! d-di di di!'

'How do you play this, then?' asked Mikey. 'I'm getting confused with all these games . . . could I have another Coke by the way?'

'Of course,' said Joyce, passing it over. 'Any more sandwiches anyone?'

'Wouldn't say no,' said Peter, who was still trying to work out this Sunday Afternoon thing. That just wasn't the name of a plane, was it. A racehorse maybe, but not an *aeroplane*.

'It's really quite simple,' Joyce went on, rustling around for more sandwiches. 'Everyone thinks of a word that they know that they think no one else will know . . .'

Mikey frowned. 'I don't know many words,' he said truthfully.

'Everyone has their own words,' Joyce insisted. 'Just think of something that you're interested in that none of us are. Honestly Mikey, if you put your mind to it everyone knows words that no one else knows, however little they think they know . . .'

Even you, she just managed to stop herself adding.

'OK, then what?'

'Then you think of two false definitions of that word, you give us those definitions together with real one, and we have to pick out the real one. Simple as that.'

'OK, I've got my word,' said Mikey without pausing for thought.

They all turned to look at him. Despite what Joyce had said, no one seriously expected him to have a word they didn't know.

'What is it?' asked Joyce.

'Jonquil.'

'Yes?' said Jonquil.

'No, that's my word. Jonquil.'

'Oh.' Jonquil went back to the *A to Z* and tried to ignore him.

Joyce was delighted. 'That's a splendid word, Mikey. Well done. Now, what are your three definitions?'

'Uh, I don't know,' said Mikey sheepishly. 'Jonquil will have to do the definitions. I don't really know what it means, I just know that it does mean something.'

Great, thought Jonquil.

'I know it means something, Jonquil, because you told me once you got your name because your dad played Scrabble. And when your mum was pregnant with you he won a game by playing *jonquil*.'

'Jonquils,' said Jonquil. 'He got the plural. Triple word score. Doubled up for using all his letters. And he didn't just win a game, he won the Southern Area Regional Final. I honestly think it was the single greatest moment of his life.' Oh, how she loved telling this story.

'And with a j and a q as well,' Mikey enthused. 'So it must mean something, then. It must be in the dictionary.'

'It's a type of flower, isn't it?' said Frank, who hadn't really been paying attention. He'd just broken into third gear for the first time since leaving the hostel as they crossed a set of lights.

'Frank!' Joyce shouted at him. 'You've spoiled the game!'

'It's OK,' said Jonquil. 'We can still play. I'll give you three definitions: A. It's a blue flower. B. It's a red flower. C. It's a yellow flower.'

Frank Muir rotated rapidly in his grave.

'It's a red flower,' said Candy, who didn't really care one way or the other but wanted to make an effort.

'No.'

'Blue flower.'

'No.'

'Yellow flower,' said Mikey before anyone else could.

'You can't guess your own word!' Riley yelled. He was getting annoyed now. Cooped up on this bus with a bunch of idiots, it was going to take them bloody hours to get to Dover at this rate. And he needed a drink.

'OK, who's going to go next?' said Joyce.

They didn't all rush at once.

Mikey cracked open his next can of Coke and did the same trick as before, turning his back on everyone so they couldn't watch him drink it.

'Maybe we need some time to think of some words. Come on, everybody think of a word. Everybody has a word.'

Candy

Jellybanging. You're at a party and you're thinking this is OK, maybe this isn't such a bad way to make a living after all, being paid to be at a party, when one of the hosts, who has paid you to be there, to entertain his guests, spikes you with Temazepam. You come to with a sore arse and a rash. There's no such thing as a free lunch. Jellybanging. Boy, am I glad I don't work the streets any more.

Mikey

Dulcet. That's another one of my favourite words. I'm not sure exactly what it means. You know, like: 'She spoke in dulcet tones.' People are often telling me I speak in dulcet tones. I think they might be taking the piss, though.

Riley

Spitroasting. There were these girls who used to hang around the pubs of Aldershot and Tidworth, near the army bases, and they wanted nothing more than to have a Para. Any Para. However pissed, however ugly. In Germany we'd had to pay for it; trust England to throw up slags who'd do it for free. And they seemed to be having a competition, some of them, to see how many green-eyed boys they could do, trying to fuck their way through the whole regiment. So we got lazy. You'd go out with the lads and you wouldn't bother even trying to pull because you knew that when you got back to barracks there'd be plenty available. And because we had to be quick, since female company in barracks was strictly prohibited – especially naked, rutting, mewing female company – and because the girls were keen to notch up a respectable score, it made sense for them to do two of us at once. So you and a mate would toss a coin, one of you would get a blowjob, the other would take the girl from behind. Spitroasting. I can't remember which you were supposed to choose if you won the toss.

08.48

'OK, I got one of your lateral drinking things,' Riley announced to the silence. Maybe if he managed to keep talking he'd forget he needed a drink, he'd forget the piece of paper in his pocket, he'd forget the mess he was in. 'This is the story: a man is going towards a field with a pack on his back and when he gets to the field he knows he's going to die . . . How come?'

They all thought for a moment. Or pretended to think.

'Say it again,' said Joyce.

'A man is going towards a field with a pack on his back and when he gets to the field he knows he's going to die.'

53

'So something in the field is going to kill him?' said Joyce.

'You could say that.'

'So why doesn't he stop going towards the field then?' said Peter. 'What's the point of that – marching towards certain death? Bloody stupid if you ask me.' First planes with daft names, now suicidal back-packers. This was the worst game he'd ever played in his life.

'That's what you've got to find out.'

'He's going to top himself then. He wants to die. There's a gun in this field and when he gets there he's going to top himself.'

'Nope.'

'What then? How's a bloody field going to kill him?'

'You've got to think a little.'

Peter gave up on the spot. 'Any more sandwiches up there?'

Jonquil felt she ought to make an effort. It was her game. How old was the man? she asked. What was he wearing? What was in the field? Where was the field? Why was the man going there? Was he with anyone else? All irrelevant, said Riley. She thought on.

A man is going towards a field with a pack on his back and when he gets there he knows he's going to die.

A man is going towards a field with a pack on his back and when he gets there he knows he's going to die.

'Anyone thought of a word yet?' Joyce asked hopefully.

Riley

Clinkers. Oh yeah, the Paras have got a word for everything. Clinkers are the little crusty pieces of shit that stick to your arse hairs after you've been living rough for a while. The only way to get rid of the buggers is with a pair of scissors, so one of the most basic survival techniques you need to learn is how to cut your own arse hair (all it requires is a steady hand and a leap of faith; you get the hang of it after a while). Otherwise you've got to get someone else to do it for you – and you simply don't want to get into that kind of debt in the army. Clinkers. Makes you want to itch just thinking about it, doesn't it?

08.59

'Blast, look, it's one of those windscreen-washing people,' said Frank. They'd been sitting in the queue for this set of lights for ten minutes. Only a couple of cars were getting through each time: it was a captive market.

'Squeegees!' Joyce exclaimed. 'That's a good Call My Bluff word.'

'Yeah, we all know what it means, though,' said Mikey. 'Scrounging bastard who makes a mess of your windscreen.'

The young man put his bucket down by the side of the road and started work on the front car, despite clear gesticulations to fuck off from the driver.

'What should we do?' said Frank. He hated dilemmas like this. He knew what he ought to do and he knew what he wanted to do and he wanted someone else to make the decision.

'Give him some money of course. It's the only decent thing to do,' said Jonquil. You're the bloody Christian, she didn't add.

'No you mustn't,' said Mikey, becoming animated. 'These are terrible people. We mustn't encourage them.'

'What do you mean, terrible people, Mikey?' Joyce asked him. 'What have they done to you?'

'They take money away from real honest beggars like myself. They're skilled workers pretending to be beggars.'

'They're hardly skilled,' said Frank. 'Not the way most of them do it anyway.'

'They're still working. They should be paying tax and national insurance like everyone else.'

'Yeah, don't give him a penny,' said Riley. 'Look at the state of him. Look at those clothes, and that hair! Can't tell if he's a boy or a girl.'

'Yes you can,' said Candy.

Two more cars slipped through the lights and the minibus pulled up to pole position.

'Clean your windscreen for you folks,' said the young man. There was just a hint of a question mark at the end of the sentence, but he'd already started smearing grey soapy water across the glass before anyone could answer.

'No! Leave our windscreen alone! You're a bloody parasite, you are!' Mikey called from the back.

'And your hair's a disgrace,' Riley added. 'You look like a horse.'

The young man started scraping at the foam.

'Go on Frank, start up the wipers. Take the bastard's hands off.'

Riley started making neighing noises. 'Champion the Won-der Horse!' he sang tunelessly between neighs.

Frank was still in a quandary. 'Joyce, what do you think we should do?'

Yeah, *Joyce*, what do *you* think? Jonquil screamed to herself.

Joyce slipped into her Little Miss Reasonable voice. 'Well, we have a small budget which is intended for everyone. The democratic thing to do is to take a vote.'

'I wasn't planning on giving him more than 10p,' said Frank.

'Don't give him a penny! He's scum!' Mikey said urgently.

Riley made some more neighing noises.

'He'll just spend the money on drink and drugs,' said Mikey.

'And you can buy a lot of drink and drugs for 10p,' said Candy.

As the lights changed, Frank's side of the windscreen was still completely covered in foam so he couldn't see out. The car behind started honking its horn. Frank started panicking. 'What should I do?' he said a final time, fumbling in his pocket for change.

'Why don't we give him a sandwich?' suggested Dougal in his whispery, hesitant voice.

'Terrific idea, Dougal,' said Joyce and she immediately produced a fresh sandwich.

Mikey conceded defeat. 'OK, but no Coke. Just a sandwich.'

'Are you sure we've got enough sandwiches to be giving them away like this?' Peter asked anxiously.

'Yes Peter. We've got *mountains* of sandwiches.'

The lights were changing back. The honks were getting louder, all the way back down the queue. You could just about see out of the windscreen now. Frank beckoned the young man over and gave him the sandwich.

'What's this?' the young man said, peering suspiciously at the limp, damp thing in his hand.

'Cheese and pickle,' said Joyce with a smile and the minibus lurched through the red light, leaving the squeegee to throw the sandwich away in disgust and start on the next vehicle. In the rear-view mirror, as they cleared the junction just ahead of the cross-traffic, Frank caught the expression on the face of the driver of the car behind. He could feel ancient gypsy curses being heaped upon him and his entire family; his ears started to burn.

They turned on to the road down into the Blackwall Tunnel. Traffic here was moving – slowly, but it was moving; the downward slope of the road seemed to give it some momentum. As they descended into the Tunnel, the noise outside rose to a crescendo. The tyres on the road, echoing around the enclosed space, sounded like the roaring of the river. Frank pushed his shades up on his forehead as the road ahead darkened; as they emerged blinking on the other side he simply flexed his temples so the glasses dropped back into position. It looked quite cool – he practised this manoeuvre a fair bit at home – but no one was watching him.

Jonquil

You knew! Didn't you? You knew. Why didn't you tell me?

I did try to suggest ... Why don't you sit down and tell me what happened.

Why has there always got to be something wrong with them? Just when you think you've finally found the guy, the one who doesn't cut his toenails in bed, who doesn't turn out to be a Young Conservative or a bisexual into open relationships, who doesn't hit you when his football team loses or drink until he's sick every Friday night, who doesn't even leave the toilet seat up ... you know, someone who'll actually *do*: why do they have to go and fuck it up – sorry – as well? I mean, why did I ever kid myself this one would be any different?

Tell me. Tell me what happened.

We went to the Tate on Sunday, you remember I told you that was our date ... ?

It wasn't such a good idea after all then?

It *was* a good idea, it was wonderful. Frank looked really smart; he looked like he'd made an effort, you know, he hadn't just thrown on his usual, slobby Sunday clothes. And we walked around the gallery and of course I know nothing at all about art, and I don't think Frank knew a whole lot more to tell you the truth, but what he did know he shared with me. He told me who the sculptures were by and stuff. Actually, I think it made it better that he didn't know too much. If he'd come out with a whole spiel, I'd have just thought, uh-oh, I'm the latest in a long line here. But he was, like, the perfect date. He was interested in me, he didn't just talk about himself the whole time, but neither was it like an interview, you know, the way some dates can be. Question, question, question and you're not sure if anyone's paying attention to the answers. I told him I worked with the homeless and he was really interested in that. He said he wished he had a job like that, helping people out. He really hates his job at the moment. He says he hates working for The Man.

Which man?

You know. *The* Man.

The man who owns — what was it? — Office Mate?

Yeah. You know, he doesn't like working for a company that only exists to make a profit; where you're just working in order to make other people rich. You know, bosses, shareholders . . . people you never actually see doing any work on the shop floor. The *Man*. He'd much rather be doing a job like mine where the bottom line is actually doing some good, not just making a buck. I thought that was a cool thing to say, it made me feel good about myself. And we were walking and talking, and then we came across 'The Kiss', you know, that sculpture of two people snogging . . . ?

Yes, I know it.

As soon as we saw it we stopped talking and just stared; I couldn't believe my eyes. I mean, *kiss* doesn't begin to do it justice. They're snogging. It ought to be called 'The Snog'. Rodin's 'The Snog'. Kiss implies a little peck on the cheek, you know, something dainty and reserved. These people are *naked*, they're wrapped around each other, he's got his hand on that, you know, that sexy, smooth bit at the top of her thigh, and her hand is flung around his neck, dragging him in. They're all over each other. And you can't see it, but you just know they're using their tongues. No question. They've got their tongues rammed down each other's throats. And you know where he's going to put his hand next, and you know she can feel the hairs of his chest against her, and you know she can feel him hardening against her leg . . . We just gazed and gazed at this thing for ages. We walked slowly around it in circles and every so often we'd catch each other's eye and smile, or raise our eyebrows. And I was getting so worked up. I just thought, what a fantastic way to tell someone you want them. Forget getting pissed and fumbling around on a sofa, you know, inching your arm around their neck — bring them to *this* place, give them some full-on, in-your-face porn dressed up as art. I couldn't believe this thing. It was this cold, white, stone, inanimate object and there were just all these sparks flying off it. I couldn't cope with anything more after this. I had to go and sit down.

I'm sure Rodin would be flattered.

Yeah ... dirty old sod.

So what did you do after the gallery?

Well it was a gorgeous day, wasn't it, on Sunday, so we went for a little walk down by the river, crossed over to the South Bank. And Frank was still chatting away, you know, asking me about this and that. And we sat and had a drink down by the second-hand book stalls just up from the hostel and I bought a copy of *The Go-Between*, which I've been meaning to read ever since I saw the film, and it was just, you know, the most perfect date ever. I was sitting there, looking out over the Thames with this tingling sense of anticipation, thinking: finally, finally it's happening to me. And then suddenly, about half past five, he announces he's got to go. I ask him why and he goes all red and sheepish. You won't laugh? he goes. I don't know, I say, is it funny? And he goes: I've got to go to church ...

So this is the great disappointment? The fact he goes to church?

No! Not at all. I thought it was *such* a cool thing to say; it just made me want him more. You know, not only was he the sweetest, sexiest, most interesting, most intelligent bloke ever, but he also has this kind of spiritual side to him as well. Because, you know, you'd have never known he was a Christian from the way he spoke. He wasn't always going on about Jesus and praise the Lord and bless you and bless this, that and the other the way some of them do. It was obviously a holier, more personal, spiritual thing for him. So I said, OK fine but I absolutely have to see you again. And he agreed. And he looked so relieved that I was OK with this, that I hadn't taken the piss out of him. So he said, when? And I said, tomorrow. I'm not sure I can wait until then and I certainly can't wait any longer.

And he grinned and said, OK where shall we meet? And I said, my place. And then I said, I'll cook us dinner . . .

And then I nearly screamed. I couldn't believe I'd just heard myself saying those words. I'll cook us dinner! Me, the worst cook in the world. So now I had to go home and persuade Katy to go out for the evening and then somehow I had to rustle up a dream supper. Or at the very least one that wouldn't put him completely off the idea of sleeping with me. Well you can guess what I was like Monday at work. Part of me was the most wildly oversexed, strutting super-bitch on heat, which I was. I mean, the smell that must have been coming off me. But equally I was the mad, neurotic housewife, desperately asking people if they knew any good recipes. You know, no one said anything, but I think I may have been a bit of a pain to work with that day.

Eventually I decided on pasta with a kind of creamy, white-wine sauce. It seemed a pretty safe option since I'd totally neglected to ask him for any clues about what he liked and didn't like. I knew he was a vegetarian – a leather-jacket-wearing vegetarian – but that was all. I was going to put spinach in it, but you know loads of people can't stand spinach. Then I was thinking about walnuts, but there's all these nut allergies kicking about these days. So in the end it just came down to white wine and cream sauce. It's one of the few things I think I've got a fighting chance of making without poisoning him or blowing up my kitchen. Also, and I think this was the clincher, I had half a bottle of white wine in the fridge that needed using up. I could hardly serve it up to him, it had only cost two ninety-nine and it had been sitting around for a few days, but in a sauce he wouldn't notice, would he.

But even then, as I stood with the carton of cream raised above the saucepan, I started panicking: what if he's a vegan? The whole thing'll be ruined. But no: vegans always say, don't they? I mean, vegetarians don't always say, but vegans *always* say. Don't they?

In the end I think he hardly noticed the food. He ate it incredibly slowly, stopping after every mouthful to ask me more questions about myself and tell me again how much he hated his job. He'd just had this massive row with his boss and he was seriously thinking of chucking it in altogether and he wanted to know how to go about getting a job like mine. I was going mad at the other end of the table. I couldn't wait to get this bloody meal out of the way. Just eat your food, I wanted to scream at him, and come over here and get your trousers off . . .

So what went wrong?

Everything went wrong. OK, here I am in my own flat, having just cooked this romantic dinner which remarkably has not been a total disaster, and of course I've done the whole bit with the candles and the music, and I'm with this amazingly attractive, beautiful, beautiful guy, who has managed to keep me at a pretty constant sexual peak for over twenty-four hours despite the fact he hasn't touched me or even been there for most of that time, and part of the reason I'm in such a frenzy is that I think he feels the same way about me, and now finally, finally, I think I'm about to get into his box of goodies . . . OK, I'm in this position. What are the scariest three words he could say to me?

Let me see . . . I've got crabs?

Worse than that. In fact, so scary that he doesn't even say them. Instead he produces this card with the words written on it. A little yellow card, the size of a credit card, and sure enough on the back there's a little strip that he's signed, and on the card it says, in big, bold, proud, black letters, the three scariest words in the world . . . True Love Waits . . . you know what this is, don't you?

It's a religious thing, isn't it? Choosing not to have sex before marriage.

Yeah, that's it.

I thought you were happy with him being a Christian.

When I thought he was a *normal* Christian. This isn't normal Christian, though, this is mad Christian. This is an insane, evangelical,

American thing dragged kicking and screaming over here, you know? I mean, calling cards! Little bits of paper that you sign and carry around with you, just in case someone tries to shag you by accident. It's so American. I half-expected a gospel choir to come bursting through the door singing 'I'm Keeping Myself Pure For Jesus'.

But the point about this – I mean the whole point about the whole fucking thing – sorry – is that it's obviously a smokescreen, isn't it. He's not really into this, he's not weird enough. If he was that weird, I'd have noticed. He's just trying to let me down gently, isn't he. And I suppose it's better to hear that rather than sorry, I think you're cute but you've got a big arse, small tits and I can get better elsewhere. I suppose I ought to be grateful to him really.

Oh Jonquil don't be silly . . .

It's true! It's the same thing they all say, he's just found a kinder, more roundabout way of saying it. I reckon it was probably the cream sauce that did it. I was probably still in with a chance up to then. But he took one look at that empty carton of full-fat double cream and he just thought, nah, she's got a lardy arse already, it's obviously going to get lardier in the future, I think I'll just cut my losses here.

This is ridiculous.

Yeah, well . . .

So what happened next? What did you do?

What do you think? I threw him out.

You threw him out? I see . . . and how do you feel about that?

Good. I mean, bad. Obviously I mean bad. I feel terrible about it. I'd wanted to have this magical experience with him and I ended up bundling him out of the door before he'd had coffee. I cried my eyes out. But I felt good as well, that I'd taken his rejection on the chin and dealt with it. I felt . . . empowered.

So you're satisfied with the way you handled things?

Yeah.

So why come back to me?

Because . . . because I suppose I don't really know how I feel. I don't know if I did the right thing or not. What should I have done?

I can't really tell you what to think and do, I can only try and help you understand what you feel.

But I said, I don't *know* how I feel. I don't know if I want to see him again or not.

Again, if you were happy with the idea of not seeing him again, would you be sitting here with me now?

So you think I should call him then?

It's your decision.

Thanks. You're a great help, you know that?

Candy

Of course it looks different by day. Everything looks a little less magical if you shine a light in its face, we've all got our warts and our blemishes, but the transformation of this place is still startling. The chairs and the tables look wasted without people cluttered around them, the stage is just a few planks of wood . . . look, there's even dust on the glitterball. Now I've seen her without her gladrags, will she ever look the same again?

I'm standing at the back of the main room of BabyCakes in my mother's soft red dress and dangly earrings, a pair of come-fuck-me shoes, one size too big, borrowed from my pal Georgette, and perhaps just a little too much make-up. (This has only occurred to me now, now that I'm standing here; I thought it looked terrific when I left Stamford Street.) These clothes don't belong to me, I don't feel comfortable in them, they're not *me* yet, whatever I may have thought when I first tried them on. Up on stage, on the bare planks of wood, a large fat man with cropped hair and piggy glasses is rapping instructions while a pretty black girl plays the piano. He appears to be some kind of musical director, which would be an enormous stroke of luck. The best I'd secretly been hoping for was to be asked to come back another day. But if he's here . . . maybe I'll get a hearing this very afternoon. Who knows.

Uh . . . excuse me? I call from the back of the room. Who the hell are you? says the man looking angry at being interrupted. I've come for an audition. You got an appointment? he says. Uh, no. Then how the hell'd you get in here? The man at the door let me in, the one with the ponytail, I tell him. He shakes his head. Tony let you in? I don't *believe* him sometimes; he'd let the IRA into Buckingham Palace if they said they were just coming to look at the portraits.

He's a rancid old queen. Believe me, I know a rancid old queen when I meet one. He's got a rancid old queeny voice, all high-pitched and snarling. The kind of voice that simply can't be *bothered* with anyone else *darling*, it's just *so* much effort isn't it. I'm clearly not going to get anywhere with him; it's a waste of time even starting. So, feeling strangely relieved at having failed so spectacularly, I start backing towards the door. He calls after me. For heaven's sake sweetie you're going to have to be a little more tenacious than *that* if you're going to get anywhere in this business. I turn back to face him. He's looking me up and down. Well you look the part, he says. Nice dress, nice face . . . can you sing though? He murmurs it to himself. Can you sing though? That's the question. Oh yes I can sing all right, I tell him eagerly, here let me show you. Well . . . , he makes a big show of thinking very hard, Simone and I have a lot to get through this afternoon. Just one song, I plead, one song won't take up any time at all, just a *verse*. I can show you what I can do with a verse. He scratches his chin and clearly enjoys holding my life in the balance. Rancid old fucking queen. OK, he sighs eventually, I suppose we should reward such enthusiasm. *Very* quickly though.

I clamber up on to the stage, the hem of my dress getting caught under my heels (it's beautiful but not practical). When I'm up there I stand up straight and try and look elegant. Right now, he says, Mr . . . ? Miss! (Mother of Mary, how long has he been doing this job?) Miss Skinn, I say proudly. Miss Candy Skinn. I give a little curtsey; I'm on Broadway already. Right then Miss uh Skinn let's hear what you can do. He signals to the pianist and she launches into a tune that's only vaguely familiar to me. Tum ti tum tum. Something that was in the charts when I was a kid, maybe even before I was born. After a couple of bars they both look at me; clearly I'm supposed to have come in by now. I'm sorry, I say with a shrug, I don't know this one. Don't know it? he says incredulously. It's 'The Winner Takes It All'! I stare at him blankly. It's *Abba* sweetie. It's bloody *Abba*! *Don't* tell me you don't know any Abba . . . I shrug at him again. I prefer to sing older songs, I tell him, a lot of French songs, Jacques Brel, that sort of thing. I look over to the pianist. I don't suppose you know any Jacques Brel . . . ? She smiles back at me, a sweet twinkling smile. The rancid old queen also smiles; I wonder what's going on. S*imone*, he says drawing her name out, do you know any Brel? Perchance? And Simone smiles even wider. Oh yes, she says, I think I know Brel.

And as soon as she opens her mouth it turns out *she's French*! That gorgeous, husky, rolling accent. This has got to be a sign hasn't it. A sign that things are going my way today. The musical director is here, he's prepared to give me a hearing (OK he's an r.o.q. but look! This is me! Up on the stage of BabyCakes having an audition!), *and the pianist is French.* So I get to sing the songs I want to sing, the ones I love. I take a proper look at Simone for the first time and though it worries me a little to admit this, she's incredibly attractive. Dreadlocked hair with a whole forest of beads, big round smiley cheeks, slim elegant figure: honey if you were a boy ... *Ne me quitte pas?* she suggests. Uh yeah I think so. I only know it in English. She starts on the piano and it's definitely the right tune although not exactly the way I know it. I'm not quite sure where I'm supposed to come in so I just plough in and hope she'll adapt. IF YOU GO AWAY – Whoops. Not there. I wait for the tune to come round and try again. IF YOU GO AWAY – No that doesn't sound right either. What the hell is this girl playing? I look over at her and she's desperately trying to direct me by nodding her head. OK I think I've got it now. IF YOU GO – IF YOU – IF YOU GO AWAY – IF YOU GO – *Shit*. What's she playing at? OK one more go. I've got to get it right this time before the old queen loses his patience with me. Just keep going whatever. IF YOU GO AWAY ON THIS SUMMER'S DAY! THEN YOU MIGHT AS WELL TAKE THE SUN AWAY! God it's in completely the wrong key, that's what the problem is. I'm growling away here like Lee Marvin. I shift up an octave and try again. AND ALL THE BIRDS THAT FLEW IN THE SUMMER SKY ... Nope. Even worse. That sounded like somebody torturing the Clangers. Simone has given up on me and moved on to the next part of the song, the big stirring bridge. This sounds more familiar, more like the version I know. Right, one more go. Take it to the bridge now ... BUT IF YOU STAY I'LL MAKE YOU A DAY! LIKE NO DAY HAS BEEN OR SHALL BE AGAIN! Keep going, keep going ... WE'LL SAIL ON THE SUN WE'LL RIDE ON THE RAIN ... Oh God what was that? What is my voice trying to do to me? This has turned into karaoke night in the deepest, darkest chamber of hell.

The fat man waves pleadingly for me to stop. Simone takes her hands from the piano and stares pitifully at me. I can't bear this. I can't cope with the shame. I step awkwardly down from the stage and march towards the door as quickly as my just-too-big high heels will allow. I want to reach the door before I burst into tears; I really want to reach the door before I burst into tears. I almost make it. See you then love! calls the guy with the ponytail after me cheerily as I bustle out of the front door with my face in my hands.

I get a couple of blocks up the street before collapsing in a doorway for a proper cry. I curl myself up and watch my dress slowly becoming ruined. It's Frith Street on an overcast April afternoon – trendy, overdressed young media people rush to and fro clutching important packages; none of them notice me. It starts to rain. Hey stop crying it wasn't that bad, says a husky accent next to me while I'm still screaming at myself inside my head. Simone has come chasing out of the club to see if I'm OK. Even in my present state I can tell that this is a very sweet thing to do. Thank you, I tell her. My eyes are all red and ballooned. You have a nice voice, she goes on, and you look great. Thank you, I say again and I even manage a smile through the tears. I think my mascara may be running; and I really screwed up in there didn't I. She shrugs. It's a difficult song, she says, and you need to rehearse it a little. You know I would love to do some songs like this at the club – Brel, Piaf, Serge Gainsbourg maybe. It would be really cool instead of all this disco shit the whole time . . .

She gets out a tissue which she's been keeping tucked up her sleeve and starts dabbing at my eyes. What a woman. You want to rehearse some songs with me? she asks casually and I have to make her repeat it to make sure I heard her properly. You really want to play with me after what you just heard? Sure, you have a nice voice: with a little practice you'll be just fine. If we get a couple of songs really good we can go back to Steven and play them for him again and he'll give us a show no problem. He always wants new singers at BabyCakes because there's always somebody leaving, some prima donna who can't get her way on everything and thinks she's going to hit the big time. It's a constant process. I make one suggestion though, one . . . condition . . . Yes? I say prepared to agree to practically anything she asks. You must sing in French. I will teach you the words and you must sing in French, not these horrible English translations . . . OK? I burst out laughing. Through the rain and the tears come howls and howls of laughter. Sure I'll sing in French. (Honey for you I'll sing in Swahili.) I give her a big hug and it dawns on me I'm sitting in the doorway of a record company's offices in Soho in the pouring rain with mascara running down my cheeks. Hey you want to go and get a coffee? I ask her. We could discuss things further. OK, she says helping me to my feet. I'm gay, I warn her – just in case she thinks I'm like trying to get fresh or something. Really? she says, I would never have guessed.

Mikey

I love singing, me, it's in my blood. Welsh, you see. We all like to have a sing-song where I come from. 'Land Of My Fathers' is my favourite, obviously, but I'll sing along to anything if people will sing with me.

09.05

On the other side of the Tunnel the road opened out a little and the traffic began to move at a fairly respectable rate. They could go just fast enough for a delicious breeze to come in through the window. Gradually the suburbs of London began to melt into green-belt countryside. They passed such exotic sounding places as the Black Prince Interchange and it truly felt as though they were on their way. And then finally they reached the M2, which they hit like a missile out of a catapult. Frank discovered the sensual delights of fourth gear and then, almost mystically, fifth. Here he found with his new sense of freedom that he couldn't keep the bus much below eighty-five (he'd have gone faster only it rattled above ninety). There was a general air of relief as the road opened up, yawningly, in front of them. The atmosphere lightened; no one had to suggest any more stupid games; people stopped deliberately trying to piss each other off. More or less.

After a while, Riley started singing to himself again:

> I love Irene, God knows I do
> I'll love her till the oceans run dry

> If Irene should turn her back on me
> Lord, I would take morphine and I would die.

It didn't seem to bother anyone now. Even when Mikey started to join in, it was absent-mindedly rather than maliciously.

Riley was adamant, though. It was his song. 'Sing your own fucking song,' he growled again.

'What is it with that song, Tom?' Joyce asked him. 'Why won't you let anyone else sing it?'

'It's very personal,' he said, and he almost looked coy. As far as Riley could ever be said to look *coy*. 'Reminds me of someone I used to know.'

There was a short, awkward silence after this, which Peter broke by asking for another sandwich. Mikey took the opportunity to get another Coke, which he drank in his regular fashion.

They clattered on down the fast lane, overtaking most other things on the road. Riley stopped his singing. They passed a groaning estate car, obviously a large family going on holiday, jammed to the roof with luggage and laughing, waving children. Most of the men waved and smiled back. The children then redoubled their own waving efforts, squeezing out from behind suitcases and toys to press their faces against the car window. Only Mikey didn't wave. He had been facing out of the window, secretively supping at his drink, but now he turned back in to face the others. He didn't like kids; they reminded him too much of his own.

'Aren't they sweet,' Jonquil cooed as the front of the minibus pulled past the car and she had to strain to keep the children in view.

'Mmm,' said Joyce, smiling wistfully and waving manically. She could just see Frank and Jonquil in that same car in ten years' time, up to their eyes in gorgeous, healthy children; and she wondered quietly and privately to herself why life was so bloody unfair.

Joyce

I honestly think it's true. Everybody has a word and mine, in case you're interested, is anencephaly. The final, damning and irrefutable proof that there is no God. Anencephaly.

10.24

Signs for Dover, Folkestone and the Channel Tunnel began appearing with regularity now, rapidly counting down the miles.

'Why aren't we going by the tunnel?' Mikey asked. He was beginning to slur his words and even the most innocent question carried a hint of aggression.

'It's dull in the tunnel,' said Joyce. 'You can't see anything.'

'Yes,' said Jonquil. 'I think it's important that we all notice the sea. It makes you realise you're actually leaving the country, going somewhere different—'

'Because *how* you go is just as important as *where* you go ... Isn't it?' Riley interrupted her. He said this leaning forward with an index finger poised in the air as though making a great philosophical pronouncement. Then he sat back in his seat, seemingly pleased with his contribution. No one asked him what he was talking about. He was fingering his piece of paper again, rolling it up and passing it from hand to hand, then unravelling it and reading it intently.

Just a name. Just an address.

There was a salty, seagully whiff of the Channel in the air. Riley couldn't wait to get off this damn bus and find himself a drink. He wasn't going to get hammered today, not today of all days. But he could use a drink, just one, to calm his nerves. This was a big day, his biggest day since ... well, a long time ago. Before his records began.

In his head he was still promising Irene, over and over again, how he'd see her in his dreams.

Riley

I'll see you in my dreams . . .

The day we met we were guests of honour at a funeral. I don't know how else to put it; that's what it felt like. The funeral of Lieutenant Andrew Stuart, Para, died in a parachuting accident. This simple, basic fact gave the whole shebang a weird kind of atmosphere. He was a Para: he died in a parachuting accident. The other Paras, myself included, felt a kind of pride at this. Not many of us got to go this way, pack on our back, sword in hand as it were. It felt right somehow – this was the way Andy *should* have died. This was the way, we kept telling ourselves tearfully over our beer, this was the way Andy would have wanted it. Only of course Andy wouldn't have wanted it like this at all, would he. It was stupid. Who wanted to be a pile of mush in the ground? He'd have given his left bollock to be drinking beer with us instead, reminiscing about some other poor cunt who'd bitten the dust. But funerals do funny things to your head, I've seen it before. There were genuine tears of pride as his flag-draped coffin was hoisted aloft and carried on its short, final journey. They wouldn't let me help carry the coffin. They said it would look ridiculous for a man in a wheelchair to be carrying a coffin. Undignified. And dignity of course is what funerals are all about.

So it was Andy's funeral and me and Irene were the guests of honour. I mean obviously not guests of *honour* as such; you don't get that at funerals. But you know what I mean. We were the ones everyone had to be most solemn around. It was us who'd known Andy, in life and in death. Irene was his widow: I was his comrade (or rather he was my superior officer; I thought of him as Andy, as my mate, but I hardly ever called him Andy to his face). I was the one who made the jump with him, his opposite number whose miserable life he saved by giving up his own. I was the one who was there, actually *there*, when he died.

You see it was a textbook Para death. That's why everyone was so choked up about it. We all wanted to go like that (only we didn't). Pack on your back, giving your life to save a mate. It was so Para. Even now, now I'm a long way removed from it all, it still brings a lump to the throat. Got to hasn't it. *He died for me*. Do you see what I mean? He was like my own personal Jesus. It was so Para it hurt. Every so often during the weeks after his death I'd catch someone's eye, one of the other lads, and they'd see what I was thinking and we'd just whisper to each other: Para, fucking *Para*. Just thinking about it gave you a glow.

Para death, bog-standard army funeral – apart from the emotion of course. Held outside in an army cemetery with full army pomp and circumstance. Those of us who'd been down south were used to dos like this by now; and this one was no different really, except every so often you had to wipe a tear away, a real stingy one. Oh and I fell in love.

What else do I remember about that day? Sweet f. a. It rained. The priest had a camp voice. The pain in my legs was fucking crucifying. And I managed to fall in love.

Later when the thing developed further, Irene tried to pretend that we hadn't fallen in love at all that first afternoon. She said she didn't believe in love at first sight (hinted that I was a pansy for even suggesting it). She said how could we have fallen in love that first afternoon? We barely said a word to each other. Which is true: apart from a formal introduction – Mrs Stuart, this is Lance Corporal Riley. Riley, this is Mrs Stuart, Andy's . . . uh, you know . . . – apart from these brief hellos I don't think we said a dickie bird. But that doesn't mean a thing. You don't need to exchange *words*, do you. You can exchange other stuff: chemistry, electricity, you know, whatever. I couldn't tell you what it was, this sudden and urgent force, but something passed between us. It was nothing to do with personality – you can't even guess at someone's personality when they're keeping schtum the whole time, and you can't go exchanging pleasantries really at a funeral. Nor was it a physical thing, and I know what you're thinking and no, it *wasn't* that neither. Sure, yeah, she looked attractive — beautiful and elegant and all that — in her black dress, black hat, black gloves. And I'm sure I fancied her: who wouldn't? But it's hard to look *sexy* at a funeral. If you know what I mean. Especially when you're the widow, it doesn't sort of go somehow.

So it wasn't force of personality, it wasn't a sex thing, what was it? Maybe . . . maybe I just transferred on to her all those feelings I had for Andy, those feelings of comradeship and devotion (and, let's face it, fucking gratitude; I owed the guy my life). No doubt this is what a shrink would tell me. I couldn't bear to see these feelings buried down with him so I allowed them to leap up out of the ground and glue themselves on to Irene, where they were transformed into sexual attraction. How about that, Mr Freud? I don't know, maybe there's some truth in it. All I know is that while she was standing next to me in the rain, I was shaking. You know, physically shaking. I probably couldn't have spoken to her even if I'd wanted to. And later that evening, back in the hospital, I caught myself composing poems to her in my head. I was a Para, for Christ's sake. A soldier. And here I was trying to write fucking poetry.

If that's not falling in love, Irene, what is it? Just because we don't know why it happened doesn't mean it never happened. If we knew why it was happening we could have stopped it, couldn't we. Neither of us wanted this, but we couldn't do anything about it. I thought of Andy and all I could think of was how I'd betrayed him. That night as I lay on my tod in the hospital ward, the pain in my legs beginning to seep through again as the drugs wore off, it felt like Andy was watching over me, I could see him shaking his head in disappointment. Poems to his missus on the night of his funeral . . . I wished he really was there so I could apologise and beg his forgiveness, so he could give me a thumping and snap me out of it.

But as the night wore on the pain eased slightly and the guilt seemed to gradually slip away, to be replaced by something else. Something like a rising sense of panic: panic that it was all over, that I would never see Irene again, that I would be left with this lonely, hollow feeling forever. And it was a very real panic. How *would* I see her again? The funeral had come and gone and I was hardly likely to bump into her moping around the barracks . . .

It took me a long time to get off to sleep that night, and when I did finally nod off I dreamed; and in my dreams I saw Irene.

10.43

Frank parked the bus at Dover port and his passengers poured out needily. They were all needy by now. Joyce needed the toilet, Frank needed a break from the wheel, Riley needed a drink – in fact they all needed a drink pretty much, even those who didn't drink.

And Mikey: Mikey needed his head examining. Even before they were out of the car park he was at it. A young couple in a red Escort pulled into the space next to them and as they got out Mikey slunk up to the husband and mumbled: 'Spare any change, mate?'

The man looked surprised, but once the request had registered he began fumbling obligingly in his pocket. Before Mikey could get his hands on the money, though, he was yanked firmly away by Jonquil.

'Mikey, leave these poor folk alone. We've got plenty of money for everyone today.'

Mikey was furious. He'd scored there; he was going to get at least a quid out of that bloke, easy. And there was a big difference, as far as he was concerned, between *we've* got a lot of money and *I've* got a lot of money.

He needn't have worried, however. As they entered the ticket hall his eyes widened like a child's at Christmas. He'd stepped into Aladdin's cave. A large room, a really large room, larger than the largest pub he'd ever been in, *full* of people on holiday. Everywhere you looked, people on holiday. Families, couples, groups, single people — all on holiday. And Mikey *loved* people on holiday: people on holiday bled money. Money fell off them like leaves from a tree in autumn. However tight-arsed folks were most of the time, for two weeks of the year they were all the same: desperate to plough through as much as they could of everything they'd earned in the other fifty weeks. This was the cycle of life. You just had to catch them at the right moment. Usually Mikey tried to get them outside Covent Garden tube, or in the queue for Buckingham Palace or Madame Tussaud's. But there was always competition in those places: everyone wanted a piece of that lucrative tourist action. Here, though, here he was pretty much on his own. In a large room. Full of people on holiday. Most of whom spoke English.

And just as the full magnificence of his situation was sinking in, Mikey noticed his companions peeling away from him. Joyce, obviously, to the ladies, fortunately situated just by the entrance. For the last stretch of the journey she'd been white as a sheet and you wouldn't have thought she could have moved quite as fast as she did when they reached the ticket hall. Frank sat down heavily on the nearest available chair. There was a group of nasty greeny-brown-coloured chairs clustered around the middle of the room. He looked exhausted, and they weren't even on the boat yet. Jonquil went to sort out tickets. Riley went to look for a drink, somewhere, anywhere. And the other three, Candy, Dougal, Peter . . . well who gave a toss where they went? They weren't going to stop him. He was all alone in paradise.

Before he started he whispered a prayer and then smiled to himself. God would be startled; He couldn't have been expecting to hear from Mikey Williams again in a hurry.

And then he set about it like a pro. A young family to his right: two quid from the father, twenty pence from his daughter, who couldn't have been more than eight. A young businessman in his shirt sleeves: fifty pence. Two French backpacking teenagers who probably didn't understand the currency yet: a quid each. A grumpy old couple standing in silence with nothing whatsoever left to say to each other: fuck all. A gaggle of middle-aged women waiting outside the newsagents: anything from ten pence to a pound each. A cheery-looking elderly lady sitting by herself: a fiver. A *fiver*!

Jonquil must have heard his whoop of delight. She was almost at the front of the queue for tickets, peering at the departure times, checking her watch, willing the queue to move more quickly. There was a boat at quarter past eleven. If the old witch in front of her would just hurry up a little they might yet make it. She spun round when she heard Mikey, like a mother able to pick out her own child's crying in a crowded playground, and yelled at him: 'Mikey, I've warned you!'

Where was Frank? Where was Joyce? Why weren't they dealing with this? How come she had to do everything herself?

Eventually she made the front of the queue, threw down a carefully counted wad of notes and asked hurriedly for eight tickets for the eleven fifteen. Clutching the tickets, she went to round up the troops . . .

And of course they were no bloody where to be seen.

In the large, packed hall the only one she could pick out was Mikey, still hitting on people despite her warnings. She scanned and scanned. Finally she spotted Frank, slumped uselessly on a chair in the middle of the room. Just slumped there. She couldn't believe it; she loved him dearly, of course she did, but he was *so* useless *so* much of the time.

'Frank!' she shrieked. 'We've got ten minutes till the boat goes. We need to find the others.'

Frank sprang lethargically into action while Jonquil hauled Mikey away from another unsuspecting punter. Mikey complained, but not too much. They'd been here not much more than five minutes and he'd made fifteen quid. Lawyers didn't get paid that much, did they?

Most of the others were at the newsagents around the corner from the ticket desk. Riley telling the assistant angrily that he ought to stock some fucking booze if he wanted to run a proper fucking shop, Peter watching and laughing, Candy flicking through a copy of *Sugar*, Dougal standing on his own, looking bewildered, being Dougal.

Joyce was the last to appear. It was eleven oh six by Jonquil's watch when she came bounding out of the ladies with an enormous, relieved grin on her face.

'Everyone waiting for me?' she said sunnily. 'Sorry, I thought I should make the most of the last civilised toilets before we reach foreign shores.'

'Civilised?' asked Candy anxiously. 'What do you mean?'

'French toilets!' said Joyce, as though *everyone* knew about French toilets.

'No!' said Jonquil firmly, sensing bladders loosening all around her. 'We don't have time for anyone else to go. You'll have to wait until we're on the boat.'

Riley

Of course I knew I had to see her again as soon as I could. As soon as my legs would carry me again to a car and operate the pedals for me to drive.

I was in the wheelchair for a month after the accident. Then the plasters came off my arms and they gave me crutches to hobble around in. My legs stayed in plaster for another eight weeks and I wasn't allowed to drive for another two weeks after that. I couldn't begin to tell you how slowly these weeks crawled by. During this time the army kept me occupied. They gave me simple stuff to do: boots to clean, reports to write, meals to prepare, menial stuff that made me think they were punishing me for having my legs smashed up. They gave me magazines to read, beer to drink. But most of all they gave me TV to watch, daytime TV. I became a world bloody expert on the subject. *Pebble Mill, The Onedin Line, Bonanza*, snooker, racing. The Commonwealth Games, kids' educational programmes, kids' non-educational programmes. I was addicted to the lot of them. There was a brand spanking-new Beta-max video recorder in the TV room and I even used to tape some of this crap, if I couldn't decide, for example, between *Hart to*

Hart and the athletics. And time – they gave me a lot of time to think about how lucky I'd been (or unlucky: I might never have had the accident in the first place), and how much my bloody legs hurt.

Finally, though, I was free to get up and walk around, free to go out on parade again, free to tab ten miles cross country at five thirty in the morning with a pack half my own body weight on my back, free to be bullied into making another jump as soon as possible. It's just like riding a bike, they said (they, the army). You never forget how. The important thing is to get straight back into the saddle.

And at long bloody last I was free to drive. I had some leave coming to me so I hired a car and I drove out to see Irene – Mrs Stuart as she still was. I could have got the address off someone, but for some reason I didn't want anyone to know. It was a private thing. I knew she'd moved back to this village in Buckinghamshire she'd lived in before she was married. Andy had spoken to me about this place, how he used to visit Irene there when they were courting. Arse end of nowhere, he said. All pretty village squares and country fêtes and maypoles. He made it sound, though, like the kind of place where everyone knew everyone else, so I thought I would be safe enough to just go there, park, and ask around.

As it happened, it wasn't that easy. No one knew her in the only pub I could see in the village. That was OK; she probably wasn't a pub kind of person. But then no one knew her in the hairdressers either, nor the butcher's, nor the jeweller's. I asked in every single shop along the small high street and all I got was blank stares. Stuart . . . *Irene* Stuart? No mate, sorry, never heard of her. I couldn't believe I'd come all this way for nothing. Somebody had to know her. Maybe she'd moved again, or maybe my information was wrong and she'd never come back here in the first place . . . but then *someone* would remember her from before. Surely. I came out of the last shop in the row and went to sit under this horrible ornamental clock-tower thing, the clear landmark of the village, in its quaint little square. It was a small, cosy place. Bustling high street for a cold winter's week-day morning. I even thought about stopping all the shoppers and asking them one by one. It really did look like the kind of place where people knew each other. But no one knew Irene. I lit a fag; it began to feel as though I was wasting my time. I thought about spending the rest of the day in the pub.

After a short while, the girl I had spoken to in the greengrocer's came out and found me. 'Excuse me, sir,' she said, polite as you like, 'did you have any luck with tracking down that lady?' She was young, about my age probably but I felt much older than her somehow. I was all togged up in my sparkling uniform and I had seen some stuff recently which made me feel very old indeed. 'You should try at the newsagent's,' she said. I told her I'd already done that. 'No, there's another one just off the main road.' She pointed over my shoulder. I turned round and I could see where she meant. A small shop in the distance, down a side street, with a yellow Walls Ice Cream sign outside it. I'd probably never have seen it on my own. 'They know everyone in there.'

I thanked her and stood up with a smile. OK, I thought to myself, one more shot and then it's down the pub. The girl hung around for a moment, breathing out cold air as thick as my cigarette smoke, and then went back inside her shop.

The newsagent was run by a grumpy old bloke who seemed to take an instant dislike to me. Probably took an instant dislike to everyone.

'Excuse me, mate,' I said confidently. I wasn't going to be put off by a grumpy bastard. 'I'm looking for a Mrs Irene Stuart, I think she lives in the village somewhere. She used to live here before she was married as well, but I don't know what she was called then. Her husband, Lieutenant Andrew Stuart, Andy, of the Parachute Regiment, he died a couple of months ago and I think she's moved back here.'

The old bloke muttered to himself. 'Stuart, Stuart . . . Why would you be asking?'

'I have some things of her husband's,' I said, indicating the uniform to show who I was. I had worn it on purpose; people trust the army.

He carried on staring at me like I was a pervert or something.

'She takes the *Telegraph*,' he said eventually, and he gave me directions to a house some way out of the village. Maybe it wasn't that surprising no one knew Irene if she lived all the way out there. 'Moved in about a fortnight ago,' he said. 'Couldn't tell you any more about her. Haven't even seen her face.'

I drove back past the clock-tower thing. The girl from the greengrocer's was sitting outside. She waved at me as I drove past and I waved back, still smiling. And on out to Irene's. A large house, but not a fancy one, about two miles outside the village. I wondered if this was the house she had lived in before, maybe even grown up in, or whether it was simply the place she had run away to when her life had fallen apart. Close enough to home to be comfortingly familiar, but a long way away from anyone else. Safe. There was a pebbled driveway at the front of the house. The car made a loud scrunching noise as I turned in and stopped. I thought this might bring her to her window – she couldn't get many people just showing up like this, not all the way out here – but there was no sign. So I went up to the door and rang the bell.

It took a while before there was any movement inside. I was just about to try again when I heard footsteps coming downstairs. The door was on a chain so it only opened slightly, and Irene – Mrs Stuart – peered out.

'Mrs Stuart . . . ?' I said, and I gazed through the gap and into her eyes . . .

. . . and you recognised me, didn't you Irene? You knew immediately who I was. How can you say that wasn't love? You'd seen me once, for one afternoon, four months earlier and you knew who I was immediately.

'It's Lance Corporal Riley,' I said unnecessarily. It seemed difficult suddenly to explain why I'd done this, why I'd driven all the way out here to see her.

'What can I do for you, Lance Corporal Riley?'

'I wanted to talk to you.'

'I see.' She wasn't taking off the chain.

'About your husband.'

She disappeared, out of my sight completely. All I could see through the gap now was the corner of a table with a telephone on it. Maybe she was about to open the door.

She wasn't. Instead, after a long pause, I heard a disembodied voice say, sadly and quietly: 'I don't want to talk about my husband. Please go away.'

'I wish we'd talked more at the funeral,' I started to say, but the door was already closing. I thought about ringing the bell again, even let my finger hover above it, but there didn't seem much point. I didn't want to be a pain and she'd sounded definite.

So that was it. I went back to the car. I drove to the nearest big town. I spent the afternoon at the bookies. I stayed at a cheap hotel. I got paralytic.

And then two weeks later I was summoned to see Lieutenant Foster. Shit, I thought to myself. This was going to be it. The *order*. The order to get back on the bike. Back up in the air. But no, it wasn't anything to do with that, it was all to do with an envelope. When I got to his office there was Foster, leaning back in his officer's leather chair, waving an envelope around. A small, white envelope, the address neatly handwritten in blue ink. Didn't look like anybody's writing that I knew. When he stopped waving it long enough for me to get a proper look, I saw it was addressed to a Lance Corporal Reilly.

'It's from Andy's widow,' Foster said in his chinless officers' accent. He was only a lieutenant, and a young one at that, but he spoke like a lieutenant colonel. 'Mrs Stuart.'

Fuck me, I managed not to say. Foster leaned forward.

'Any idea *why* Mrs Stuart would be writing to you, Riley?'

'No sir ... I, uh, I went to visit her a couple of weeks ago ... but she didn't want to speak to me.'

He stood up suddenly and looked at me. Blurting it out like that made me realise just how bloody ridiculous it sounded. I just went and visited her, just like that, completely unasked and uninvited. Like a complete berk. Foster was still looking at me. His eyebrows were arched and they said *why*? *Why* did you go and visit her, Riley? He still didn't hand the envelope over to me.

'I needed to talk to her, sir,' I said, to answer the question he hadn't even asked. 'About Lieutenant Stuart.'

'Jesus, man, there are army counsellors for that sort of thing.' He glared at me and then lowered his voice. 'Look Riley . . . we know what a time you've had, but you can't . . . you can't go around harassing a grieving woman like that. Especially not an officer's widow.' He approached me. He was still clutching the envelope. We were both still standing. 'There are people here you can talk to. Professional people. There's no shame involved. It's quite a . . . natural reaction to your circumstances.'

'I don't need to speak to professional people, sir,' I replied quietly. 'I wanted to talk to her. I thought . . . I thought she might want to talk to me.'

Lieutenant Foster carried on looking at me, as though the answer to some vital question or other might be written on my face. Then, then he gave me the envelope.

'Well I should think this will be an end to it. But if you have any problems Riley, do please bring them out into the open. You can always come and talk to me if you like. I'm perfectly approachable, you know.'

'Yes sir. Thank you, sir.'

'I mean it.'

'Thank you, sir.'

Not if you were the last man on Earth. Sir.

I waited till I was back at my bed before I tore the envelope open. It was still gummed down. If Foster had opened it and read it, and you had to assume he had, then he had somehow managed to reseal the envelope.

But he hadn't read it, had he. He couldn't have done. If he'd read it there would have been none of this rubbish about that being an end to it. Would there. Because this was the letter, Irene . . . I burned it immediately, but I can still remember every word. This was the letter that asked me to come and meet you in London. You were sorry you had been so *brusque* with me before. (Brusque! I read that word over and over. I never even knew you spelled brusque with a q.) You

83

were sorry you'd been brusque. It had been unexpected, that was all. But you did want to talk to me. You knew what I meant to your husband, you knew some of the stuff we'd been through together.

Yeah, some . . .

And you wanted to meet me in London. You had to take care of some business things there from time to time, so it would be easy to arrange a date. London. It was perfect. I could come down on my next leave. I could say I was visiting friends, Foster would never know. No one would know.

I phoned that evening from a call box in town. We fixed a date and a place to meet. A restaurant. A Saturday night. Right. What business were you planning to do in London on a Saturday night, Irene?

11.06

'Passports please . . .'
   'Thank you.'
   'Thank you madam . . . passports.'
   'Thanks.'
   'Thank you sir . . . passports . . . thank you . . . thank you . . .'
   'Cheers mate.'
   'Thank you sir . . . passports . . .'
   'Here mate, spare any change?'
   'Mikey!'

Mikey

Only asking. Nothing wrong with asking, is there.

Jonquil

And . . . did you call him?

Yeah. I called him.

And . . . ?

And . . . I don't know. I don't know how I feel about it all. I suppose that's why I'm back. To try and figure it out . . . I mean, I saw him again and everything. I've seen him a couple of times. To all intents and purposes we're Going Out together . . . whatever that means . . .

What do you mean, whatever that means?

Well, that's all we do, isn't it. We go out together. And then we come home together. And then he gives me a little peck on the cheek, and then he goes back to *his* home, his grubby little flat in Stockwell. Without me.

Ah, the sex thing.

Yeah, the sex thing . . . Is that going out or isn't it? I don't know. I've never done it like this before. Not since I was fourteen anyway, and my mum would give me hell if I wasn't back before ten o'clock, and there was no chance of anyone spending the night with anyone else . . . I just don't know how to handle it.

You're not happy with the way things are going?

No. That's the weird thing, I'm very happy. That's the thing I can't get a hold of. I'm very happy. He makes me feel . . . good about myself. I don't know how to explain it. I feel useful. I feel like he needs me. That first night we saw each other again, for example . . . and I know, I owe you a huge debt of gratitude. You made me call him again and I'm so glad I did, even with the sex thing and everything. Anyway, we went out and he really, like, opened up to me, you know? Told me some of his problems. And I answered as best I could and it seemed to help. Bit like what you do really . . . only cheaper . . .

What sort of problems?

Work mainly. He turned up at the pub in his work clothes. We were meeting at six thirty and he hadn't had time to go home and change . . . In a pub up in town. We were back on neutral territory, that's how much of a step backwards we had taken. And he turns up in this yukky pale yellow T-shirt with the company logo on it. And I stared at him. They make you wear that? I asked him. And he just looked at me longingly – and this was before he'd sat down or we'd got a drink or discussed our last date or even said hello really – and he goes: You've got to get me out of this place. I don't think I can take it any more.

I made him get the drinks in before I asked him what place and what exactly he wanted me to do. Office Fucking Mate, he goes. Sorry . . . but you know, that's exactly how he said it. OFM, the staff call it. They all hate it there by the sounds of things: the long hours, the low pay etc etc. And, you know, how much fun can stacking shelves with computer disks and doing endless bits of photocopying be? What do you want me to do? I asked him. And he asked me how I got my job. It's what I've always wanted to do, I told him, I did a social work course at college, I did volunteer work, I did some locum shifts at various hostels around London to begin with and then I got my first regular job. Well can you get me some of these shifts? he goes. Help me get into it. And I asked him if he was sure that was what he wanted to do. And he's like, yeah of course, what do you mean? The way they all do. So I give him the whole story. I tell him what the homeless are like, generally, and what working with them is like. I tell him a lot of them are drunks. That means drunk the whole time, not just nicely pissed on a Friday night like me and him might get, but you know, totally, permanently, wake-up-in-the-morning-and-reach-for-the-White-Lightning *pissed*. I tell him how much they stink. How I get home every night and my clothes reek of stale cigarettes, BO and extra-strong lager. It's that kind of sweet, cheesey smell, it's the same wherever you go, wherever the great unwashed congregate, you know? You recognise it straight away. And it kind of lodges itself in your nostrils and just sticks there, so even if you're away from work for a couple of days the smell still follows you around. I tell him the homeless are regularly threatening and occasionally violent. I tell him they lie and steal and cheat. I tell him how *irritating* they can be. How transparently manipulative and pathetic. How downright dislikeable a lot of them are.

And he stares at me incredulously. The way they all do.

Because, you know, homeless people have become such a fucking *cause*, haven't they ... excuse me, but I'm clambering on to my soapbox here. Everybody likes the homeless, don't they. Because they're all cheery chappies who stand outside tube stations with their dogs selling *The Big Issue*, having a laugh, wishing you a nice day even if you don't buy a copy. So everybody likes them. Everybody except the people who actually have to deal with them on a day-to-day basis, who know what a pain in the arse they can be. It's like all those wankers on the telly with their red ribbons – you know they'd all run a mile if they actually ever met anyone with AIDS. It's all, oh yes I met a homeless person once and he was quite a decent chap actually; such a shame. And it *is* a shame. That's exactly what it is – it's shameful the way the poorest people in society are treated. It's fucking despicable – sorry – but that doesn't alter the fact that a lot of these people are drunken, sad bastards who've just been nannied all their lives and you've got to be paid to look after them because no one in their right mind would give a toss about them if they weren't being paid for it ...

You managed to put him off, then?

No ... no, not at all. Played right into his hands. He just gazed at me in admiration and said he thought it was wonderful what I did. And I thought, yeah. Of course. He's a Christian. This only makes it more attractive for him.

So what now? You're going to try and fix him up with a job?

He's started already. They interviewed him for a locum position last week, added him to the list and he's done a couple of night shifts already.

And ... ?

Hugh Brune

And he loves it. He can't afford to give up his other job until he gets more regular work, so he comes off the night shift and goes straight into Office Mate. And then I see him in the evening and he's still all fired up about it. He's sat up all night talking to a manic depressive and this is, like, the best thing that's ever happened to him. He keeps telling me how fantastic it all is, how I've been so good for him, how I've helped him turn his life around, sort him out, nobody's really taken such an interest in him before etc etc . . . and, you know, it's hard to hear those kinds of things over and over again without warming a little to the person saying them.

Sounds like Frank's more suited to the work than you are.

Oh I'm still suited to it OK. I just like to moan. Most of them are sweethearts. I was just exaggerating to make a point, you know? I get so many people saying to me, oh yeah, I'd love to work with the homeless, and you know they'd hate every second of it, you know they wouldn't last five minutes if they actually had to do it, so you kind of develop a defence mechanism. But Frank meant it and he's stuck with it and, you know, fair play to him. In fact I've been getting a lot more positive about my job this last week because he's been so, you know, enthusiastic about it.

You haven't done any shifts together yet?

No! No, God, I can't imagine that . . . No, he's been working at completely different places, and always during the night so far. No, I can't really see us working together. It'd be unbearable for the people around us. I mean, our relationship is at a kind of weird stage right now. We're really kind of lovey-dovey, but we're not, you know, touchy-feely.

So you still don't understand his feelings about sex?

No . . . Well, yeah, a little maybe. But not completely. Not yet. But, you know, I suppose it doesn't feel quite as important as it did. I was making such a big deal out if it before. I'm a little more laid-back now. It's new territory for me, so I'm just going to see how it goes. If we can't sleep together, maybe we'll just be good friends for a while – I do enjoy being in his company.

And if I can't get it with Frank, who knows, maybe I'll get it somewhere else ... He couldn't have any complaints about that, could he?

11.11

They set up a base on deck, at the side of the ship. Jonquil's idea. She was still full of this notion that you needed to watch yourself travelling to see how far you'd come. There's a point on this crossing, she told Peter who wasn't remotely interested, where, on a clear day like today, you can see France in front of you and England behind you and you really get the feeling of being nowhere in particular, you know? Neither here nor there.

'Neither here nor there,' she said again.

Peter shrugged. It wasn't even as important as that as far as he was concerned.

Anyway it was a lovely day: they ought to be sitting outside, making the most of it. It struck Jonquil how British they all looked. Despite the baking heat, they all had their just-in-case jackets and jumpers. She had her trusty cardy; Joyce was wearing her black denim jacket which didn't even reach her hips and looked about three sizes too small for her (and didn't, to Jonquil's mind, go at all well with the rainbow dress she had on underneath – for someone who liked to talk at length about her 'time in the fashion industry', Joyce had appalling taste in clothes). And some of the men – Peter and Tom especially – had coats so thick you had to wonder if they knew what season it was, let alone what kind of day. Or maybe they just liked being warm; maybe a life on the streets taught you to appreciate warmth.

They spread themselves over a dozen of the bright red, hard seats that clung to the deck and sat in silence as the boat pulled away from England, listening to the gentle, friendly grumbling of the engines. The other passengers gave them a wide berth. In fact by the time the boat was clear of Dover port there was no one else sitting anywhere near them. They looked kind of funny, the group of them all together. They looked like they didn't belong – here or anywhere else. And even in competition with the sea, that smell was something.

From her brightly coloured bag, which up to now had seemed to contain nothing but sandwiches and Coke, Joyce suddenly, startlingly, produced three juggling balls the same bright red colour as the seats. Jonquil looked on in expectation. What on *earth* had Joyce brought juggling balls with her for? Was she really going to start throwing them around? Here? And wouldn't it simply be hysterical if one of them was to slip out of her hands, roll overboard and drop into the sea . . .

'Does anyone want a go at juggling?' Joyce asked loudly.

The question was greeted by an appropriate silence. Unperturbed, Joyce began to toss the balls carefully into the air. She began with the simple three-ball manoeuvre, the classic juggle, keeping the spare ball directly in front of her face, gazing at some magic vanishing point directly under her nose, face locked in concentration, hands barely moving. Then, gaining in confidence, she attempted some more complicated routines – throwing the spare ball in a high arc above her head, releasing two balls simultaneously so they crossed at her midriff. Perhaps if they hadn't been so close to the water she'd have attempted her favourite trick of all, the behind-the-back release.

Jonquil, meanwhile, watched the show slyly through her sun-glasses. What she wouldn't have given for the power of telekinesis now. *Drop you bastards, drop*, she found herself silently urging.

'I didn't know you could juggle,' said Mikey.

'Oh yes. One of my many hidden talents,' said Joyce, not letting her eyes shift for a second. 'I picked it up when I was in India.'

'They juggle a lot in India, do they?'

'Uh . . . well, the people travelling through India do. I'm not sure about the locals.'

At this point one of the balls slipped. Joyce cursed under her breath. Jonquil almost fell off her seat with delight.

'Is it difficult then?'

'Not really. Not once you've got the hang of it,' said Joyce, scrabbling on the deck for the escaping ball. 'At least, it's not too difficult while you keep it going. Stopping's the hard part, catching them all again without letting them go all over the floor.' She held the balls out to him. 'Have a go.'

Mikey shook his head. 'I can't even catch,' he said.

'Oh don't be silly. Everyone can catch.'

To prove her point, Joyce threw one of the balls very gently towards him, perfectly pitched at chest height. Instinctively, Mikey thrust his arms out, then he panicked and crossed them at the wrists, allowing the ball to drop between the backs of his hands, making a strange whimpering sound as he did so. The word *spastic* sprang unbidden to Joyce's lips and was ushered quickly away by her inner wardens of good taste. She didn't know what to say next.

'Bet it makes you hungry, don't it, all that juggling,' Peter said thickly, picking up the ball which Mikey had failed to catch and handing it back to Joyce.

'I . . . what? No, not really. What do you mean?'

Peter was staring intently at Joyce's bag. Eventually she took the hint. 'Oh, you want another sandwich.'

'Well, wouldn't say no . . . you know . . .'

Joyce looked at her watch. 'I suppose it is pressing on to lunch time.' Sensing that it hadn't been a terrific idea to take them out in the first place, she put her juggling balls back into her bag and started handing out sandwiches. She'd spent an hour this morning making these sandwiches, getting up at some ungodly hour to do so. There was something for everyone; she'd made cheese sandwiches, cold-meat sandwiches, sandwiches with just salad in them (she couldn't remember: was Frank a vegan or just a vegetarian?). She'd used brown and white bread. Some had margarine but not others. Then she'd cut the whole batch into triangles. They'd looked delicious as she wrapped them carefully in cling film, soft and crisp, each one rising to a satisfying peak in the middle. They looked slightly less delicious now, warm and squashed from a morning spent in her bag, but everyone took a couple and made polite murmurs of approval as they ate. No one asked what the fillings were; they all just took what they were offered. They were all, Joyce felt, itching to go inside. Despite the sunshine, despite the fresh sea air. There were bars inside, there was a duty free shop: there was drink.

It was Peter who broke first. Still chomping away on his last large mouthful, he said: 'OK if I go and, uh, stretch my legs?' Most of the food stayed in his mouth.

'No Peter,' Joyce said firmly. 'Stay where we can see you. Otherwise we'll simply lose everybody.'

'Oh I don't think it matters if people go off for a wander,' said Jonquil. 'They can't exactly go far, can they. And it'll give us some time to ourselves.' She had taken off her cardigan and crossed her arms behind her head so the world could appreciate how carefully she'd shaved her armpits, and was now squinting up at the sun through her shades. Frank, who had pushed his sunglasses up on to his forehead to eat his sandwiches, did his trick again with his temples, making the glasses fall neatly into place, and *again* nobody noticed him. He too sat back and gazed up at the sun.

Joyce felt her skin prickle from being so flatly contradicted. What did Jonquil mean, they couldn't go far? There was a shop full of bottles of vodka in there: you could go a very long way on a bottle of vodka.

'Go on, scram, the lot of you,' Jonquil went on. 'But make sure you're all back here by the time we arrive in Calais. I don't want to have to come and look for anyone.'

They vanished like cartoon baddies disappearing from the scene of a crime. All except Dougal, who went to stand by the railings to feed the rest of his sandwich to the gulls; and Mikey, who just stayed where he was for a few moments and then went to ask Joyce for another Coke.

Joyce had drifted off; she was miles away. Thinking about that car full of children they had passed on the motorway. That one cold, virtually unpronounceable word that still held such sway over her life. From somewhere behind her eyes she felt tears coming. She wasn't sure if they were caused by Jonquil being so horrible to her just now or by her own painful memories. Or maybe it was just the sea breeze making her eyes water.

'What?' she said, suddenly aware that Mikey was speaking to her.

'I said, could I have another can of Coke . . . ? Are you OK?'

'Yes . . . yes, I'm fine,' said Joyce, reaching into her bag. 'It's just, you know . . . it's just the wind.'

Jonquil looked over at her through her sunglasses and then looked quickly away again. Nothing to do with her if Joyce was crying, was it?

Mikey also turned away from the others and mothered his can of Coke like he'd been doing on the bus.

'For heaven's sake, Mikey,' Frank said, 'you can do that in the open, you know. We know what you're up to under there with that bottle of rum.'

What he was up to, of course, under cover of his jacket, was taking a glug out of the Coke and then topping the can up from the half-bottle of Bacardi stashed away in his inside pocket. He brought forward the bottle sheepishly. There was only a small amount left sloshing around in the bottom of it, maybe a mouthful at most.

Joyce stared in horror. She hadn't known, not at all. If she'd known, she might have held back on the Cokes a little. She'd just assumed he was thirsty.

'Gosh Mikey, have you really drunk all that this morning?' Jonquil said. It was quite impressive in a way.

Mikey nodded yeah. He didn't feel the need to mention that this was his second bottle actually. Nor to point out that he'd have drunk a lot more given more money and more opportunity. It wasn't easy keeping your booty concealed in a confined space like that minibus. And now he was nearly completely out – and it was a long afternoon ahead.

'But why, Mikey?' Joyce asked.

Jonquil snorted. Frank shook his head. He'd only be doing the job a few weeks but even he knew this was a bloody stupid question to ask. There was no *why*. If there was a *why* there wouldn't be such a problem; there'd be a reason, you could address it, sort it out, overcome it. It was this lack of why that was so scary.

Mikey looked for an answer, though. 'Because . . .' he said with difficulty. 'Because if I didn't drink, I'd have to stop.'

There. That said it all really. Made perfect sense to Mikey. If he didn't drink, he'd have to stop. He drank because the only alternative was to stop drinking, to *not* drink. And Mikey could envisage many things in this world – he could envisage himself getting a job, a place to live, another wife maybe, more kids (inevitably more bloody kids), he could see aliens landing, a cure for cancer, Swansea City back at the top of the league. But to stop drinking? Think of the pain, think of the loss, think of all that free time with nothing to do, think of the *sobriety*. It was . . . unthinkable.

'What do you mean?' Joyce asked.

'I just . . . have to drink,' Mikey tried to explain. 'It doesn't have to be Bacardi and Coke, although that's my favourite. But I have to . . .'

Joyce still didn't understand, but she didn't ask further. She didn't want to think about this any more. After a few moments she went over to talk to Dougal, who at least was teetotal. He was still working his way through his sandwiches, taking a bite out of each one and then feeding the rest to the seagulls which flew alongside the boat, chaperoning it and preventing everyone from being able to relax completely. These weren't sandwiches from Joyce's mountain, these were extra sandwiches, ones he'd brought himself.

'What have you got in these?' Joyce asked him.

'I don't know. My sister gave them to me yesterday. These ones are corned beef and apple, I think.'

'Hmm, that sounds . . . interesting.'

'Oh yes, she's very inventive when it comes to food, my sister.'

'She must be,' Joyce said.

Dougal took another, small bite of sandwich.

'These are disgusting, though.'

Dougal

Whatever happened to ham sandwiches? Can somebody please explain to me what the ham sandwich ever did to offend anyone? When I first came to London, twenty-five years ago, you could pop into almost any church in the city around eleven thirty, twelve o'clock and they'd give you a ham sandwich. Or maybe a cheese sandwich. But that was it: ham or cheese or ham and cheese. Nowadays at the day centre where I usually go for my lunch they get leftovers dropped in from these fancy delis and it's all goats cheese and sun-dried tomatoes, Tandoori chicken, aubergine and hoummus on warm ciabatta bread. I can't remember the last time I had a ham sandwich. Of course I know I shouldn't complain, it's very kind of these people to donate anything at all, and some of these things don't, I suppose, taste too bad . . . but if you're feeling a little delicate, they play havoc with your insides.

11.39

Actually Dougal wasn't the only one not drinking, Candy wasn't drinking either, not today. She was too fucked up to drink today. Her arm was giving her hell where George Johnson's men had been stamping on it. The bruise and cut on her face weren't as bad this morning, but she knew she looked a picture. She felt like a battered wife, too ashamed to admit what a mess her life was.

And now, to top it all, she felt sick. Not sea sick. Not even Candy could manage to get sea sick on a day as still as today. She was sick with worry, a worse kind of sick. What was going to happen with that gun? She'd been fretting about this all day. On the way down in the minibus she'd been promising herself that getting through passport control would be the worst bit. Once they were on the boat everything would be fine. But now they were on the boat and everything was not fine. Everything was a very bloody long way away from being fine. Now she was telling herself getting into France would be the worst bit. Once they were inside the country, *then* everything would be fine. But then the gun still had to get itself from Calais to Orléans without being noticed . . .

She stood in the middle of the main lounge, almost faint from her worry, being ignored. People brushed past her on their way from seat to bar to toilet to shop. No one paused to consider why there was someone standing slap bang in the middle of this large, crowded room, bruised and shaking and wide-eyed with terror.

She looked around. She tried to pick out someone who might have a spare cigarette.

12.39

French time. Jonquil adjusted her watch, wiping an hour from its face. It was another one of those processes that made you feel like you were *going* somewhere. Somewhere different. In fact it was one of the fading ways in which Little Britain still sought to differentiate itself from the rest of Europe, wasn't it. The Imperial time-change. What happened to that hour you lost every time you crossed the Channel? Where did it go? Of course, it didn't *go* anywhere. It was a deposit. Little Britain held on to it safely for you; and you only got it back when you came home.

12.42

Gilbert was bored. Bored, bored, bored, bored, bored. They'd been in this boring shop for days and days. There were no toys in here, no sweets – well, there were some large fancy boxes of chocolates and Toblerones made for giants, but no proper sweets, no Jelly

Tots – no comics, no nothing. There were just incredibly large packets of cigarettes, which everyone knew were terrible things. You got two hundred cigarettes in these packets. Gilbert tried to think about how long it would take to smoke two hundred cigarettes. Could you smoke two hundred cigarettes in your whole life? Then there were bottles. Bottles were boring. And then, worst of all, there was perfume. Perfume was a *girls'* thing. He wasn't quite sure how it worked, but it was something *girls* did to make themselves smell funny.

They had stopped by the perfume racks.

'What do you think then, Gil? Shall we get Mummy some perfume as a nice surprise?'

Gilbert didn't think. He wasn't entirely sure what perfume was; perfumes all seemed to be called after words only grown-ups used, words he didn't understand like Obsession and Contradiction and Eternity. In any case he didn't have any money, and there were signs up all over the place saying you had to be seventeen years old to buy anything. It wasn't his decision.

He was only seven, but he wasn't stupid.

'I think we'll have some of this,' said his dad, picking out a small bottle with a picture of a lady on the front that cost thirty-four pounds ninety-nine. You could get an Action Man *with* all the Arctic Adventure accessories for thirty-four pounds ninety-nine.

'Hey Daddy, what's that man doing?' Gilbert said, tugging urgently at his father's sleeve. Something was actually happening in the boring shop.

'What man?'

'That man over there ... The one putting those bottles into his coat.'

'I don't know.'

'He's stealing, isn't he?'

'Now we don't know that. He could be working here.'

'In those clothes?'

'Come on, let's just pay for this and leave, shall we? There's no need to make a fuss.'

What's more, the man was singing to himself. Gilbert always got into trouble if he sang to himself, except if it was in the bath or in the car sometimes on long journeys.

Riley

You know what, I don't think I was ever happier than I was on that boat going down to the South Atlantic. Not even later on when I was with Irene. I think I always knew things were doomed with Irene, but on that boat – the Canberra, the Great White Whale – with those boys, I felt anything was possible. I was nineteen years old and I was on top of the bloody world.

The moment we arrived at Southampton it was clear something big was up. There were people shouting, crying, a regimental band playing, orders being barked, general chaos. Me and Hughie Gibbs got roped into a chain gang, loading crate after crate of Double Diamond on board. I'd never seen so much beer in all my life; it felt like we were going on the biggest almighty piss-up in history. I couldn't keep a straight face as all this booze passed right under my nose.

I suppose Irene must have been there, with that long, sad gaggle of birds lined up along the dock to see us off. We'd all been given strict orders not to wave as the boat pulled away. We were going off to war, not on a pleasure cruise, and it wasn't *army* to wave. Not everyone took notice of this, but Andy would have done; he was a pro like that. Irene, though, she would have waved. Maybe not as hysterically and as tearfully as some of the others lined up with her, but she'd have waved all right and smiled the best smile she could, and she'd have made sure Andy saw her smiling and waving. Imagine that. Imagine leaving someone like her behind to go eight thousand miles to some poxy islands you've never heard of before. Doesn't bear thinking about. Of course I didn't know her then. She was just a face in the crowd. Me and Gibbsy were leaning on the deck railings, just laughing at the warbling, wailing old slappers.

Pointing out which ones we'd shag when we returned, which ones would be widowed and available. It never occurred to us, not for one second, that it might be us not coming home. We were the fucking Parachute Regiment. I was nineteen years old and I was on top of the bloody world. And anyway, I don't think we really believed at that point there was going to be a war. We were all very gung-ho about it of course. Every night we raised a glass to Maggie for giving us the chance to go and kick some dago arse, for giving us the opportunity to go and do our fucking job for once. But deep down I think we knew there wasn't really going to be a war. There were never wars these days, not in the so-called civilised world. People threatened wars a lot, but they didn't actually do it. Everyone was barking, no one ever bit: it was too expensive – in all sorts of ways. As we sailed, we knew there were men in suits scurrying around Buenos Aires and London, cobbling some kind of deal together, some lily-livered compromise that would stop us from getting our hands dirty. The Yanks were supposed to be helping us negotiate something, so were the French, the Japs, the UN. Something would get sorted out. No one'd fire a shot. We weren't going down there to fight a war: we were going down there to look hard for a little bit and then come home again.

Anyway they couldn't keep us away too long. There was a World Cup that summer and for the first time since I was a kid, England had actually qualified. They couldn't expect us to miss that.

So we settled down to enjoy the trip. It was an amazing boat; a real proper cruise liner, the sort of tub the likes of us wouldn't normally get to see in a million years. There was a pool and a cinema and everything. And it was an OK life on board, once you'd got used to the stupid way the navy spoke (port, starboard and so on). They'd get us up early and we'd do manoeuvres in the morning – usually running up and down the deck with full kit on, and weapon drills, map-reading, medical instruction and so on. Then we'd have lunch – and the food here was a hundred times better than the usual army slop, although you had to wait around for a bit to get fed. Then in the afternoon we'd soak up some rays. Heading south, the sunshine got a little brighter every day and we started to get some serious tanning in.

The lack of skirt was a drag. A few of the ship's staff were female, but they were strictly out of bounds. (Although they must have fancied some. Imagine it from their point of view: two thousand of the hardest men in Britain locked up in a confined space, sweating their guts out every morning, bronzed and half-naked every afternoon. They must have been fucking panting.) So we had to make do with the post. Post like you wouldn't believe. They started air-dropping them in shortly after we set off. From every corner of the country, from Bristol to Rotherham, Aberdeen to Watford, it seemed like every patriotic bird in Britain had decided to do her bit for the lads by sending us a picture of herself with her tits out. It was a nationwide Get Your Tits Out For The Lads campaign; made you proud to be British. And I mean there was *sackfuls* of this stuff. Linda from Gravesend: I just want to say that I think you're all incredibly brave and you're doing a fantastic job and we're all thinking of you back home. Joanne from Rusholme: Pop an Argie for me boys! They didn't come addressed to anyone, just 'A Soldier', or maybe 'A Para'. We passed them around, we laughed at them, we pocketed the pretty ones for ourselves, we took bundles of them openly with us when we went to the khazi. Hughie told everyone he was keeping a master list of the acceptable ones and he was going to fuck them all, one by one, when he got back. After the World Cup was over.

Who were these slags? Whoever they were, they made us happy. They couldn't satisfy us physically, but they satisfied our egos. At last it seemed like people were taking us seriously. You could see this in the older soldiers especially. For years it had felt like the British people had forgotten they even had an army. Once it stopped being compulsory it stopped being noticed. Now, though, now we were the boys again. Now it seemed – to us at any rate – like everyone wanted a piece. That April if you were a bloke and you weren't a soldier, you were no one. And if you were a girl and you weren't fucking a soldier, you were no one. You were fucking no one. Listen to some of these slags. Paula from Southend: I really wish I could be there with you. I wish I could do things for you, help relieve your stress and anxiety . . . all of you!

Imagine. You're nineteen and there are birds you've never met before writing stuff like this to you. I'm sorry Irene, but that's why I was on top of the world on that boat. It was the single most important place you could be at that time. Everyone was looking at us.

Apart from the skirt, the only other problem was the beer problem. There wasn't a shortage, not as such (there was a fucking mountain of Double Diamond on board, I knew that, I'd humped it on myself), but there was an availability problem. Top brass was frightened that cooped up on this boat with nothing to do except eat and drink, we'd all get too wobbly-arsed to fight a war at the other end. So we were rationed to two cans per man per day. Fuck all, in other words. Twenty minutes' supply at most. This went for everyone except ranks major and above (after all they were just going to bark orders at other people at the other end rather than do any fighting themselves, so what did it matter how fat they got?) and the press and the handful of civilians on board.

So every sunny afternoon was filled with dreaming up inventive ways of scoring some tins. The officers were dodgy – they had the power to make your life a misery, and possibly, depending on how things went, very short indeed, so you didn't want to get on the wrong side of them. The journos on the other hand, they were fair game. No one liked the journos. It seems strange when you look back on all the support they gave us, all the Gotchas! and what have you, but we were suspicious of them. Army doesn't like the press. It's a tradition. Journos: nothing but scruffy lefties out to promote their own names by trying to write about the 'horror of war', which of course they know fuck all about, dampening the public's natural patriotic fervour and undermining the whole caboodle. Of course that wasn't the case with the Falklands as it turned out, but how were we to know that? So we were allowed to run rings around these boys. There was this one guy in particular, Ken Nightingale from one or other of the posh papers, he never seemed to learn. We pulled scam after scam on this poor bloke. We'd play cards with him for beer and mark the deck; we'd offer to sell him little titbits of army gossip for beer; we'd creep into his cabin most afternoons while he was wiring his regulation thousand words and simply nick his beer. Nothing he could do about it. In fact he seemed to admire us for it: when we sneaked a look at some of the stuff he was wiring home, it was all about the indomitable, never-say-die, bulldog spirit of the British Tommy, keeping his chin up in the face of adversity, blah blah blah. Whereas all it was, of course, was a natural, basic human desire to get pissed.

It was Gibbsy who kept all this going; he really came into his own on that trip south. If one of us was flagging, it was him that cheered us up, got us through those long nights spent cooped up in our cabins, drinking our illegal beer, listening to the World Service for any clues as to what was actually going on. It was Gibbsy whose mad stories about top brass got the on-board magazine closed down; it was Gibbsy who replied to all the *really* ugly slappers from the post bag using someone else's name, usually a Marine's; it was Gibbsy, allegedly, who took all the white feathers out of his pillow and posted them off in a bundle to 1 Para, who were sat twiddling their thumbs in Northern Ireland.

About ten days into the trip we stopped off for some r and r at Ascension Island. An unbelievable place: a sort of Robinson Crusoe paradise island stuck in the absolute bloody middle of nowhere. We did exercises in the morning, nothing too strenuous, just a few runs, and then beached it up in the afternoon – which of course was a right laugh, but hardly the best preparation for what was to come on Falkland (where it was cold and wet the whole time we were there, and where I spent one entire night lying still on frozen ground being fucking *snowed* on). It was while we were laid up on Ascension that shit began to happen. Firstly we heard that 2 Para had been given the nod to come and join us. Although none of us said so out loud, this was a relief. The rumour was that there were three times as many Argies in and around Stanley as there were in the Task Force. Even allowing for our technical superiority (which we never doubted, not for a second. They were all conscripts, weren't they. Kids. Not to mention cowardly-arsed dago sheep-fuckers), those numbers didn't add up.

Then we heard that the *Belgrano* had gone down. The whisper went around the island base like a dose of the clap. By the time the official announcement was made, the parties on the beach had already started. We christened a piece of driftwood the *Belgrano*, pushed it out into the waves and bombarded it with bottles and pebbles. Even now it was still a game, a movie, a newspaper story, a crisis to be averted. Actually the sinking of the *Belgrano* seemed to signify the *end* of everything, not the beginning. Surely the Argies would just give up now and fuck off back home . . .

And then the following day, while a group of us were waiting to give blood, we heard that the Argies had exoceted the *Sheffield*. So much for giving up. Now it was real; some of our boys had actually died. We hadn't had to deal with this for a long, long time – not for as long as I'd been in the army anyway. Occasionally someone'd get done by a sniper in Belfast or something, but only in ones or twos, the sort of statistics you could ignore because that's all they were: statistics. I hadn't known anything like this before, a whole shipful of men, our boys, blown out of the water. Later that same day, while I was searching on board for some anti-tank equipment for an exercise, I came across half a store cupboard full of packages labelled BAGS: HUMAN REMAINS. I froze. I fell into a deep, still panic which not even Gibbsy could shake me out of. It was true, then: we were going to war. No drill, no exercise, the real deal.

When the boat set off again at the beginning of May there was a completely different atmosphere on board. There was no more pissing about, everyone put their back into training every day. As a sign of the new situation, top brass even banned us from watching any more grot films. Hughie tried to respond to this the only way he knew how – he fixed up a Wank On The Biscuit competition, Paras versus the Cabbageheads; but no one showed up. That's how seriously we were all taking it.

Hughie never made it back by the way. He had half his head

blown off in the fight for Longdon. He never got to fuck those girls on his list; never saw Keegan miss that header against Spain.

12.52

'Hey mister, have you ever been on a boat before?' Gilbert asked.

'Yes,' said Riley, 'but not like this one.'

'This is my first time,' Gilbert said proudly.

'Now Gil, don't bother the gentleman,' said his father, who was furious that Riley had come to sit with them. There were plenty of other free tables. Why did he have to pester them? They'd seen him blatantly steal four half-bottles of whisky and hadn't said anything; he shouldn't push his luck.

'Don't mind me,' Riley said amiably, his secreted bottles clinking as he sat down.

'Were you stealing in that shop?' Gilbert asked.

'No,' Riley replied.

'You were! We saw you! You stole four whole bottles!'

'No, I wasn't stealing. I, uh . . . I work there.'

'See Gil. I told you . . .'

'Why were you taking those bottles off the shelf then?'

'Because . . . they were past their sell-by date.'

'Whisky doesn't have a sell-by date.' This was Gilbert's mother, who ought to have known better.

'It does now . . . New EEC regulations.' Riley took one of the bottles out of his coat pocket. 'Of course that doesn't mean that I can't enjoy a little drop. Staff perks. I don't suppose you've got a glass anyone . . . ? Paper cup . . . ? No . . . ? Oh well, tastes just as good out of the bottle.' He tipped and swallowed. A man-size gulp. Then he offered it around. 'Anyone . . . ?'

'No thanks, no . . . *no*, Gilbert.'

'Okey doke. Suit yourselves.'

Riley took another big swig.

That was better.

13.00

'Looks like Tom Riley's made some new friends,' said Jonquil, coming inside.

'Yeah,' said Frank. 'He can be quite personable when he wants to be.'

'Oh Tom's not so bad . . . He's had a hard life.'

Jonquil had said this before about some of the residents and Frank didn't buy it. *He'd* had a hard life. His family hadn't exactly been loving and supportive; they hadn't been, as the Americans would say, *there* for him. But he didn't feel the need to kill himself with drink. It was rubbish: wet, liberal, soft-minded, university-student rubbish, the kind Jonquil was quite prone to come out with. God gave you adverse circumstances in order for you to overcome them and better yourself, not for you to simply get pissed and hope they might go away.

But he didn't pursue it. They'd come inside for some quiet time to themselves and he didn't want to pursue an argument. They sat down at a spare table, a long way from Riley. Frank offered to get some drinks, but Jonquil shook her head. She just wanted to sit and think for a while. England was now out of view behind them; France was inching closer. What were they going to do when they got to Calais? There had been vague ideas about shopping or going to the beach. They seemed hopelessly naïve now. These people didn't want to shop or build sandcastles. They wanted to drink. And then drink some more. And then drink some more. And then fall over. And most of them were well into stage two of this plan already.

'Not sure if it was wise to let everyone just go off like that,' said Frank in his usual clumsy, tactless, *male* way. 'We'll have a hell of a job to round them all up at the end.'

'Don't you start,' Jonquil snapped at him.

'What do you mean . . . ?'

Jonquil leaned forward, fizzing. 'I came in here to get away from

Joyce whinging on at me like that. I don't need it from you as well, you know? I know I'm the youngest one here but I've had the most experience of dealing with this client group and I think I know what I'm doing. OK? They'll be fine on their own. Honestly. And anyway we shouldn't be treating them like babies. If they want to go off and do their own thing it's not up to us to try and stop them. We're here to give them an opportunity, not dictate to them.'

Rubbish: wet, liberal, soft-minded, university-student rubbish. Apart from anything else, it didn't seem to Frank particularly fair on the French to let this drunken rabble loose in their country without at least making a token effort to get them home again. 'I'm not sure I agree with you entirely,' he said, still trying to avoid that argument, but sensing it was on its way whatever.

'Look, you and Joyce think what you want to think. I'm fed up of the two of you ganging up on me.'

'We're not ganging up on you.'

'You are! You always listen to Joyce more than you listen to me.'

'I don't!'

'Well I think that you do . . .'

'Our personal relationship shouldn't have any effect on our professional relationship. I shouldn't be listening to you more than any other member of staff just because I'm going out with you . . .'

'But you don't listen to me *more*. You listen to me less. That's the whole point.'

'I don't!'

'You do!'

Frank was exhausted, but he kept on fighting. Battles like this always exhausted him but he didn't know how to stop. He felt like he was skidding at great speed towards a large hard thing. A wall. He was kicking his legs, his arms were flailing, but he couldn't stop himself. His head was reeling: *how* had he ended up back here again? He'd seen this coming – how had he not managed to stop it?

Jonquil, on the other hand, was exhilarated. She was on complete auto-pilot. In a funny way she was paying Frank a compliment by going at him like this. Other people she would tut inwardly and smile sweetly at. Other people didn't matter. Of Frank she expected better. He was supposed to know when she was feeling vulnerable, got-at, when she was feeling jealous and spiteful for no logical reason at all; when her feelings were completely unknowable and she didn't even know herself how she felt, Frank was supposed to know and act accordingly. That was his job, his function: that was the point of Frank. She did the same things for him. She knew because he'd told her so. And she managed to do them without even thinking about it. So when Frank failed to perform, justifiably she got pissed off and lashed out at him. It was only normal.

Outside on deck Joyce dozed, unaware of the sparks going off in the lounge. She could hear what sounded like Mikey and Dougal arguing about something, but she pretended she couldn't. She wanted to doze. The sun was warming her face and lighting the inside of her eyelids. Blocking out Mikey and Dougal, she could hear the splash of the sea and the gulls and, somewhere, children playing. It was a lovely, lovely day.

Riley

I'm not a restaurant person. I don't know enough about food to really make the most of them and even in the old days I always wanted to drink more than you're supposed to in a restaurant. I don't like the stuffy atmosphere, I don't like being called sir – I'm used to calling other people sir – and I don't like the fact they always end up costing you more than you think they're going to.

So, no, you could say I wasn't entirely at home as I sat there reading a menu for the fifteenth time, waiting for Irene to show up for that first Saturday night rendezvous, waiting for our secret date to begin. I'd got there early and ordered a scotch and lemonade which I was trying not to polish off in two gulps. All I could do was read the menu. If I tried to look around the room I ended up making eye contact with one of the army of waiters who were getting impatient with me, I could tell, for not getting the show on the road. You could tell it was a posh place because there were almost as many waiters as there were people eating. It was both sparse and cluttered at the same time. There was no decoration – no paintings, nothing on the walls at all – but I think the sparseness was supposed to be a decoration in itself. A statement of some kind. On the other hand, it was full. Full of tables, packed so close you could smell someone else's main course while you were having your pudding; full of waiters squeezing back and forth between the tables; full of diners dining. And it was bright: white, bright, gleaming, with an individual spotlight burning down on each table. I'd thought there'd be candles, soft lighting, music, a gentle rhubarb rhubarb – restaurants are usually quiet, aren't they, even when they're jammed full of people; this place wasn't. But this was a smart restaurant in London in the early eighties and I think that was the fashion for restaurants then.

Irene arrived bang on time. She looked, of course, stunning. She was wearing black again, like she had at the funeral. Black dress, black shawl, black clip in her hair. But a different black. A deep, dark, triumphant black. All black apart from the simple silver sparkle of her jewellery – small earrings and one chain necklace, nothing too fancy – and for the first time, a smile. And Irene, that *smile* . . .

'Corporal Riley,' she said after some hesitation.

'Mrs Stuart,' I said.

And then we both laughed. We weren't going to get through a whole evening like that. I stood awkwardly while she was seated by a waiter, then retook my seat. Still smiling, she asked for a gin and tonic, and I took the opportunity to order up another scotch and lemonade. I began to relax, just a little.

'You can call me Irene,' she said. Still smiling.

'And you can call me . . . well, everyone just calls me Riley.'

'My goodness, you really are an army man, aren't you.'

'It's not just the army . . . everyone calls me Riley, they always have done, since I was a kid . . . all my mates, everyone.'

'Haven't you got a first name? Is it something terribly embarrassing?'

'It's Thomas . . . Tom.'

She thought about this. 'Don't you think I could call you Tom? It's such a waste of a name if you don't use it.'

'You can call me Tom if you want.'

Irene, I hated the name Tom. I hated my mother for giving me that name. I hated anyone who used it and I usually responded violently when I heard it. But I loved it when you called me Tom: how do you work that out?

After that we made some small talk. No, it wasn't really small talk; it was friendlier, more intimate than that. But it definitely wasn't the stuff we'd come to talk about. We didn't want to rush into that, we had the whole evening ahead of us. It was polite just to natter a little first. I can't remember what we nattered about, but we seemed to hit it off OK. I don't remember any of those big silences you often get when you're with a woman, a woman you're trying to get to know better. At one point Irene threw her head back and sniffed loudly. Isn't the smell in here *divine*, she said. I sniffed too. I had chicken and spuds on my left and some kind of hot ginger pudding thing on me right; they didn't agree. I told Irene this and she laughed. Yeah, it seemed to be going OK.

And then all of a sudden they were clearing away our main courses and we were still talking about trivial things. Still getting on famously, still talking about trivial things. I began to get scared that this would be it, that we would simply be nice to each other and then go our separate ways and that would be the end of the story. *I know why I came here*, I wanted to blurt out. I came here, Irene, to tell you that your husband, who you loved, saved my life. Not once, more than once. Yeah, he gave his life in that accident so I would survive, which you know about. *But he had saved me once already before then.* When we were on Falkland together. I don't know why I have to tell you this, but there it is. I do. I just . . . I feel it's important you should know.

I tried to yank the conversation away – away from the nonsense and on to the real stuff. Andy. But she still wasn't comfortable with this. Her smile disappeared and she stared down into her lap.

'I'm sorry. I don't want to talk about him. Not yet.'

'But he saved my life, I have to tell you—' I tried to explain.

She reached out and touched my hand. 'It'll keep for another time. When I'm ready.' I looked at her and tried to work out what she meant by this. 'After all, this isn't going to be the last time we see each other, is it?'

I laughed nervously. 'No, guess not.'

That's when the first big silence arrived, just pulled on up and made itself comfortable; and was broken only by a waiter with dessert menus.

We had pudding, then we had coffee, then we had brandy. Conversation was a lot more stilted during this. Must have been: I remember a lot more of it. I told Irene a bit about my childhood, growing up in a small town on the south coast where it seemed like everyone else was an OAP, spending my days gazing out at the sea, dreaming of getting away. I told her why I'd joined the army; told her I was trying to do a little writing from time to time, which intrigued her. (I told her I was writing poems. I didn't tell her what the poems were about. Not yet.) But mainly I asked her questions about herself. It descended into typical date stuff, the stuff I'd talked about on a hundred different evenings with a hundred different women. I'd had it drummed into me at a young age that this was how you treated a lady on a date. Ask her questions about herself. Ask questions, look interested.

And then the bill came. Naturally it was presented to me, in a large leather folder, but before I could open it, Irene snatched it out of my grasp.

'Hey, what are you doing?' I said, but inside I was jumping up and down. If we could go Dutch, I might just about be able to eat for the rest of the month.

'Tom, let me explain,' she said quietly. 'This business I do in London . . . I have a small private income and the investments need some managing from time to time. Now, I know what the army must be paying you and I think, given the circumstances, it's only proper I should pay for the meal.'

She produced a very shiny, gold credit card and slipped it inside the folder. What was I supposed to do? I was relieved and flattered and humiliated at the same time.

Shortly afterwards a waiter came up and discreetly removed the folder. While he was gone, Irene leaned towards me and said: 'Can I ask you a question?'

'Sure.' You can't really say no when someone asks you this, can you.

'Does it bother you that I'm Andy's wife?'

'I don't understand . . .'

'Does it bother you that you're sitting in a restaurant with the wife of one of your friends?'

'But he's dead.'

'Yes . . .'

'And that's why I had to see you.' At last we seemed to getting on to the meat. 'I had to tell you some things about how he died and what he did for me while he was alive. I wouldn't be here with you if he wasn't dead.'

'So it doesn't bother you?'

'Well, yeah, the whole thing bothers me. Andy being dead *bothers* me.'

'Yes . . . yes, of course . . . Good.'

She murmured *good* a few times to herself. I still didn't get it. The credit card slip arrived for her to sign, which she did. The waiter hardly glanced at her signature before returning her card. Then he went away and we sat in some more big silence while we finished the brandy. I didn't have a clue what was supposed to happen now.

'What about you?' I said. 'Does it bother you to be with me?'

'What do you mean?'

'I mean, the accident and everything. Andy saved my life, but I could just as easily have saved his. If I'd have been more experienced, if I'd have thought a bit quicker, if I'd have been a bit braver maybe . . . maybe you'd still have a husband. I could have saved him and I didn't. He saved me. Again. You must hate me just a little for that. Even if you think you've forgiven me, you must hate me just a little for that. Don't you?'

She looked into my eyes, bored right down deep inside my head. It scared me a little. 'Tom, I don't hate you.' She took my hands across the table and stroked my knuckles with her thumbs. 'I think you're . . .' She paused. Obviously she couldn't find the word to describe what I was. So instead she said: 'I think it was very sweet of you to come and see me that afternoon . . . and I *will* talk to you about Andy. When the time is right.' She said some more nice stuff about me in her soft, soothing voice, and I was enjoying listening to it so much that I almost didn't notice her asking, as we were being helped on with our coats, if I wanted to go back to her hotel room for a nightcap.

13.33

Joyce was humming to herself, quietly, almost inaudibly. I was right, you were wrong . . . tum ti tum ti tum.

The boat had docked. Over the tannoy the chief steward had invited foot passengers to leave by the door next to the gift shop; invited them in a haughty tone of voice that suggested that he wouldn't mind if they hurried up a little actually. And most of them did hurry. Most of the passengers hurried towards the exit, or back down to their cars, as though they couldn't bear to spend another second on board. But not Joyce and her friends; they were still missing half their party; the steward was giving final instructions to disembark; Jonquil and Frank were doing their nuts; the bastards were nowhere to be seen.

Joyce and Dougal were sitting apart from the others, not involving themselves in the hair-tearing that was going on around them. I was right, you were wrong, tum ti tum.

'OK, let's do one more circuit each, Frank,' Jonquil said. 'No doubt they're hiding in one of the bars somewhere, finding this all terribly funny. If we don't find them this time round . . . well, they can all go to hell.'

Frank nodded.

'They can't have gone far,' Joyce couldn't resist saying. Her voice was sing-songing.

'Can I help you look?' Mikey said eagerly. 'I don't want to hang around here. I want to get down on to the beach.' They'd been able to see the beach as the boat pulled into the port, and now Mikey wouldn't shut up about it.

'No!' Frank practically shouted. Then a little more quietly: 'No, Mikey, you stay here with Joyce and Dougal. We don't want to find some people only to lose others again.'

'Okey dokey,' said Mikey. His words were so slurred now they sounded like they were bobbing in the waves like the boat. 'I just want to say that I think it's terrible what they're doing. You've brought us all on this lovely day out and they're just taking advantage of it and it's terrible . . .'

'Thank you Mikey.'

'Because you're all lovely people and you deserve better than this.'

'Thank you Mikey.'

'You're all so hardworking—'

'*Thank* you Mikey.'

'Look, why don't we just forget about them, you know?' said Jonquil. 'They can find their own way off the boat and we'll probably meet up with them on the way back. I don't know if I can be bothered chasing round after people playing silly buggers.'

Mikey shrieked with laughter. Jonquil said a rude word!

'We can't do that,' said Frank.

'Why not? I told you, people are free to do what they want.'

Frank and Jonquil moved closer to each other. It looked like it might turn nasty. Then a message came over the tannoy. 'Would the customer who left their cigarettes at the duty free shop please call at the information desk.'

Jonquil sighed wearily. 'I'll go and get them,' she said.

But Mikey was way ahead of her. By the time she'd looked around to work out where the information desk was, he'd already spotted the sign and bolted off down the stairs. Before she got to the desk, he was already there, jostling with the others, shouting at the steward.

And the expression on that steward's face – Jonquil wished she could have taken a photograph of it, to keep and console herself with on days when things weren't going her way. She could then look at this expression, a mixture of confusion, anger and *why-me* self-pity, and take comfort from the fact that, however badly things were going for her today, at least they weren't going *this* badly.

His name was Paul, he was twenty-one years old and he'd been working on the ferries for nearly a year. He'd seen a lot of ugly things during this time, or rather he'd seen one ugly thing – vomit – but he'd seen a lot of it; he certainly hadn't been prepared for anything like this. It had seemed so routine. On tidying up the shop they'd discovered a forgotten box of cigarettes. He'd made an announcement. Then, instead of a grateful old lady telling him what a dear young man he was (and everyone in the shop was pretty sure they'd been left by a dotty-looking old lady; they could remember her buying them), he'd found himself confronted by three screaming drunks. He looked from one red, belligerent face to another and wondered what on earth he was going to do.

'Look, can anyone tell me which *brand* of cigarettes they think they bought?' he tried.

The three men screamed brand names at him. Every brand of cigarette under the sun. Marlboro, Bensons, JPS, Embassy, Luckies, Raffles, Berkeley, Camel, Rothmans, Silk Cut . . .

'OK, Silk Cut,' said Paul the steward. 'What kind of Silk Cut?'

'Silk Cut Lights,' said Peter, first off the mark.

Paul shook his head.

'Extra-Special Namby-Pamby For Poofs Only Ultra Light Silk Cut Nancy Boy cigarettes,' Riley growled.

Paul shook his head again. 'Nope.' He didn't really know why he was bothering with this. As far as he could see, however he chose between them, the two who didn't get the cigarettes were going to let him have it.

'Regular!' shouted Mikey from the back. 'The normal, regular, purple ones. The ones I always smoke.'

The box was produced from under the counter. 'Fuck!' said Riley. Before Paul could hand it over, though – in fact his plan now was to simply lob the box at them and then run for his life – Jonquil intervened. She put herself between him and the men. 'OK, it's time to leave the boat now,' she said in a friendly yet authoritative tone that carried, she hoped, a senior-member-of-staff-on-this-trip air about it.

'But they're my cigarettes,' Mikey protested. 'I bought them and paid for them and everything.'

'Mikey, you've been up on deck the whole time with Joyce. You haven't even been down to the shop, let alone bought anything.'

Jonquil started to usher them, still protesting, away from the desk. She cast an eye back at the steward. The evident relief on his face made him look kind of cute. He was young, spawny-looking, stiffly smart in his uniform.

Virgin, almost certainly.

On the way back up to the gift shop, it occurred to her that there was still someone missing. 'Hang on, has anyone seen Candy?'

The other three looked blank.

Then Riley had an idea. 'I think I saw him over this way,' he said and started back towards the information desk.

'Tom!' Jonquil yelled at him before he'd got very far. Riley stopped immediately: this girl had something of the army about her. 'We'll all go up to the exit together and then *I'll* go and look for Candy.'

Candy was already found, however. As they rejoined the others on the deck, a member of the ship's crew was asking Frank if he knew anything about a young man in floods of tears in the amusement arcade. 'At least, I assume he's a young man, sir, it's a little . . . you know . . . hard to tell. I just thought that . . . you know . . . looking at the other members of your party, he might be with you . . .'

'Yes, he's with us. Perhaps you could show me where he is,' said Jonquil briskly while Frank was still shaking his head and tutting. He looked up, startled. Jonquil was pointing at him and Joyce and she was issuing orders like a teacher. 'OK, you two keep an eye on the others and for heaven's sake don't let them out of your sight until I get back with Candy. Got that?' she barked. Frank nodded and looked over to Joyce. Surely your girlfriend wasn't supposed to speak to you like this, even if you were colleagues?

Jonquil followed the crewman down to the amusement arcade. Another one who'd barely started to shave. Was no one over twenty-five allowed on the crew? Or any women? They found Candy in, as the crewman had said, floods of tears, sitting in front of an extravagant-looking game called *The House of the Dead*. Blinking rapidly, she was staring at a large screen depicting a handsome young man (handsome anyway for a computer-generated young man) with a large gun wandering around a gothic haunted house pursued by various hideous ghouls, partially obliterated by the words Insert Coin(s) in large, blurry white letters. It didn't look much like Candy's cup of tea. It looked as though she'd been walking around in a daze and simply sat down on the nearest available chair when the tears had come.

Jonquil went up and put an arm around Candy's shoulder. 'What's the matter?' she said gently.

There was no reply. The machines around them spluttered their high-pitched electronic gunshot sounds and annoying mechanical jingles. Further along in the arcade two teenagers were being led away, protesting loudly, from an equally violent-looking game called *Virtual Cop*.

'Candy, we're here. We have to leave the boat now.'

Candy looked up at the young crewman, who was standing right beside them, stared at him intently. Jonquil got the message. 'Uh, perhaps you could give us a moment . . . ?' she said to the young man. Then when he was gone, and with a note of irritation creeping into her voice: 'Now Candy, tell me what this is all about.'

'I can't get off the boat,' Candy said quietly.

'What do you mean, you can't get off the boat?'

'I mean . . . I just can't.'

'Why not?'

'Because . . .' Candy pressed herself closer to Jonquil and whispered: 'I can't go through customs.'

'But you don't have to, there aren't any customs any m—' Jonquil's heart froze as she realised what Candy had just said. Why didn't Candy want to go through customs? *How many reasons could there be?* He probably had bags of heroin taped all over his skinny body. Cocaine sewn inside the lining of his jacket.

The flow of tears seemed to have abated. Candy was looking up now, peering through puffy red eyes. 'They don't have customs any more?'

Jonquil was thinking rapidly. She wasn't a schoolmistress; this wasn't, as she kept telling herself, a school trip. These men were individuals, free to do as they liked, make their own mistakes, responsible for the outcome of those mistakes.

Free to smuggle large amounts of drugs into mainland Europe . . . well, why on earth not: it was all a learning experience.

Jonquil sighed, thought, and found she couldn't just let this happen. Candy was free to make mistakes, yes, but only up to a point. Maintaining a level of calm in her voice, she asked: 'What have you got that you don't want to take through customs, Candy?'

'Nothing . . . I'm . . . I'm just worried about some of the others, that's all.'

Bracing herself. 'You haven't got any drugs on you, then? You can tell me, you know.'

'No!'

The force of the denial took Jonquil aback. She was convinced by it. Although of course she wanted to be convinced.

'So why all the fuss then?'

'Well . . .' Candy turned back to look at the handsome man on the video screen while she searched for the right words. 'I'm worried about some of the others. They do silly things sometimes, some of them. And they've all been drinking. I was thinking maybe we should just turn back and go home . . . but if you say there's no customs to go through . . . ?'

Jonquil smiled. It was touching in a way, and of course a relief. Candy was, you had to keep reminding yourself, a delicate flower, one who could get upset by the slightest of things. And he was probably still in a state following whatever had happened to him last night; his bruises were still shining like beacons through his make-up.

'I think the others are OK,' she said comfortingly. 'I mean, I know they do stupid things, but none of them are *that* stupid.'

Candy didn't look so sure. 'Well, as long as there's no customs . . .'

'I think we're pretty safe.' Jonquil held out her hand. 'Come on, let's get you off this boat before they really do turn round and take us home again.'

As they walked back up the stairs, Jonquil asked: 'So, how's the singing going?'

Candy's face brightened noticeably. 'Yeah . . . yeah, good. I enjoy it.'

'I should think you'll be coming over here on tour pretty soon, won't you.'

A moment of genius on Jonquil's part. Candy forgot instantly about the tears and the worry and the bruises. A tour of France! Imagine that . . .

The others were restless when they got back to them. And surrounded now by spickly spanly uniformed members of the crew – some of them maybe as much as forty years old, still none of them women – who were really quite eager for this shower of drunks to get the hell off their boat.

Here comes the prima fucking donna, Riley thought to himself and Candy appeared, grinning inanely, although you could tell he'd been bawling his eyes out about two minutes ago. Riley was impatient; he had a job to do today; he simply didn't have time to wait around for temperamental shirtlifters.

Behind them an elderly lady was trying to manoeuvre three large cases towards the exit. She was also clutching a box of Silk Cut to her bosom.

Riley didn't care about the cigarettes any more, but he saw an opportunity to speed things along. He went up to the lady and grabbed the largest case. 'Excuse me, madam, would you like a hand with this?' he asked, and before she could answer he ran up to the gift shop and off down the gangway with it.

'Tom!' Frank called after him.

But he was away. And, as he was counting on, Peter couldn't allow himself to be out-gallanted, not by Riley, so Peter took another case from the bemused-looking lady, saying, 'Allow me. That one looks even heavier,' and he set off down the gangway after Riley, shouting: 'I think my one's even heavier than yours!'

Mikey also approached the lady, but only to ask her if she was sure those cigarettes were really hers.

'Oh yes,' she replied, and the sandpapery rasp of her voice suggested she hadn't been smoking Silk Cut all her life, 'I've been such a silly this trip. First I left these on the counter in the shop and then I stupidly fell asleep in one of their very comfy chairs. This very nice young man over here had to wake me up.'

Mikey looked dejected. 'Don't suppose you've got any change then?'

'Change . . . ?'

'Francs or pounds, I don't mind which.'

Without saying a word, Frank yanked Mikey away.

'I know Mikey,' said Jonquil, who was full of good ideas just now. 'Why don't you take the last of this lady's cases for her?'

Mikey pulled himself away from Frank and gave him a just-you-try-that-again look. He brushed himself down and picked up the lady's final case. 'Of course I will, Jonquil, of course I will. I was just about to offer anyway.'

And so, one by one, finally finally, they made their way down the gangway on to the unsuspecting soil of France.

Candy was the last one down. She paused for a while at the top of the gangway. A tour of France! Imagine that . . . She pictured hordes of fans and well-wishers turning out to greet her, bringing her bouquet upon bouquet of flowers, demanding autographs until her arm was sore. Her number-one fan, Mr Potts multiplied a thousand times, a thousand *French* Mr Pottses. So: not flabby and moustachioed, but smartly dressed and inconspicuously groomed. Open-necked shirts with labels instead of Marks and Spencer ties. Tapered trousers with turn-ups instead of flares which halted around the ankle. Red-eyed still from her crying and with the roar of the crowd in her ears, she turned to the handsome young man in his crisp white uniform, standing rigidly next to her, and she smiled warmly at him.

And the short-haired, apple-cheeked young sailor leaned forward and murmured to her: 'Fuck off the boat. We want to go home.'

Candy

Old Compton Street, three thirty Sunday morning. I'm walking – no I'm prancing – down the street handing out flyers for my opening night at BabyCakes. They're small white pieces of paper with the BC logo (a naked waiter holding a tray of drinks aloft: *so* tacky) stamped officially in the top left-hand corner and then my name in big *big* pink letters underneath:

MISS CANDY SKINN

sings for you . . .

Then there's a photograph of me. A smudgy photocopied black and white one but still – a photograph! And then the words *ne me quitte pas* . . . also in pink letters underneath that. They're gorgeous. I want to frame every single one of them and put them on my wall.

And everybody wants one. People are taking two or three extras to pass on to their friends. BabyCakes isn't going to know what hit it Thursday night. Even the straight boys posing on their scooters outside Bar Italia show an interest. BabyCakes . . . where is that again? one of them asks, brylcremed and nonchalant, sucking on his cigarette like he just walked straight out of a black and white French film from the fifties. I point. He nods. And he passes some flyers around his friends and they nod. Jacques Brel's the man, he tells me. His friends nod in agreement. A voice calls my name from behind me. It's my gang. They're thinking of moving on. We're thinking of going down to Turnmills. Coming? I don't know. I've got to finish handing these out. I want a big crowd for my opening night don't I. So? Hand them out in the queue down Turnmills. People down there'll want to come. Yes look sweetie there can't be a single solitary soul in the whole of Soho who hasn't got one of these hateful little things now. Yes come *on* Candy, come with *us*. I beam and I look at my friends and I beam some more. Come on Candy . . . come with us. *Come with us.*

A week ago these people weren't bothered where I went or what I did. Now they can't wait to tell all the leather boys at Trade how long they've known me. I tingle.

13.56

If the day had stopped seeming like a terrific idea to Jonquil on the boat, by the time they reached Calais it looked positively mad. A complimentary bus from the ferry took them about half a mile into the town and deposited them at the end of a long street lined with restaurants. These establishments had low-key, European-sounding names: Café le Champagne, Café Malaga, le Monaco, le Pinnochio, le Venezia. Walking down this street felt like running a gauntlet. The restaurants weren't inviting as such: they were too homogenous, too gaudy, too transparently inauthentic to actually be welcoming or tempting, but they did in their way seem to *dare* you not to be hungry. Go on, give it a go, they seemed to taunt, see how far you get. The kitchen smells were propelled out through the open doors (you could almost imagine people in each of the kitchens with giant sets of bellows, forcing the smells out on to the street), large menu boards blocked the pavements, some even had little men with moustaches to usher you inside. Jonquil found herself picking up speed as she marched purposefully past these places. Not hungry, she muttered to herself, not hungry. She was worried that the men – Peter in particular – would be seduced by the doughy, garlicky aromas floating about them and start complaining that they hadn't had lunch properly. They'd only had Joyce's sandwiches, and sandwiches could be misconstrued as a snack, elevenses sort of, rather than as lunch *per se*. But none of the men appeared to notice the restaurants as they ambled past each one in turn. Only Mikey, who paused to tap each of the small men with moustaches for a couple of francs if they approached him. Jonquil didn't seek to stop him from doing this: it seemed fair dos.

At the end of this street was a large square with a modest funfair in the middle of it and a pointless-looking tower in the corner, where the group came to a natural stop and waited, herd-like, for someone to take charge. Indecision reigned. In fact it was a tyranny of indecision. An indecision *reich*.

Jonquil thought hard. As senior member of staff, it was up to her to lead the way here. They couldn't just stand around on this street corner all day. She caught a couple of pairs of eyes straying towards the bumper cars in the middle of the square, but letting the men loose on the funfair would be asking for trouble. They could go up this silly tower thing in front of them . . . but then what? She carried on thinking hard. Actually it was quite obvious what to do, the first thing they needed to do was . . .

'Money,' said Joyce.

. . . get some money changed. They hadn't thought to do it on the boat, what with one thing and another.

'Does anyone have any French money? I think we should go to a bank before we do anything else,' Joyce added firmly, looking over at Jonquil. 'What about you blokes? Do any of you want to change some money?'

The men all laughed. Even Candy, who looked like she was still crying, laughed. They all laughed except Mikey who looked anxiously at Jonquil and said: 'But you told us we wouldn't need any money! Didn't you? You said it was all being paid for. I haven't got any money!' This wasn't true, not in the least. Mikey had odd notes dotted all over the place, picked up here and there, and two deep pocketfuls of loose change that jangled like wind chimes when he walked and which he rustled annoyingly with his hands when standing still. But that was *other* money. Real money. His money. That wasn't money to be changed into foreign rubbish and spent on things he didn't need, things that weren't even alcoholic. He wouldn't have come on this bloody trip if he thought he was going to have to *pay* for stuff.

Jonquil smiled. 'Don't worry Mikey. Of course it's all paid for.' Then she became brisk and business-like again. 'Look. There's a bank over there. We'll go and change some money and then we'll figure out what we want to do with the rest of the day.'

'I don't see a bank,' said Peter.

'Over there. Look.'

Peter did look; he still couldn't see a bank. But he was looking for the wrong thing. He was looking for black horses and griffins and sickly turquoise-coloured signs. English banks. Usually Peter could spot banks a mile off. He'd spent some of his most profitable days hovering, hungry-looking, next to cash machines. Cashies were the business. You didn't have to say anything most of the time, you didn't even need 'Homeless – Please Help' signs. Ninety-nine out of a hundred people would ignore you anyway. But the hundredth, the one who took pity on you, the one who was having a good day, who'd just got a pay raise or just asked the person they really fancied out for a drink after work or had just checked their bank balance and found they had more than they thought, *they would have to give you a note*. The trick was – and it took Peter a long time to figure this out – the trick was to find one of the rare cashies that still dispensed five-pound notes. If people only had tenners to give away, your odds shot up from one in a hundred to about one in a thousand and that could make for some very long mornings. But with fivers you could pretty much guarantee the one per cent, whatever the place, whatever the weather; it was almost scientific. So all you had to do was find a cashie that would get through a hundred punters in an hour, and there were plenty of those in London, especially on a Saturday, and you were bound to make five pounds an hour. At least. And, of course, free of stupid things like tax and national insurance. It was better than working in McDonald's. And on a day like today you could even pick up a tan while you worked. Peter liked banks; cashies were the finest inventions ever.

'Nope,' he said. 'Don't see one.'

'There!' said Jonquil. 'The building with the word BANQUE in large letters on the side of it.'

Peter peered at it. 'That's not how you spell bank,' he said. He was crap at spelling, but he was pretty sure on this one. It wasn't Barclays *Banque*, was it.

Jonquil sighed. A drunk trying to be funny was one of the most tiresome things in the world. 'It's the *French* way of spelling bank, Peter.'

'You mean . . . all the signs are going to be in French?'

Jonquil glared at him; she was bored of this now. But as she glared, she caught the genuinely bewildered look in his eye and she was reminded of the two fundamental and contradictory rules of working with this client group: 1. Never underestimate their intelligence, their cunning, their ruthlessness, their ability to turn any situation to their advantage. But 2. Don't underestimate their stupidity either, which at times can verge on the devotional. 'Yes,' she said heavily. 'We're in France. Of course the signs are in French.' Actually it was rather sweet, wasn't it, to be *that* ignorant. And wasn't that the reason she had brought them here? To show them what abroad was really like, to give them these little insights into other cultures.

Peter looked around. Bloody hell, it was true! The signs *were* all in French. Road signs, shop signs, billboards, road names . . . all incomprehensible. 'What's the point of all this?' he said. 'None of us speak French, do we.'

'Uh, I speak a little,' said Dougal nervously. He didn't really want to spend the day translating for everybody. 'Just a very little. I did it at school.'

Candy also thought about piping up. She *sang* in French. But if Simone didn't tell her what the songs were about, she wouldn't have a clue.

'It's OK. I think between us we speak enough to get by,' said Jonquil, starting across the road to the bank.

The others followed. When they reached the *banque*, without thinking, Joyce, Jonquil and Frank all went inside together.

'Hang on,' said Jonquil when she realised what had happened. 'We shouldn't leave them on their own out there. Joyce, do you want to wait outside while Frank and I change our money, then you do yours . . . ?'

Joyce ignored her. No, she didn't want to wait outside. She didn't want to be ordered around like a schoolgirl either.

'I said—' Jonquil started again.

'I'm already in the queue,' Joyce snapped. 'If you want to wait outside, go ahead. Although I thought you said we weren't going to behave like this was a school trip.'

Jonquil's mouth started goldfishing. Did Joyce just say that? In that tone of voice?

Frank intervened. 'I'm sure they'll be fine. We'll only be a few minutes. And anyway we can see what they're getting up to through the window, look.'

It was a spacious, open-plan bank, not like the bullet-proof cages you got at home. There was a soft, plush carpet and people-sized pot plants dotted about, and two whole walls were made entirely of glass, through which sunlight poured copiously. So you could see everything that was going on outside. In one corner of the room a wildly over-made-up middle-aged woman sat smartly at a desk with absolutely nothing on it, not even a telephone. Seeing three foreigners looking unsure of themselves, she stood up and went over to them.

'Can I help you?' she asked in perfect, although not particularly helpful-sounding English.

'It's OK. We're queuing to change money,' Jonquil said firmly.

'Ah . . . OK. Then please stand over here.'

The woman pointed to an unattended position at the far end. Then, without pausing to smile, she went back to sit primly at her barren desk.

Both Joyce and Jonquil moved at the same time. Frank went to stand between them. It looked like he was going to have to do a lot of standing between them today.

Outside, through the large, moneyed window, the others were getting restless. They were bored *and* all the signs were in French *and* there wasn't a pub anywhere in sight. Peter and Mikey both looked around the building for a cashie. There wasn't one. This bank, this *banque*, didn't even have a fucking cashie. That was it: Peter was going home now. What was the point of a country with no cashpoints? Riley took out a bottle of whisky and swigged.

'Here, give us a gulp,' said Mikey.

'Fuck off.'

'Aw . . . go on.'

'Fuck off. You've been drinking your fucking Bacardi all day. Didn't spot you handing that round.'

'I gave you some this morning . . . Anyway, it's finished now.'

Riley wiped his mouth with the back of his hand and swigged again. Then he had a thought: 'Tell you what, I'll swap you a gulp for some ciggies.'

'I haven't got any ciggies,' said Mikey. 'You know I haven't.'

'Anyone else? A drop of the hard stuff in return for some good, honest nicotine. Dougal . . . ? No, you don't smoke, do you.'

'Or drink whisky,' said Dougal.

'You, what's your name, Candy, you've got some fags, I know you fucking have, I've seen them.'

'I don't want any of your whisky.'

'So? Just give me the fags then.'

Candy started backing away. 'I need them!'

'I'm only asking for one or two.'

'I've only got one or two left!'

126

Not true. She had almost a whole packet in her bag and a completely unopened packet stashed away in the pocket of her chinos. But Candy started to panic if she wasn't surrounded by cigarettes. And anyway, why should she just hand them over? She'd been a couple of rounds with George Johnson and his thugs: she could deal with this drunken idiot.

'There's a shop over there with a Marlboro sign outside,' said Peter. 'I reckon you could get some fags in there.' Marlboro still meant Marlboro presumably, even in this place.

'I haven't got any fucking money, have I,' said Riley, still advancing on Candy.

'So? Nick them then. Just because it's a foreign country, doesn't mean we have to stop behaving normally. Nick them.'

Riley thought about it for a moment. No, he decided on reflection, it was easier to beat the shit out of the kid than to try and rob places in a foreign language.

But then Peter had to go and say: 'Or maybe you're too chickenshit to do it.' The bastard. And so that was that. He had to do it. The bastard: it would have been so much easier to beat shit out of the kid. He gave Candy one last, longing look. Just a couple of little slaps, that's all it would have taken, maybe not even that, maybe he'd have just needed to raise his hand . . . The kid was cut and bruised enough as it was. But no, Peter had to *challenge* him, to egg him on, put him in a position where he couldn't back down.

So wearily he muttered, 'Just you fucking watch then,' and he trudged over towards the Marlboro sign.

Peter

I mean, it's taking the piss, isn't it, signs in French. Some of us have a hard enough time reading them in bloody English. They should put up translations or something. I know, I know. I should learn to read better. Course I should. But I can't, see. I can't because I'm stupid. Yup, stupid. Thick as two short planks. Mr Shit-for-Brains. Johnny

Fuckwit. A cobblestone short of a pavement, a sandwich short of a picnic, a goalie short of a football team. I make no bones about it: I've been stupid for ages, me. Since I was, oh let me see, thirteen? That's how old I was, I think, when Mr Neville told me. Of course around that time a lot of people were telling me I was stupid, but mostly they were just having a laugh, you know, taking the piss. But Mr Neville though, he told me so there was no arguing with it. You see, he *proved* it to me. Beyond any reasonable doubt.

'YOU'RE STUPID FREEMAN!' he shouted at me.

We'd just done a test in English. You had to read a piece of a story and then answer some questions on it, circling the answer you thought was right out of a, b, c, d and e. One of those tests. I got fifteen per cent.

'Freeman, do you know what would happen if a baboon took this test?' Mr Neville asked.

'Uh . . . no sir.' They wouldn't make a baboon do an English test, would they? What would be the point of that? I couldn't see what he was getting at. See: *stew*pid.

'Well, let me tell you. If a baboon took this test, just circling answers at random, he would score on average twenty per cent . . . What was your score again, Freeman?'

'Fifteen per cent, sir.'

'So you understand what this means?'

'No sir.'

'IT MEANS YOU'RE STUPID, FREEMAN! IT MEANS A BABOON WOULD HAVE GOT A HIGHER MARK ON THIS TEST THAN YOU! A BABOON!'

I've never forgotten that.

14.01

It was just like a newsagents, this Marlboro shop. It sold sweets and newspapers and cans of Coke and cigarettes. Only it was called a *tabac*. There was a red, cigar-shaped sign outside which said *tabac*. This was a good thing, a reassuring thing. Most newsagents these days seemed embarrassed about selling fags. They'd hide them away right on the top shelf, less accessible even than the jazz mags. But here was a shop that proudly announced: TOBACCO! Come inside. Smoke. Feed your cancer.

Riley paused for a moment outside the shop. There was a strange flutter inside his stomach, a flapping of wings, a scampering of hooves. After a brief moment of confusion he realised what it was: he was *nervous*. He dismissed the feeling angrily. He'd been ripping off newsagents regularly and profitably since he swiped his first *Fiesta* when he was twelve. This one was no different just because it was in a different country. He pushed the door open and marched in.

The shop was divided into two. The newspaper half smelled musty and damp; the Coke and sweets half smelled sugary, almost sickly. It smelled pink. And at the far end of the shop, past the rows of strange-smelling things, behind the counter, was an impossibly attractive fair-haired girl, seventeen at most.

She said something in French.

Riley took a moment to compose himself, then said confidently: '*Bonjour, Madame.*'

'*Mademoiselle,*' said the girl.

She really was stunning. Her hair was wild and frizzy, her face an expertly arranged collection of moles and freckles, and her large green eyes sparkled like fireworks. Riley was halfway down the shop before he realised who she reminded him of.

Irene.

Irene as he had never known her. Young, carefree, unmarked by tragedy . . .

No, it was ridiculous. The girl looked nothing like Irene. She was just pretty, that was all. And Riley had allowed his head to become flooded and sentimental with all the whisky. He'd promised himself he wasn't going to do that today. It was a big day, he needed to be able to think straight.

So what was doing in here then? Was this thinking straight? OK, it was a fairly straightforward thing, pinching a few ciggies from a newsagents. But what if he got nicked? It was a small risk, yes, for an old pro like him. He'd been doing this for twenty years, only ever been caught twice and he'd talked his way out of both of those. But what if he did get nicked? That would be it, wouldn't it. He'd be sent home. And he wouldn't get another chance like this in a hurry.

He must have been out of his mind. It was all that bastard Freeman's fault. He'd egged him on, hadn't he, forced him into it. Riley didn't even want a cigarette, now he thought about it. He'd been planning to quit as it happened. He'd only had five or six all day, so really he *had* practically quit already.

In fact he was just about to turn around and walk back out of the shop – and Freeman could say what he liked; Freeman could go fuck himself – when he realised he'd reached the counter and the girl was looking at him expectantly.

'*Oui, Monsieur?*'

God she was beautiful. Even if she wasn't Irene, she was still beautiful. He had to say something to her; otherwise he was just going to look like an idiot. Anything would do.

'Uh . . . *je voudrais* . . .,' he began falteringly. Then he had a flash of inspiration. '*Tabac*!' he said.

See. It was easy. He didn't know what Freeman and the others were moaning about. This language was a piece of piss if you actually stopped to think about it.

'Ah, you are English?' said the girl.

How did she know?

'Yes . . . yes I am,' Riley admitted.

'And you want some tobacco?'

'Yes.'

She turned around to indicate a number of brands of rolling tobacco stacked up behind her. There were cigarettes too, hundreds of different types of cigarettes, some familiar, some exotic-looking. But now she was pointing at the rolling tobacco, Riley decided that that was what he fancied. As a non-smoker now it hardly made any difference; he was only getting the stuff to show Freeman he could, to prove he still had it. He picked out a brand he'd never heard of before. The girl took a pouch and placed it on the counter.

'And papers,' he said.

The girl looked like she hadn't heard him.

'Papers,' he said again.

'Uh ... we have *Figaro*, *Le Monde* ... no English papers, I think.'

'No; cigarette papers.' Riley made the rolling motion with his two forefingers and thumbs.

'Oh,' said the girl. 'You don't need. They are in the bag.'

Free papers with your tobacco: this was the mark of a civilised society.

So there it was then. The tobacco was on the counter. What was Riley going to do now? He couldn't just pick it up and run ... Could he?

Well, he could ...

He'd make it out of the shop OK, he was pretty sure of that. And the girl probably wouldn't even bother to chase him. But he didn't want to. He didn't want the last thing this girl saw of him to be his cowardly arse scampering out of the door.

He had an idea. Delving into his pocket with one hand, fingering the tobacco pouch with the other, he said hurriedly: 'There you go, love, a pound'll cover it, won't it?' And in one movement he threw a pound coin down on to the counter, picked up the tobacco and turned to walk purposefully out of the door.

'Wait,' said the girl.

'Yes ... ?'

'This is English money.'

'Yes ... You don't take English money?'

'No. This is France.'

Riley made a show of looking perplexed. He was hoping she wouldn't recognise the coin and accept it in good faith. Or Plan B: she was so charmed by him and his child-like error she let him have the tobacco anyway. 'But ... I don't have any French money.'

'I need twenty francs.'

'You know, you have beautiful eyes.'

'Yes, and I need twenty francs. Please.' How stupid did he think she was?

'They remind me of someone I used to know.'

Riley had returned to the counter and put the tobacco down. The girl put her hand on it. That was OK; as long as she had her hand on the tobacco she was prepared to talk further about her beautiful eyes. At length even.

'So . . . they remind you of someone?'

'Yes. Someone I loved.'

'Your wife?'

'No . . . someone else's wife.'

'Someone else?' This was getting interesting.

'Yes. A friend of mine.'

A friend of his. Even better. He didn't look like the type, but you could never tell. 'So, what happened?'

'He died. He died trying to save my life. It could have been the other way round, you know. I could have died saving his life. But I didn't. He died; I lived.'

'So you killed your friend because you loved his wife?'

'I didn't kill him. It was an accident. I couldn't have killed him; I loved him.'

'You loved your friend?'

'Yes.'

'And his wife?'

'And his wife.'

The girl raised her eyebrows.

'Her name was Irene,' Riley said. 'You know, like the song. "Goodnight Irene".'

He sang a few bars. The girl shook her head; she didn't know it. And it sounded horrible.

'She lives in France now,' Riley went on. 'I'm going to see her.' He produced the crumpled piece of paper from his pocket. 'She lives here . . .' he said, showing the girl the address. 'St Omer. It's not far from here, yeah?'

'No,' said the girl. 'Not far. Thirty or forty kilometres . . . you will see her?'

'Yes. I hope so.'

'And you don't see her for how long?'

'Uh . . . let me see, must be something like fifteen years.'

'Fifteen years!'

'More or less.'

'And you love her?'

'Oh yes.'

Fifteen years. And he *loves* her. 'So . . . what happened? Why fifteen years?'

Riley shook his head. 'Things,' he said. 'Things happened.'

They fell silent for a moment while the girl tried to make sense of this confusing story. She wasn't sure she'd understood everything he'd said. Not only was her English limited, but he had a peculiar way of speaking: she might well have missed something important that would explain it all.

'Well, I'd better be going,' Riley said finally. 'There are people waiting for me. You're sure I can't pay with English money?'

'No.' The girl gave him his pound back. Then she handed over the tobacco. 'And you can take this. You say I have beautiful eyes.'

Riley grinned broadly. 'Thank you,' he said. 'And you do have beautiful eyes. And a very beautiful face in general.' He was still grinning broadly as he walked out of the shop.

Riley

Lying in Irene's bed, with Irene's head on my shoulder, about a month after I'd started seeing her properly, I told her about that night on East Falkland.

Sometime in the middle of the night there seemed to be a lull in the fighting. At the time I couldn't see any real reason for it. I just thought it was natural, I suppose. People who'd been firing guns at each other for six hours straight had to stop and take a breather some time. The truth was, we'd made very little progress in the last hour or so. Mostly we'd just been running out our dead and wounded; and what a fucking job that was too. Giving morphine to some poor cunt who's just had his foot blown off by a mine and your hand is shaking so much you can't fucking administer the stuff properly and the guy is fucking howling at you, fucking howling his guts up. Or you're carrying a wounded mate of yours over your shoulder – and this didn't happen to me, but it happened to someone I spoke to later, a young private – you're carrying this mate of yours, like I say, and he's wounded and he's screaming but, you know, he's OK, he's going to make it. And then a round of fucking rifle fire comes in and he takes a couple of bullets; and the first thing you think is, fucking hell, that's my mate dead; and the second thing you think is, if he wasn't on my back that would've been me. How are you supposed to feel about that? Now I realise that this brief period of relative calm must have been the point where we captured the first peak of Longdon – Fly Half – and were regrouping before pressing on to take the rest of the mountain. It was tactical, it was necessary, you can see that with hindsight, but there on the ground, without the luxury of the bigger picture, it felt like stalemate. A cold, icy stalemate blowing across the ridge.

In a way that lull was the worst bit of all, worse than the actual nitty-gritty. While it was all going off around you, you didn't have time to stop and think about what was happening, you just got on with it. Now, though, now we just seemed to be standing around. Worst of all, the terror started to disappear . . .

I use the word terror because it's the only one I know, but it doesn't really do the job. I'm not sure there is a word that does the job properly. How can I explain what it feels like to be under continuous, sustained shell-fire if you've never been there yourself? Terror doesn't do the trick. The nearest I can get is . . . well, you know those giant chess games they have for the tourists in the gardens of some of the posh country houses? The ones with people-sized pieces on a carefully mown lawn . . . yeah? Well being fired upon on unfamiliar terrain in the middle of the night is like playing Russian roulette on a similar scale. Giant guns, giant bullets. Each shell that brushes past your face and lands somewhere else feels like the huge click of a hammer on an empty chamber. Whoosh . . . BANG!! Echoing around you. Only instead of playing with one bullet in six chambers, or ten chambers or whatever, here the number is unlimited, which of course increases your chances of survival but actually makes the whole thing worse since there's no end to it: the game can go on forever. Whoosh, bang. Whoosh, bang. Whoosh, bang. Again and again and again. Whoosh, bang. No letting up. Whoosh, bang. Nearly got you that time. OK . . . ? That's what I mean by *terror*.

Only like I say, when the terror subsided it was even worse because the one thing about the terror was it kept out the pain – which once again is a completely useless word to describe how my feet felt after we'd been tabbing across the Falkland swamps. People who see me nowadays around the streets of London often make a comment about my shoes. I've always got a good pair of shoes on me. Whatever the state of the rest of my clobber, I look after my feet. Always. Even in summer, when everyone else is going around in sandals and last year's discarded designer trainers, I've got a pair of Doccers on. Always Doccers. And if one pair wears out I'll blag or nick a new pair. I'll even buy them if I have to. I'll go without drink for a few days to get a new pair of Doctor Martens; I've done it before. Because if I feel even the slightest splish of dampness on my feet, I'm transported instantly back to those fucking islands, where my feet turned into an icy blue, slimy mush the night after we landed, as we made our way up to Windy Gap while the SAS lit up the sky with cover-fire, and they didn't return to anything like normal until weeks after we got back.

Now, however, as we tried to sort out some treatment for the wounded, I started feeling *guilty* about being in such pain. At least if my feet hurt like hell, that meant they were still attached to my legs. How come I still had my feet when there was all these people around me who'd lost theirs? What made me so special? My head started spinning with stupid questions. After a while I couldn't take much more of this, so I went up to Andy, who was waiting by the radio for our next orders, and said: 'Just going to go and take a shit while it's a bit quiet, skip.' I didn't need one particularly but it was something to do, something to take my mind off things, and I didn't know when I'd get the chance again.

And Andy said: 'Yeah, all right ... hang about, I'll come with you.'

So off we went, the two of us, into some bushes right next to where the company was regrouping. I mean, no more than thirty, forty feet away. If it had been light, we'd have still been able to see them. We could certainly fucking hear them, mainly the groaning from the wounded. We found a spot, dug our holes and started peeling off our webbing, then we squatted, back to back, and went about our business.

It was quiet. I mean, it wasn't *quiet*, not like it is right here in the countryside in England with Irene – we could still hear the other men, like I say, and there was still the occasional burst of fire, but there wasn't stuff whizzing past your ears any more. And it was cold. With all the adrenaline I hadn't really been noticing the cold, but with my arse cheeks suddenly exposed to it, I really felt how bitter it was. I was scared about getting tired; tiredness was something to fear almost as much as the bullets.

'How much longer have we got, do you reckon?' I asked Andy.

'There's about four hours till dawn,' he said.

'Not going quite to plan, is it.'

'Wasn't ever going to. These things never do. We're doing OK, though. It's only a question of time.'

We concentrated and shat some more.

'Gibbsy's dead,' I said.

'Yeah ... Don't think about it, Riley. There's plenty of time for thinking about the dead later on. Think about yourself. We've still got an objective.'

'Yeah, you're right. When I think about myself, though, all I can think about is how cold my feet are and how much I stink of shit.'

And I did: I was fucking humming. Earlier in the night we'd been crawling through what I guess must have been an Argy shit-pit. It was disgusting, but it was easily the most sheltered approach to that part of the mountain; and if it's crawl in shit or get shot at, believe me, you get down on your hands and knees. You enjoy it.

Andy laughed at this. 'I wouldn't worry about it. Shit's a friendly smell.'

Still squatting, I turned my head towards him. 'What do you mean?'

'You're used to shit. You smell it at home, you smell it all the time. Believe me, if it wasn't for the shit all you'd be able to smell would be the blood and the morphine and that would be a whole lot worse. A whole fucking lot worse. Honestly. Don't worry about it.'

'Yeah, life's too short to worry, eh,' I said. It had been a favourite phrase of Gibbsy's, one he used when he'd just really wound someone up badly. Don't worry, be happy, that was the other one. He'd sneeze into someone's pint or nick their clothes from the shower, or some other really juvenile prank, and then tell them not to worry about it. Life's too short to worry.

'Yeah,' Andy said with a little laugh. 'Life's too short.'

Right in front of me there was a rustling. I froze. My hand went to my rifle. My cheeks clenched so tight I thought they'd burst.

Then a head appeared. A head! Slap bang in front of me, peering out of the undergrowth, a startled fucking rabbit-in-headlights Argentinian head. Instinctively I picked up my gun and shot him in the face. He was blown backwards and the head kind of popped like a balloon, sending his blood spurting up in the air. There were yelps from behind him and immediately three other men stood up.

They had their hands in the air, these three men. I want to make that absolutely clear before I go on. They had their hands in the air and despite the dark they were close enough that I could see perfectly well that they had their hands in the air, and were therefore, obviously, surrendering. So there really is no excuse for what happened next.

I stood up as well, trousers still around my ankles, knob waving at these terrified Argies in the cold and the dark, shit starting to drip down the back of my legs because I hadn't had time to clean myself. And then God only knows why, and if he *does* know why I wish the bastard would tell me because I haven't got a fucking clue . . . then I shot the first of them. Clean in the stomach, blew the cunt away. Then I jumped over to them, no, I *sprang* over to them and I was still waving my rifle around and letting out some kind of war cry and these two other Argies dropped to their knees and they started wailing, pleading with me, praying, begging on their mothers' lives, whatever they thought would work, and I tell you, I have never seen two men look more fucking petrified in my entire life, and behind me Andy has done himself up and he comes over to me and he's going, they're surrendering Riley, they're fucking surrendering, and he's fumbling around with the sheet of Useful Spanish Phrases they'd given us all, trying to *interrogate* them for Christ's sake, and I'm still waving that rifle around and the Argies were still screaming and Andy was still shouting.

And then I shot the other two – bang, bang.

The shots were still ringing in the air, the smoke hadn't even cleared, when Andy leaped up to me and punched me in the face. I went down like a sack of shit, the cold grass stinging the backs of my legs.

Andy hunched down beside me, pulled my face close to his and said: 'They were surrendering, Riley. They had their hands in the air. That was fucking *murder*.' He was whispering, but shouting at the same time. 'What the fuck did you do that for?'

I started gabbling. 'I don't know . . . I just saw them and I didn't know what they were doing . . . and I know they had their hands in the air, but I thought I saw one of them twitching and he might have been . . . I don't *know* . . .'

Andy stood up and went over to where the four dead men were lying, propped up slightly on each other like logs for a fire. 'Jesus, Riley, they weren't even *armed*.'

I didn't stand up, but crawled my way over to where they were.

They still looked terrified even now they were dead. They were nothing more than boys: lost, frightened, dead boys.

But you know what, I couldn't even bring myself to feel guilty. Or ashamed. Or any of the stuff you're supposed to feel when you've just murdered four innocent teenagers. The only thing I could think of was, shit, I've blown it now, haven't I. I've let everyone down. Given the big occasion I've lost it completely. Lieutenant Stuart thinks I'm a cunt. When this is all over everyone'll be going on about this and that heroic deed and no one's going to want to talk to me. As soon as we're home there'll be a court martial, prison, and then I'll be out of the army on my fat, yellow arse. And that's the only way anyone'll remember me. Riley. He couldn't hack it when the going got tough. Lacked the big match temperament. Started shooting people left, right and centre.

'I'm sorry,' I said. In fact I think I was just whispering it over and over again. But I wasn't sorry for them, I was sorry for *me*.

Andy let out a long, exhausted sigh. 'Come on,' he said. 'We can't let anyone find them like this. There'll be a fucking scandal.' And he started pulling the bodies apart.

I looked up at him.

'This never happened, OK?' he said. 'I don't want to hear about it ever again. You were scared, you were tired, it was an error of judgement. Just . . . just wipe your arse and pull your fucking trousers up, OK?'

As he moved each of the bodies he had a quick go through their uniforms to see what the men were carrying. Two of them had envelopes which read PARA UN CONSCRIPTO and which contained short letters, obviously written by schoolkids, with innocent, childish crayon drawings of trees and suns and houses and smiling stick-people. My heart broke all over again. Another one had a box of matches with a picture of the *Belgrano* on the front and a list of statistics underneath – dimensions, weight, capacity, top speed, that kind of stuff. It reminded me of that card game I used to play as a kid, Top Trumps. I had visions of these poor, lost and frightened conscripts sitting in their sangars, gambling on matchboxes, trying to collect the set of Argentine warships, waiting to be blown to fuck. Suddenly, and coldly, they didn't feel like the enemy any more.

So we moved the bodies back into the undergrowth and set them apart so it would look, hopefully, as though we had shot them with one round as they tried to crawl past us, so it would be OK that we had killed all four of them before realising they were unarmed. I mean, *unarmed*. What the fuck were they doing crawling around in the middle of a war unarmed anyway? Deserting? They were lucky to have got this far: the rumour was that Argie officers were having to shoot their own men in the legs to stop them running away. At least that's what we'd been telling ourselves to keep our spirits up.

I tried to thank Andy but he wasn't having any of it. He put his hands up and said it was over, it was finished. It had never even happened. And true to his word, he never spoke about it again. I thought we'd have to come up with something to explain the four gunshots, but when we got back to our company no one had heard a thing. Four more shots that night, just four more drops in the ocean.

After the orders came through, me and the three privates under me were given a low-level recce mission as the company advanced on the second peak of Longdon. Basically Andy had seen to it as best he could that I would be kept out of trouble for the rest of the night. And that was about it for me and the Falklands War. Oh yeah, I was involved for the rest of it. I functioned. Followed orders, laid down cover fire etc etc. But I never really got stuck in again; Andy made sure that I never had to. And I felt detached from the whole thing now, as though it was happening to someone else and I was just watching. I've got memories of what happened for the rest of the war, lots of them, stark and vivid memories, but they're memories of *watching* it happen somewhere else, not actually being there myself. For example, Longdon as the sun came up after the battle: I won't be forgetting that in a hurry. We were sore and exhausted and we'd just heard that the whole of the mountain had been taken. It ought to have been a moment of triumph – we'd hardly won the war yet, but this was an important, decisive battle and the end of a long, hard night – but the shit that greeted us as the mist cleared stopped any celebrations. Under cover of darkness you can kid yourself on that it isn't really happening, the enemy are just statistics, it's just another exercise, but the daylight rubs your face in it. We just sat and gaped open-mouthed at the scene for about half an hour before we could even move. There was battle shit strewn up and down the whole mountain: guns, torn pieces of uniform, half-eaten rations and smashed-up hexie stoves, mis-matched boots, tents, sleeping bags, syringes, blood and med dressings. And everywhere, everywhere you fucking looked, there were dead Argies. Making our way back to company HQ we had to pick our way through this shit. There was no escaping it, it was round every corner, in every gully and shell-hole. The mountain stank. I've still got the stench lodged somewhere at the back of my nostrils. It stank of blood and shit and smoke and morphine, of damp earth and cordite. But it wasn't *me* seeing this and smelling this, it was someone else, someone who belonged there, someone who could cope with this assault on their senses. Similarly, the night we spent watching 2 Para overrun Wireless Ridge – it became pretty clear early on that they weren't going to need any help, so it was just a case of sitting back and watching the fireworks while the ground froze beneath us and the snow fell; that night seemed longer than the night of the fighting – that wasn't me either. It couldn't have been me. I couldn't have hacked it.

The only time that I actually felt like I was *there* again was when we suddenly realised it was all over. Before we got any official announcement we started noticing the boys around us were wearing berets instead of helmets. People were smiling, slapping each other's backs, congratulating each other on a job well done. We marched down into Stanley and as we did so I realised that *this* was what I'd joined up for. The chance, just once in my life, to march into a town which I'd just helped liberate. Liberate: just think about that word for a moment. It's one of the best, most noble things you can do as a human being, isn't it. Liberate. And how often do people get to *liberate* each other these days? So even if my own personal war hadn't been particularly noble or brave, I still couldn't help a little glow of pride as we marched in. This was an honour and it was *my* honour and I was right there as it happened and despite everything no one's going to take that away from me.

When we got into Stanley it was in a right state. Most of the islanders had moved out when the Argies had moved in, gone to stay with people on other parts of the islands. Those that stayed had to put up with Menendez and his mates making themselves right at home. There were makeshift signs all over the place – all the Port Stanley signs had been taken down and replaced by clumsily drawn *Puerto Argentina* signs. All the shops were forced to display their prices in pesos. Along the roads were hand-painted signs reminding you to KEEP RIGHT. And the place was crawling with Argie top brass: so many of the fuckers we couldn't guard them properly, so they all to keep their rooms in the best hotels, got to come and go pretty much as they pleased. They were even allowed to hang on to their revolvers, having managed to convince our top brass that they were at risk from their own troops. Fucking nobility looking after its own again. I mean, there may have been some truth in this – I'd have wanted to have a pop at an Argentinian general if I was one of their lads – but, you know, so what? Everyone felt this was outrageous. *We'd* won the fucking war. No one was suggesting we go Japanese and introduce starvation diets and slave labour camps or nothing . . . but, you know, *we'd* won the war.

So we spent a few days holed up in Stanley feeling hard done by – tidying up, drinking beer, eating mutton (yeah, mutton; they were living it up in swanky hotels, we were eating mutton. Who won the fucking war?), listening to the football on the radio. Hardly anyone had a telly there. In fact one of the islanders told us they'd all been offered tellies by the Argies when the troops first arrived – in time for the World Cup and everything – in return for their support. And they'd all refused, the berks. What were they thinking of? I mean, you could have taken the telly and then carried on plotting behind their backs couldn't you – accepted it with your fingers crossed as it were. But these islanders had some weird ideas. You know, living on these godforsaken islands with mutton instead of TV was a pretty strange thing to do in itself. We also found out later that one of Haig's proposals before the war kicked off had been to hand the islands over to the Argies, *but* if any of the islanders wanted to resettle in Britain the Argies had to pay them fifty thousand pounds to do so. And the bloody idiots turned that down too. That is, they were being offered *fifty thousand pounds* – fifty fucking grand – *not* to live on a shivering shit-hole eight thousand miles from the people they claimed to share a country with. And they said no. It's no bleeding wonder we found some of them a little difficult to get along with when we were billeted in Stanley. Some of them weren't even from the same planet as us.

I couldn't wait to get home. That little glow of pride didn't last too long and I started getting seriously spooked by the faces of those four boys. I felt I had more in common with the beaten Argies than I did with my back-slapping comrades. During a couple of quiet moments I tried to talk about it with Andy, but he still wasn't having any of it. It never happened, he'd tell me fiercely, and then he'd change the subject or walk away. It never fucking happened.

'And you know what, those four kids were the only people I killed, personally, in the whole of the campaign.'

'Well, that's good,' she says. 'It's not about how many people you killed, it's about the part you played in a noble enterprise.'

'Yeah ... the parties afterwards were a nightmare, though. Everyone had a story to tell and everyone could tell their stories except me ... Did Andy ever tell you about the Four Mad Fuckers?'

She thinks and smiles a little. 'I don't think so.'

'Well, here's an example of the stories people were telling. The Four Mad Fuckers were these four guys in 2 Para who were stonking out enemy positions during the fight for Wireless Ridge, when the base plate of their mortar starts to slip on the rocks. Now, if your mortar fire is going to be accurate your base plate has got to be completely secure, otherwise you're just going to be firing all over the shop and it's a waste of ammo. So: you know what these guys did?'

'. . . ?'

'They took it in turns to stand on the plate as the rounds were fired. Put their body weight down on it to hold it fast. And as they did so, each one of them got their ankles broken by the recoil shock, one after the other . . . Crack, crack, crack, crack.'

'My God . . .'

'That was their Falklands War. The Four Mad Fuckers; they were famous throughout the Parachute Regiment; probably are still. They had their war, I had mine.'

Irene props her head up on her arm and runs her other hand through the hairs on my chest.

'Andy told me once that *you* had saved *his* life . . . now I think I understand why.'

I shake my head. 'Nah. I never saved his life.'

'You were quick-thinking enough to take out the first of the men when his head suddenly reared up in front of you. That was good soldiering.'

'He was unarmed!'

'You weren't to know that. There was no way you could have known that. You could hardly wait for him to come up and pop a bullet in your head to find out. No, that was a necessary piece of fighting and I think Andy appreciated it. Especially as the two of you were in such a vulnerable position . . .'

'And then I shot the other three as well. In cold blood.'

'Well, if Andy says it never happened, it never happened. Who knows. Maybe it did never happen.'

And she puts her head down again, nuzzles into my shoulder and does whatever she can to take my pain away.

14.06

'What's that? It's fucking rolling tobacco,' said Peter. 'I thought you were getting ciggies.'

'Changed my mind,' said Riley, opening up the pouch of tobacco. 'Anyway, makes no difference to you, does it. You're not getting any.'

At that moment Joyce, Jonquil and Frank emerged from the bank. Jonquil immediately caught sight of Riley's tobacco.

'Tom! Where did you get that? I thought you didn't have any money?'

'Yeah. I got it at the shop over there. You know. The *tabac*.' Riley placed a heavy French emphasis on the last word.

'But you don't have any French money . . . Tom?'

'Uh, no, not as such.'

'Tom, did you steal this?'

'Course he stole it. He's a thief! Nothing m—'

'Shut up Peter. Tom, did you steal this tobacco?'

'No. The girl in the shop gave it to me.'

'Yeah, right . . .'

'Shut *up* Peter. What do you mean, she gave it to you?'

'She gave it to me.' Riley's broad smile returned. 'I may not have any money, but I'm a millionaire in natural charm.'

'So if I go over there and ask the girl in the shop, she'll tell me she just gave it to you as well, will she?'

'Should think so.' The smile grew even broader. If he could encourage Jonquil to make a tit of herself in front of everyone else, maybe she'd get off his back for a bit. He didn't like the way she'd been ordering people about all day. 'Why don't you go ahead?'

'Yeah. Go over there and ask her,' said Peter.

Jonquil hesitated. She didn't like the confidence in Riley's voice; nor the smug grin he had draped across his face. But she couldn't back down now. 'Yeah . . . OK, I will. Uh, Frank, why don't you see what everyone wants to do this afternoon while I'm gone.'

'OK, right, yeah.' Frank cleared his throat and while Jonquil tried to cross the road to the *tabac*, he announced generally: 'OK, what does everyone want to do today?' He didn't want to do this. It was going to lead to arguments and he hated dealing with arguments. He could sense one bubbling up, like a kettle on the verge of boiling. Maybe he shouldn't have asked such an open-ended question. Maybe that was the problem. Maybe he should just have said, OK, people, why don't we just do . . . whatever.

Surprisingly it was Dougal who piped up first. 'I thought we were going to go shopping.'

'I thought we were going to go shopping,' said Mikey in a sneering, high-pitched, piss-take of Dougal's voice.

Dougal glared at him. 'My sister has asked me to do some shopping for her,' he explained patiently, 'and I need to go.'

'Well I'm not going shopping,' said Mikey. 'It's stupid. There's shops at home. What do you want to come all the way over here to go shopping for? Anyway,' he looked over at Peter, 'all the signs will be in French.'

Frank could feel the panic rising. How could they go shopping and not go shopping at the same time?

'Well, I know what I'm going to do,' said Riley. 'I'm going to answer a call of nature.'

'Wait a minute, Tom. Where are you going to go?' said Joyce.

'Over here. There's a toilet just up here.'

'Where?' said Frank.

'Right here,' said Riley, pointing at a wall directly in front of them.

'That's a wall,' said Frank.

'No, it's not, it's a *pissoir*.'

'No, it's not, it's a wall.'

'It's a *pissoir*,' Riley insisted. 'They have them over here. I've read about them. They look just like walls, but they're really public toilets.'

'I don't think they have them any more,' said Frank. 'And anyway, that's definitely not one of them. It's a wall.'

'There were some proper toilets by the funfair,' said Candy, pointing a way down the street.

Riley peered. 'I can't see that far.'

'Just down there, at the end of the street, on the left.'

'I'm really not sure it's such a good idea—' Frank began.

But Riley was already off, still muttering that he couldn't see where Candy meant, but promising to find it. And no doubt planning to go up against a wall in any case.

So Frank turned back to sorting Dougal and Mikey out. Dougal had a fiery look of real determination in his eyes; Frank had never seen him like this before, not remotely like this. And Mikey: Mikey was just pissed; he was looking for trouble wherever he could find it and Peter was egging him on.

'I know,' said Candy. 'Why don't we split into two groups?'

Split into two groups. Of course. That was the thing to do, Frank realised. Why hadn't he thought of it? It would satisfy both Dougal and Mikey. And, perhaps more significantly from a quiet-life point of view, it would enable Joyce and Jonquil to be kept apart for most of the rest of the day.

'One group could go shopping with Dougal,' Candy went on, 'the other can go with Mikey and do . . . whatever he wants to do.'

'Go to the beach,' said Mikey firmly.

'OK. Go to the beach. Whatever.'

'Hmmm, I'm not sure—' Joyce said.

'It's perfect,' Frank interrupted. 'It'll help keep the troublemakers apart.' He didn't specify who the troublemakers were. 'Which do you fancy, Joyce? Shopping with Dougal or beach with Mikey?'

'Well, I'm not too sure—'

'I think Jonquil and me would quite like to do some shopping,' Frank continued, picking up speed. 'You know, get some nice French cheese and wine and stuff. How about you take Mikey and whoever else to the beach?'

Joyce felt steamrollered. It seemed she wasn't going to be

consulted about anything today. But she was happy enough to take Mikey to the beach. As long as it was just Mikey and maybe one other, and not Mikey *and* Peter *and* Tom Riley. She wasn't sure she could handle those three together.

'Well, OK . . .,' she said.

'Fine,' said Frank. 'So who's going to be in which group, then? Candy . . . ?'

'Uh, ask Peter first.'

'Okayyy . . . Peter?'

Peter took a step towards Candy. Why did he have to go first, what was the point of that? Bloody little shirtlifter; what was his game?

Candy took a step back. It went no further than that.

'Well, I want to do whatever *she* isn't,' Peter said gruffly.

'Fine by me,' said Candy.

'Okayyy,' said Frank again, drawing the y out even longer this time. 'So who's in which group then?'

'I fancy the beach,' said Candy.

'I'll go fucking shopping then,' said Peter.

'Well that's that settled then.'

'What about Tom?' Joyce asked. 'Which group do you think he'll want to go with?'

'I think he should go to the shops,' Mikey said quickly. 'He's starting to get on my wick, to be honest.'

'Well I think he should go the beach with you lot,' said Peter, who was just looking for a scrap with anyone now.

'Let's just see when he gets back, shall we.'

Shortly afterwards Jonquil returned, looking slightly nonplussed.

'It seems as though she did just give the tobacco to Tom,' she said. 'As far as I could understand. The girl didn't speak any English so I don't know how Tom managed to charm her . . . where is he by the way?'

'At the *pissoir*,' Mikey said gleefully.

'I'm sorry?'

Frank explained. And then he told her about the plan to split into two groups. Jonquil wasn't sure about such a major decision being taken in her absence, one that wasn't even her idea, but once she'd been reassured that it hadn't been Joyce's idea either, she was able to see that possibly it had its advantages.

Candy

I'm not sure which is going to happen first. Whether I'm going to hit Simone first or she's going to hit me. LA, she keeps singing at me. LA LA LA! And she plays a note on the piano and then sings that note. LA. That's the note, she says, that's the note you should be singing – LA – but you're singing this note – LA. And she plays the black note right next door to the first one. They sound ghastly one after the other. LA! I try. No *LA*. LA. NO *LA*. Ne me quitte *PAS!* LA! Lalalala*LA*! She plays the black note and the white note over and over again, one after the other. Can't you hear the difference? she says. Well they are very close. Exactly – so it sounds even worse when you don't get it quite right. Listen . . . And she goes back to playing the two notes again. They sound like a police siren! LA – LA – LA – LA.

We're in the flat of a friend of hers. A friend with a lot of money, a very expensive flat and most importantly a piano we can use. The place itself is pretty unchic to be brutally frank (there's nothing wrong with the building, it's one of those ultra-trendy loft conversion jobs, but it's been interior-designed by a lunatic and you can't help but bristle at the *waste* of so much money). And Simone and I in our own sweet way are also going slowly insane in here. It's our fourth rehearsal. It's one day until my opening night at BabyCakes. It's not going well. Simone is sitting at the piano hitting keys and saying LA a lot and I'm standing beside her desperately trying to resist the temptation to slam the lid down on her bony fingers.

OK, she says with a sigh, let's try it again from the top. You know what I think? I tell her, I think there's too much singing in

149

this song. She looks at me as though we may well be approaching the final straw. What do you mean? Well there's no instrumental breaks in it at all. It's a song, she says simply. Yes but it would be good if there was a pause in the middle so I can strike a few poses. You know – communicate the *feeling* of the song without actually having to concentrate on the singing for a bit.

Because if we're being honest these songs take some fucking concentration. How did I ever let her talk me into singing them in French? It's impossible. I'm trying so hard to remember the words and roll my rs correctly and hit the black notes instead of the white notes or the white notes instead of the black notes or whichever way round it's supposed to be that I scarcely have time to pose. And frankly what is the point of getting up on stage in the first place if you're not going to do a little posing? I strike a few right here and now for Simone; she watches me and her eyes become thinner.

You have to get the song right and worry later about the posing, she says, because if you don't get the song right everyone will laugh at you. I freeze mid-pose as though the wind has suddenly changed direction and now I'm stuck like this. I wish she hadn't said that; that *wasn't* a nice thing to say at all. So – shall we try it from the top again? she suggests. She plays the opening bars and then stops suddenly. That's where you're supposed to come in. It is? Yes! Listen . . . She plays it and sings it. That husky voice is beginning to get right on my tits now. OK, now you. She starts up again and I come in where I've been told to, exactly where I've been told to. Then *again* she stops abruptly. No! It's LA. She hits the piano key. I was singing LA! You weren't, you were singing LA. Are you sure that fucking piano is in tune? Yes I'm fucking sure the fucking piano is in tune. Well it doesn't sound in fucking tune to me. It's fucking you who's not in fucking tune. Maybe I'm just singing the wrong songs. Maybe it's the wrong fucking singer . . . Maybe it's the wrong fucking accompanist . . . Ha . . . ! And with that I storm off into the bathroom.

(And upset as I am right now I should just take a moment to

tell you about this bathroom. Firstly it's large. It's not just larger than other bathrooms I've seen, it's larger than most other rooms I've seen. It's certainly larger than any of the bedrooms I've ever had. In fact it's probably larger than all the bedrooms I've ever had put together. The few bits of wall which are tiled are tiled black. Deep black tiles with white surrounds. But by far the majority of the wall space is mirrored. Mirrors fucking everywhere. I mean OK above the sink so you can see yourself while you're shaving. But in front of the toilet? What kind of person likes to watch themselves shit?)

I slam the door behind me and lock it and run a sinkful of water. Beautiful warm clear water straight from the tap; rich people's water. Oh and of course I burst into tears. I don't know what's the matter with me – I've cried more during the last month than I probably did in the whole year before that. I blame the lack of heroin: I never used to blub like this when I was on smack. I get so *emotional* these days.

Simone starts rapping on the door and asking if I'm OK like I knew she would. Yeah I'm *fine*, I shout back at her bitterly in a what-do-you-care-anyway kind of voice. I didn't mean to be horrible, the bitch says. Yeah well I just don't think you understand sometimes what it's like to be me . . . Come on out Candy and let's try again. I'm not sure if I can— I start to tell her. And then standing bent double over the sink I become suddenly aware that I'm about to throw up. What is happening to me? I stagger over to the toilet open up and yawn. A gush of yellowy liquidy stuff comes out – I had two glasses of orange juice for breakfast this morning and nothing to eat since – and it splishes into the bowl some of it splishing over the side and on to the fluffy thing that sits uselessly around the edge of the toilet. Outside Simone shouts my name and then she's shouting my name and banging on the door. So I guess she doesn't hear the splishing. I slump down by the toilet and gaze putridly at myself in the mirror.

Candy! Candy open up! Candy . . . ? Are you going to answer me . . . ? I'm trying to answer; but my throat is so dry I can't speak.

151

And then I retch again. Just dry retching – there's nothing left to come up except my innards and they don't feel too secure at the moment. Mother of Mary what's going on? Was it something I ate? I haven't even eaten today. Well look I'm going to go now, Simone says, give me a call if you want to meet up tomorrow otherwise I'll see you at the club.

At the club . . . ? Oh sweet Jesus fucking Christ *at the club*! Don't go, I try and call to her, we can't finish yet. But my *fucking* throat won't make a *fucking* noise. So while I'm croaking and wheezing on the bathroom floor Simone is turning briskly away putting her jacket on and walking out of the door. I hear it slam with a very final-sounding thud. And then I throw up again some foul-smelling acidy stuff dregged up from somewhere in the pits of my stomach.

Oh fuckety-fuck *fuck*.

Now at least I know what the problem is. It's nothing to do with what I ate or didn't eat or the orange juice or anything else. It's terror. Pure and simple. Who ever told me I could sing anyway? No one that's who. Not a damn soul. I've been so caught up in what I *want* to do and what I *need* to do that I haven't stopped for a moment to consider what I actually *can* do. Just a teensy-weensy oversight. So now here I am the day before I open and everyone I know is coming to the opening night, all my friends, all their friends, everyone with a flyer from every gay bar in London – and even my accompanist thinks I'm going to be a laughing stock. I have that peculiar dread I used to get when I was a kid when I had been naughty and I knew I was going to get found out. I sit and I cry and I retch and I panic.

14.12

The supermarket turned out to be a bus ride away. It didn't take them long to find the bus stop, despite the language barrier, which became steelier every time one of them opened their mouths. The 'little bit of French' which Dougal claimed to remember from school amounted to nothing more than the sentence *Madame Bertillon est dans la cuisine*, which sounded correct, and his accent wasn't bad either, but wasn't terrifically useful under the circumstances. And Jonquil was refusing point blank to try any more French after her failure to communicate with the girl in the tobacconist's.

So it fell, as these things so often seemed to, to Frank to approach a grizzled-looking man on the street and say, 'Supermarket?' in a vaguely inquisitive tone of voice.

The man was perfectly used to ridiculous English people wandering around his town looking lost. However he objected to Frank's choice of word.

'Hypermarket,' he corrected.

'*Hyper*market,' said Frank. He had visions of a Sainsbury's that had drunk too much coffee.

'Hypermarket. Bus,' said the man.

'Bus. Where?' responded Frank.

'Bus. Train station,' said the man confidently.

'Bus. Train station?' Frank mouthed this silently to Jonquil, as if to say, what's he on about now?

'Perhaps he means the bus leaves from outside the train station,' suggested Jonquil.

The man nodded vigorously.

'Ah . . .' said Frank.

'Number five bus. Number seven bus,' said the man.

'From outside the train station?'

'Yes.'

'Ah . . .' They were back on the right track now. Just one more question: 'Train station. Where?'

The man pointed up the road. 'Five hundred metres.'

'Thank you very much,' said Frank. '*Merci beaucoup.*'

Sure enough five hundred metres up the road (or probably something like five hundred metres; none of them were really sure how far this was) they discovered the train station, and sure enough just as they got there a number seven bus was pulling away, blindly

153

and happily oblivious to Frank running along behind it, banging on the back window, screaming for it to stop. When it had pulled out into the traffic and out of his reach, Frank turned round, red-faced and fuming, to see a completely empty number five bus pulling calmly into the vacated bus stop.

'Well, uh ... we'll take this one then, shall we,' he said puffing.

Jonquil smiled sympathetically at him. Peter also smiled, and then, well he couldn't help himself, he burst out laughing.

Dougal said nothing.

They clambered aboard. Clearly no one was going to attempt the French word for 'four' so Frank held up four fingers and said: 'Hypermarket.'

'Four to the hypermarket. Certainly sir,' said the driver perfectly.

They settled down towards the back of the bus. Jonquil and Frank sat together; Peter refused to sit next to Dougal; in fact he made a point of sitting two rows away from everyone else.

'So, Dougal, what have you got to buy for your sister?' asked Jonquil as the bus set off.

Dougal produced a short list with half a dozen or so items scrawled on it in fussy, near-illegible handwriting.

'I thought you didn't have any money, though?'

'Oh yes, my sister gave me some money she had left over from her last trip,' said Dougal, 'but I didn't want to say anything outside the bank because ... well, you know.'

'Very sensible,' said Jonquil.

'I haven't got any money,' said Peter from behind them.

'Oh well, never mind Peter, you can, uh ... browse,' said Frank, wishing at the end of this sentence that he hadn't started it.

'Yeah, right,' said Peter, and he went back to staring glumly out of the window. He should have insisted on going to the beach. What was the point of going to a supermarket with no money? He'd let himself be hoodwinked by the little shirtlifter hadn't he. The others would all come back with a suntan and he'd have spent the afternoon wandering aimlessly round a bloody supermarket. And he bet the others got beer. Joyce was a pushover for stuff like that, whereas these two bastards in front of him . . . Jonquil especially . . . Yeah, he bet the others were lying, right now, drinking beer on the beach, eyeing up the talent . . . and of course it would be *topless* talent here, wouldn't it. Peter held his head in his hands. He really was the fuckwit of the century. He'd come to France, the home of Topless Beach Talent and been talked into going to a bloody *supermarket* instead; while Candy – fucking *Candy* who didn't even know how to appreciate a decent tit – was sitting around in tit heaven, oblivious. It made you want to weep.

No, it made you want to drink.

The two bastards in front of him, meanwhile, were now deep in conversation with each other, whispering so not even Dougal could hear.

'I'm glad Tom didn't come with us,' Frank was saying.

Mikey was suddenly very, very drunk. Not that he'd been particularly sober all day, but now he was *extremely* drunk, staggering down the street, humming whiningly to himself, and Joyce was beginning to lose patience with him.

'Come along, Mikey, we're nearly there. You can have a rest and a sleep when we get to the beach.' She turned to Candy. 'Where exactly do you think this beach is?'

'I don't know. We're heading back towards the boat. That's a good sign. The beach was just near where we docked, wasn't it?'

Candy was happy now. They were here, in France, the sun was shining . . . she was glad in a way that George Johnson had made her come. And the gun thing, well that was out of her control. It would happen or it wouldn't happen and she hoped she wouldn't be around if it did happen, but there was nothing she could do about it. So why worry? Life's too short to worry – that was one of the things Riley liked to tell people, usually just ahead of inflicting physical damage on them.

Hugh Brune

For no good reason at all, Mikey started to sing 'I'm The King Of The Swingers' from *The Jungle Book*.

'Oh Mikey, please!' said Joyce.

Mikey stopped, but he didn't look happy about it. 'Why won't anyone let me sing today?' he complained. 'It's only singing. I'm only singing because I'm happy.' Then, happy, he broke out into song again. 'SING WHEN I'M HAPPY! I ONLY SING WHEN I'M HAPPY!' He looked over to Candy for support. 'You understand, don't you. You're a singer.'

'It's a different kind of singing,' said Candy.

They walked on a bit. Mikey contented himself with humming.

Joyce took hold of Candy's arm. 'I'm glad Tom Riley didn't come with us, aren't you?'

'Yeah, he can be a bit of a handful,' said Jonquil. 'Especially as they've all been drinking now. And him and Peter really don't get along, do they?'

'Yeah, because him and Mikey really don't get along with each other,' said Candy.

'I hope Joyce will be OK,' said Frank.

'I hope Frank and Jonquil will be OK,' said Candy.

'Oh they'll be fine,' said Joyce with a smile. 'Don't worry, they'll be fine.'

'Joyce'll be fine,' said Jonquil, and she returned to staring out of the window. Calais viewed through a bus window looked almost surreal. It was as though the people here were *trying* to reach out to the invading English hordes, whose willingness to part with the unfamiliar local currency must have seemed miraculous to them, but couldn't bring themselves to try too hard because these invaders were, after all, English. They passed a pub with a large Union Jack outside it and a sign proclaiming WELCOME IN

156

OUR PUB: there was something profoundly alienating about that word *in*.

Meanwhile the traffic in the other direction seemed practically non-existent – Dover and Folkestone weren't overrun with eager French shoppers snapping up cheap English tea, were they. You got the occasional party of French teenagers wandering glumly around Trafalgar Square on enforced school exchanges, but that was about it. Looking back to the ferry, Jonquil realised that everyone on board had been English; or at least those who weren't were keeping quiet about it. The staff were English, the shops on board sold English goods for English money; it was a little piece of England floating menacingly across to France. While England, humiliatingly, had to *beg* French people to come and visit. As the bus trundled out through the suburbs of Calais they passed large billboard advertisements for, of all things, Kent. Jonquil hadn't realised that Kent was a product which could be bought and consumed like any other. But here they were: enormous colourful posters enticing you to investigate *Kent historique, Kent romantique* ... even *Kent authentique*, as though South East England were plagued by other, less serious counties trying to pass themselves off as Kent. It was embarrassing.

It took about a quarter of an hour to reach the hypermarket. Frank had been keen to see what a hypermarket looked like, as opposed to a plain, dreary supermarket, and he wasn't disappointed. It was vast. It was like all the Tescos he'd ever been into all rolled into one. He felt his jaw drop.

Peter was less impressed. A big fuck-off supermarket was still a supermarket and, more importantly, still very much not a beach. However, he was pleased to notice what looked, unless he was very much mistaken, like a bar, right outside the shop. Tables and chairs and men drinking beer. That was a bar, wasn't it?

Jonquil took the lead and marched them all inside. Unbelievably the place looked even bigger from the inside than it did from the outside. There was aisle after aisle as far as you could see, and hundreds and hundreds of signs screaming at you in brightly coloured letters. Although, as Peter would have pointed out if he hadn't been too busy weighing up whether to try and swipe a couple of bottles from the spirits section or head back outside to that bar, the signs were all in French. And what was the point of that?

Jonquil grabbed a trolley. Even the trolleys were enormous. Like supermarket trolleys at home, you had to insert a coin to release one from the snaking chain of trolleys, to ensure that you returned it afterwards. Unlike the ones at home, inserting the coin did actually release the damn thing; you didn't then have to pull and tug at the lock and kick the wheels and then get some spotty youth from the cigarette desk to give you your quid back. 'OK, let's shop,' she said.

Dougal took out his shopping list and wandered off in the opposite direction.

'Uh, Dougal, this way,' said Frank.

'Actually,' said Jonquil, 'it probably does make sense if we split up. We all want different things.'

'Yeah, good idea,' said Peter.

Something about the eagerness of his tone should have alerted her. 'Right, we'll meet back here by the trolleys in *exactly* half an hour. OK?' she said. 'Has everyone got that? Peter, you're not going to do anything stupid, are you?'

No. He was going to get himself a drink. It would be the most sensible thing he'd done all day.

But she made him promise to be good, so he did. Good was relative anyway. And then Dougal went off one way and Frank and Jonquil went off the other way and Peter was left alone – blissfully alone – to make his mind up.

Bar, spirits . . . bar, spirits . . . bar, spirits . . .

Bar.

Jonquil

Frank . . . ?

Yeah, Frank. You know he's started working at the hostel.

No ... What, your hostel?

Yeah. Stamford Street, yeah.

Days?

Yeah, days. A proper, regular job. Packed it in at OFM and he's come to work with the homeless. Loving every minute of it.

And how's it working out?

It's brilliant. It's honestly no problem at all, you know? We're professional at work and then outside work we're good friends. When we're together maybe we talk a little too much about work for my liking. But, you know, that's because it's early days; I'm sure it'll ease off. Frank is still new to the job, he has to ask about things.

And that's not a problem for him? Presumably you're his boss, in a way?

No, he's so free of all the usual macho bullshit it's amazing. He's the new boy, he's got loads of questions to ask and he just accepts it. Anyway, I'm not his boss. Philip wouldn't allow anyone else to be a boss ...

Philip?

Oh God, I've told you about *Philip* before, haven't I?

So what about the other people at work? How are they taking this?

Taking what?

You and Frank. You said you thought they might find it unbearable if the two of you were working together.

I did? Well ... I don't think they notice, to be honest.

Really?

Really. No one's said anything, you know? As I said, we're professional about it. Work is work, play is play.

And play is going . . . OK, is it?

What, you mean the relationship? God, yeah. I can't believe how well it's going. I have to pinch myself sometimes. We've even said the l word.

The l word?

Lurve. It just happened as we were coming home on the night bus. We were sitting on the top deck and there was no one else around and we were going past Big Ben and it just sort of slipped out. It was like . . . what was it like? It was like that thing when you're eating absent-mindedly, an apple say, and – do you ever do this? – you forget you've already got a mouthful, you're reading a magazine or something, so you put another one in and a bit of the first mouthful falls out, half-chewed, on to your plate. It was kind of like that. Only not as gross obviously. I was staring out of the window and feeling all happy and warm, and I think we may have been holding hands, and the words just fell out my mouth. I love you . . . I mean, it wasn't even news for me. I'd known for ages. All my friends knew. I told you, didn't I? I told you way back, when I'd first met him. So I hardly noticed that I'd said it. But Frank: Frank practically jumped out of his skin! He turned round to me and made sort of flustered, grunting noises for a bit, and then he said, you do? And I thought about it, realised what I'd done, and said, yeah! And he said, well I love you too then. And I said, you're not just saying that because I said it? And he said, no I really mean it. So I said, great, give us a kiss then. And that was that; it hasn't made a huge difference. Things were pretty cool before; now they're even better.

The sex thing isn't a problem now?

No. No, not at all. I can't believe I was making so much fuss about it before. Well, I can believe it. That was the old me. But no, I think it's a brilliant idea now.

You do? Honestly? You think not having sex before marriage is a brilliant idea?

Yeah. Once you've realised the advantages, it's so obvious. I mean, it's only a question of having some degree of will power, isn't it. And things are so much less tense without sex getting in the way, you know? I was thinking about this the other day. Me and Frank haven't started rowing yet, not proper, stand-up shouting rows. And we should have done by now, shouldn't we. Especially as we've got work stuff we could be rowing about on top of all the normal stuff. But we don't. We're completely cool with each other.

And this is all down to not having sex?

Must be.

How long are you planning to abstain for?

I don't know. I don't really look upon it as abstaining, you know? See, we still . . .

. . . Yes?

We've reached a kind of compromise. I examined his little calling card in detail and, according to the small print, the pledge has only to do with *sexual intercourse*. Not sex itself. And of course there's a world of difference between the two things. So we . . . you know, we explore that world. We abstain from sexual intercourse, but not the other stuff.

Other stuff?

I'm not going into details.

And Frank's OK with this?

Yeah . . . He was a little concerned at first, you know, that we were following the letter of the law and not the spirit. So I said to him – it was a Friday night after a long week at work and we'd had quite a bit to drink – I said to him, why don't we just try a few

161

things? Just gently. And if you feel compromised, fine, we'll get dressed and carry on as we are ... So we did: we tried stuff. It was round at my flat, Katy was away for the whole weekend so no chance of being disturbed, we got the atmosphere right and ... yeah, I think Frank's pretty OK with it. If you know what I mean. I'm not too sure what the people at his church would think, but, you know, fuck them. Or not, as the case may be.

So how do you get on with the people at Frank's church?

I've never met them. I'm not sure they're my kind of people, you know?

You don't go to church with Frank?

Are you kidding?

That's a very big part of his life, though. How does he feel about that?

Fine. He's completely cool about it. In fact he wouldn't want me to come even if I asked, if he thought I was just coming to keep him company. It's more important to him than that – you know, you should only go if you *truly* believe in it, no one should be faking it. But on the other hand he doesn't have a problem at all relating to someone who doesn't share all his beliefs. He's got this total live-and-let-live outlook on life, which I really admire. You know. He's got his church thing, and I've got my spiritual side too and we respect each other.

Your spiritual side?

Yeah. You know, I've studied Buddhism and stuff. And Frank respects that.

You've studied Buddhism? Really? You've never told me about it.

Yeah ... well, I've read a couple of books on the subject. I wouldn't necessarily say I was *practising* ... you know. They have some pretty weird ideas about who you can and can't shag as well.

14.25

The people in the hypermarket were, not surprisingly, entirely English. English people were here in all their various, gory beauty. There were posh Surrey English people: men who wore jumpers over their shirts – even though it was eighty degrees outside – and then turned the collars of their shirts up; and women who didn't wear their jumpers at all, but draped them casually over their shoulders, tying the sleeves lazily over their cleavages. There were loud Essex English people: violently coloured shell suits for the women, ill-fitting shorts for the men, lobster-red skin for everyone. How, you were forced to wonder, had they managed to get themselves *that* burned just walking in from the car park? There were shifty-looking Londoners, poor-looking Northerners, black English, Asian English, students, geezers, old folk, impossibly large families, proudly childless young couples, all defying magnificently the concept of an English nation.

Except they were all buying wine. *This* was what united them. Bottles and bottles and bottles and bottles of wine. Red, white, rosé, sparkling, dry, dessert – but mainly red. *Cheap* red. And if they weren't buying wine they were buying beer. Beer came in dinky little green bottles that looked like they contained about two mouthfuls each. There were twenty-four bottles to a crate; you could fit six crates into a trolley, seven if you were good at balancing stuff, so everyone did. Most people had two trolleys. That is, two trolleys each: four trolleys per couple: twenty trolleys per large group of ten. One for the beer, one for everything else. Even the 'reassuringly expensive' brand-name stuff only cost fifty francs a crate.

Jonquil and Frank were somehow managing so far with two trolleys between them. Buying the cheese had been fairly straight-forward. Frank had made the startling discovery that bries were round and not triangular and had tried to use this new intelligence to persuade Jonquil to let him buy a whole one, but she didn't want to spend the rest of the day lugging a whole cheese around. Instead they got a small selection of various types. Inevitably they ended up choosing the creamiest, squelchiest, most alive-looking ones; the ones that oozed full fat.

Then the wine. Where did you start with all this wine? There were acres and acres of the stuff, endless corridors with red on one side and white on the other.

'Now, we mustn't go mad here,' Jonquil warned. 'We've got to carry all this back, remember.'

So they set about trying to pick. They chose according to two criteria: prettiness of label and cheapness of price. It was funny to think you could go on courses at home, long courses at that, to learn all about wine, how it was produced, how it was stored, the good regions, the good years, how to develop your palate . . . Etc etc. When all you really needed to know were these two things: how much does it cost and does the label look cool?

They enjoyed choosing. It was a tough job – there was so much to bloody choose from – and they didn't really know what they were doing, but they enjoyed it. Jonquil especially. She liked the domesticity of it, the routine day-to-day pleasure of it. Shopping for groceries, even cheap French wine, with someone else was actually quite intimate. They discussed each bottle that caught their eye, laughed over the ones with the stupid names or stupid pictures, argued about what they might have to eat with each selection.

'We should do this more often,' said Jonquil.

'What, come to France?'

'No, this. Shopping.'

Frank looked at her. 'You think we should go *shopping* more often?'

'Well . . . yeah.'

'Why?'

'I don't know. Because it's nice . . . don't you think? Doing this together . . . oh forget it, never mind.'

The thing was they didn't even drink that much wine. How long was it going to take them to get through six whole bottles? But they were surrounded by wine, everyone else was buying wine. So they bought wine.

Of course the hypermarket didn't only sell cheese and wine – how *hyper* would that have been? It sold pretty much everything you could think of, from mid-price country and western CDs to children's clothes. Every inch of this immense hangar was filled with stuff to buy, aisle after aisle after aisle, and no one was buying any of it. There were clever customer-service gimmicks, also being largely ignored. A few of the more obscure products – mainly bizarre-looking cleaning implements – were demonstrated by unwatched videos running on an endless loop. There was a tank dispensing drinking water to no one at all. Every aisle was deserted apart from the ones with cheese and alcohol in them.

Or almost. In fact there was one soul, standing alone, lost and bewildered in this vast consumer emptiness, who was not buying cheese or wine. An old man in a shabby old suit, tie resolutely straight despite the blistering heat outside, half-full shopping basket in his hand and an increasingly panicked look on his face. People did notice him as they zoomed past the end of the aisles in the desperate hunt for booze, but they didn't pay him much attention. Perhaps they just took on board, mid-zoom, the quaint observation that France also had its share of weird blokes who hung around supermarkets looking like they'd been there for a couple of weeks.

Eventually, however, someone took pity on him. A middle-aged, peroxide-blonde woman from Canterbury called Sheila, who was here with a small group of her girlfriends who were beginning to get on her nerves.

'Are you OK?' she asked, approaching the man.

There was no reply.

'Are you English?'

'Scottish!' said the man fiercely. Fiercely but quietly.

'I see . . . and do you need any help? You look a little lost.'

For the first time Sheila noticed the piece of paper the man was holding. He looked at it sadly. 'I have to get some things for my sister,' he said.

Hugh Brune

'What things? Here . . . let me see if I can help you find them.'

The man wouldn't relinquish his shopping list, but Sheila persuaded him to move his hand around so she could read it. The handwriting was atrocious and she had to strain to work out what all the items were. She checked the list off against the contents of the basket. Actually he'd done remarkably well considering the hugeness of the place and the variety of the items; pretty much everything was here.

'I'm having a problem with the pâté,' the man said.

Sheila checked the list and the basket. Sure enough, the pâté was missing. 'Okay . . .,' she said, 'there must be pâté around here somewhere.'

The man indicated behind her. She turned round. They were in the pâté aisle. Behind her was an entire wall of pâté: there must have been a hundred different types at least. Surely this was some kind of joke. Surely there weren't *this* many different types of pâté in the world?

'They haven't got the one I want,' the man said.

Rubbish. There had to be every different type of pâté ever produced anywhere right here in front of them. He just hadn't been looking properly. Sheila made a note of the name, as best she could read it, and started searching the shelves.

'I've checked,' he added. 'I've been here for twenty minutes.'

OK . . . well, he could buy a different kind then, couldn't he. 'What kind of pâté is that, liver pâté?'

'Yes.'

'Why don't you get another kind of liver pâté then? Your sister won't notice the difference.'

It was immediately clear from the man's expression that actually his sister would notice the difference and this had been very stupid thing to say.

OK . . .

'She'll be very upset if I don't get her what she wants,' said the man, who seemed genuinely worried.

Sheila thought about it for a little while. Actually there was a very simple solution to the problem, as there was to most problems if you thought about them for a little while. All the chap had to do was buy a different kind of liver pâté and then tell his sister that this new kind had *replaced* the one she had asked for on the market. In fact it was still exactly the same stuff, but it had been given a brand new name for marketing purposes. That should keep the old bird quiet.

However, before she had a chance to share her brainwave they were interrupted by a voice from the end of the aisle.

'Dougal! There you are. We've been looking all over for you.'

It was a girl and a rather sullen-looking young man. They appeared to be in some kind of hurry.

'Have you got everything?' the girl said. 'We really ought to be making a move.'

'Almost everything,' said Dougal.

'I've got an idea about your pâté—' Sheila began.

But the girl talked over the top of her. 'Thanks very much for your help. I'm sorry to cause you all this trouble, but he's with us.'

Suit yourself, thought Sheila.

'Well . . . good luck,' she said to Dougal, backing away slowly.

Dougal was too preoccupied to respond.

'Good luck,' said Sheila again.

Jonquil hated that. She hated it when do-goody members of the public stuck their noses in and meddled. It was *her* job; she was trained to do it and they weren't and they usually ended up causing trouble.

'Come on Dougal,' she said. 'You've got enough things there, haven't you? That'll do.'

14.25

For Joyce and Candy and Mikey, all three of them, the beach was a wistful experience. They hadn't been anywhere near a beach since they were children and the sounds and the smells and the glint in their eyes from the sun brought back heady memories. It was low tide. The sea was a long, long way out and the beach was quite crowded, so they had walked a fair distance across the softening sand before settling themselves.

It was tough on Joyce. Not only had this brought back memories of her own childhood, but she was physically surrounded by children: playing, laughing, happy children. She couldn't complain, of course. What else would you expect to find on a beach on a day like today? But it was tough none the less.

And to make it worse, Candy and Mikey were nattering away like old women. About children.

'So this operation of yours . . .,' Mikey was saying. He was slurring his words badly now. The word 'operation' came out in a flurry of phlegm. It was hard for Candy to concentrate on what he was saying without moving closer and risking getting sprayed. 'Is it, like, the full deal?'

'What do you mean?'

'They, like, take your bits off and put other bits on you?'

'I'm not sure those are the correct gynaecological terms, but, yeah, that's it essentially.'

Mikey didn't understand any of this last sentence, but he persevered. 'So you can have kids and everything?'

'Uh, no . . . no, it doesn't stretch quite that far.'

They watched a young boy and girl, directly in front of them, busily building a sandcastle. Both children had fixed looks of intense concentration as they turned out their buckets of firm, wet sand; then, if they were successful, they would giggle with delight and proudly show the other one.

'It's a shame,' Candy went on, 'but there we are: even the wonders of modern science have their limits.'

'I wouldn't worry,' said Mikey, frowning. 'Kids are a pain in the arse.'

'How many have you got again, Mikey?'

Mikey squinted at the sun while he tried to count them all up. He was wasting his time. Even when he was sober he didn't have a clue any more how many of the little bastards there were.

'I don't know,' he conceded. 'More than fifteen, though. Once I'd got my rugby team together I stopped counting.'

This was too much for Joyce. 'You don't *know* how many children you have, Mikey?'

'Uh, no . . . not exactly.'

Fifteen, seventeen, what difference did it make?

'That's terrible.'

'Yeah . . . most of them were born in the seventies,' he offered by way of explanation. 'And, you know, the seventies are a bit of a blur for me.'

Joyce couldn't believe she was hearing this. It wasn't just unfair; it was monstrous. What kind of despicable evil had her previous incarnations committed for her to end up with karma like this? She couldn't be Mrs Thatcher; Mrs Thatcher was still alive. Stalin then. Yes, she'd have to be the reincarnation of Joseph bloody Stalin to deserve this. 'But . . . don't you know their *names*?' she said.

'Some,' said Mikey, reclining in the sand. 'The boys mainly. There were two other Michael Williamses. I always wanted a boy called after myself, so my first son was Michael Williams Junior. Then about ten years later, when I was on something like my ninth or tenth I forgot about the first one – just for a moment, mind – so there was another one. It hardly matters; they don't know each other; they don't even know me. In between they were mainly called after rugby players of the time – that is, if I was around to have a say in what they were called at all. You know, Phil Bennett Williams, Gareth Edwards Williams, J. P. R. Williams Williams, that sort of thing. But the girls . . . the girls I don't remember so well. I know there was one called Lena after Lena Zavaroni . . .'

'Don't you ever see them?'

'No. Mostly they live with their mothers. Some in care. Of course a lot of them have grown up now so who knows where they are . . . One of them, the second eldest, was in prison last I heard.'

'You've never given the mothers any maintenance or anything?'

Mikey burst out laughing. The laughter turned into a coughing fit. 'What with?' he said when he could splutter the words out.

169

'I haven't got enough money for myself, have I, let alone any-one else.'

'You could get a job,' said Joyce.

Mikey thought about laughing again, then decided it hurt too much. 'Philip wouldn't even give me a job sweeping up the hostel, remember?'

Joyce fell silent.

Mikey did too. He closed his eyes and tried to remember some more about his children. This was affecting him more than it ought to be. This was, he decided, simply his brain's way of telling him he hadn't drunk enough yet today. A simple message. One he'd heard before.

Joyce watched the two children at work on their sandcastle. She took out her three red juggling balls and tossed them absent-mindedly, hardly noticing when she dropped one and dented the sand. She stared and stared at the sandcastle. It was all she could do to stop herself going over there and stamping on those perfect little turrets.

Joyce

I suppose the final, damning and irrefutable proof that there is no God can take many forms. In my case I know exactly what it was. It was a wooden box, maybe twenty inches long by ten inches wide, maybe not even as big as that, sitting on a table in front of me. As I looked at the box, shifting uncomfortably in my hospital-issue wheelchair, Mark holding my hand and not letting go, the thought just struck me. Not a dramatic revelation or anything, not a blinding flash on the road to Tunbridge Wells, just a banal observation, like taking in the colour of the curtains: there is no God. There *is* no God.

Inside the box was the half-formed body of my daughter, and I mean body, I use the word intentionally. One of the younger doctors, like all the medical people, had kept referring to her as a *foetus*. I suppose he was trying to be helpful in his way, trying to lessen the impact or something like that, but I wanted to bloody hit him every time he said it, especially given the attitude of my sister Margaret to the whole thing. Everyone, it seemed, was trying to differentiate this bloody, lifeless mass of tissue from the housefuls of happy, healthy children I was sure to have in the future. Dali and van Gogh were both substitute children, the young doctor took great delight in telling me. These facts were obviously useful weapons in his job; probably you had to learn lists of substitute high-achievers (*who might not have lived* . . .) at medical school for deployment in just this kind of situation. So bloody what? I thought. So – he seemed to be implying – a world without miscarriages and failed pregnancies is a world without *Sunflowers*. But this was absolutely no trade at all as far as I was concerned. What was a painting compared with what I had lost? Show me that world, I wanted to yell; take me there.

We had named the baby Elizabeth, to be shortened to Beth. Not Betsy or Liz or Lisa or anything else – Beth. The fact that she would never hear her name spoken made it all the more important somehow to get it right. We were allowed to hold her before she was taken away and put in her box. We had our photo taken with her, were given a lock of her hair to keep. She was the tiniest thing you can imagine. If you held your two palms out flat she could lie across them, her feet just hanging off the edge. Her head was large, her arms and legs thin and spindly. She looked like a puppet, a doll – it was like seeing a rejected prototype of yourself.

Her funeral service was held in the small hospital chapel not far, appropriately, from the mortuary. It was a white, disinfected, impersonal room (the curtains were orange, by the way), which served as a multi-faith chapel, which meant all the specific religious symbols had to be temporary. For our lapsed Catholic purposes a cheap-looking cross had been hung from the picture rail to offset the candles and the flowers. A young priest, the son of an acquaintance of my father's, had been drafted in for the occasion, and he did his best to look comfortable under the circumstances.

Ironic, of course, that my anti-Damascus should occur so suddenly like this in a place of God. In a way it was a relief: a relief to finally *know*. No more apologetically seeking refuge in agnosticism, no more wondering what if, perhaps even no more guilt . . . For however lapsed you become, it's still not the same as severing your ties completely. Now, though, I was free. Free to do all those forbidden things I had secretly been longing to do, free to covet my neighbour's ox if that's what I wanted to do. I found I had to stop myself – and I can scarcely bring myself to admit this – I found I actually had to stop myself *smiling*. At the irony, at the relief, at the sheer ludicrousness of the situation. A dozen people, none of whom had been anywhere near a church since the last time someone they knew got married, trying to sing along to a hymn they'd never heard before, played on a wonky cassette through a battered cassette recorder.

Can you imagine that, though – if I'd started giggling at this point? How would I have explained it? What on earth could I have said? In the end I had to force myself back to the dark thoughts which had prevented me from sleeping a wink the last few nights: *Your baby's dead, Joyce. You failed. You failed as a mother. You're barely even a woman.* That put paid to any thoughts of laughter.

I don't know if the funeral helped or not. Probably it did in the long run. It was our choice to have it; it wasn't necessary (she was only a *foetus* after all). I had insisted on it when agreeing to the termination, and my dad said if we were going to do it, we should do it properly, so he'd chosen this bloody awful hymn that no one knew. After it was finally over, he stood up and read a lesson from the Bible. Then the priest said a few words. Then Dad stood up again and read a short poem. He'd had a permanently bewildered expression the last four days, my dad. He hadn't slept any more than I had, but he hadn't cried either. He'd been bottling it all up, coping only by organising everything around him. It was a terrible time for him. Beth would have been his first grandchild; Mum was not long dead and he was still getting to grips with living alone; and now my bloody sister Margaret was tearing what was left of the family apart. The thing was, he looked like he *wanted* to cry, but he simply didn't know how to go about it any more.

After the poem the priest said a few prayers. The one that starts 'Our Father', which even our bunch of miserable sinners was mostly familiar with. Then I was terrified there was going to be another hymn. But no, when we emerged blinking from our prayer and from our minute's silence for personal reflection, we were already being ushered outside. Mark wheeled me out and the twelve of us – our immediate families (except Margaret), a few people from work and my best friend Rosie and her husband – squeezed into three cars. There was a brief pause while I was hoisted inelegantly from my chair and into the car, and everyone tried not to look. While the chair was being folded up and put into the boot, one of the hospital staff started to complain that we were taking hospital property off the premises. Until it was pointed out to him that I was still so weak that without the chair I wouldn't be able to watch my own unborn baby being buried, and that I would be coming back, with the chair, later that afternoon.

Then I caused a huge fuss by insisting that Beth's coffin come with me, on my lap. Dad said it would be too upsetting for me. And I told him the whole business had been too upsetting for me and it was a little late to be worrying about that now. Mark asked if I was sure and I said yes. And that was it: I was. *Sure*. I was starting to be sure about a number of things. And it felt good to be sure.

In the end they relented and I was deposited in our old Ford Cortina. Beth was placed on my knees. We hadn't hired hearses or anything, so we made the short trip to Dad's house in the dirty red Cortina with the Mark and Joyce windscreen stickers. Mark drove. My dad and my Uncle Brian got in the back.

And no one said a word for the whole twenty-minute drive. What on earth could we have talked about? What would have been considered a suitable topic for discussion? I thought about mentioning the weather a couple of times – it was grey and overcast and not worth mentioning unless you were desperate to talk about something. But I didn't. I just sat there in silence, stroking the box, feeling the smoothness of the wood, crying softly.

The burial itself was very short and straightforward. One of Dad's neighbours had dug a small hole – it was deep, but very small; too small – under one of the apple trees at the end of the long, tidy garden. The coffin was placed in the hole as gently as Mark and a couple of the other men could manage; and then Dad read another poem. I don't know where he was getting this stuff from. I'd never known him to have anything to do with poetry before, not even when Mum died. The earth was thrown back in the hole, patted down, and then we all trooped Englishly inside for tea and Swiss roll. Only much later did it occur to me to wonder what we would do when Dad sold his house. This didn't cross anyone's mind at the time. This wasn't a decision based in logic – it just seemed like the right thing to do.

On the way inside, Mark said he wanted a word with me. He was pushing me very slowly indeed and once we were out of earshot he stopped altogether and crouched down to speak to me.

'I just wanted to say . . .,' he said, 'I'm glad we got married. And I want to stay married.'

I smiled and told him I was glad too.

This might seem like a strange thing for him to say. After all, it would have taken a very special man indeed to ask for a divorce on that particular afternoon. But you see, we only got married because I was pregnant. Before that we were utterly opposed to the idea. It was old-fashioned and reactionary and sexist and all of the other things we were Against. But then I got myself up the stick and all our principles seemed to disintegrate. We'd got married, sold out, so Beth wouldn't be born a bastard and she didn't even have the good grace to be born alive.

So it was good of Mark to say what he did. It was.

Shortly after tea, just as people were starting to drift away, we had a visitor. A golfing buddy of my dad's had heard we were planning to bury Beth in an unmarked plot in the garden and thought this was terribly sad (although *we* would know where the plot was, that was the whole point), so he had brought us a cross which he had carved himself. A cross. I could have rammed the bloody thing down his interfering throat. How dare he be so intrusive, so presumptuous. How dare he force his unwanted symbols into our lives. Somehow, though, I managed to keep it together while we were all dragged back up to the end of the garden to see this ugly, disrespectful thing hammered into the ground. And I became surer with each whack of the hammer: surer, surer, surer, surer . . .

Because you can argue round and round for hours about this, about God's great plan and the importance of faith and free choice and human beings being able to distinguish for themselves between right and wrong. I went to a Catholic school, I went to university in the seventies and smoked pot; believe me, I know how long it's possible to talk about this stuff for. You can point out that if God had to prove his existence (and no, I'm not using a capital H for *his*, not any more), there wouldn't be any reason for him to exist. You can tell me that the thing is to *believe*, and that you either believe or you don't, and that's the whole point of God in the first place. But there is no sane way you can argue that if there was a benevolent and omnipresent God – however much he wanted to challenge our faith, however mysterious the ways in which he chose to move – there is no way you can argue that he would allow there to be coffins as small as the one I had sitting on my knees in the car that afternoon. They simply wouldn't exist. There is no room in the same universe for God and baby-coffins. It really is as simple as that.

So you're left with two alternatives: either God *isn't* benevolent and omnipresent (in which case, what's the point? As far as I'm concerned, benevolence and omnipresence are the minimum requirements for being God). Or he doesn't exist. Either way, I decided that afternoon I wouldn't be spending too much more of my time in the future glorifying his name. And as soon as they let me out of the hospital, I went round to my dad's house and I tore that fucking cross out of the ground.

If I thought that was the end of it, though, I was dreaming. Two days after the funeral, my milk came in. I went back to Dr Ross, leaking, half-crazed with rage and humiliation, and demanded that she make the damn stuff go away. She did all she could, which was absolutely nothing. She was a tiny Jamaican woman with a large, friendly smile who gave the impression that she would remain permanently chilled and in control, whatever rumpus was going on around her. It was a useful demeanour for a doctor to have. She let me shriek insults at her and then sob comprehensively on her shoulder, to hit her and hug her in quick succession. Of all the doctors I saw at the hospital – and it felt like I had seen pretty much all of them at one stage or another – Dr Ross seemed to understand me the most. It had fallen to her to break the news of our baby's condition to us, and even at the time I appreciated the sensitivity with which she had done this. When I had calmed down a little, she advised me that even expressing the milk was a bad idea since this would only stimulate the supply. I was stuck with it until it decided to go away. I could express a little if I was feeling particularly sore or tender, but only the minimum to make things bearable. And then she smiled. And I smiled too, although my smile was a sadder, more bitter one. This seemed to be what my life was reduced to now: the very best I could aim for was *bearable*. And I was way off that – way, way off. Every time I thought I was over the worst, something else cruel and unexpected (or at least unplanned-for, unthought-about) would come along. A month after the milk dried up, the blood returned. Only much heavier than it had ever been before. I got clots, I got stomach cramps, I got headaches – I got extremely pissed off. During this time I became, perhaps not unsurprisingly, obsessed with babies (and, I suspect, at the same time somewhat difficult to live with). Babies and pregnancy and miscarriages and abortions and everything to do with it all, these were the only things I could think of. At least, looking back I can see it was an obsession; at the time I didn't notice anything out of the ordinary. I thought it was just me dealing with stuff, working stuff through. I dreamed about babies and I had vivid nightmares about walking, bloody, aborted foetuses. I relived the operation over and over again, the injection becoming larger and more painful each time

I recalled it; and the final moments when my body simply refused to push, *refused* to participate in this charade which would end in my, our, baby being taken away and destroyed like radioactive waste, *knowing* that once the baby was expelled that would be it, she would be dead and it would be over — these final moments became ever more agonising. I joined a self-help group for women who had miscarried or had had selective abortions, but I don't know if this was a good idea or not. All I found out was that, compared to some of the other women, my experience had been a walk around the park. None of these other women had buried their babies. About half of them had not even *seen* their babies. One woman had had her head held back during delivery so she couldn't see, and once the cord had been cut, she said, the stillborn body had been passed out of the room like a rugby ball coming out of a scrum. Passed out of the room to God knows where. All of these stories did not make me feel better; I felt ashamed. I felt, somehow, as though I was making a fuss about nothing. I felt — if you can believe this — as though I ought to count myself lucky. Lucky the whole experience wasn't even worse. I didn't tell the group that I had dug out Mark's copy of *Never Mind The Bollocks, Here's The Sex Pistols* and was playing the song 'Bodies' over and over again until it felt like a rusty nail being driven into my head. I didn't tell them that I had, in a subconscious state, walked into our local video shop and rented one of those dreadful *Look Who's Talking* films and that when I got home I had no memory of having done this. I didn't tell them I was re-reading *The Weather in the Streets* and *The L-Shaped Room*, re-reading them compulsively, learning entire passages by heart. I didn't tell Mark any of this either. He didn't seem to notice.

Then one night, suddenly, it stopped. I woke up sharply at about three thirty and found myself being led, in a similar sleepwalking state to that which had taken me to the video shop, down to the kitchen, where I spent an hour and a half writing a poem to Beth. Well, I don't know if you'd call it a poem or not. It was part poem, part prose (it didn't rhyme, but neither did the lines go all the way to the end of the page. Is that poetry? It doesn't matter). But it was everything, absolutely everything, that I thought or felt about Beth. I've never written anything like it before or since. I'd never been much good at writing things down before. Even in letters to my friends I always made mistakes, found it hard to make myself properly understood. But this: this said *exactly* what I wanted to say, *exactly* how I wanted to say it. And staring at these pages of scrawlings I realised for the first time why I'd never been much good at writing things down before. Nothing I'd ever written or read prior to this poem – and nothing since either – had ever come close to representing my real thoughts and feelings. This wasn't my fault, I now realised, this was the fault of language. Language up to now had merely tried to describe what I wanted to say, it hadn't actually said it. But this did. This poem did. It was spot on. For the first and only time in my life language had lived up to its hollow and preposterous boasts. It had actually done its job for once. I felt like I had smashed through a glass sheet above my head and into a world of true meaning. I felt elated, free, bursting.

So with this poem it stopped, or rather the worst of it stopped. Of course things didn't return to normal after this. They would never return to anything that could be recognised as normal again. But they did, to use Dr Ross's word, become bearable. I began going to see my father again, began visiting that small, crossless plot in his garden. People who had been nervous about speaking to me, not knowing how I would react, began to be visibly more comfortable around me. Mark especially. Poor Mark: he looked so relieved when finally we were allowed to watch television again in the evenings, when we no longer had to spend all our time together staring at the walls, barely exchanging a word.

I wrote a letter sometime after Mark left to the priest who had been kind enough to conduct Beth's funeral, explaining my abandonment of his faith. I don't know what I expected him to do, but I wanted to get it down on paper, make it official. He replied promptly, telling me that it was perfectly normal to feel like this after such a deep personal tragedy and I wasn't to worry; my faith would be returned to me in the fullness of time, and when that happened it would be stronger than ever. He used some convoluted analogy to do with a tree shedding its leaves. Occasionally – every time I think about that box – I consider writing back to him to let him know how wrong he was.

14.25

Peter approached the bar with trepidation. He was going to try his regular pub trick and see if it worked as well here as it did at home.

The trick was simple: it was simple enough that Peter had mastered it entirely. You went into a pub and ordered a pint. While the barman (or lady) was pulling your pint, you tried to engage him (or her) in conversation. Any subject would do, but it had to be something that would get the barman (lady, *person*) talking. Him talking, not you. Politics, the weather, last night's football, how business was going, whatever. The important thing was that when he handed you over your pint, he had to be telling you something so interesting and important he couldn't possibly interrupt it to tell you how much you owed him. So while he finished his interesting and important story, you could sup away at your drink – anything between a third and two thirds of your pint depending on how chatty the bloke was, and barblokes tended to be chattier in this respect than barladies. And also depending on how surreptitiously you could drink: Peter himself could drink very surreptitiously indeed. Then when he told you how much it was, you put your hand in your pocket and – oh my God! – discovered you didn't have any money. And then you ran.

Obviously you couldn't do it in the same pub twice. But there were a lot of pubs in London.

He hovered by the bar and waited to be served. The barman was washing some glasses and ignored him. Eventually Peter coughed to get his attention.

'*Oui?*' said the barman.

'Beer,' said Peter firmly. He wasn't sure what the French for beer was, but he reckoned it was a pretty universal term.

The barman let fly with a stream of French.

When he had finished, Peter said, 'Beer,' again, a little more firmly this time. He was worried now, though. The fatal flaw in his plan had just occurred to him: if the barman didn't speak any English, how was he going to engage him in interesting and important conversation?

But the barman, a sad and bitter man called Jean-Louis, had found it impossible, however hard he tried, to work in the bar next to a hypermarket near Calais and not pick up any English. So he said, very reluctantly: 'You must sit down and I will come to your table.'

He pointed to the terrace behind Peter. Peter turned round to look. There were ten or so small round tables with umbrellas sticking out of them. About half were occupied, all by men on their own, smoking and reading newspapers, presumably waiting for their wives to finish the shopping inside.

'Please,' said the barman. 'Sit.'

It wasn't going exactly to plan, but Peter felt he couldn't back out now, and anyway he needed the drink, even just a sip. So he took a seat and bummed a cigarette off the man at the next table. The barman washed a few more glasses and then came over to him.

'Yes please?'

'Beer,' said Peter, really firmly now.

'Small or large?'

'Large.' Obviously.

The barman went away, washed a couple more glasses, then reappeared with the largest glass of beer Peter had ever seen. It was a huge, towering, shimmering thing. It was a pint of lager with another pint smuggled in on top. It was beautiful; it was the sort of thing you wanted to write a poem to. Whoever made that stupid comment about size not being important hadn't seen this glass of beer. Peter could feel his jaw scraping the ground.

When he tried to speak, his voice was high-pitched and faltering.

'Business been good lately then?' he said as his trembling hand reached out for the glass.

But the barman was already walking away, totally uninterested in anything Peter had to say. Peter drank as much he could in one gulp, then called after him: 'I said, business been good for you recently?'

Jean-Louis turned around, annoyed.

'Good win for France in the World Cup,' Peter tried. 'You know, football . . . ?'

'Yes. We knew we would win.'

Another crafty couple of sips. About a quarter of the drink had disappeared now. Peter felt it would be pushing his luck to drink any more. He couldn't understand, though, why he hadn't been asked to pay. Maybe he was supposed to offer, maybe that was the custom over here.

So he did. Starting already the fruitless fumblings in his pockets, he nodded at the glass and said: 'How much?'

'It's OK. You drink what you want and then pay at the end.'

Peter gave a little laugh. He had to be pissed, didn't he. He thought for a second there the guy had said he could drink as much as he wanted and then pay at the end.

'No, really,' he said. 'How much is it?'

'You are in France now,' Jean-Louis the barman explained patiently, as he had done to so many Englishmen in his bar before. English patrons, who formed the majority of the bar's clientele, were referred to by the staff, with no affection whatsoever, as *les fuck-offs*, and a twenty per cent Stupidity Tax was generally added to their bill. 'You can drink how many beers you want and then pay at the end.'

There. How complicated was that? It was a system, like driving on the right and preserving polite forms of address, that worked perfectly well throughout the whole of the rest of Europe. Why then did the English fail so comprehensively to understand it? What was wrong with them?

Peter felt a huge surge of excitement rush through his body. *He*

181

could drink as much as he wanted and then pay at the end! Why hadn't he had the foresight to be born French? What a civilised system of drinking: he was emigrating immediately.

'Oh well, in that case I'll have another one,' he said.

'Another *formidable*?' said the barman. 'Another large one?'

'*Mais oui.*'

14.43

Of all the many good games they had discovered at the beach, this was turning out to be one of the very best. They had decided to call it Flicking Sand At The Fat Sleeping Tourist. It wasn't a great name – it didn't trip off the tongue even in French – but it did sum up the game pretty accurately. The idea was simple: you took it in turns to flick sand at the snoring Englishman and the one who eventually woke him up lost. It had everything you could ask for in a game: fun, skill, unpredictability and just a hint of danger.

The man's two friends didn't seem to mind. One of them, the woman, the slightly scary-looking beady one in the colourful dress who'd been juggling like a clown earlier on, was also asleep; they could have broadened the scope of the game and made it more interesting by incorporating her – but that seemed just too dangerous. If the man woke up and gave chase they were fairly confident of outrunning him, but the woman might be more difficult. The other one, the one who was made up like a girl and had a girl's handbag but was wearing boys' clothes, was wide awake and watching. He/she obviously thought the game was a terrific idea, egging them on and even joining in occasionally.

So they flicked and they watched and they tried to stop themselves from giggling too loudly. If you woke the sleeping man by laughing, you still lost; that was in the rules.

After a while, though, it began to get boring. It seemed you could flick sand at this man all day without stirring him. They stopped worrying about suppressing their giggles and laughed as loudly as they wanted. Still nothing. Soon it stopped being funny enough to laugh at. But they were too competitive to stop – there had to be a winner. Or rather there had to be a loser. Someone had to wake this silly man up.

As they got bored they stopped taking it strictly in turns and began to flick willy-nilly. Eventually it was a combined spray from both of them, followed by a raucous, high-pitched peal of laughter which shook him. He made a snuffly, sneezing, coughing sound and wriggled so the sand fell off him. Then he suddenly lunged out like a snake, barking and chomping his jaws.

The children screamed and ran away, still screaming, still laughing, and when they were a safe distance they slowed down and began arguing about whose grain of sand had actually woken the man. Behind them they could hear the man shouting at them something which, had they been older or better versed in the English vernacular, they would have recognised as fuck off.

Candy howled with laughter.

Mikey, once he realised he was in no immediate physical danger, growled softly and tried to go back to sleep.

Joyce didn't stir, not even with all the commotion going on around her.

Mikey tossed and turned a couple of times and then gave up. Bloody kids. He had a head like a block of ice now and he could feel his legs beginning to shake. He needed a drink. He searched in his pockets in the forlorn hope that this would yield some untapped, weightless supply of alcohol he had conveniently forgotten about. It didn't. All it produced was his usual collection of worldly goods – this stock-taking was a regular activity for Mikey. There were some coins, in fact there were a lot of coins and quite a few yellowing notes as well, a set of keys, a crumpled pack of Marlboro Lights with a few dog-ends in it and a couple of scraps of paper. He stared at them wretchedly, these emblems of his life. The sun glinted off the metal of the keys and made the ice in his head burn.

He picked up the pieces of paper and tried to read them. He felt if only he could read what was on these pieces of paper, he could convince himself that he was sober enough to go and find a drink to get drunk enough to make his forehead stop throbbing. He tried to steady his eyes. The words zoomed in and out of focus. Then he realised it wasn't his eyes that were the problem, it was his hand, his bloody hand was shaking like a pneumatic drill. He transferred the paper from his left hand to his right; his right hand promptly started shaking. He passed it back. Still no luck. Both hands didn't shake at once, but whichever hand held the pieces of paper shook. Then it occurred to him: it wasn't his hands that were shaking, it was the *paper* itself. He scrunched the pieces up and threw them into the sand in despair. He thought he could feel tears coming.

'What are these?' Candy asked.

'Bullshit,' said Mikey sadly. 'Just bullshit.'

'Do you want me to read them out to you?'

Mikey shrugged. It didn't count if Candy read them out. That was conceding defeat to the shakes. On the other hand he didn't have a clue any more what was on these pieces of paper and he was curious. 'OK,' he said.

The first one had the name and the time of a television programme. 'Oh, I know this,' Candy said. 'It was one of those fly on the wall documentary things, wasn't it, about the West End underworld. You know, one of those nosey-parker programmes. One of the girls at the club was talking about it the other day. It was supposed to be really good. Lots of silver-haired gangster types talking in that sexy, rough trade accent of theirs . . .' Mikey had written it down so he wouldn't forget to watch it, and then he'd forgotten to watch it. He shook his head. Was there much point in carrying on? His children and their names and where they lived, he could cope with not remembering those. In a sense it was a conscious decision not to remember those; it was his way of shirking his responsibility. But was there really much point in carrying on once you'd reached the stage where you wrote down the name of a TV programme you wanted to watch so you wouldn't forget to watch it and then forgot that you had written it down?

The second scrap contained a name and an address written in a different, even more illegible scrawl. A Mrs Irene Stuart of somewhere, squiggle, St Omer, France.

'Is this yours?' Candy asked.

'Course it's mine,' Mikey said defensively.

'It's just . . . isn't Irene the name of Riley's woman?'

'Maybe.'

'You didn't take this off him then?'

'Uh . . . maybe.' Mikey wasn't trying to be awkward or evasive: he genuinely couldn't remember.

'I think you did. It's not your writing.'

Mikey thought hard. 'Oh yeah, I know . . .,' he said, and then there was a long pause. 'He wouldn't let me sing on the bus. He was singing his song about Irene and he wouldn't let me sing along.' His mouth was having trouble forming the words, which now he had remembered something were tripping over themselves in their hurry to get out. 'And he kept looking at this piece of paper while he was singing. So later, when he was being all cocky because he'd stolen that tobacco, I took it.' Mikey slowly took his head out of his hands and beamed triumphantly.

'Did you really see Riley go off with Jonquil and the others?' Candy asked.

'Uh no . . . no, I thought it would be kind of funny if we left him to get lost.' Mikey had thought this would be hilarious and looked over at Candy to start the guffawing, but nothing happened and he found himself feeling slightly ashamed. 'I'm sure we'll find him easily enough, though,' he added. 'He'll just be sleeping it off on a bench near where we left him.'

Candy could feel the clouds gathering around her. Riley wouldn't be sleeping on any bench. Assuming he could remember the address, or at least the name of the town, having lost the piece of paper, he'd be on his way to this place, St Omer, to see his girlfriend, wouldn't he. Now, add this to the gun thing, which had presumably happened by now, and shit was going to hit the fan like it had been fired out of a very large cannon. She felt a little sorry for Joyce and Jonquil

185

and Frank; they didn't deserve any of this. A ferry pulled out of the port and alongside the beach. The people on the deck waved at the sunbathers.

Candy looked over at Joyce, who was still fast asleep, blissfully unaware of how horribly wrong her day was about to go.

Mikey was looking at Joyce too. 'She won't mind if I go and find myself a little drink now, will she?' he said, beginning the long and laborious process of clambering to his feet.

Candy didn't reply. At this rate she was going to be the only one going home with the party.

'What do you reckon?' Mikey asked again.

'I don't know. Where are you going to go?'

'There's a bar near that block of flats there,' said Mikey, pointing to the ugly grey apartment building that ran along the sea front. 'Do you see where I mean?' He'd just about struggled to his knees now. 'Just behind where those kids are playing basketball.'

'OK . . . Don't do anything daft though.'

As though Candy was going to stop him.

Mikey nodded towards Joyce. 'Tell her I'm sorry if she wakes up. And say I'll be back really soon. I don't want her to get angry with me again . . . I don't think she liked it that I couldn't remember the names of all my kids.'

'Don't worry. Joyce just has this thing about children.'

'Yeah . . . why's that?' But by the time he'd asked the question Mikey had finally, heroically, staggered to his feet and he stomped off in the sand, leaving deep prints where his feet landed, without listening to the answer.

'I don't know,' Candy said, allowing her voice to drop as she realised she was talking to herself. She watched Mikey disappear up the sand and into the cluster of shabby white beach huts by the road, carrying on talking to herself: 'She just has this thing about children. I've noticed it. Maybe she had an abortion or something when she was younger.'

Joyce

'It's what they call a *selective* abortion,' I tried to explain. 'I give birth, but she'll be born dead and then we can have a funeral and bury her, just like a real baby.'

I kept saying that. She *was* a real baby.

Margaret's voice at the other end of the telephone was adamant. 'You can tie yourself up with semantics if you want. The bottom line is you're going to murder your baby.'

I couldn't see her face, but I knew exactly the expression she had. I'd seen it before, though rarely directed at me. The fierce, indignant, horrified self-righteousness. My dear little sister who always knew best.

'She's not going to live. I'm not killing her,' I said.

'You should still let nature run its course and leave it to the will of God.'

'She hasn't got a skull, Margaret. She hasn't got a brain. She's hardly even got a spine. *That's* the will of God . . .'

There was a short silence at the other end. Then Margaret said: 'Well, I can see my talking to you isn't achieving anything. But Joyce . . . just take some time to think before you make a decision like this. Please.'

'The decision's made,' I told her and I hung up. And I burst out crying.

Mark had been sitting on the stairs behind me and at this he leaped forward to give me a cuddle. I held him tightly and buried my head in his neck. I shouldn't have called her. I should have waited until it was all over and done with and then told her. In the past tense. But I had foolishly believed I could appeal to her sisterly feelings and get her to give me her blessing. With Mum gone I had no one else to really talk to about it and Margaret's blessing would have meant a lot to me.

I tried to explain this through the blubs to Mark. He nodded and patted and stroked. He was getting good at understanding what I was saying while I was crying.

It was a Saturday night. I know it was a Saturday night because *Blind Date* was on the telly in the front room with the sound turned down. I remember watching it while my sister lectured me on Jesus and morality and realising suddenly that what had happened to me called into question the validity of so much in my life. The whole game, in fact. This was life, as far as I could see it: you worked at a job in order to get money; you got money so you could make yourself look good; you made yourself look good in order to attract someone of the opposite sex; you attracted someone of the opposite sex so you could have sex with them; you had sex with them to get pregnant, to have a kid, to fulfil your most basic, primal human need. That's what all those people were doing on *Blind Date*, that was their final destination. And then this happened. And suddenly the whole game was up in smoke.

Everything had been a blur for the last twenty-four hours, mainly a blur of tears. Actually I suppose it had really all started a week before that. I had gone along for a routine scan. Purely routine; I had no reason to suspect anything. Of course, with the benefit of hindsight I can see there were all sorts of things wrong. I hadn't put any weight on for a start. I was over four months gone and I hadn't gained a single extra pound. I wasn't broody either, not remotely. I wasn't cooing at strangers' children on the bus or knitting clothes the way some of my friends had done. But I just thought I was being grown-up about it. I hadn't expected this sudden life change, hadn't planned for it, but now it was happening I was dealing with it in a calm, rational, mature manner. But part of me clearly knew something was up. Mother's intuition, call it what you will, but deep down, I *knew*.

So when I noticed Dr Ross's severe expression as she peered at the ultrasound screen, I started shaking.

'What's the matter?' I asked as calmly as I could.

Dr Ross carried on peering. She wore large round glasses and spoke in a thick Caribbean accent. 'I don't know,' she said. 'I'm not sure the foetus is developing quite as it should be. I'd like you to come back so we can do some more tests.'

'What do you mean, not developing properly? Is it serious?'

'It's too early to tell, I'm afraid. Come back next week and we should have a much clearer picture.'

With that she smiled. Dr Ross had a friendly, sincere smile, but surely she had enough experience to know a smile wasn't any bloody use to me. Despite my protestations, though, she wouldn't tell me any more, and I was ushered from her room to spend a whole week sick with worry. I hardly slept at all. (They say having a baby costs you sleep. No, *not* having a baby costs you real sleep.) I was moody and irritable and Mark and I barely exchanged a word. He fussed around me and demanded to be helpful. In the end I asked him if he would come with me to the next scan. More for his benefit than mine, to let him feel useful, although when we were there I was relieved to have his company. So when Friday finally rolled around he took the day off work and drove me up to the hospital. He held my hand while various tests were done on my trembling, exhausted body. I noticed Dr Ross peering at the scan in the same severe manner as before. The screen was turned away from me; I could only imagine the horrors displayed there.

'What does it show?' I asked nervously. I was scared that these tests would prove inconclusive too and I would be forced to endure another sleepless week.

Now I wish they had been inconclusive. It would have given me another week of innocence, another week of hope, of love, of normality. Instead she said: 'I'm afraid it's bad news, Joyce.' I was standing next to the reclining ultrasound chair, wiping the conducting jelly from my stomach with a tissue. I didn't sit down, but I clenched the arms of the couch behind me for support. 'The foetus isn't going to survive,' she said in a text-book monotone which not even her sunny accent could alleviate. 'The skull hasn't formed properly.' She said it so matter of factly it didn't really register. Then she handed me a photograph of the scan. In order to take it, I was forced to take my hands off their support, which caused me to fall backwards on to the couch, giving us both a shock.

'Are you all right?' she said.

I didn't answer. I'd just lost my baby. Of course I wasn't all right. I stared at the photograph: it was a blurry black and white mess of Rorschach blobs with a large, grey smudgy thing in the middle, which I guessed was supposed to be my baby. I wasn't even sure if I was holding it the right way up. I couldn't possibly see how this meant what she said it meant. It looked exactly the same as the photograph from the first scan six weeks previously, which we had excitedly taken home, shown to our friends and eventually stuck to the fridge door with a magnet. That photograph had meant everything was OK – how could this one mean something different?

Mark too was shown the photograph, and he too failed to comprehend it.

'I'm just going to ask a colleague to have a look at these,' said Dr Ross. 'In cases like these it's obviously very important to get a second opinion. Although I have to say, I'm afraid, there's no doubt in my mind.'

Mark and I held each other while she was away. We didn't speak. Words weren't remotely adequate for what we were feeling. A complete stranger was about to come into this room and pronounce a judgement of life or death on our unborn child.

Presently, Dr Ross returned with a large man with a dark, bushy beard, who introduced himself with a grim smile as Dr Joslyn. It took him no more than a couple of minutes to agree with Dr Ross's diagnosis. I didn't need to be scanned again; the photographs were sufficient for him to reach his conclusion. 'I'm sorry,' he said, shrugging his shoulders.

My brain took this on board and immediately began brain-like damage limitation exercises. There had to be a way out of this. If it only thought hard enough, there had to be a way to make this not be real. It thought and thought and thought, but it was no good. Eventually it had to give up and accept the truth: there was no escape. This couldn't be a joke, it couldn't be an error, it couldn't be a dream, it couldn't be anything else. If two professional medical doctors told you your baby was dead, your baby was dead. Dead. Dead baby.

And with this simple, shining realisation, my whole world caved in around me and I collapsed.

I was brought round by the three of them flapping over me and heaved back on to the chair. A glass of water appeared and was practically forced down my throat. There were more silences and shrugs and I'm sorrys. Mark decided to deal with it by being practical. 'So what do we do now?' he asked.

'You have two choices,' said Dr Ross. 'You either let the pregnancy take its course or you have a termination. If you opt for termination, which I think is the course we would recommend . . .' She looked over for support from Dr Joslyn, who nodded, '. . . then you need to decide fairly soon.'

'Fairly soon?' said Mark.

'Within the next few days.'

'And if we continue with the pregnancy?' *We*, he said.

'A still birth is the most likely outcome,' said Dr Joslyn, 'although there may be a miscarriage before then. It is possible that the baby will be born alive, but if this is the case it will almost certainly die within a few hours. No baby with this condition has ever lived more than a couple of days. And I should point out that it will be . . . quite deformed.'

Mark asked a few more, increasingly desperate questions about the nature of the operation, there were more long pauses. Dr Ross tried to play down the medical implications. She said all I needed was a simple injection to induce labour, which at this stage of pregnancy would be no more painful than severe menstrual cramps (which was a barefaced lie; it was agony). She said that in Jamaica they called pregnancies like this 'false bellies', as though it was something slight and mildly embarrassing – what we might call 'women's troubles', or 'down-below problems'. I didn't give a damn what they called it in Jamaica.

Then Dr Ross suggested gently that we go home and try to think about what we wanted to do. She probably had other patients to see, maybe even other people she had to break horrific news to. So, holding on to each other, we made our way slowly down to the car park. Inside the car, Mark started crying. He slumped forward over the steering wheel with his forehead on his arms and I realised that this was the first time that one of us had cried. We had known for something like forty-five minutes that our child wasn't going to live and this was the first time either of us had managed to cry. I tried to join him. It would be therapeutic to cry; surely my body had a physical need to cry now, to expel liquid. But nothing came. I strained my eyes and tried to squeeze the tears out of their ducts. I shook my head and slammed my fists repeatedly against the dashboard. Mark tried to put his arm around me and I pushed him away. I opened my mouth and howled. And still nothing came. Inside my head I was yelling myself hoarse, I yelled and yelled and yelled, but I could produce no more sound than a high-pitched croak, like a broken doorbell.

That evening Mark's mother drove up from Southend to see us and it was her, Esther, who really, in the most practical sense, pulled me through. She said that if the doctors advised termination, I should take their advice. But she also insisted that I lay down my own ground rules for the termination. If I was going to cope with this at all, I had to take control of some aspect of it. I couldn't just allow it to happen, allow myself to be told what to do, otherwise I'd end up hating myself and everyone around me. So we devised this scheme of giving the baby a name, having the funeral and then the burial in my dad's garden.

'They'll never agree to that, will they?' I said.

'They will if they possibly can,' said Esther. 'I think you'll find people are going to want to say yes to you over the next few weeks. I should make the most of it.'

We talked and talked, planned and plotted, me spread out on the sofa, Esther on the floor with her back resting against me, her head on my tummy. Mark joined in as best he could, sitting stiffly upright in one of the armchairs, but by about one o'clock, absolutely shattered, he went up to bed. Esther and I carried on talking and drinking white wine through the night. It was Esther who made me promise not to be ashamed about any of this. I could be upset and angry and devastated and even guilty (and I was), but I should never, ever feel ashamed. No one would want to talk to me about this, she warned. Miscarriage was a combination of society's two strongest, dirtiest taboos – gynaecology and death – and therefore not a popular topic of conversation, but that was society's problem, not mine. Even when everyone else was sweeping the episode under the carpet, desperately looking on the bright side, I should never let myself be shamed into pretending it had never happened. I listened until I was drunker from her talking than from the wine. Eventually we both fell asleep where we were on the sofa. We became friends, firm friends. I still see her occasionally, even now Mark's long gone.

The following afternoon the three of us went for a long walk from Highgate cemetery up to Hampstead Heath and Parliament Hill. It was a blustery, kite-flying day. We walked and talked (as far as we could) about other things. We stopped in the grounds of Kenwood House and ate a picnic, which was harder work in the wind than it was worth. Later we sat on a bench at the crown of Parliament Hill, gazing at the smoggy panorama, and Esther produced from her bag a copy of Sylvia Plath's *Collected Works*. 'Oh no,' Mark groaned, 'not the poetry.' He made it sound like the comfy chair in the Monty Python sketch. 'Not the poetry! Anything but the poetry!' Obviously this is what happens when you suffer a tragedy like this; the people around you suddenly develop a need to inflict poetry on you. They don't know what to say to you any more so they read you poems. They let other people do the talking for them.

The poem she chose was called, appropriately enough, 'Parliament Hill Fields'. I don't remember much about it now. Esther read it well and I found the soft, formal tone of her voice more comforting than the words themselves. The only phrase from it that has stuck with me is *your absence is inconspicuous*, and I only remember that because it seemed so wrong, so false. I didn't feel that the absence in my case *was* inconspicuous, I felt like the whole world could see what I lacked, I felt like I had my tragedy tattooed across my face.

We walked down into Hampstead village. It was already starting to get dark. At Esther's suggestion, I had resolved that if I hadn't changed my mind by six o'clock, that would be it, decision made. Six o'clock came and went as we sat in a café eating chocolate eclairs. We got the tube home and started phoning our friends and family to tell them the news.

And first thing Monday morning I went to see Dr Ross and told her I had decided to have the abortion.

She looked up from the forms she was filling in and gave me one of her Dr Ross smiles. 'It's what we call a *selective* abortion,' she said.

14.55

Exactly half an hour after they had entered the hypermarket, Frank and Jonquil stood impatiently by the trolleys near the entrance. Dougal was also there, still fingering his dog-eared shopping list glumly. Frank had re-locked the trolley and got his ten-franc coin out – in fact it had sprung out at him as he reattached his trolley to the others. He had pocketed the coin carefully. As they had come out of the shop, a grubby-looking young boy had appeared from nowhere, lifted out their two bags of wine and tried to make off with the trolley. Frank wasn't prepared to let him have ten francs – a quid – for simply lifting two bags on to the ground, not in the mood he was in. So he clung firmly on to the trolley and gave the boy some centimes he had in his pocket.

'Come on Peter, where are you?' said Jonquil, half to herself, half to the others.

'I'll go and look for him,' said Frank.

'No, give him a few more minutes. It'll take ages to look through the whole place.'

They waited in silence. Almost silence: Jonquil began to tap at her watch in a particularly irritating way. When it became clear that no one else was going to think of this, Dougal said: 'I saw a bar outside. He could be in there.'

'A bar?' said Frank. The word struck fear into his heart. Peter. Bar.

'Let's go have a look,' said Jonquil.

He was there all right, sitting at the sunniest table, his heavy jacket draped over the chair next to him, his legs stretched out, eyes closed, gently talking to himself. There was no evidence on the table, however, that any drinking had been going on. Frank immediately felt ashamed of himself for jumping to suspicious conclusions. He was going to have to watch himself if he was going to make a success of this job. You couldn't go around being judgemental like that. It was important to think the best of people until proved wrong, even when the weight of experience and common sense pointed you firmly in the opposite direction. OK, Peter was a drinker, he was annoying, he smelled funny. That didn't make him dishonest. He still deserved the benefit of your trust. Anyway this probably wasn't a *bar* bar; more like a terrace where people, men, could wait in the sun for their loved ones.

'All right Peter,' he said cheerily. 'You forgot you were supposed to be meeting us, didn't you.'

Peter opened his eyes and looked up groggily.

'Have you been drinking?' Jonquil asked.

'Jonquil, give the guy a break. There aren't any glasses on the table, are there.'

Jonquil looked. It was true, the table was entirely glass-free. Proved nothing.

'Is it time to go?' Peter asked innocently. 'Sorry, I haven't got a watch. Don't really need one most of the time, you know, don't have that many important appointments. So what's the point of having one, know what I mean?' Muttering softly, he dragged himself to his feet.

Jonquil thought about asking him again if he'd been drinking.

She looked around and saw most of the men at the other tables looking back at her strangely; she decided not to ask.

They got maybe a hundred yards off the terrace before they were stopped by a loud, barking voice: '*Excusez-moi Monsieur!* Excuse me please!' A short, snarling Frenchman in a barman's uniform marched straight up to Peter. 'You must pay your beers now please.'

'What beer?' said Peter, who wasn't quite as out of it as he looked.

'Your beer. Five *formidables*.'

'Peter, is this true?' said Jonquil.

'No. I haven't drunk no beer. I've just been sat here, minding me own business. Don't know who this bloke is, don't know what he's talking about. You don't want to believe him anyway, do you, he's a bloody frog.'

'*Mais si!*' said the barman and he gave a little stamp of his foot. 'You have five *formidables*.' He held up all the fingers of one hand.

Frank sighed wearily and took out his wallet. 'How much do we owe you?'

'One hundred fifty francs.'

'Don't pay him!' Peter protested. 'He's a lying . . . ! You taking a frog's word over mine, is that what you're doing? I'm telling you, he's just trying to rip you off. He's—'

'Shut up Peter!' Frank was trying to do a mental conversion as he counted out the notes. Ten, twenty, thirty . . . a hundred and fifty francs, that was . . . sixty, seventy . . . hang on, that was fifteen quid. *Fifteen quid.* 'For God's sake Peter, we were only gone half an hour.' How could anyone drink fifteen pounds worth of beer in half an hour?

Peter kept wisely quiet. Frank thrust the bundle of notes into the barman's hand. 'Come on, let's go meet the others,' he said and stomped off. When they reached the bus stop Frank suddenly turned round and waved his finger in front of Peter's face like a lunatic wielding a knife. 'I'm having that money back off you, you know. Fifteen quid. It's coming out of your giro week by week till you've paid me back.'

Frank was becoming angry. He could feel his face turning red and his brow furrowing and his ears prickling. Calm, he told himself, calm, don't give the bastard the satisfaction ... But he found he couldn't help himself; he turned round and yelled at Peter some more anyway.

14.25

Riley was confused. He stood, looking confused, outside the bank where he could have sworn he left the others. Maybe somehow he had got the wrong bank. Maybe all banks looked the same over here and they were waiting for him, looking at their watches and tutting, just around the corner outside a completely different but identical-looking bank.

What, with the same people working in it and everything? He recognised the severe woman sat doing arse all at the empty desk. No, this was the place all right. There was the little shop just over the road, the one with the pretty girl, where he had bought – or rather acquired – his tobacco. Where the hell had they gone then? He looked both ways up and down the street, peering into the distance, willing them to emerge from the long mid-afternoon shadows. I know, he thought, they're pissing around. This is some kind of stupid hide and seek game.

'OK you bastards,' he shouted suddenly, his voice rough from a full morning's whiskying. 'I know where you are. Come out, you ... bastards!' He tried to think of another word to describe them, but his vocabulary failed him.

He drew a few startled looks from passers-by, who then hurriedly looked away again, but that was all.

After a little more time spent peering into the distance he had an idea. Perhaps something had come up, they'd all had to leave suddenly, but they'd left a message for him with the girl at the tobacconists. His friend. Pleased with himself at having worked this out, he turned and crossed the road.

The girl looked up as he entered the shop.

'No,' she said immediately. 'No more tobacco.'

Riley held his hands up. 'No more tobacco,' he agreed. He approached the counter slowly, still with his hands up.

'My friends—'

'Your friend very angry with you,' she said.

He looked puzzled.

'Your friend, the young girl, she is very angry with you. She think you steal the tobacco.'

Well she can fuck off. 'Where are my friends?' Riley asked.

The girl shrugged gallicly. 'I don't know . . . you lose them?'

'Yes . . . they didn't leave a message here?'

She shrugged again. 'No.'

The final no came just as Riley reached the counter. He turned around slowly and began shuffling his way out again.

'They will find you,' the girl called after him. 'Have a cigarette and wait.'

As he stepped out of the dingy tobacconists, the sunlight hit Riley full in the face like a boxer's punch. When his eyes had adjusted and he could open them as far as a squint, he spotted a bench. He went over and sat down and tried to think. Where were they then? He tried to retrace his steps. They'd all been standing around here, arguing, talking rubbish, waiting. He'd gone off for a slash – telling everyone exactly where he was going. He hadn't, despite the clear temptation, gone up against a wall; he'd walked all the way back up to the proper toilets and done the thing properly. He'd been gone no more than ten minutes; OK maybe a quarter of an hour; twenty minutes tops. Then he'd come back here to find the others had all fucked off somewhere. Charming.

He began peering up and down the street again, still half-expecting them all to jump out from behind a lamp post and shout ha! It didn't make any sense.

The sun beat down on him. It seemed to be shining in a straight, concentrated line directly above him, burning through a compass into his head. He stretched out on the bench; stretched out and made himself comfortable. He decided after a short time that he wasn't really worried by the others' disappearance. Here he was in a foreign country with no money and no way home and he wasn't remotely worried. In fact, now he thought about it . . . now he thought about it, wasn't this all part of some kind of plan of his? To lose the others, shake them off and make his getaway . . . Yes, now that he thought about it even more, he remembered he had some kind of plan, some reason why he absolutely *had* to get shot of the others . . . In fact they hadn't left him, *he'd* deliberately lost *them* . . .

He yawned. The sun and the drink and the fact that this was really an exceptionally comfortable bench were all making him drowsy. He really ought to try and remember what this plan of his was, though, before he fell asleep . . .

Riley

'Up to anything tonight, Riley?' asked Lieutenant Foster as we came back in from some routine exercises on Compton Down. It was a Friday night coming up; we were all heading back to Aldershot.

'Don't know, sir . . . just down the pub with the lads, I guess.'

'Not seeing your girlfriend tonight then?'

'No, sir.' This didn't look too good.

He paused to let the others get out of earshot and it was clear he expected me to pause with him.

'I wondered if you'd come out for a drink with me this evening,' he said when the coast was clear. 'There's something I'd like to discuss with you.'

I'd been in the army long enough to tell the difference between an invitation and an order: this wasn't an invitation.

'Yeah, sure. Cheers,' I said, my mind racing.

'Fine. Eight o'clock then. I'll see if I can sort a car out.'

A car? The alarm bells started ringing louder. If we were just going out for a pint, normally we'd go to one of the handful of pubs

199

in Aldershot that welcomed Paras, and (most importantly) had girls in them who also welcomed Paras, the Fives or the Rat Pit or one of them. You could walk there, or at the very least five of you could pile into a cab. That way no one had to stay sober, because on the kind of Friday nights out we had, you didn't really want to be sober, not if you could help it. So when Foster turned up in a flash-looking BMW blagged off one of the senior officers it was clear it wasn't going to be a typical Friday night down the boozer. He drove us to a small village a few miles south of Farnham; a large, grand country pub he'd obviously been to before. I wished I'd found a reason — any bloody reason — not to go. This was trouble. It was clear what he wanted to talk about: he'd told me, *ordered* me not to see Irene any more and instead I'd started sleeping with her. Andy, his friend, my superior officer, hadn't been in the ground six months and already I was fucking his wife. This had to breach some kind of army protocol.

As soon as we were in the pub, the pints were in and we were settled at a large, solid-oak table, close enough to the open fire to feel the glow on our faces, he came right out with it: 'You know what I want to talk to you about, don't you?'

I didn't answer him straight away. It wasn't that I was about to deny anything, I just wasn't quite sure how to play this. I think I was still holding out some kind of pathetic hope that he would throw his hands up in the air and say, well I tried to warn you off her but you clearly don't need my advice so good luck to you, mate.

Huh.

'Come on, man!' he said. 'You're still seeing Andy's wife. Admit it.'

'Yes, sir.' I didn't see why I had to *admit* this. I wasn't ashamed about it. It wasn't illegal.

'After what we discussed . . .'

I must have let a little smile slip at this point. Something about the way he said *discussed*. I certainly didn't remember any fucking discussion. Whatever, I must have let my feelings show somehow because the next thing he said to me, suddenly sounding like my old geography teacher, was: 'Oh so you think this is funny, do you?'

'No, sir.' I said this with about the same amount of respect as I used to show my geography teacher. You can make *sir* sound like the worst insult in the world if you know what you're doing.

'I told you, Riley, if you need help we can get you help . . .'

I drew a deep breath and took the first sip of my beer. This wasn't going to be easy. Fuck it, *you* try and explain falling unconditionally in love to a lieutenant in the Parachute Regiment. I interrupted him. 'I don't need help, sir.' *Sir.*

'I beg your pardon?'

'I don't need help. I'm not doing this because I'm fucked up or anything. I'm doing it because . . . me and Irene just have a thing. I don't know how to explain it.'

'Of course you're fucked up,' Foster said in his brisk, business-like voice. 'And so is she. How could you not be? Only a year ago you and Andy were in a war together. From Mrs Stuart's point of view, she's seen her husband go off to war, worried about him, prayed for him, finally got him home in one piece again only to lose him six months later in a stupid training jump. It's bound to affect her in some way; obviously this is how she's choosing to deal with it . . .'

'We're in love, sir.' I interrupted him again. I felt like a berk saying the words; they sounded so corny. But how else do you put it? There are no synonyms for love, that's the whole point.

Foster stopped mid-sentence and took an angry gulp of beer. 'I'll pretend I didn't hear that,' he said when he had swallowed.

'It's true. We're in love.'

'Oh for God's sake, man. Don't be ridiculous! How old are you?'

'Twenty-two.'

'And how old is she?'

'Uh, thirty-one, I think.'

'Well, there you go then,' he said as though this proved his point beyond all argument. 'You're both young, you've both been through a traumatic time recently. I'm not a psychologist but I should think it's only natural, under these circumstances, that the two of you should develop a . . . an affection for each other. But that doesn't make it wise and it certainly doesn't make it right. There are other considerations here.'

I looked at him. Foster probably wasn't any older than Irene. Who was he to come on like he had a whole world of experience on his shoulders?

'Not least of these considerations,' he continued, 'is the fact that she's Andy Stuart's wife. Your officer, your friend . . .' He leaned towards me. 'The man who saved your life, don't forget.'

'I've thought about that, sir.'

'Well don't you think he'd mind?'

'He's not around to mind.'

'His friends are around to mind on his behalf.'

I fixed him in the eye. 'None of his friends are closer to him than Irene was.'

'But she's not thinking straight!' He looked fed up now rather than angry. 'Riley . . . Tom . . . don't you see this can't ever work? She's using you to try and replace the irreplaceable and once she's over the worst of the grief, once she's realised that you're not Andy, she's going to lose interest in you. It's hard to accept, I know, but it's the truth, believe me. Meanwhile all you're doing is affecting your ability to be a good soldier.'

'How's that?'

'By dwelling on the past. You were involved in a tragic accident, in which your superior officer died . . . died *saving your life.*' He emphasised the point again. 'You need to move on from this, put it all behind you. All this woman does is remind you every time you see her of the circumstances that brought you together.'

I let this sink in. This was the first sensible point he'd made.

'OK, I'll have a word with her,' I said. 'I'm seeing her next week. For Easter. I'll have a word with her.'

'No,' said Foster, shaking his head. 'No having words. It's got to stop.'

'OK, I'll tell her it's over.' I hadn't decided this yet, but it didn't look like we were going to leave the pub until I'd promised.

'No. You mustn't go and see her. It's got to stop immediately.'

'But . . . I can't just not see her. We've got to talk about it.'

He kept on shaking his head. 'I can't allow it.'

I couldn't believe this. It wasn't his thing to allow or to not allow. 'Why?' I said eventually. 'Why?'

You don't say *why* to a lieutenant.

'Because . . . because I won't allow it!' he shouted.

We glared at each other over the forgotten beer.

Then he leaned in towards me again. His voice dropped to a whisper so I had to lean towards him to catch what he was saying. Our noses almost touched in the middle of the table.

'I know about that night on Longdon,' he said. 'Andy told me.' He let me register this and then went on. 'I don't want to say anything to anyone, it hardly shows the regiment in the best light, but I will if I have to, if it's the only way of making you realise how serious this thing with Mrs Stuart is. Do you understand me? There are plenty of people who would like nothing better than a nice juicy story about unarmed soldiers being shot in cold blood. If this was to come out . . . well, let's just say your future in the Paras wouldn't look as rosy as it does now.'

I slumped back in my chair. I felt beaten and wounded. So Andy hadn't kept it to himself after all. At the end of the day he couldn't keep it bottled up. You couldn't really blame him — it's a hell of a thing to carry around with you. But it had to be Foster he told, didn't it. Couldn't he have seen a counsellor or something, or told Irene, or just written it down somewhere. It had to be bloody *Foster*. What did he hope to gain by telling this bastard?

Foster also sat back. 'Promise me you're not going to go next weekend,' he said.

I stared straight ahead, blankly, not at him, through him. I promised.

And that was that: business done. He stood up abruptly and headed for the door. If I wanted a lift back to barracks I was going to have to go with him. Neither of us had even half-finished our pints. It wasn't the greatest Friday-night session I'd ever been on.

And maybe that would really have been it. Maybe if it had ended there I wouldn't have gone to see her that Easter, never seen her again. I didn't like being blackmailed, but I think the point about dwelling on the past made some sense. Maybe Irene was more fucked up than I had allowed myself to notice. Maybe it was true: we were just using each other to compensate for the lack of Andy. Why else, if I was being honest with myself, why else would Irene be with me anyway? I didn't exactly have a lot else to offer her.

So, yeah, that could well have been the end of it, and perhaps that wouldn't have been such a bad thing. It would have been a whole lot cleaner certainly to have stopped it there. But then Foster blew it. In the car on the way back, with his victory wrapped up and secure, he went and blew it.

He had to go and start gloating. 'Of course,' he said, 'there are any number of other reasons why this thing with Mrs Stuart would never have worked . . .'

I didn't encourage him. I just looked out of the window.

'I mean, background for example. Andy and Irene both have a very . . . *different* background to yours.'

As Foster had said himself, he wasn't a psychologist. If he was, if he'd had any fucking insight at all into human character, he'd never have started down this road. It wasn't that I disputed the fact; far from it. I'd known since day one that top brass of the army was largely a club for people of *different* backgrounds to my own and I was only likely to go so far up the greasy pole. On Falkland it had been starkly clear: all the voices barking the orders were posh, most of those screaming in pain weren't. Also, most of the strategic positions around Longdon were named after rugby positions: Fly Half, Wing Forward, Full Back and so on. When we set off that night, they called it the *free kick*. That should give you a pretty good idea of who was in charge.

But Foster should never have brought the subject up. It was stupid of him. Whatever else he said, he should never have suggested that somehow I wasn't *good* enough for Irene.

15.43

Both groups were late for the rendezvous, having both had to drag one of their number out of a bar. Mikey had managed to find a bar called *Le Welsh* nestling among the tobacconists and beach-ball shops along the sea front. He couldn't believe his luck when he saw the name – they'd have to serve a Welshman in a bar called *Le Welsh*, wouldn't they. However, he was unable to convince the barman, who unfortunately wasn't remotely Welsh, of his creditworthiness. Not when he uttered the few disparate phrases of the Welsh language that he knew, not when he stressed the innate superiority of the Welsh rugby team over the French, not even when he launched into a spirited version of 'Land Of My Fathers'. He was just ignored. When Joyce and Candy finally found him he was still pleading with his outstretched arms, hopping desperately from foot to foot, as though prolonged alcohol deprivation might spontaneously combust him at any moment. When Joyce tried to suggest gently that it was time to go and meet the others he simply looked at her and growled and made it quite clear that he wasn't going anywhere until somebody had bought him a drink. To be fair, it didn't look like he'd be capable of going anywhere until somebody had bought him a drink. So Joyce stood him a beer, a regular-sized beer with a large, frothy head, which he despatched cleanly in one. And then he started apologising. And he went on apologising all the way back into town.

He was *still* apologising as they turned the last corner to find Jonquil and the others waiting outside the bank. The two groups greeted each other uneasily, each of them aware, consciously or subconsciously, that something was wrong. Something was missing.

It was Jonquil who noticed it first.

'Hang on, where's Riley?' she said.

They all looked around.

'Well, where did you leave him?' Joyce asked.

'What do you mean? We agreed he was going to the beach with you.'

'Yes, but Mikey saw him coming out of the toilet and joining your group. We thought he had insisted on going with you . . . Didn't we Mikey?'

Everyone turned to look at Mikey.

'I'm sorry. No really, I am. I'm terribly sorry.' Mikey's apology for demanding a beer at *Le Welsh* blended seamlessly into his apology for fucking up everyone's day completely by losing Riley. 'I thought that was him, honestly I did. I mean someone who *looked* a lot like him came up to your group, didn't they . . . or reasonably close anyway . . .'

They stood and listened to Mikey's rambling excuses; all except Candy and Peter who were standing apart from the others, deep in discussion about something or other.

Then Frank said, without apparent purpose, simply because he had to say it, he said, very loudly: 'FOR FUCK´S SAKE!' And everyone turned round to look at him.

Jonquil took his arm, and took command of the situation. 'It's OK,' she said soothingly. 'He can't have got that far. Not in the sozzled state he was in. He'll be crashed out somewhere not far from here.'

They all looked, cheered on by Jonquil's calm, sensible words, expecting Riley to suddenly materialise. He didn't.

'Right,' said Frank, the redness slowly beginning to disappear from his face. 'I'll go and look in those loos back by the funfair. That was the last place we saw him, maybe he never made it any further than that.'

'Good idea,' said Jonquil. 'I'll go and check down some of these side streets, see if he's hiding down there. Joyce, you stay here and make sure we don't lose any more.'

Joyce nodded. Mikey carried on apologising until Joyce threatened to hit him.

Five minutes later Jonquil and Frank returned, neither with anything to show. Now it was serious. Arguments developed. Frank was all for going straight to the police and reporting Riley as a missing person. Jonquil was sticking with her line that they were all responsible adults and Riley could bloody well find his own way home.

Then Candy broke away from her high-level talks with Peter and said: 'I know where he is.'

'What?' said Jonquil. 'What do you mean?'

Candy opened her bag and produced Riley's scrap of paper, which she had swiped in turn from Mikey when he was too busy needing a drink to notice. She handed it to Jonquil. 'He's visiting his girlfriend.'

Jonquil read the scrawled name and address. 'Oh God,' she said. 'Is this the Irene he's always singing about?'

Candy nodded. 'Yeah.'

'And where on earth is . . .' She struggled to read. 'St Omer?'

'I don't know. I don't think it's too far from here.'

'How do you know this is where he's gone?'

'I don't,' said Candy. 'But he's gone somewhere, hasn't he. And he *was* singing about this woman the whole way over.'

'Do you know how we could get there? Is there a bus or something?' asked Frank.

Jonquil turned to him. 'Don't be silly. We can't go chasing off after him. If Tom's chosen to go off and see this . . . old flame of his, whatever . . . then that's his choice.'

Frank sighed. He wished there were some way he could avoid saying what he knew he was going to say next. 'I'm not sure . . . I'm really not happy with this. We have a responsibility . . .'

'Yeah, only to do our best. That's where our responsibility ends. Only to do our best, you know? Not to go chasing around France after someone who's deliberately given us the slip. Anyway, we don't even know where this St Omer place is. What if it's miles away? What if there isn't a bus?'

'You could hire a car,' suggested Candy helpfully. 'At that square

207

where we first stopped, the one with the fair in it, there were a few car-hire places there. I noticed them.' She'd been looking out for them.

'Oh Candy, don't be ridiculous. Hiring cars is expensive. Where would we get the money from?'

'Credit card,' said Candy and Frank together.

Jonquil looked at them, bewildered that this conversation had proceeded beyond the first exchange. She felt trapped. Surrounded. She looked from Candy to Frank and back again. Then she settled on Frank. 'We still don't have enough money. Even if we use a credit card we'll have to pay for it later on. We can't afford it . . . Frank?'

Frank shrugged. 'We'll have to find the money. I'm sorry . . . Perhaps we could get some of it back from Philip, from the Residents' Fund or something . . .'

Yeah, *right*. Philip just loved paying out money from the Residents' Fund. And he'd been *so* supportive of this trip the whole way along.

'I just feel this is our responsibility and we can't walk away from it,' Frank concluded.

'Look, I told you,' said Jonquil, who was starting to get angry now about being told by someone with less experience than her what the responsibilities of her job were, 'we've done all we can. If one of our party has chosen to disappear, we all have to learn from that.' Then she added firmly: 'We have responsibilities towards the rest of the group as well, you know.'

'*And*,' said Frank, who was raising a hand and in severe danger of wagging a finger in Jonquil's direction, 'we have a responsibility towards this poor woman Riley has gone off to see.'

Jonquil thought quite seriously about throttling him. If she caught even the slightest wag of that finger she was going to do it.

Frank pressed on regardless. 'We brought him over here, gave him the means to go off and try and find her. Suppose she doesn't want to see him . . . We've no idea what their relationship is, or was . . . Tom could be stalking her for all we know.'

Jonquil fought for an answer to this. She still hadn't ruled out the possibility of strangling Frank.

'I don't mind taking the others back on my own,' said Joyce, who assumed quite rightly that if she didn't offer her opinion of her own accord she was unlikely to be asked for it. 'If you give me the keys to the minibus I'll pick it up at Dover . . . then I could come back and pick you up later . . . or you could get the train back to London . . . whatever . . .'

There was a protracted silence. Then Frank handed her the keys. It seemed to signify a decision being reached.

Jonquil watched this happening as though it was happening somewhere far, far away, on a TV screen or in a book or something like that, something unreal, something that didn't actively concern her. 'OK,' she said blankly.

'Peter should go with you two, though,' Candy said suddenly. 'The rest of us will go back with Joyce, but Peter should go with you two.'

'Why?' said Frank. The only advantage that he'd seen so far to this insane turn of events was that he was getting shot of most of the drunks for the rest of the day. He'd about had it with drunks, and Peter Freeman especially. Freeman had aroused dark and violent thoughts in Frank that were best left well alone. It was almost worth blowing a hundred quid on a hire car just to get shot of the drunks for the rest of the day. There was no way Freeman was coming *with* them.

Joyce was pleased, though. Three of them to look after on her own would be a whole lot easier than four. Dougal and Candy were sweethearts anyway and Mikey looked like he was just going to dribble and apologise for the rest of the day. She could deal with that.

'Because . . .,' said Candy, thinking hard. 'Because Peter's been to St Omer before. Haven't you Peter?'

'Uh . . . yeah. Yeah, that's right. Been there,' said Peter.

'When?'

'Uh . . . quite a few years ago. I can't quite remember where it is, like, but I'll know it when I get there. I reckon I'll be able to find this house, you know, where his girlfriend lives . . . Irene, whatever. Me and Riley have spoken about it before.'

Frank eyed him up, trying to work out what was going on.

'Anyway, I reckon I owe you,' said Peter. 'You know, for the beers and that.'

Frank didn't respond to this. He was thinking, yeah, you do owe me, but the way you pay us back is by *not* coming; but he didn't air the thought. No one aired their thoughts for a while. They all stood still, on the spot, staring at their feet. No one was going anywhere until a final, final decision had been reached. They weren't past the point of no return yet: all it took was for one them to say, no, this is bloody stupid, let's just go and get back on the ferry and let Riley do whatever the hell he wants.

Instead, Jonquil said, finally: 'OK. Peter can come with us. You three go back with Joyce. OK with everyone?'

Everyone nodded; although it was not OK with them all.

'You still owe us the fifteen quid for the beer, though,' Frank told Peter, to clarify the situation.

Mikey

I am sorry, though . . . no, I am . . . really, really sorry . . . I'm really sorry . . . AND SORRY SEEMS TO BE THE HARDEST WO-ORD . . .

Sorry.

Riley

But what if. What if Foster *hadn't* suggested in the car that I wasn't good enough for Irene. What if I'd been the honourable soldier and obeyed orders and not seen her again. What if I'd stayed in barracks that Easter weekend. What then. Would it have made any difference?

All these questions were shooting through my head as I made my way up to the khazi on the train. I was on my way back to Aldershot after the break. The smoking carriage was packed full: mainly squaddies heading back to base, but one or two civilians too. I'd been drinking steadily all journey, cans of warm Stella from the buffet car chased down with some scotch from my own hip flask. Once I judged it was safe to go for a piss without losing my seat, I made my move.

As I stood up, two other blokes a couple of rows further along stood up as well. I'd clocked these two earlier giving me strange looks and I wondered if we knew each other from somewhere, some army thing or other. Down south maybe. As I made my way up to the end of the carriage, squeezing past the people who were trying to make themselves comfortable in the aisle, I had the sense I was being followed. I didn't want to turn around to make it obvious I'd noticed. It was probably completely innocent: they were probably just going for a piss too. But something about them made me uneasy.

The bog was still vacant when I reached it so I went inside and locked the door quickly behind me. I had a routine beer-drinker's fast, intense slash. Then, when I was finished, I lingered for a couple of moments before flushing the chain. If they were still waiting for me outside now, I'd know they were up to something.

In fact I never even made it outside. As soon as I opened the door I was forced back into the tiny room by the first, larger bloke. The other one came in behind him and turned the lock again.

Three of us stuffed into that tiny space didn't leave them much room to swing their kicks and punches, but they found a way. Where there's a will. It was a banal beating, only memorable for the fact that we were all squashed up together like slow dancers. Three slow dancers all together, making a crowd. After they'd drawn blood in a couple of places, I was crumpled up on the floor trying to get my breath back, one of them crouched down beside me and, just in case I was in any doubt at all who I had to thank for this little work-out, whispered beerily in my ear: 'You're a fucking soldier,

211

you cunt. When an officer gives you an order, you obey it.' And then he grabbed me by the collar, shoved my head down the khazi and pulled the chain. The pool wasn't big enough to try and drown me so, disappointed, he yanked me back out, stopped to consider his next move, and then cracked my head on the rim of the bowl twice rapidly in succession.

I yelped with pain and thought for a moment that I would black out. This was moving beyond teaching me a lesson now; it looked serious. I was going to get bones broken here. When I could see again through the blood in my eyes, I noticed the other one, the one standing up, had pulled out a knife.

The weekend had been a disaster from the word go. Irene had been in a strange mood. She had seemed distracted, as though there was something on her mind that stopped her from giving me her full attention. We'd had no concrete plans, we spent most of the weekend fussing around her house, moving from room to room, not being allowed to settle anywhere. Now and then I'd suggest doing something, because this was starting to do my head in to be honest. I'd suggest going for a walk, or to the pictures, or down the pub, and Irene would say yes, and look relieved that we'd finally decided on something, and then immediately say no and come up with some reason why she couldn't possibly. And I'd have to rack my brains and try and think of something else. Then when I told her about my little chat with Lieutenant Foster she became really agitated.

'So what are you going to do?' she asked.

'I don't know,' I said. Because I really didn't.

'Are you going to leave me? Is that what you've come to tell me?'

We were sitting on her patio, on her elegant garden furniture, sipping at long drinks. Good Friday evening. It had been a beautiful day; the sun was hazily putting its head down. Irene's voice was becoming more and more distressed with each sentence.

'Are you going to leave me?' she said again.

'No, I never said that.'

'What then? Are you going to leave the army?'

'No . . . I don't know. Well . . . no. I thought I might put in for a transfer.'

'Away from the Paras?'

'Yeah.'

'Tom . . . you told me once this was all you had ever wanted to do since you were a little boy. You told me that when you joined up, as far as you were concerned you were joining the Paras rather than the army.'

'Yeah . . .'

'So . . . ?'

I was trying to be grown up about this. 'You know . . . things change. I didn't know then that there was going to be a war. I didn't know I was going to be involved in an accident, I didn't know someone was going to save my life. I didn't know I was going to . . . you know, fall in love.' I said this last bit quietly; I still wasn't comfortable with saying it.

'Why don't you leave the army altogether?'

'Yeah? And do what?'

Irene took a long sip of her long drink. 'I'm thinking of moving to France,' she said.

I looked over at her. I didn't really see how this helped.

'I want to move away from here,' she went on. 'I thought it might work, moving back to where I grew up, but the whole place has changed. I don't know anyone here any more. I feel like my whole life has come full circle and stopped. And I'm too young for that. I need a fresh start, a new life. I've always dreamed of living in France . . . I've got enough money to do it . . .'

I still couldn't think of anything to say to this, so she carried on talking.

'And it's not as if I've anything to keep me here. No family. No friends to speak of in the village . . . there's only you.'

'What would I do in France?' I said.

'Whatever you like ... Nothing if you want. I've got money enough for both of us.'

Should have been perfect, shouldn't it? A life of luxury in a village in France with a beautiful woman. But the way she put it, it sounded terrifying.

I shook my head. 'Couldn't do that. I'd do my nut.'

'OK then, we could get you a job.'

'I don't even speak French.'

'You could learn.'

Yeah, right.

'There are hundreds of things you could do. Everything you could do over here, you could do over there. France is just like England really ...'

Only it's France. 'The Paras are the only job I've ever had,' I said.

'You're still young.'

'Yeah, but ...' I was struggling to explain. I couldn't even explain it to myself at this point so I guess I had no chance of making her understand. It's only now, with the benefit of alcoholic hindsight and the excessive wisdom of middle age, that I know what the problem was: I was shit scared of having my own life. Of not being told what to do every minute of the day. Of having to make my own decisions. That was it. I was *scared*.

'Have a think about it,' said Irene. 'We'll talk about it later.'

And we did talk about it later. We talked about it the following day as Irene drove me at white-knuckle speeds in her Rover up and down some country lanes. (We *had* to get out of that house on the Saturday. Otherwise we'd have ended up killing each other.) We talked about it that evening on the way to a boring, stuffy dinner party given by people who used to be closer friends of hers than they were now. We talked about it Sunday on the way back from church (yeah, I know, church. Irene wasn't a believer either, not really, but she said she'd taken some comfort from it since Andy had died; and it was Easter). We talked and talked and fucking talked about it.

Irene was trying to get me to give up the army and become her pet, kept toy-boy. My idea was that if she wanted to move, she should move somewhere else in England, somewhere she'd never been before. That would still be making a fresh start, wouldn't it. Meanwhile I would get another posting with the army, maybe get a promotion soon, and we could carry on as we were. We talked backwards and forwards around these two points of view. Neither of us moved; neither persuaded the other to move. I don't think Irene could bear the thought of having another soldier for a husband. And I couldn't get my head around not being a soldier. I couldn't make that leap of imagination. This was the thing: I'd done P Company. As an eighteen-year-old I'd spent sixteen weeks away from home, family and friends doing the most punishing physical training there is on God's earth, being shouted at by some of the hardest men I'd ever met. I'd conquered the trainasium – an evil thing: a giant mass of scaffolding, see-saws, ropes and leap-nets which they used to put raw recruits through their paces, see what kind of nerve and head for heights we had. It scared the shit out of me. I fell off it more times than I can remember and each time I fell, getting back up was a little bit harder. But there was no let-up. If you froze on it, you got piss-takes from below; if you fell off, you were sent straight back up again. No let-up. It was one of the hardest of the hard bastards who used to take us on the trainasium, a guy called McKenzie. He had a catch phrase he used to bellow at anyone who was looking a little shaky on it; we heard it from him maybe half a dozen times a day and you could tell he enjoyed using it. We used to repeat it to each other later on when we were out drinking – drinking with relief that we weren't on the fucking trainasuim any more. It became a running gag. Don't worry about falling, McKenzie would yell at you while you were clinging on by your fingernails to a rope suspended twenty feet above the ground, or even while you were lying sprawled on the grass, having already fallen, trying to work out how many of your bones you'd broken. Don't worry about falling, he'd yell, the ground will always stop you! There was a rumour a kid had died once from falling off the trainasium, but that's all it was, a rumour.

So, yeah, I'd fucking *earned* that beret. That's why I was so scared to leave it behind. While for Irene the Paras had meant the Federation of Army Wives: committee meetings, stalls on Airborne Forces Day, living on giant estates with other left women, the forced jollity of the Sunday lunches that the regiment put on while we were all down south. I'd never seen this side of the coin, being single the whole time. It made me think. But thinking only made things more complicated.

We were still talking about it as she drove me to the station on Monday afternoon.

'So . . . have we reached any decisions?'

'I don't know,' I said. 'Have we?'

She didn't take her eye off the road. She was driving too fast again. 'I guess we haven't.'

We drove on in silence until she parked the car outside the station. 'So what are we going to do?' she said, switching off the engine.

'I don't know . . . keep on thinking about it, I suppose.' I leaned over to kiss her and as I kissed her it struck me we hadn't slept together all weekend (or rather that's all we had done: slept). This was only about our fourth kiss. We'd spent all that time talking instead. I wondered if this was a sign. I wondered with an increasing sense of panic as I kissed her whether this was the end of everything; you know, our last ever kiss.

'I love you,' I said as I pulled away from her. I hadn't meant to sound that desperate.

'Yes,' she said, 'I know.'

We had another hug and Irene had a little cry. Then I got my grip bag out of the boot and waved goodbye to her from the station entrance.

'Safe trip!' she called to me.

Safe trip. When the two blokes were done with me I was left curled up in a mess on the floor, wedged between the sink and the door. I had a cut to my face and one to my arm and bruises all over my body from the kicking. I heaved myself over to the toilet, pulled the seat down and rested my head on that. The blood seeped out of the cut under my eye and stained the lid. Shortly afterwards the train pulled up at a station and I suppose the two blokes must have got off there. I don't know how long it was before I was found. It felt like about ten minutes but I probably blacked out at some point so it may have been longer than that.

When they did find me, I still had enough of the Para in me to pretend everything was OK. You should have heard me. This smartly dressed young bloke was helping me to my feet and I was bleeding all over his crisp white shirt, refusing to let him pull the emergency cord or even go and find the guard and tell him what had happened. 'No, no, it's fine,' I was going, 'just a scratch.' Just a fucking scratch. I had this beautiful notion that I would have a little wash and brush-up, a couple of hours' rest and by the time I got back to barracks no one would be any the wiser. So the bloke hauled me back down the carriage to my seat. I could hear people gasping as I passed them, but I didn't take any notice. They were just civilians, what the fuck did they know. They'd never seen a *real* injury before. When we reached my long-empty seat (there were still people standing; no one had taken my seat; the British are so fucking British sometimes) I noticed that on their way out my two friends had taken the trouble to remove the small, melting Easter egg that Irene had given me from my bag and smear the chocolate across the seat like a turd. What the other three passengers sitting around my table must have thought of this, I can't imagine. I can't imagine either what they must have thought of the sight of me as I staggered, bleeding, towards them. The young bloke slowly withdrew his arm and lowered me into my seat. He lowered me gently most of the way, but I simply dropped the last little bit and as my backside hit the soft, chocolatey material I heard a series of cracks, like toppling dominoes, across my stomach. My eyes bulged. I felt a searing pain across my body, the worst physical pain I have ever known in my life. I started howling.

And I carried on howling until the medics arrived and gave me a shot. I think I was still howling when they slotted me into the ambulance like a cake going into the oven; I didn't stop until the drugs kicked in and I found myself back in hospital, dreaming again of Irene.

15.38

'*Monsieur . . . ?*'

No reply.

'*Monsieur . . . ?*'

Still no reply. Lots of snoring, a little bit of spluttering and the occasional fart; but nothing that could be mistaken for a reply.

A little louder this time. '*Monsieur . . . ?*'

'*MONSIEUR!*'

Riley was dragged awake by gentle slaps across his cheek and somebody shouting something foreign at him. As soon as he realised what was happening to him, he lashed out and shouted what he imagined to be, 'What the fuck do you want?' but what came out sounding like the low, unidentifiable rumble of a single being played at thirty-three.

The Frenchman jumped back in fright.

Riley glared at him. 'Speak English,' he growled. It was a statement rather than a question. A command.

'Ah . . . yes. Yes,' said the Frenchman. 'You were sleeping.'

'I was sleeping, yes. Then some bastard went and woke me up.'

Satisfied that this puny-looking man in little round students' glasses posed no serious threat, Riley put his head down and tried to get back to sleep again. The man carried on talking. Riley waved him away. He felt a stirring in his bladder and thought about relieving himself on the bench. That usually got rid of unwanted attention.

'Now leave me alone,' he said. 'I want to go back to my dream.' He'd been dreaming just now, he was pretty sure of it, and nice dreams too, not the awful one he usually had about falling out of an aeroplane. No, these had been nice dreams, dreams you would want to return to . . . He sat bolt upright suddenly. Yes. He *had* been dreaming. Dreaming of Irene.

Irene.

Oh shit . . .

He began searching his pockets for Irene's address, cursing himself loudly for having drunk so much. He'd promised himself, he'd fucking *promised* himself that he wasn't going to drink today. He had things to do today; people to see. OK, he had *a* thing to do, *a* person to see. He couldn't afford to get drunk. Not today. He couldn't afford to fall asleep on a bench.

He couldn't afford to lose this piece of paper.

Not *this* piece of paper.

The one with Irene's address on.

Not today.

Please.

Disgusted with himself, Riley stood up, went over to the Frenchman, who was still jabbering on about why it had been his civic duty to wake Riley up, and grabbed him by the shoulders.

The Frenchman stared at him, terrified.

Riley stared back, not quite sure what to do next.

And then it came to him. From the deepest, darkest recesses of his abandoned brain, from somewhere far out in the ether, maybe even from that God who was usually so content to cloak his existence so thoroughly, it came to him. 'Mrs Irene Stuart,' he blurted out. 'Mrs Irene Stuart. 8 rue des Moulins. St Omer.'

The Frenchman looked bewildered. '*Pardon, Monsieur?*'

Riley said the address again, just because he could. Then he said more clearly: 'St Omer.'

The Frenchman still looked bewildered.

'St Omer,' said Riley again. 'St O-fucking-mer.'

'ST OMER!' he shouted.

'St Omer,' he said more quietly.

'St Omer,' he said for what was obviously going to be the last time, gripping the man's shoulders tightly.

219

Suddenly it clicked. '*Ah! St Omer,*' the Frenchman said with obvious relief. '*Oui, bien sûr.*'

'Yeah, that's what I said. St O-fucking-mer.'

'You want to go there?'

The man was a genius. 'Yes,' Riley explained patiently. 'I. Want. To. Go. There.'

The Frenchman started a long and complicated explanation of which train to get and where the station was. Riley did his very best to concentrate and understand; then a thought struck him.

'No, forget it,' he said, holding a hand up for silence. 'I can't take the train, can I. I've got no money . . . No. Mon. Ey,' he said again, more slowly. 'I'll have to use my thumb.' He showed the man his thumb.

The Frenchman tried not to laugh. 'No, you cannot go by autostop.'

'Why not?'

'Because . . . Because it is too dangerous.'

Now Riley laughed. 'Too dangerous!'

'Here. I will give you the money. It is only forty or fifty francs, I think.' The Frenchman handed over a crumpled fifty-franc note. 'And I will show you where is the station.'

'St Omer?' said Riley, just to check.

'St Omer.'

Then Riley said the full address again. Mrs Irene Stuart. 8 rue des Moulins. St Omer. He couldn't remember if he had ever felt so pleased with himself.

Riley

Dear Tom

This is a very difficult letter to write. A braver woman would come and tell you these things in person, or at the very least telephone, but I'm scared. I'm scared that if I try to talk to you, you'll talk me out of it.

I have decided to put my house here on the market. A friend of mine has been looking at properties in France for me and believes she may already have found a suitable one. It sounds gorgeous. It's in a small town in the north of France called St Omer, which is not too far from the ports so I'll be able to pop back across to England easily whenever I want. The house is a converted water mill. Apparently there's a stream which runs alongside the road and each house is connected to the road by a bridge. Almost Venetian. Doesn't that sound picturesque? And there's a ruined church within view of the house, and a shady park at the back where I'll be able to read in the afternoons. Obviously I shall have to go and look at the place myself, but assuming it's even half as nice as my friend says it is, as soon as I've managed to sell here, I'll be off.

I realise now that it was very unfair of me to try and put pressure on you to come with me. The army is your life and your career and you must do whatever you feel is right. I am sure your Lieutenant Fisher or Foster or whatever his name is has his reasons for telling you the things he did. In all the years I was married to Andy I never understood the army and I don't suppose I shall now. What is clear to me, though, is that it will not be possible for you to have a life in the army and a relationship with me. You will have to choose one or the other. If I remove myself from the scene completely, this forces you to make that choice.

Oh dear, I sound like I'm putting pressure on you again, don't I? I really don't mean to. It is your decision and your decision alone. I will write again when I know for certain where I will be living. If you are not able to come and stay with me, I will truly understand. However, I hope you will at least write from time to time and that we will stay friends. You have been a great comfort to me during the darkest and saddest time of my life and I would hate it if we lost touch.

I love you and I will always love you. Sometimes this is enough. Sometimes I fear it isn't.

This will probably come as a shock to you and I am sorry for this, but I look forward to hearing what you have to say when you have had time to think things over.

Yours ever
Irene

16.12

They hired the cheapest car on the books from the first car-hire shop they came across, back in the square with the funfair. A Japanese make none of them had heard of before. It was a tiny car with a small, squashed-up boot. It looked like someone had hacked it in half with a giant meat cleaver. It looked, in fact, as though someone, an eight-year-old child probably, had built it that morning from a kit. Still, though, Frank thought to himself: Japanese, it'll have a good stereo at least.

It didn't have a stereo. It barely had a dashboard.

A salesman who looked like Manuel out of *Fawlty Towers* and whose English was almost as good showed them around the car's features. It didn't take long. His English, as well as being limited, also had a curious time-warp flavour to it, as though it had been learned entirely from Frank Zappa records.

'Of course she don't look like much, man, but once you get to know her, she move like a baby . . .'

He sat in the driver's seat and went through the gear changes and the headlights and the windscreen wipers, introducing each one with enthusiastic zeal, as though they were the very latest breakthroughs in motor-vehicle technology. When he got out they asked him a few questions (of the 'Yeah, but does it actually go?' variety). Jonquil asked all the questions; Manuel directed all his answers to Frank.

Then he produced a piece of paper with two identical pictures of a car on it. 'OK,' he said, pointing to the top car, 'on this car we gonna mark all the scratches on the car when you take her away.' Then, pointing to the second one: 'And on this one we gonna mark all the scratches on her when you bring her back.'

He walked slowly around the vehicle, inviting them to point out any marks they could find. There weren't any. It still looked like it had been built that morning from a kit.

'Oh yeah, man, I can't believe you didn't spot this one,' said Manuel, leading them towards an infinitesimal nick on the passenger's door. 'This is a really bad one.' He didn't, unfortunately, have the language to get across just how much this scratch appalled him, so he tried to convey it with facial expressions. The war crimes of Pol Pot, he seemed to be suggesting, didn't disgust him as much as this scratch. He showed Frank, then he showed Peter, then he even showed Jonquil.

Frank got the message. 'OK, we'll try not to damage the car.'

Manuel marked the scratch in lurid red pen on the top car, then filled in the mileage, wrote PLEIN next to the petrol-gauge symbol and handed it over for Frank to sign. Frank did so nervously; it felt like he was signing his entire life away. He was even more alarmed when he was asked to surrender his passport as surety.

Then finally it looked as though they were ready to go. Just as they were climbing into the car, though, it occurred to Jonquil that they had no idea where they were going.

'Do you have a map?' she asked.

'Yeah, we have cool map.' Manuel disappeared into his office and reappeared with a sizeable road atlas. 'Only eighty francs.'

'Nothing smaller?' asked Frank.

'No.'

'I don't suppose you could throw it in with the car as a gesture . . . ? We'll bring it back in perfect condition. No scratches.'

Manuel's face took on an anguished expression which effortlessly crossed all language barriers. He ought to have been working for the UN. He'd *love* to throw the map in, his expression said; in an ideal world he'd have happily killed his own *mother* in order to give these lovely, lovely people a free map; but there were, *frustratingly*, outside forces way beyond his puny control which prevented him – and this hurt *him* more than anyone else – which prevented him from doing this.

Frank handed over a hundred-franc note.

And then, at long last, they were off. Jonquil suggested planning a route before they left the forecourt, but Frank was eager to get away from the greasy, moustachioed salesman. He figured he could drive around for a bit and while he was getting used to the car, Jonquil could work out where they were supposed to be going. And then it struck him: here they were again, him attempting to drive, her attempting to map-read. Tears and fights and tantrums could only be moments away.

'Comfy in the back?' Jonquil asked Peter to try and put off for as long as possible the moment where she had to pick up the atlas.

'Yeah, suppose,' said Peter, who wasn't comfortable at all; he was crumpled up in the back seat of a car which had been designed by bitter, revenge-bent dwarves. But he was far too busy being scared to worry about whether or not he was comfortable.

For the moment had come for Peter. The moment he'd been putting off all day, the moment he'd tried — and partially succeeded — to forget all about by drinking. He hadn't managed to drink enough, though. How much would have been required to forget about this completely? He'd have needed to drink until he was dead, wouldn't he. And he wasn't dead: he wished he was dead, but he wasn't dead. So with Candy's help he'd remembered what it was he had to do. And he was just sober enough to be aware that once he'd done it, his life would never be the same again.

Now was the time.

'What's that smell?' said Jonquil, turning the map upside down to see if it made any more sense that way.

'Sorry,' said Peter.

They drove back up the street with all the restaurants on it, the first street in Calais they had walked down what already seemed like a very long time ago. At the end of the street was a road sign. 'Here we go,' said Frank, nodding at the sign. 'Up ahead, look. St Omer. Forty-four kilometres. You can probably put the map away.' Well, that was a waste of eighty francs, wasn't it.

Frank indicated towards the turn-off.

OK. Now, Peter. *Now*.

'Look, sorry right, but we're not going to St Omer.'

'What do you mean, Peter?' said Jonquil. 'Of course we're going to St Omer. That's where Riley's gone. Don't be silly.'

'No we're not,' said Peter.

'Yes we are,' said Frank firmly.

'No we're not,' repeated Peter.

'No we're not,' agreed Jonquil, who had just had a look over her shoulder.

Frank looked sharply at her. She was white and paralysed and had a vaguely apologetic smile slapped across her face, as though the very fact of her knowing before Frank implicated her in some way. It was a guilty, sorry, knowing smile. Somehow in the few seconds since he had last looked at her Jonquil had gained some terrible new knowledge, some new insight into the way of the world. It could only have come from where she had just been looking just now, over her shoulder. So, readying himself to see whatever she had seen (and how bad could it really be? It must have come from Peter, mustn't it, this new information, and how bad could it really be if it came from Peter? Jonquil must be overreacting), Frank looked in the rear-view mirror; and nearly skidded off the road.

He had a gun.

Peter had a fucking *gun*.

'Sorry,' Peter said. 'We're going to Orléans instead.'

Frank could feel his head clouding. When he could speak, he said: 'Hold on a second, I'm going to pull over and we can talk about this.'

There was still no sound or movement from Jonquil. Frank drove on for a couple more minutes until he came to a lay-by at the side of the road. He brought the car to a stop and turned round in his seat to face Peter.

'OK, what's all this about?' The thing was to be calm and authoritative. Peter had had a skinful today. Christ knew where he had got this weapon from, but he could be made to see reason; he was drunk, that was all, on some kind of mad, alcohol-fuelled fantasy, but he could be made to see reason.

'We're going to Orléans.'

Only he didn't sound drunk any more. He sounded terrifyingly sober. He was even making a reasonable stab at pronouncing *Orléans*.

'OK ... Peter, please put the gun down. We're just talking.'

This only served to make Peter tighten his grip on the weapon. Frank tried to reintroduce a note of calm into his emasculated voice. 'We're just talking,' he said again.

Slowly Peter took this on board and lowered the gun. Didn't loosen his grip any, but lowered it.

Frank breathed a sigh of relief. 'OK ... Now, why do you want to go to Orléans?'

'Got to deliver this gun to someone ... A man in Orléans.'

'Where did you get it from?'

'Candy gave it me.'

'Candy?' Where in God's name had *Candy* got a gun from?

'Yeah ... He was supposed to do the delivery, but he made me do it.'

Frank struggled valiantly to make any sense out of this. Candy couldn't hurt a fly, not even a fly that had really pissed him off; how had he managed to *make* Peter do this? And ... and and and, where in the name *of fuck* had Candy got a gun from?

'Is it loaded?' Frank asked. First things first.

'Oh yeah,' said Peter. 'It's loaded.'

As if he was going try and threaten them with an empty gun. What would be the point of that?

Frank thought some more. 'Orléans is a very long way from here,' was all he could think of to say. Actually he didn't have a clue where Orléans was, but a few minutes ago St Omer had seemed like a totally insane trip to be making at this point in the day and St Omer was only forty-four kilometres away. Orléans, he was fairly willing to bet, was further away than that.

Peter immediately raised the gun again. 'We're fucking going!' he said.

Suddenly Jonquil found her voice. Or rather she found *a* voice:

it didn't sound like hers at all. 'You'll never dare use that,' she said.

Frank slapped a hand over her mouth. You simply didn't say 'You'll never dare use that' to a man with a gun, not unless you were in a film and the script made it explicitly clear that he wouldn't use it. That kind of gamble just didn't pay off in real life.

'Yes I fucking will,' Peter said.

'Yes he fucking will,' Frank agreed.

And then they sat there for a bit, the three of them, in an oddly shaped car parked in a lay-by just outside Calais, Peter clenching a gun at arm's length, Frank and Jonquil frozen to their seats with a mixture of anger and terror.

Finally Peter said: 'How far is it, then, to Orléans?'

Slowly and deliberately Jonquil picked the atlas up off the floor and started to flick through it. 'Fifty-nine pages,' she said.

'How far's that?' asked Peter.

Jonquil turned round to show him. She showed him Calais, where they were, in the top left-hand corner of Page 2, open armed and welcoming, the first place you hit when you came to France, so homely and close to England, the last piece of France to actually belong to England. And then she riffled quickly through fifty-nine pages to show him Orléans, where, fantastically, it seemed they were now going, which nestled fortress-like in the heart of Page 61, surrounded by grey roads and unfamiliar terrain and unpronounceable place-names. There were only a hundred and eighty pages in the whole book: they were talking about a third of the entire country.

'That's not far,' Peter said hopefully.

'It's bloody miles,' said Frank, who still didn't have a clear picture of how far it was. 'We'll never get there today.'

'Yeah, we will. We have to. Today's the day the delivery's got to be made.'

Frank had a brainwave. Maybe Jonquil was right; maybe he wouldn't dare use the gun.

'You won't shoot me,' he said as confidently as he could.

'You can't drive. If you shoot me, who's going to drive you to Orléans?'

'Good point,' said Peter, swinging the gun across so it pointed directly at Jonquil. How stupid did Frank think he was? Hadn't he seen any films at all? 'I'll shoot her instead then.'

Frank hit the steering wheel in frustration at his own stupidity. Jonquil was now shaking visibly.

'You'll just have to drive fast,' Peter suggested.

'OK, we'll go,' said Frank. What the hell, it wasn't the first completely mad decision they'd made today. 'But put the gun down, all right? You have to put the gun down. If I'm going to be driving fast I don't want it going off accidentally.'

Peter thought about this, thought it sounded reasonable and slowly lowered the gun again. But he kept a tight grip on it. Jonquil flicked the map back to Page 2 and plotted a course in the vague general direction of Orléans. She hadn't stopped shaking any. Frank peered over her shoulder. According to the small map of the whole country at the front of the atlas, Orléans was due south of Paris. So it would be easy to get to then. They just had to follow signs for Paris, then go through Paris – straight down the Champs-Elysees probably – and then go even further the other side. Piece of cake.

Inside Frank, anger began to take over from terror. He slammed the car into gear and shot off down the road. He straightened his leg, hammering his foot to the floor, and pushed the poor little Airfix car until it shook, whipping past any cars that got in the way without letting up on the gas for a moment.

He was driving like a lunatic. In the back, Peter whooped like a kid on a funfair ride. Maybe this wasn't going to be so bad after all. Maybe . . . maybe it was even going to be *fun*. Next to Frank, Jonquil was too numbed to notice Peter's whooping; or too numbed to say anything anyway.

And Frank: Frank's head was a long way away. This was the only way he could deal with this situation, by having his head a long, long way away. He was trying to work out how he had got himself into this; how Peter had managed to smuggle a gun into

France; how Candy had managed to make him do it. How Candy — *Candy!* — had managed to get hold of a gun in the first place.

Candy

First night. Standing in the wings at BabyCakes with butterflies the size of eagles in my stomach. The crowd's a bit restless tonight is the word backstage; the compère is dying on her cute queer arse every time she goes out there. But the good turns are still being appreciated. Simone standing next to me clutching my hand looking at me from time to time and winking. Waiting to go on. Waiting . . . The previous act finishing finally. The compere, an embittered old queen called Dolly, taking the stage reluctantly and announcing in her sarcastic Home Counties accent that tonight ladies and gentlemen we have a special *treat* for you a *new* singer to BabyCakes a fine interpreter of the French *chanson* please give a *warm* BabyCakes welcome to . . . Miss Candy Skinn! Marching out on to the stage like I was born to do it hand in hand with Simone. Blinking in the lights. Unable to see the audience for those lights shining in my face; the polite ripple of applause the only indication that there's anyone there at all. Taking an age to get ready; Simone dropping her music; the loud scraping of the piano stool across the wooden floor; Steven the rancid old queen giving us a thumbs up from the wings. Impatient coughing from around the room. Then finally . . . finally . . . ready. The first chord. The brief introduction to the first song. My first note pitch perfect. The song taking over, existing outside me and around me. The warm glow of appreciation coming back from the audience. And then the magical moment at the end where the song dies down the last note fades slowly out and there's a tiny split-second pause for this all to sink in before the clapping and hollering rise up at me like a seventh wave.

Enjoy it, I remember Sally telling me as she cooked me up my first shot, it's never the same after the first time. And I remember Richard saying a similar thing to me after he had just to all intents and purposes taken my virginity. All the good things in life it seems are never the same after the first time. Maybe this is true of life itself. Maybe all this reincarnation hoo-hah is true but the snag is we're doomed to lead ever more unfulfilling lives, locked into an eternal downward spiral forever trying to recapture the innocent joyousness of our first existences, our first experiences. Who knows? Whatever – I was fully expecting that first night at BabyCakes to be the best night of my life. The best night or the worst night depending on how it went. And it had gone even better than my wildest dreams. So I knew deep down that this was it. This was likely to be the night I looked back on from my old age as the pinnacle of everything that happened to me. It was downhill all the way from here. Nothing would ever be this great again. I was so obsessed by this thought that I was hardly able to enjoy my success at all. It felt like I was at the top of the mountain and I was giddy from looking down – it was a hell of a way to fall.

But now I don't know. Now I'm not so sure I don't prefer things the way they are. It's mundane now; it's a job. It's something I sometimes have to drag myself in for. Something I can do without thinking. Something I look forward to finishing and going home from. OK it's not as exciting. Like the drugs and to a lesser extent the sex you don't get the rush any more. But there's a permanence now which is in its own way just as much of a thrill. You wouldn't enjoy that first shag half as much if you knew it was the only one you were going to get. Would you. So the singing's a job now with all the routine and responsibility which that entails but it's a damn sight better job than walking the streets at night offering your arse to strangers. I'm finally starting to sort myself out. I'm clean. Completely clean apart from the occasional celebratory g and t . . . oh and the fags. But I only smoke because I happen to think I look glamorous with a cigarette hanging out of my mouth; I don't need the nicotine any more. I've got a regular pay packet and I'm near the top of the list for a council flat. I'm even starting to save seriously for my operation. Things *are* getting better; they're getting better all the time.

I had this blinding flash of revelation just a few moments ago as I was checking my make-up after yet another routinely brilliant performance. This isn't the top of the mountain at all, it's base camp. There's a lot of climbing left to do. I start to unbutton my yellow satin top; I've decided on a blue dress for the second set. Evening wear. Something really classy. I'm going to knock them dead. Johnny the stage manager knocks on my dressing room door. (OK it's not *my* dressing room; I share it with the other artistes; it's not the London Palladium yet.) Two fellers waiting to see you Miss, he says. I shake my head looking back at him in the mirror. Can't do it, I tell him, I'm shattered. I need to prepare for the next set. Tell them I'm very sorry.

And then once he's out the door – wham – it hits me. Candy what have you just said? You don't *want* fawning admirers at your door? You don't have *time* for people like this any more? Your *fans?* Not that long ago you didn't have *fans*, remember? Not that long ago the people you encountered were divided into two clear groups – people who didn't beat you up for dressing like a girl and people who did. And I stop my unbuttoning and I think back on the road I've come down the last six months. The first night here with the ugly punter – the audition – practising with Simone – my opening night. And I think to myself: *now* you've made it girl. Now you'd rather sit on your own deciding which dress to wear next than meet your public. *Now* you're a star. And it feels good I have to say; it feels really, really good.

Johnny comes back into the room this time without knocking. I'm sorry Miss these fellers really do want to have a word with you, he says. His voice sounds frightened. Who are they . . . ? I start to say. But just then they burst through the door anyway. Two young guys burly mean-looking. Skinheads. Trouble. One of them grabs Johnny flicks a knife out and holds it to his throat. The other one grabs my arm. You're coming with us! I'm still sitting at my dressing table. I've got another set to do yet, I point out. The man squeezes tighter on my arm and yanks me out of my chair. I SAID YOU´RE COMING WITH US! And you, the other guy tells Johnny, are going to show us the best way to get out of this place. We don't want to have to go back through the main room. Too many people. It's e-easy, Johnny stammers, it's just out of the dressing room turn left down the corridor and leave by the fire exit at the end. Show us! Lead the way!

Once outside they throw Johnny to the ground and give him a kick in the ribs for fun and then bundle me into a car which pulls up from nowhere. Where are we going? I ask when I can find my voice. Rebuttoning myself. Our employer wants to see you, one of them says, about a gun. Your employer? Yeah . . . George Johnson. Know the name faggot?

George Johnson. I'd guessed of course but that doesn't stop me being paralysed by fear. I remember my old RE teacher Miss Devlin once giving us a lesson about pride coming before a fall. I remember not having a clue at the time what she was talking about.

17.10

On the boat back to England, with everything more or less sorted, Candy decided to have a drink. She was proud of the way she had handled the situation. Less than twenty-four hours ago she had been beaten and broken and ready to kill herself before George Johnson's men did it for her. But instead of buckling under she had sat down calmly, worked out what needed to be done and got on with it. This was good: this was yet another sign, perhaps the most telling yet, of the new, confident, sorting-stuff-out Candy emerging from the drug-addled, fucked-up ashes of the old. She had solved the problem of Johnson and his stupid gun and, most importantly of all, she had solved it without laying her own neck on the line. This would earn her some respect. In future Johnson would be more likely to pick on someone else to run his errands. It was just another little way in which Candy's life was straightening itself out. For the first time ever some kind of normal life seemed almost within her grasp. Perhaps that operation, on which she had previously been pinning all her hopes, would not now be necessary. Perhaps she could be just as happy as a gay man with an extravagant taste in clothes as she would be as a biologically altered woman . . . Certainly as her savings grew and she explored the possibilities of a sex change with her shrink and the whole thing became more real, it also became more terrifying. Either way, she felt she could now look upon it as a positive, life-affirming choice rather than as a final act of desperation.

Of course she was feeling ever so slightly guilty about ruining the day so utterly for Frank and Jonquil. They were nice people; they didn't deserve the shit she'd just laid at their door. But what else could she have done? She had been coerced, she had no choice. If they ever had the chance to sit down, the three of them, and talk it over, Frank and Jonquil would see that. She wondered if Peter had pulled the gun yet. She wondered what the reaction had been. She had dreadful visions of Jonquil fainting with fright, Frank's heart giving out from shock. You couldn't really rely on Peter to do things in a tactful manner – assuming there was such a thing as a *tactful* way to pull a gun on somebody.

Of course it was equally possible that Peter had simply forgotten about the gun again. She'd been expecting him to make his move when there was just the four of them at the supermarket, but no, he'd forgotten he had a loaded weapon in his pocket at that point and gone down the pub instead; he'd needed reminding. So it was entirely possible that he was sitting in the back of the car, happily watching the countryside floating by, wondering what he was doing there, knowing he had some sort of mission to accomplish but unable quite to remember what it was. Candy felt a lot less sorry for fucking up Peter's day. In fact she'd be mildly disappointed if it was only a day that was fucked up for him, a mere twenty-four-hour period as opposed to the rest of his life. She felt that the mission she had sent him on had an air of permanence about it and she would be hard pushed to feel remorse if she never saw him again at the end of it. Not that she wished him dead, Mother of Mary no, just surgically removed from her life, that would do fine. She was going to make it perfectly clear to George Johnson when she got back that she had placed the matter in Peter's hands and so it was on Peter's head what happened to the gun. She didn't care one way or the other. For her, it was over.

So Candy decided to have a drink. They were sitting in the second-class lounge and Joyce, who was almost as relieved as Candy that the day was finally drawing to a close, had decided, perhaps unwisely, to treat everyone.

'Right then,' she said. 'Who wants a drink?'

And Candy, officially clean but still allowed the occasional celebratory g and t, said: 'G and t, please. And some crisps: I'm hungry.'

'Right . . . Dougal?'

'Oh, nothing for me . . . well maybe an orange juice.'

'OK . . . Mikey?'

'That's very kind of you Mrs . . . er, Joyce. Pint of lager please.'

Joyce thought about this. 'A pint? Are you sure, Mikey? With all you've had already today, wouldn't you be better off with a half?'

Mikey looked devastated. 'OK . . . Actually no, I don't think I'll bother. You're right: I've had enough to drink, haven't I. I think I'll just go for a little walk instead.'

'It's quite all right, Mikey. I don't mind buying you a drink. I just think you ought to be careful, that's all.'

'No, really, it's fine. I've been so much trouble to everyone today. I really appreciate you all looking after me . . . No, I fancy some fresh air. I think I'll take a walk on the deck.'

He stood up and wandered off. Joyce went up to the bar and bought the drinks and some crisps. It struck her that they hadn't eaten since her sandwiches had run out on the way over – not that she felt at all hungry herself, and no doubt if the others had felt the odd pang, they'd have let her know about it. She brought the drinks back to the table and tore open the bags of crisps for everyone to share. She tried for a while to engage Candy and Dougal in a conversation. When that failed, she suggested playing some more games. They still hadn't solved, she pointed out, Tom Riley's riddle about the man going towards a field knowing he's going to die. Candy said it was pointless thinking about it while Riley wasn't there to tell them if they were right or wrong.

So that fizzled out too and they sat there in silence, drinking and munching. Dougal was still upset over not being able to find the type of pâté he wanted. And Candy, despite insisting to herself that she didn't care one way or the other, found she couldn't stop thinking about that gun.

18.45

'I've got to stop and take a rest,' said Frank.

'Are we nearly there yet?' Peter asked suspiciously. He was still gripping the gun sweatily, but not actually pointing it at anyone.

'No, we're not nearly there yet. It's still bloody miles away. But we're making good time: I'm sure we'll be there before midnight when your precious gun turns into a pumpkin or whatever.'

Good time was an understatement. Frank had continued to drive like a lunatic, bringing his foot up only when pure survival instincts demanded or occasionally to check the route, balancing the map on his lap and steering with his knees. Instead of trying to go through Paris he had plotted a vague course around it. He had memorised a string of names – Abbeville, Beauvais, Mantes, Dreux, Chartres – and was following signs for each of these in turn. And driving fast, he had found, was the only way to deal with the abject terror. It was a scientific thing. The fear of the gun was cancelled out by the fear of the imminent high-speed road crash. He had been surprised to discover he had it in him to drive so fast for so long. He was even more surprised that the car was up to it.

'Why do we have to stop then?' asked Peter.

'We just do,' said Frank. 'I need to rest. I need to check where we're going. It's dangerous for me to keep on driving when I'm tired. And we should get some more petrol . . . Look, there was a sign back there for a garage a couple of kilometres up ahead. I'm going to pull in there, OK?'

Peter thought about this. Now he was presented with the opportunity, his bladder seemed suddenly full. 'OK,' he said.

'That OK with you?' Frank asked Jonquil gently.

Jonquil nodded mutely. She hadn't said a word since they left Calais. She had given up the map-reading almost immediately and after that wouldn't respond to Frank at all, however he phrased the request. It was a good job one of them was keeping it together, Frank thought to himself as he turned the car off the main road. And as he thought this, he realised with a faint sense of shame that a teeny, tiny part of him was enjoying this. *He* was the one keeping it together and somewhere mixed up with the fear and the anger was just a little piece, the smallest piece imaginable, of warped pride.

The garage looked deserted. He stopped the car by one of the pumps and got out. Before he could even get the cap off the petrol tank, though, a large man in blackened overalls appeared and ushered him away. It was a garage with at-the-car service; they really were a long way away from home.

Peter also got out of the car. His hand was still clenched tightly around the handle of the gun, but he had taken the trouble, Frank was relieved to notice, to hide both hand and gun away in one of his coat pockets.

'Toilet?' he said hopefully to the man in overalls.

'*Toilette*,' the man corrected him and he pointed round to the back of the main garage building.

'Yeah, me too,' said Jonquil, also climbing out of the car, and she followed Peter across the forecourt.

Round the back of the garage there were two doors, one marked H, one marked D. Unfazed by this, Peter confidently opened the door marked D. It made little difference, they were both the same inside: small, dark, damp, unbelievably foul-smelling cupboards with nothing in them but a hole. Peter's first thought was: Bloody hell, someone's nicked the toilet. But then he remembered what Joyce had said in the ticket hall about French bogs and consoled himself with the thought that he'd pissed in a lot worse places in his time.

Outside, Jonquil hung back. She could feel the day cooling down around her, a false sense of normality setting in, their hopes fading with the daylight. Time was running out: the longer these insane circumstances prevailed, the less insane they would seem, the easier it would be to go along with them. She had to act before they just gave up and accepted this ludicrous situation. She had a plan – probably not the kind of plan that stood up to close scrutiny, but she was purposefully not scrutinising it closely. It was the only plan she had. And of course it was no good relying on *Frank* to come up with anything better. He looked like he'd happily drive Peter to Timbuktu if asked; in fact Frank looked like he was actually *enjoying* this in some perverse way. Taking several deep breaths, she prepared to do the stupidest, most dangerous thing she had ever done in her life.

She gave Peter twenty seconds to overcome the undoubted horrors that lay behind the door and get a reasonable flow going. She counted out the time in her head like she used to do when she was a girl. One elephant, two elephants, three elephants ... On twenty elephants she lunged towards the door marked D and flung it open. As she had been banking on, Peter was using both his hands to try and direct his stream somewhere vaguely near the hole, and his gun was left exposed in his coat pocket.

It was still a huge risk. Peter could still have whipped out the gun and shot her before she could get a foot in the door. However, he was sunk by a woefully misplaced sense of modesty. Realising that this must be Jonquil coming in behind him, thinking that it was probably his fault for coming into the wrong cubicle, he had to finish his business and do himself up before he could turn around. And that was his mistake – almost a fatal error. He felt the gun slip out of his pocket. He struggled to finish, shaking himself to squeeze the last drops out; and in his haste he forgot one crucial aspect of putting yourself away after taking a piss. The zipper bit into his flesh like a child might bite into a toffee apple, wide-mouthed and hungrily, and Peter's scream was audible halfway back to Calais.

Frank certainly heard it, leaning against the car bonnet watching the numbers on the pump whizz round, and was chilled. The attendant also looked shocked and pulled the nozzle out of the tank, but Frank held a hand up to him. 'It's OK,' he said. '*Ça va*. I'll go and sort it out.'

He ran off before the attendant could argue. Round the back of the building he found Jonquil with the gun held, trembling, at arm's length, pointing it at Peter, who was staggering outside the open door of the toilet, cross-legged, knees bent, flying at half-mast, eyes bulging. He was still trying to scream but was now too dry-throated to make a noise.

Jonquil was repeating softly to herself, like a spiralling mantra: 'You bastard. You fucking bastard. You fucking fucking bastard. You fucking fucking fucking bastard . . .' And so on.

It took a moment for the scene to sink in, then Frank started prioritising things. The first thing, clearly, was to get that bloody gun out of sight. The attendant was bound to come round any second to see what the hell was going on.

'Jonquil,' he said as commandingly as he could, 'I want you to put the gun down now . . .'

However, Jonquil chose instead to swing the gun round and point it at him, ordering: 'Don't come any closer!'

Frank instinctively raised his hands in the air.

'We have to put the gun away now,' he explained gently. 'If the man comes round here and sees it we're going to be in trouble.'

He ignored Jonquil's order and continued to walk steadily towards her.

'It's OK,' he told her. 'You did a great thing, you got the gun. We're in control now. But you have to put it away.'

Still talking soothingly to her, he reached out for the gun and pushed it slowly to her side. She carried on staring, wide-eyed, directly at him. He tried to take the gun out of her hand, but she wouldn't relinquish it, so he guided it instead inside her cardigan and out of sight.

'OK?' he asked.

She nodded.

That was that, then. The next thing was Peter, who had now collapsed to the ground in agony. Slowly he was able to disentangle his swollen, purpling flesh from the harsh metal. He folded himself back inside and then *extremely* gingerly pulled the zipper up again. Frank gave him a couple of moments to get his breath back before helping him to his feet. Peter tried to speak, but he was still too hoarse. Frank heaved him up and then clung on to him to support him while he tottered and groaned and eventually straightened himself out.

'Right, this is what we're going to do,' said Frank. 'We're going to walk slowly back to the car and act as though nothing out of the ordinary has happened.' He didn't think for a moment that this would work – the attendant was bound to ask something, and would probably be able to make out the gun-shaped lump in Jonquil's cardigan – but he couldn't think what else to do. If worst came to worst, he supposed, they could always just point the gun at him and then screech off into the sunset. Free petrol that way too.

He needn't have worried. As the man in overalls watched the three of them coming back – one with her arm tucked inside her cardigan like Napoleon, one hobbling slightly, all of them looking nervous and guilty – the only thought that struck him was maybe they'd been involved in some kind of strange sex game. He'd heard stories about the English.

Frank followed the man into the shop and paid for the fuel, then returned to the car. The other two were already sitting sheepishly inside like a couple of naughty children. Jonquil still had her hand clamped inside her cardigan. Frank drove to the edge of the garage forecourt, then stopped again.

'OK,' he said, staring straight ahead through the windscreen. 'What now?'

'We go home,' said Jonquil.

'No!' cried Peter from the back. His voice was still a notch higher in pitch than was normal.

'Peter, it's over. I've got the gun,' Jonquil said loudly. The colour was beginning to come back to her face; the confidence was returning to her voice. She'd done it. She'd fucking *done* it. Just when it looked like she'd come up against a situation that was out of her control, when it looked like it was Frank who was coping, Frank who was holding it all together, *she'd* come through.

She was going to tell people about this for years.

'I have to go to Orléans,' Peter said. 'They'll kill me if I don't go.'

'No Peter. We're going home.'

'He may have a point,' said Frank.

Jonquil glared at him. Obviously Frank was just being difficult because she had saved the day and not him. How pathetic; how predictable. 'Frank, we don't have to do what he says. I've got the gun.'

'Yeah . . . but like I say, he may have a point.'

'What do you mean?'

'Well, look at him.' Frank indicated Peter, who was curled up foetally on the back seat. 'He's scared out of his mind.'

'*I'm* scared out of *my* mind,' Jonquil pointed out.

'Yeah, but . . .'

'But what?' Jonquil couldn't stop herself raising her voice now.

'Look at him. He's scared for his life. He wouldn't have made us do this if he wasn't scared for his life.'

'It's true,' Peter said. The quietness and soberness of his voice was chilling. 'They'll kill me if I fuck this up. If we're not going to Orléans, you may as well shoot me here. Cut out the middle man, know what I mean?'

'But it's seven o'clock,' Jonquil said. 'We ought to be getting the boat back now. No, we ought to be halfway home by now. I bet the others have landed already. We shouldn't be driving around a strange country with loaded guns.' She took the gun out of her cardigan and looked at it, as if aware for the first time what a horrible thing it was.

'What are we going to do with it if we don't take it to Orléans?' Frank asked.

'Take it back to England. Hand it in to the police.'

'You *really* don't want to do that,' Peter advised. 'This is an order from George Johnson.'

'So? Who's he when he's at home?' said Jonquil.

'A gangster,' said Peter matter of factly.

'Yeah right,' said Jonquil, working on the shaky principle that if he hadn't bothered to give himself a proper, scary gangster name, he couldn't be a proper, scary gangster. George Johnson sounded like an accountant. 'He can't be above the law, whoever he is.'

Frank, on the other hand, knew exactly who George Johnson was and where he stood in relation to the law. About a year previously a nervous-looking journalist had come into Frank's shop to photocopy a lengthy article denouncing Johnson's so-called business interests. Frank read bits of the article as he was copying it and was interested enough to follow the story closely as it broke. The gist was that Johnson, in addition to his legitimate business of importing and exporting electrical components, also ran prostitution rings and drug supplies and had close links with far-right groups all over Europe. Different forms of the article appeared in various newspapers and magazines over the next fortnight and the police began an extensive investigation into Johnson's business affairs; but they were unable to link him with any nefarious activities whatsoever and six months later the investigation was dropped. One month after that, Frank heard on the news, sixth or seventh item down, the journalist in question was found burned to death in his own flat. It was put down to an accident. George Johnson's name wasn't mentioned.

'Oh I think he may be above the law,' he said.

'Yeah,' Peter agreed. 'He is.'

'So what exactly are you supposed to do, Peter?' Frank asked.

'I've got to take this gun to a bar called Le Chat Noir on . . .' Peter checked his piece of paper. '. . . Avenue de Paris, near the train station. And give it either directly to Mister le Blanc or to one of his men.'

'And how are you going to know what this Mister le Blanc looks like? It's his gun, I take it . . . ?'

'I ask for him, don't I. I tell them at the bar that George Johnson from England sent me.'

Frank looked across to Jonquil. 'That sounds simple enough . . . Come on, let's do it. I reckon we can be in Orléans in a couple of hours. Three hours tops. A couple of hours to sort this out, then we'll make even better time driving back through the night. We'll get an early boat and be home in time for breakfast tomorrow. How about it?'

Jonquil couldn't believe what she was hearing. This was supposed to be *her* day. She was in charge of this trip to France; so how come they weren't doing what she wanted to do? In fact at no point during the day had they done what she wanted to do. Had they? If she'd put her foot down outside the bank they'd have never hired this stupid car, giving Peter the opportunity to hijack them.

'No,' she said firmly. 'We're going home.'

'I really think we ought to help Peter out,' Frank insisted.

Which left Jonquil no option. Shaking her head sadly, she raised the gun and pointed it at Frank's head. 'No,' she said evenly. 'We're going home.'

And Frank snapped. Just like that. Snap, and he was gone.

He could take so much, but no more. Not this. It was one thing having a scared, drunk nutter point a gun at you; it was quite another to have your *own fucking girlfriend* do the same thing. This was no way to sort out disagreements.

He fired up the engine, slammed the car into gear and screeched out of the garage, back up to the main road and continued the way they had been going.

'We're going to Orléans!' he said tauntingly.

'Frank, I'm warning you, turn the car around.'

'What are you going to do, Jonquil? You going to force me to turn the car around?'

'Don't make me.'

'Make you what? Shoot me? Is that what you're going to do – shoot me? That'll stop the car all right.'

'Frank . . .'

'Only way you're going to stop me . . .'

The car was accelerating rapidly. The engine was screeching.

'*Frank . . .*'

'Joan of Arc was from Orléans, you know . . . Do you know about Joan of Arc . . . ?'

Frank was in a road movie all of his own. From somewhere in the dregs of his memory there surfaced an old Orchestral Manoeuvres In The Dark song about Joan of Arc. He started humming it. It was strained and tuneless; the other two wouldn't have recognised it anyway. Then he started taunting her again. 'We're going to Orlé-ans,' he said in an hysterical, sing-songy voice. Jonquil pressed the gun against his head and screamed for him to stop. The metal felt exhilarating against his cheek.

In the back seat, Peter buried his head in his hands. He'd envisaged many awful things going wrong with this escapade. He hadn't really expected it to be successful at all, that's why he'd tried to drink his way out of it and to hell with the consequences. You couldn't really hope to just hijack your way across France if you'd never done that kind of thing before, especially if you were a useless fuck-up anyway. So *something* was bound to go wrong somewhere along the line, he was quite prepared for that. But he wasn't prepared for *this*: the two people in the front of the car, two people who were reputedly in love with one another, threatening to take them all to Kingdom Come. This was just crazy, plain and simple.

Jonquil

I'm scared. You have to help me. I've just discovered something about myself and it scares the shit out of me.

What is it?

Murder. I think I'm capable of murder.

What do you mean?

Just that. I think I'm capable of taking another human being's life and not feeling any remorse.

But you obviously know you would feel remorse; otherwise you wouldn't be scared by this. You wouldn't be here.

Maybe . . . I'm not sure if it's the remorse that scares me, though, or just the fear of getting caught. You know?

Are you talking about murder in general? Or one person in particular?

One person, really . . . There's a new girl at work . . .

Ah . . .

I say *girl*; she's a woman. She's about . . . well, I'd say she was in her late thirties; mid to late thirties. But she's one of these people who tries to dress ten years younger than she really is, you know? She's spent some time in India and she has all these beads and tie-dye stuff. But she's not really a hippie; she's too straight. And she's so *sensible* and *calm* and *nice*, and everyone likes her . . .

Except you. You want to kill her.

Yeah.

What about Frank? Does Frank like her?

Oh yeah, *especially* Frank. Frank can't keep his fucking eyes off her – sorry. But I mean, it's true. They spend the whole time together at work. By some means or other – Joyce would say it was karma no doubt, but I reckon they've fixed the rota – somehow all their shifts coincide. Isn't that funny? So Frank's always off with her, showing her the ropes, when he should be doing other things.

Jonquil, this kind of jealousy is perfectly normal in a relationship.

It's not jealousy . . . I mean, obviously it's jealousy, but I've been jealous before. This goes way beyond that. I can't stop thinking about it. Which method to use – poison, stabbing, a whack on the head with a blunt instrument; how to dispose of the body; how to cover my tracks. You know . . . it's not healthy, is it? I've been browsing the true-crime shelves of bookshops: that's a clear sign if ever there was one. You ever seen any of these true crime books? These are not for normal, balanced people. They're for people who are, on some level, however deeply buried in their subconscious, planning to bump someone off. Probably they don't even know it yet, but they are. It's like if you get a really exotic recipe book and you think, oh no I'll never make any of these in a million years, the recipes are too complicated or the ingredients are too obscure or whatever, but the pictures are kind of nice, I'll just look at the pictures – even so, you're still open to the *possibility* you might make one of them one day, under the right circumstances. Just by owning the book.

Is it Frank you want to do away with, or Joyce?

I don't know. Both, ideally. If I just kill one of them, the other'll suspect. Won't they? God, listen to me. See, I've practically decided to go ahead and do it . . .

Honestly Jonquil, this is perfectly normal. It's nothing to worry about. It really is nothing more than an obsessive jealousy. If you actually wanted to go ahead with this, you wouldn't be telling me all about it first. Now that you've told me, if either of these people drop dead suddenly, I shall have to go to the police.

You'd do that?

Of course.

What about patient confidentiality?

It only exists within the boundaries of the law. I'm not a priest at confession. If I didn't tell the police what I knew, I'd be an accessory.

I see . . .

So you see you can't do it now. And deep down you knew that. You knew that by coming her and telling me all about it, you were removing any possibility that you might actually go ahead.

I was?

Yes.

Of course I could always kill you as well.

Well . . .

See? I really am fucked up.

What is it about Joyce that you think Frank finds attractive?

I don't know. Everything, I guess. Her whole being.

Yes, but specifically. Do you think she has qualities Frank admires which you don't possess?

Yeah, like I told you. She's calm, sensible, polite . . . all the things I'm not.

But Frank loves you the way you are.

Does he, though?

I don't know. You've been telling me solidly for the last six weeks that he does.

Well . . . yeah, maybe.

So why would he suddenly start admiring a completely different set of qualities in someone else?

I don't know . . . she gives off this air of vulnerability. She's had a really tough time of it. She had a baby that died, and then her husband left her, so, you know, everyone feels sorry for her . . . And she's slim.

You're slim!

I'm three quarters of a stone overweight.

Medically possibly. Not noticeably. Has Frank ever made any comment about your weight?

No ... but he wouldn't *say* something like that anyway. Doesn't mean he isn't thinking it. Look, this is ridiculous. You can't say with such authority that it isn't possible for him to fall for someone else just because they're different from me. It doesn't work like that. Logic hasn't got anything to do with it.

Have you tried getting to know Joyce as a person?

What?

I mean it. Have you tried to get to know her a little better?

No ... If you don't like someone, you don't like them. You can't suddenly decide to be best friends just because it'll make your life easier. If anything it'll make things worse. You'll just get on each other's nerves even more.

OK, but you can make a bit more of an effort than I think you're making at the moment to get along with her. If you could get to like Joyce, even just a little bit, you wouldn't feel so threatened by her.

Yeah? How?

I don't know ... Try spending some more time with her at work?

Huh. She spends all her time at work with Frank.

Are there any activities you could do together?

Activities?

Yes ... There must be something.

Well, I suppose ... I've had this idea for quite some time. But I haven't said anything to anyone yet because I'm sure Philip will just say no outright ... I think it would be a really nice idea to take some of the residents to France for the day. So many of them haven't even been out of London, let alone England. Or else they came to London from wherever it was they were trying to escape from and they've never left. So I think it would be a real eye-opener for them, you know, even if we just went to Calais for lunch . . .

That's the kind of thing. Would Joyce come?

Oh yeah . . . I'd thought about this already. In fact, it might be one of the reasons why I've never mentioned it to anyone. If I do organise this, the only people who are likely to volunteer to go are me, Frank and Joyce. We're the only remotely interested people on the staff at the moment. The others couldn't give a toss.

This sounds ideal. You'll have the whole day together, the three of you, and you'll have problems you'll have to overcome together.

Problems . . . ? Oh, I see what you mean. Well, yeah, I suppose one or two of the residents might enjoy a little drink on the way. But nothing I can't handle – you get used to the drunks fairly quickly. No, the real problem is going to be persuading Flipping Philip that this is a good idea and getting his support. Persuading him to give us a day away from the hostel and some cash from the Residents' Fund. That and spending the whole day with Frank and Joyce: that's going to be something of a problem as well. I'm not exaggerating this, you know – I really do have some very dark feelings indeed towards them.

Compared to that, anything the residents can throw up will be a doddle.

Joyce

I was so excited I phoned Mark at work. One of his colleagues took the call and told me Mark was on the other line.

'Is it urgent?' he asked.

'No, it's OK . . . what am I talking about, of course it's urgent, it's Joyce.'

'It's Joyce,' I heard the man tell Mark.

There was a click while I was put briefly on hold; then Mark picked up.

'I'm on another call,' he said briskly. 'You'd better make it quick.'

'OK, I'm pregnant. Quick enough?'

'You what? What do you mean?'

'I mean, I'm pregnant . . . One of your sperm has fertilised one of my eggs and we're going to have a baby.'

'Yeah, but . . . hang on a sec.' I was put on hold again while he told his other, important call he'd get back to them. 'OK, I'm back.'

'Terrific.'

'So . . . how'd this happen?'

'Oh come on Mark. You gave me a special kiss, remember?'

'Yeah, but you know . . .'

'The pill is only ninety-eight per cent safe. Look it like that, this was a statistical inevitability.'

'Yeah . . .' He sounded bewildered. Then a thought struck him and he announced cheerily: 'I've got super-sperm, haven't I?'

I couldn't help laughing. I didn't even mind too much when I heard all Mark's friends laughing behind him and realised he'd turned the whole thing into a laddish office joke. 'Duh-duh duh-duh duh-duh duh-duh Super-Sperm!' he was singing. 'No contraception strong enough to stand in their way!'

'Mark,' I said, trying to regain his attention and calm him down a little. 'Mark, you are pleased, aren't you?'

'Pleased? Yeah! Course I'm pleased,' he said, trying to sound as definite as he could. 'I mean, I'm more shocked than anything. I had no idea.'

'No. That's why I phoned to tell you.'

'I mean, I didn't even know you were late or anything . . . I'm sorry, I should take more notice of these things.'

'Yeah . . . I didn't want to tell you until I was sure. I thought I was just being silly.'

I don't know why I hadn't told him of my fears and suspicions earlier on. Probably because I didn't honestly believe in them myself until I saw the test result. I thought there'd be some other explanation. I thought I was just being emotional. Deep down I didn't *feel* pregnant (and there was a clue, surely, if I could have seen it).

He dutifully bought me a large bunch of flowers on the way home. We had a serious talk, during which neither of us could stop grinning, about where we were going to go from here and what this meant to our relationship. We did talk about whether we were sure we wanted to keep it, but it was no more than a cursory aside, purely in deference to the women who had fought for our right to have this option. I don't think either of us was in any doubt. Even though it was entirely unplanned and unexpected, and even though we'd never seriously discussed children before, I think we both knew this was the right thing to happen to us.

Then later that night a delivery boy from the local pizza restaurant turned up with a banana and tuna-fish pizza and a card, signed by all Mark's friends at work, which read: YOU MIGHT AS WELL GET USED TO IT! CONGRATULATIONS! A sweet thought, although rather a bizarre way of expressing it – and, frankly, a waste of good pizza.

We had a week of getting used to the idea before the m word reared its ugly head. A week during which Mark was unbearably excited almost constantly. 'God, I feel so virile!' he told me at least three times a day. He started wearing aftershave, taking cold showers first thing in the morning and doing odd jobs around the house that didn't need doing. On the Sunday I even caught him tinkering underneath the bonnet of the car.

Then one evening as we were doing the washing up, he turned to me and said: 'So: surname?'

'Ye-es?'

'Whose surname is the poor brat going to be saddled with?'

'Oh . . . I don't know.'

I'd been assuming mine actually, but I suppose it was perfectly reasonable of him to ask.

'We could see which sounds nicer,' he suggested.

It was Peacock against Tompkinson. So there weren't really aesthetic considerations.

'Or we could go for a double-barrelled,' I said.

Mark shook his head. 'Short-term solution. What'll happen to our grandchildren? They'll end up being Peacock-Tompkinson-Something-or-other-elses. Within a couple of generations the whole thing'll be completely out of hand.'

'We could get married.' I said it casually, almost apologetically.

OK, so it was me. It was *me* who first mentioned the m word. I hadn't thought about it beforehand; it just kind of spilled out.

Mark didn't bat an eyelid, though. After all, we were just talking. 'But you wouldn't necessarily take my name. That wouldn't solve the problem.'

'If we were going to do it, I'd want to do it properly.'

'Seriously?'

'Yeah . . . I mean, it's one man's name or another, isn't it. It's no big deal. Either you or my dad. And at least I have the luxury of loving both of you.'

'But what about your principles? Our principles. What about the inherent sexism of marriage and the historical oppression of women?' Said Mr Super-Sperm.

'I don't know.' I stared into the dishwater. I'd been scrubbing the same pan for about five minutes. 'I'm not saying I definitely want to, I'm just saying we ought to think about it.'

'OK . . . Best not think about it for too long, though. These things take time to organise.'

'OK.'

Twenty-four hours. Is that a reasonable length of time to take over a decision like that? The following evening at pretty much the same time we were standing again at the sink. Swapped around this time; he was washing, I was drying; boy, did we have a democratic relationship. 'I've been thinking about it,' I said. Then I took a deep breath. 'I think we should get married.'

He nearly dropped a cup. 'You do?'

'Yeah . . . For the sake of the kid. I think it'll be simpler. I can't bear to think of him or her being called a bastard by other children in the playground . . .'

'Joyce, it's not the 1950s any more.'

'Yeah, but . . . Our parents'll be happier.'

Mark turned towards me with a soapsuddy wine glass in his hand. 'But the entire purpose of our lives is to wind our parents up and disappoint them in every way we can,' he reminded me.

'Well, my dad's having a tough time.'

Mark carried on staring at me.

'Oh come on, Mark. It's not as though I'm proposing we vote Conservative or anything. I just think it's a nice, clean answer to our situation.' It dawned on me for the first time around now that this part wasn't my decision alone. I needed his consent. 'Will we?' I asked him.

It took him a heartbeat to answer. 'OK.' Obviously he'd been thinking about it too.

So that was it then. OK. Fine. B-boom: decision made. I still can't quite believe, actually, how fast it happened. Twenty-four hours from first suggestion to 'OK'. When I think how long it took us to make all the other big life decisions: you know, moving in with each other, buying a car . . . even deciding where we were going to go on our holidays usually took longer than that. In fact, I found it all rather anti-climactic. I had wanted to do the thing properly and stumbling half-heartedly to a conclusion while doing the washing up isn't really fairy-tale stuff, is it. No, I didn't want a white wedding with a church and flowers and stuff, but I did – for some repressed and no doubt deeply anti-feminist reason – want *him* to propose to *me*. And bless him, Mark understood. The following Friday he came home from work late, a little drunk from having been out with some of his mates, bearing yet another large bunch of flowers. He dropped to one knee in front of me while I was sitting on the sofa, produced a modest ring in a very handsome black display box and said, quite solemnly: 'Joyce, will you marry me?'

And three months after that, in Lewisham Registry Office, wearing a preposterous velvet waistcoat, he promised a whole roomful of people that he would stay with me until death did us part.

He didn't of course. I didn't expect him to, not even when he told me at the funeral that he would. That still doesn't mean it wasn't a nice thing for him to say at the time; I just knew that once something like that funeral had happened it was going to be terribly difficult for us to be happy together again. Once you've been that distraught with someone, it's a long, long road back. At least he didn't disappear drunk in the middle of an argument. He waited until the worst of it was over for both of us, until the scars had been healed as far as they were likely to, then he packed a bag quietly one night and left without ceremony while I was lying in bed, zonked out on Valium. Leaving me a couple of months short of my thirtieth birthday with something of a life crisis on my hands. On top of the vacuum in my domestic set-up, I was becoming increasingly disillusioned with my supposedly glamorous (to those who didn't actually have to do it) job as a PA to a fashion designer. So I quit. The Friday after Mark walked out, I quit on a whim. Daniel said to me: 'Have a nice weekend, Joyce. See you Monday.' And I said: 'Er . . . no you won't, actually.'

I drifted aimlessly for a couple of weeks, completely baffled by what to do with all the time I suddenly had on my hands, before I found myself a place on a Buddhist retreat in South Wales, where I immediately felt at home — so at home I ended up staying the best part of a year. If you'd told me five years earlier I'd spend eleven months on a Buddhist retreat — in Wales! — I'd have asked you to roll me one too. But I loved it. It was really good to get out of London, to get far away from where anyone knew me, to clear my head. During this time I managed to earn a bit of money from making and selling my own jewellery and as soon as I had enough saved up I travelled around India for three months. Then when I returned to London I decided that instead of launching myself into another high-stress, dead-end secretarial job, I would try and find something a little more rewarding. A little less hollow.

And that's how I ended up at Stamford Street in a job which I love and which fulfils me in so many ways it's impossible to describe.

And which, I suppose, I owe entirely to Beth.

17.35

Yeah, Joyce was always going on about how much she loved her job. What do you do? strangers would ask her. I work with the homeless, Joyce would answer, proudly. Really? That must be *so* challenging and rewarding. And Joyce would close her eyes and say: it is, yes; it really is.

But there were times when she hated her job. There were times when it bored, frustrated and antagonised her; when she could gladly have strangled the miserable, ungrateful little bastards. And this was one of those times. Standing in the ticket hall at Dover, with Candy and Dougal waiting patiently by her side, wondering where the hell Mikey had got himself to.

She hadn't seen him for most of the crossing. He'd declined her offer of a drink and wandered off somewhere on his own and she hadn't seen him after that. Instead of trying to hunt him down on board when the boat docked, she and the others had come into the ticket office to wait for him. All the foot passengers had to file past where they were waiting so there was no chance of missing him. But the stream of people became a trickle and eventually dried up completely and there was still no sign of him. Joyce found somebody important-looking in a uniform behind the ticket desk and asked him: 'Excuse me, is that everyone off the five-fifteen landing from Calais now?'

The man looked at his watch. 'Oh yes, I should think they'll all be off by now.'

'It's just that one of our party is missing.'

'I see. Give me a second and I'll phone through for you.'

He disappeared into an office. Joyce continued peering around the large hall for Mikey, but to no avail. And the place wasn't busy now: if he was here, she'd have been able to see him.

When the man reappeared he was shaking his head. 'Yes, they're all off the boat now,' he said. 'However, I understand the police apprehended a drunk and disorderly gentleman. A middle-aged man, quite short and tubby, with a Welsh accent. Very, very drunk apparently. Could that be your, uh, friend?'

Joyce sighed deeply. 'Where will they be holding him?'

'Come with me. I'll show you where the port police station is.'

As they followed the man through the hall, Joyce felt the eyes of the other passengers on her, as though she were the criminal. She consoled herself with thoughts of ripping Mikey's arms off and rubbing salt on the stumps.

Outside the ticket hall, they were shown a grubby brick building the other side of the car park. 'He'll be in there, I'm sure,' the man said. 'Just knock on the door and ask for Sergeant Watkins.'

They crossed the car park. The building had a blue Police lantern outside it; Joyce further amused herself by imagining Mikey swinging from it. Maybe having been hanged, drawn and quartered first.

'Do we have to go and find him?' asked Candy, who had fairly extensive experience of police stations and knew just how long even a routine thing like this could take. Once a policeman started filling in forms it was usually very difficult to get him to stop.

Joyce looked horrified. 'We can't just *leave* him here.'

'But Jonquil was saying earlier on about each of us being responsible for our own actions . . .'

'I'm not Jonquil,' Joyce said firmly.

Before they even reached the door they could hear Mikey's voice, shouting belligerently. 'It's bloody mine! I bloody told you!' The windows of the police station were open and his lilting, musical tones floated out into the warm evening air. Joyce marched straight through the station's small reception area and into the office on the right, where, it was audibly apparent, Mikey was holding court. The sleepy policeman manning the desk did attempt a half-hearted, 'Er, excuse me, you shouldn't really . . .,' but he was easily ignorable. She flung open the door and barked out Mikey's name – 'Mikey!' – like she was calling him in for his tea. The room fell silent.

The office was a cluttered mess of chairs, desks, files and pieces of paper. Alongside Mikey, who was slouching by the open window with his hands in his pockets, there were two policemen in the room and also a shortish man with blond, cropped hair and a pencil moustache who was wearing a different kind of uniform.

Mikey looked relieved to see Joyce standing in the doorway. Having been halted mid-flow by her sudden entrance, he found his voice again. 'Thank God you're here,' he stammered drunkenly. 'I've been wrongfully arrested.'

'You haven't actually been arrested yet.' Presumably this was Sergeant Watkins, the slightly overweight, smug-looking one sitting at the largest desk with his hands locked behind his neck.

'What's the problem?' Joyce asked him.

'A slight altercation over a bottle of Bacardi,' Watkins said. He indicated the offending bottle, Exhibit A, which stood, trophy-like and defiant, on a table in the centre of the room.

'He *stole* it,' said the man with the silly moustache. Joyce guessed he worked in the boat's duty-free shop and had caught Mikey shoplifting. There was something about his appearance, the smartness of his uniform, the precision of his hair, the whininess of his voice: it was a fair bet his colleagues called him Hitler behind his back.

'I told you, it's mine,' said Mikey, making a grand effort to speak in words and sentences rather than grunts and dribbles.

Watkins turned to Joyce to explain. 'Apparently your friend brought his own bottle of rum on to the boat. He didn't want to carry it around with him during the voyage so he cunningly concealed it on the shelves of the duty-free shop. Then when the boat docked he went to retrieve his property and that's when Mr Weller here apprehended him.' He turned back to Mikey. 'Would that be correct?'

'Yeah, course it is. Told you already,' said Mikey. 'Sensible place to hide it.'

'Preposterous!' blurted out Mr Weller nazily.

Watkins looked over at his colleague. 'What do you reckon, George? Number seven?'

'I'd put it top five, sarge. Easy.'

The two policemen grinned at each other, a knowing, exclusive, Masonic grin.

'What do you mean, top five?' Joyce asked. 'What are you talking about?'

Watkins' expression grew, impressively, even smugger. 'It's a lonely, boring life in this little outpost of the British Empire,' he explained, 'so we like to keep ourselves amused by compiling a Top Ten list of the most ridiculous excuses offered to us by the people we bring in here. I have to say we haven't had a New Entry for a few months now, but *this* one . . .' he tapped a biro against his teeth, '. . . is really not bad at all.'

'It's true!' Mikey managed to shout before letting out a long, loud belch.

Watkins carried on talking to Joyce. 'Now, madam, what is your relationship to this . . . gentleman?'

'Mikey – Mr Williams – is in my care. I work at the Stamford Street hostel for homeless men in London where Mr Williams lives. We've just been to Calais for the day and we're on our way home.'

Home . . . yes, that's where Joyce wanted to go. Home.

The fat, smug plod stroked his chin and did his annoying tapping thing with the pen. 'So what you're saying is that if no charges were pressed, you'd take Mr Williams back to London with you immediately.'

'Immediately,' Joyce confirmed: the word had a good, get-out-of-jail feel about it.

'Hang on a minute—' Mr Weller started to protest.

But Sergeant Watkins silenced him with a hand, then stood up from his desk and walked over to him. He put a hand on Mr Weller's shoulder and drew him to a corner of the room. He pretended to speak privately but it was a small room and his

257

voice was perfectly audible to everyone else. 'Look, sir, between you and me the only reason I picked this gentleman up is because he was D and D and I didn't want him wandering around the streets of our little town pissed out of his head, if you'll pardon the expression. Now, if this kind lady is going to take him back to London that does rather alter the situation. Do you see what I mean?'

'No—'

Again the hand to silence him. 'Of course, a crime *has* been committed here and it is entirely up to you how you wish to proceed . . .'

This seemed to appease Mr Weller slightly. He looked over his shoulder at Mikey. Clearly the way he wished to proceed involved sharp instruments of torture, and didn't involve, not at all, either judges or juries.

'You have two very clear options, sir. Either you press charges, which means I have to take a statement from you, I have to take a statement from him, we all have to phone our wives, get home late . . . *Or* you forget about the whole thing, in which case you can go home now.'

Mr Weller shook his head in a whatever-is-this-country-coming-to fashion. 'A *crime* has been committed,' he said.

'That doesn't alter your options. Sir.'

Mr Weller looked Mikey directly in the eye; not an easy thing as Mikey's eyes were shooting all over the place. It all depended, Joyce realised suddenly, on Mr Weller's home life. Didn't it. If Mr Weller had a cosy, comfortable home with a hearth and a hearth-rug and a garden with inviting garden furniture and a loving, waiting wife and a well-stocked drinks cabinet, they were laughing. If, on the other hand, and as she strongly suspected, he lived a sad, lonely existence in a barren, sterile, modern flat and didn't get out quite as much as he ought to, they were here for the duration.

Mr Weller threw his hands up in the air. Maybe he realised that people were going to draw conclusions about his life in general from the decision he made now. 'OK, whatever,' he said. 'Let's leave it.'

'Thank you, Mr Weller,' said Joyce. 'That's very Christian of you.'

'I'm Jewish.'

OK, maybe they didn't call him Hitler behind his back.

Mikey immediately moved away from the window and picked the bottle up off the table.

Mr Weller moved towards him. 'Where do you think you're going with that?'

'It's my bottle,' said Mikey. 'We've just agreed.'

Weller looked to Sergeant Watkins for support.

'I'm afraid he does have a point, sir.'

Mikey headed for the door. Pushing his luck just slightly, he added on the way out: 'Lucky I don't sue you for wrongful arrest.'

'We didn't actually arrest you, sir,' Watkins pointed out. 'You were merely helping us with our enquiries.'

Mikey sauntered out of the door. Joyce, seeing there was nothing else to be gained from the situation, followed him.

Outside, Candy and Dougal were waiting quietly, but as soon as Candy saw Mikey she began to shout at him for wasting even more of their time. She'd just about had it with Mikey. She'd had it with having her time wasted. Candy didn't consider her time to be particularly precious, perhaps because it was the one and only thing she seemed to have a lot of, the only thing that seemed resolutely and irreversibly on her side. But there comes a point when even the people who have seemingly inexhaustible amounts of time on their hands resent it being pilfered from them, just like that, for no reason at all. They object to being swindled; it's a natural human reaction. Even if you have no attachment to the thing you're being swindled out of, the point is it's *yours*, you don't want to just give it up, especially not to drunks. Mikey did begin to apologise – he had a programme that kicked in automatically in situations like this – but then he realised who he was doing the apologising to and stopped. He clasped his hard-won rum to his bosom and growled like a lioness protecting her cubs. Joyce gathered the three of them up and ushered them away from the police hut, back towards where they had left the minibus.

They got maybe a hundred yards before she broke down completely.

'WHAT WERE YOU DOING?' she shrieked at Mikey. 'YOU KNEW YOU´D GET CAUGHT. WHAT WERE YOU THINKING OF?'

Mikey and Candy stopped their bickering. Candy was awed: this was how she'd meant to sound when she'd started in at Mikey. This was real, *proper* having a go at someone. She didn't know Joyce had it in her.

The programme whirred into action. Mikey started apologising again.

This was the last straw for Joyce. 'SHUT UP!' she warned him. 'I SAID SHUT UP!' She was bawling hysterically, eyes scrunched up, fists clenched, the classic posture for bawling someone out. They'd never heard this tone of voice from her before.

Mikey couldn't stop, though. Apologising was like pissing: once you'd got into your flow, halting was a physical impossibility. So on he went: 'I'm sorry, Joyce, no, really I am. I'm really, really sorry. Because this has been such a lovely day and you have been so nice in looking after us and I've been nothing but trouble all along and I'm really sorry . . .' On and on and on . . .

Until Joyce seized his Bacardi bottle and smashed it on the ground. That shut him up.

Mikey watched the clear, thick liquid seep into the gravel. It was like watching a child die. Joyce watched it for a moment too, then she burst out crying. Her legs buckled under her and she sat down on the ground heavily, sobbing.

The other three stood around her uselessly, uncomfortably, trying to work out what to do. Wondering how they were going to get home.

Mikey

Oh God. Women crying. I hate it when women cry. What are you supposed to do? Should you put your arm around them? Usually they just push you away. Should you just let them get on with it? But what if you're responsible for the crying? And I usually am responsible: women seem to cry a lot around me.

I'm sorry, Joyce . . . no, really I am . . . I'm really, really sorry . . . *really* sorry . . .

17.35

Riley was crying too. It was the crying time of day, the melancholy, drawing-in time of day. The sun had all but vanished over its hazy horizon, but there were still three hours of sunlight left: three hours of phoney, phantom, missed-the-boat sunlight, sunlight without warmth, that only served to remind you that the real thing was long gone. If you were prone to crying, now was your time. Of course it was rarer for Riley to cry. In the circles in which Riley moved tears were not often a viable option.

The train to St Omer had taken about half an hour. There were no guards or barriers or anything so he hadn't felt a pressing need to buy a ticket and had instead pocketed the fifty francs the little Frenchman with the John Lennon glasses had given him. His main concern was that the train was so smooth and comfortable that he might fall asleep and miss his stop. On reaching St Omer he spent the first hour or so walking around, proudly reciting Irene's address to passers-by like an amateur Hamlet. Everyone seemed scared of him; the few who managed to understand what he was saying simply pointed him in the right direction and then scurried off. However there seemed to be some confusion as to which the right direction was. He would follow one person's finger for a short while, before being spun around and sent in completely the opposite direction by someone else. He was being bounced around the town like a pinball. In particular he kept finding himself back at a large cathedral, surrounded by cobblestones which were rough and hurt his feet. After a while he stopped asking and just kept walking, mumbling the address over and over to himself as though it were a spell and he was trying to summon the house into being by magic.

Eventually he stumbled across rue des Moulins, more by luck than anything else. It turned out to be not far from the station. He'd been walking around in happy, unflustered circles. It hadn't been bothering him unduly that it was taking him so long to find this road; he knew he'd get there in the end. This was meant to be. But now he was this close, if he was brutally honest with himself (and he was trying his hardest not to be honest with himself, but for some reason he couldn't help it; the honesty kept bursting through in a most brutal fashion), now he was here he was starting to get a little nervous. Although he'd been planning this trip for years, just waiting for the right opportunity to come along, to present itself, in truth he'd never really expected to make it. It was too unreal for him. France was an imaginary country, somewhere you saw on TV, or you read about, somewhere other people came *from*, not a real place you could go to. Or if you could go there, it was only in your dreams. Riley had been here plenty of times before in his dreams. It didn't look like this when he dreamed about it, but this was the place all right. He remembered Irene describing it, before she had even moved here, in that last letter of hers. The mill, the stream, the little bridges from the houses to the road. At the end of the road stood two grand willow trees and the ruined church Irene had spoken about – it all came flooding back now – and an imposing statue of a stern-looking man in flowing robes. Irene would have given this man a deflating nickname, Riley knew – Bob or Henry or something like that. He could picture her walking past the statue every day, on her way to the shops or to the park to read, with a cheery Morning Bob! Morning Henry! How are we today? Still upset about something, I see . . .

So he walked slowly down rue des Moulins, wondering what he would say to Irene when they finally met again. Would he still recognise her? Yes, of course he would. More to the point, would she recognise him? He would be the one that had changed. His hair had grown, his belly had grown, his face had become fuller and redder, he now wore unwashed Oxfam clothes instead of his smart army togs. A black donkey jacket with plentiful pockets for stashing hidden booze, a plain bottle-green T-shirt and dark, scuffed jeans. Would Irene be shocked by the marks of the drink? Instead of welcoming him with open arms, maybe she'd send him away in disgust and her memory of him would be sullied for ever. Riley stopped walking. Momentarily he considered giving up and going home. But no, that would be a stupid thing to do now he'd got this far, wouldn't it. If he was going to entertain doubts about this, they should have been entertained a long time ago.

Number eight was, naturally, the prettiest house in the street. Riley knew it was the right one immediately; he didn't even need to check the number. In each of its four windows stood a tidy, well-maintained flower box, bursting with colour. The footbridge over the small river also bore boxes of plants and seemed to have been recently repainted a fresh, French green colour. It was Irene's house; everything about it spoke of Irene. Riley stood outside it for a while, composing himself, making a token effort at presentability by pulling his straggly hair into some sort of shape with his hand, trying to work out what to say to Irene first. He had to be prepared, he kept reminding himself, for there to be a man. It was only natural. Irene was an attractive woman; there was bound to be someone in the town who wanted to look after her. But Riley had convinced himself this didn't matter. He hadn't necessarily come here to relight the relationship anyway. The important thing was to be with Irene again, to touch her, to tell her that she was important to him even now; even now he'd fucked up so entirely, she was still important to him. If there was a man there, then Riley would shake his hand and the three of them would get along.

He took a swig of whisky from the last of the four small bottles he had liberated from the boat, to calm his nerves. He wished he hadn't drunk so much today, but one more swig wasn't going to make a lot of difference.

Then he strode up, over the bridge, to the front door and knocked on it.

There was no answer.

He knocked again.

Still no answer.

He pressed his ear against the door to see if he could hear any movement inside. Nope. Nothing.

He sat down on the doorstep. This was OK; it was late afternoon, there were any number of places Irene could be. He would wait. He took out his tobacco and shakily rolled himself a cigarette, listening to the soft gurgling of the water underneath him and thinking of the girl in the tobacconists.

After he'd been sitting there for some time, smoking and taking occasional glugs, he heard a voice calling him from the next bridge along. At least he assumed it was calling him: of course it was doing the calling in French. It belonged to a handsome, tanned woman wearing a white blouse and a yellow, flowered skirt – she looked like the embodiment of a childhood summer – who was now coming towards him. Probably thought he was a burglar or something.

'Irene . . . Irene Stuart,' Riley managed to say and he pointed at the house.

There was another barrage of French gobbledygook.

'English . . . ?' said Riley without much hope.

'Ah. You are English?'

'Yes.'

'And you are a friend of Irene?'

'Yes.'

Conversations with foreigners were great. Riley had noticed this before, talking to some of the Europeans who had made their homes on the streets of London, Portuguese and Italians mainly. They pronounced each word clearly and they stuck to the basics, the essentials. Your regular English speakers dressed up their sentences with all sorts of fancy adjectives and socially-required niceties (like please, thank you etc, what a waste of tongue those words were) and supposedly humorous add-ons. Foreigners stuck to the point. You could be as pissed as you liked and talk to a foreigner.

'What is your name?' See, nice and simple. Not, what's your name *mate*? Or I say, would you possibly mind telling me what your name is? Or what's your handle? Or by what monicker are you generally known? *What's your name?* Easy. *What's your name?*

'Riley,' said Riley. Now they were getting somewhere.

'Riley . . . *Tom* Riley?'

'Yeah . . . that's right.' Don't call me Tom, though: no one calls me Tom, not any more.

The woman sat down next to him and put her hand on his knee. On his knee, no less. Riley was curious to see how things were going to develop from here. 'I must tell you something,' she said.

Riley waited patiently, watching the last of the sun shimmer through the drooping greenery of the willow trees, while she searched for the right words. This really was a beautiful spot.

Finally the woman said, bluntly: 'Mr Riley, Irene is dead.'

It took a moment for this to penetrate the clouds of his mind. Dead . . . He forgot momentarily what the word meant. When he remembered he rejected the meaning as absurd. He tried to think of what else it could mean, what the woman really meant to say.

His next thought was for the house. He turned round to look at it, at the perfect patterned curtains, the pretty vases, the polished front door. He cast his eye again along the boxes of plants that adorned the bridge. So this *wasn't* Irene's . . . ? Somebody *else* lived here . . . ? It didn't make sense. It seemed disrespectful, almost cannibalistic. As if someone had tried to climb inside her skin and pass themselves off as her. This house was Irene's. No, more than that: this house *was Irene*.

Despite his best efforts, the truth did eventually touch base and when it did the questions tumbled out of him: how, when, what happened, was she hurt . . .

'It was the cancer,' the woman said softly. She moved her hand from Riley's knee to his arm. 'She didn't want to spend all her time in the hospital so she died quite quickly. It was in . . . nineteen four—, nineteen twenty . . .' It took her a few goes. Eventually she said 1988.

'1988?'

She thought about it. 'Yes. 1988.'

No, that wasn't possible. Towards the end of 1988 Riley had moved into a run-down bed and breakfast place near Brighton. He had often looked out across the sea and thought about Irene leading her life on the other side without him. She had been very alive to him then.

No, 1988 simply wasn't possible. If she had died in 1988 that would mean that by the time he received her Christmas card during that strained last visit to his parents she had already been in her grave for two years. But he had seen her address, this address, and thought about writing back to her. When he decided he didn't know what to say in a letter he made a note of her address, which he kept with him always, and vowed to come and see her here. *He'd imagined this house*. Almost exactly, like one of those mind-reading tricks where somebody draws a picture and the magician tries to reproduce it on his piece of paper from brainwaves. The town, the country, these had not seemed real, but the house . . . he knew this house. Somehow Irene had managed to send him pictures of this house. So she couldn't have been dead then; she'd never been more vibrant in his thoughts. And he had *seen* her, right there, in his dreams.

A bewildered expression crossed Riley's face as he tried to take this in. The woman stood up and patted his shoulder. 'I will leave you now,' she said. 'I will leave you to think. But when you are ready, please . . . come and visit me here, next door. Irene and me were very good friends. She spoke about you many times. I thought you might come . . . I have been waiting for you . . .' She let a sad smile appear. 'My name is Natalie.'

As she walked away Riley's head fell between his legs and just for a moment he thought he might throw up. He clasped his hands around the back of his neck and rocked, gently, backwards and forwards. He polished off the whisky in two long, needy gulps. He could feel it beginning to drill holes inside his head.

So Riley cried. But it wasn't now that he cried; he was still too shocked to cry now, too unfamiliar with the process of grief. It wasn't until later, until he had called on Natalie and she had held his hand, given him badly made tea and a hot meal and suggested politely that he take a bath. It was the first bath Riley had had in as long as he could remember, maybe since that night at his parents' house. He lay back in the warm water, he felt it cling to him and cleanse him, and he felt the regret begin to smother him. And that's when it happened. At first he mistook the tears for bathwater, so alien to him was the notion of crying. But after he dabbed at them with a towel he found that his face was still wet. His eyes felt red and stingy, and his mind kept casting itself back to the night he had lain with his head buried in Irene's breast and told her about Longdon; and that's when he was forced to accept what was happening to him. He was crying. Once he realised this, he felt a strange sense of relief. It was OK, he was safe here, no one would ever need to know. He could simply lie here and let it happen.

By the time he was able to arrest the flow of tears the water was growing cold, but he hardly noticed. He was struck by an urgent, very specific and familiar need. He called out to Natalie.

She came to the door and said, 'Yes?'

'I want to ask you something.'

'You don't mind I come in?'

'Uh . . . no.'

It hadn't occurred to Riley there was anything to mind. In any case nothing untoward was visible through the stagnant grey bathwater.

'What do you want?' Natalie asked. Just like a foreigner. Direct. Brilliant.

'I need a cigarette,' said Riley gruffly. 'Is it OK if I smoke?'

'In the bath?'

'Yeah.'

She thought about this for a moment, then shrugged. 'OK ... why not.'

'The thing is ... could you roll it for me? My hands are a bit wet.' He showed her. His fingers still bore traces of years-old embedded dirt, but the skin was red and dripping and wrinkled like a pensioner's.

She held up a finger. 'I have a better idea.'

She reappeared a couple of moments later with an ashtray, a lighter and a shiny silver cigarette case which she opened up to give Riley his choice of small, elegant, filterless French smokes. Riley felt like he was being offered a Cuban cigar or a line of top-quality cocaine. He took one gingerly; Natalie took one also, then offered him a light. She sat down on the toilet with the ashtray in one hand and her cigarette in the other and they both smoked in silence, looking intently at each other. She had also brought in a small pink plastic box, which she referred to as a *cassette*, which she placed on top of the toilet cistern. She had been putting these all over the house since Riley had come in; they gave off strong wafts of lavender which she claimed were to repel mosquitoes, but which, Riley had a sneaking suspicion, were actually being used to counter his own, distinctly non-lavendery smell.

Finally Natalie said: 'You can stay here ... as long as you want to. No: I *would like* you to stay. As long as you want to.'

No fucking about. Straight to the point. You just come out with it, old girl.

Riley nodded.

'And when you are ready, I want you to tell me about you and Irene. I like to listen to the stories of other people.'

Riley stubbed out his cigarette and sank back into the water. 'I'll tell you now,' he said. 'I'll tell you anything you want to know. It's no big secret. Where do you want me to start?' He thought about it. 'At the beginning, I suppose.'

'No,' said Natalie with a smile. She was already fishing herself out another cigarette. 'At the end. Start at the end.'

'The end?'

'It's the best way to tell the stories of love. You start with the last time you saw her, or spoke with her, or wrote her a letter. Then you tell me about the time before and then the time before and so on, until you finish with the first time you saw her. Or, better, the first time you fell in love with her . . .'

The first time he saw her: the first time he fell in love with her. 'Same difference,' Riley said. He thought about this. It was going to be complicated. Remembering things the right way round was hard enough. At least he knew where he was going, though. The funeral. He had to end up at Andy's funeral; as long as he kept focused on that he couldn't go far wrong.

'OK. So: the last time?'

'The last time . . .' Riley put his hands behind his head, spilling some water on the floor. 'The last time, yeah. I got this letter from her, right?'

Riley

I got this letter from her, right? I was still in hospital. Irene had addressed it to me at the barracks, but I was still in the army hospital at Wroughton recovering from the attack on the train when I got it. This time the envelope had obviously been opened and then clumsily sealed up again. The letter inside already had a second-hand reek about it. As with Irene's first letter to me, I read it once and then quietly burned it.

When I was discharged from the hospital, Lieutenant Foster had me in for another one of his little chats. He congratulated me on my recovery, welcomed me back to active duty and told me that in his opinion I had a bright future in the Paras ahead of me if I could keep focused on it. I thanked him. Our visit to the pub, my promise, the beating on the train, he never mentioned them. Just a few more things in my life that Never Happened.

I wandered around in a daze for a couple of days, not sure what I ought to do, how I ought to be taking this. Then, that Friday night

I went down the pub and, what with one thing and another, I never came back.

Officially I went AWOL; no doubt there's some bureaucratic berk in glasses sitting in an army office still trying to track me down. But I didn't just go AWOL from the army, I went AWOL from my entire life. From my mind.

I'd love to tell you what happened during the next few years, but the specifics of it are long, long gone. Not that they'd be of much interest anyway. What happened was: I drank. I drank until I forgot what it was like to be sober, that there was even such a thing as sober. I forgot also that there was such a thing as Irene; it was easier than you might think. She disappeared so completely from my thoughts it was like she had never existed. I drifted around London, on and off the streets, in and out of hostels, until one summer I decided to move down to the south coast. Just on a whim. Some of the blokes I was hanging around with had done it and I fancied a change of scene. I stayed in a B&B on the outskirts on Brighton, signed on, supposedly looked for work, actually spent all my time sitting on the beach, staring out at the sea, like I used to do when I was a kid. Still drinking. I was supported in this move by Social Security: we were all supposed to be 'getting on our bikes' to look for work, and if they didn't mean getting on our bikes down to the seaside, well, they should have said so. I ended up staying for ages; if things had worked out differently, who knows, I'd probably still be there.

Then, this one day I got talking to a bloke called Alec. We were both trying to work the same pitch outside the Odeon. I was getting annoyed with him to be honest. There weren't enough pickings for two people in that spot and I had got there first. But then during the course of one of his ramblings, just as I was getting really pissed off and was thinking about decking the bastard to get rid of him, he let on he was from Eastbourne.

'Oh yeah?' I said. 'So am I.' And we went through the usual palaver of naming everyone we'd ever met from there to see if we knew anyone in common. We didn't.

Then he asked me: 'So, do you still have family there?'

'Yeah. My folks.'

'Go back much?'

I gave him a funny look. 'No ... I don't think it'd be a great idea.'

He gave me a funny look. 'What do you mean? They're your parents; you owe it to them to let them know once in a while that you're still alive ... And I bet you'd get a good nosh up out of them as well. Fuck's sake, it's only a few miles up the road.'

I thought about it some, then shook my head. 'Nah. Don't think so.' I'd managed to live down here the best part of two years and never felt the need to go the few miles home. Didn't see why I'd want to change that now.

He wasn't going to be swayed, though. 'Look, I've had a good day today,' he said. 'Here, take a fiver, fuck off my patch for the rest of the day and go and see your old girl ... yeah?'

I took the fiver; grabbed it out of his hand. I wasn't sure about the going home bit, but I didn't need to think twice about taking this bloke's money.

I did go, though. Not that day, but a couple of days later. He'd said just enough to make me feel guilty enough to go. I think I had some mad vision of the return of the prodigal son ... you know, fatted calves and fine wines etc. Forgetting for a moment that it was my *parents* I was going to see. Forgetting why I'd marched out on them in the first place. I was reminded as soon as I walked through the door: the old girl started slapping me around like I'd been sent home from school for being naughty rather than shown up out of the blue after seven years. Where had I been? she shouted at me. Why didn't I ever phone? Why didn't I have a job? What were these clothes I was wearing? I stood in the hallway, the front door wide open behind me while she shouted and punched and screamed and cried. My dad stood at the foot of the stairs, smoking a fag, looking confused. When it had quietened down, I tried to give my mum a hug, but she pushed me away and said: 'Go and have a wash first.' That's one of the things about life on the streets, one of the crosses you have to bear: people keep trying to bathe you.

So I had a bath and then we had our family hug and then we even had that big nosh-up that Alec had promised, which was absolutely spot-on. I used to hate my mum's cooking when I was growing up, but after all those years of army food and hand-out slop, a simple home-cooked shepherd's pie was the business. While we all chomped away, and while things seemed to have calmed down a little, I tried to explain what had happened. Why I didn't have a job or a home or any of the other things they might have expected me to have. I tried to tell them that now I was free from the army, there was no way I could ever go back to working a regular job. Whatever it was. I didn't have it in me to be at a certain place at a certain time every day, to be sober and presentable, to be answerable to a pompous bastard who hated my guts and whose guts I hated. I couldn't even imagine, in the foreseeable future, living with a roof over my head. Once you got a flat you immediately had hassle: bills and repairs and poll tax and what have you. I didn't care a lot about money and I didn't give a shit about how I looked and I was quite happy to sacrifice both of these things for the freedom to get up in the morning and go where I pleased. From the expressions on their faces, it was clear my folks hadn't got a clue what I was trying to say. The old girl looked like she was about to become hysterical again so I shut up.

After the meal, as we were cleaning the dishes away, my dad suddenly had an idea. 'Just a minute,' he said, and he went rummaging in the cluttered drawers of their rickety old sideboard. He searched through all of them before he found what he was looking for, a crumpled piece of card which he presented to me proudly. 'This came for you,' he said.

I couldn't help a small smile. I hadn't been home in seven years and this was it, the sum total of all my mail. I took it and uncrumpled it. It was a Christmas card with a picture of a stable and a couple of round, rosy-cheeked cherubs on the front. Inside there was an address and the simplest message: Happy Christmas, My Love. Irene. Immediately I felt the tears burning at the back of my eyes.

'Came . . . ooh, five or six Christmases ago I should think,' the old man said. 'We didn't know where to send it on to.'

Later I tore out Irene's address from the rest of the card and carried it with me. Always. When that card got too tatty I copied it out, carefully, on to another piece of paper. I suppose you could say it was worth the trip home just to get the card, to get that address. But overall it was a depressing experience. I left the following morning and I haven't been back since. I don't think they're waiting up for me.

I left Brighton too. I'd been there a long time. After that visit it seemed a little too close to home; or maybe I just fancied another change of scene. I went back to London and set myself up in the Bullring at Waterloo. It was a funny old summer. First of all stories began appearing in the papers, serious allegations now, about war crimes supposedly committed by members of the Parachute Regiment during the Falklands War. These centred around the murder of one or more prisoners of war, depending on who you believed, and then expanded to include wild and lurid tales of Argies being suffocated in their own shit-pit and ears being removed from corpses as trophies. They reappeared even more forcefully the following year when one of the other ex-Paras wrote a book about the war, but I was never able to work out if they were referring specifically to me. There were stories about POWs being lined up on a cliff above a body pit and shot, one by one, down into the pit; stories about American mercenaries being systematically murdered to cover up Yank involvement in the war. I half-expected to see Foster's face in the papers one day, smearing my name all over the place – it wouldn't have been any more far-fetched than the stuff that was being reported – but it never happened.

Then, later that summer, Saddam invaded Kuwait and the rest of the year was taken up waiting for the Gulf War to happen. And what a war that turned out to be: that huge, horrible, long build up, just waiting for it all to go off, and then wham, bam, blink and you've missed it. I found myself feeling a little jealous of the boys going out to the Gulf. Once again it was OK to be a soldier. I saw this thing on TV which said that army recruitment centres up and down the land were being besieged by eager, patriotic young blokes. The recession was starting to kick in and there was no end of unemployed, unemployable thugs who wanted nothing better than to get out there and fuck up some towelheads. I was sorely tempted to join them. But I knew it wasn't really on. The army had records, they'd have been on to me as soon as I signed my name and I'd have spent the whole war in a military prison for desertion. Anyway, there were still nights when I closed my eyes and saw the faces of those Argie conscripts, those letters, those matchboxes with the ships on them; and every time I saw them I knew I'd never go soldiering again.

I kept myself reasonably straight during this time. Not teetotal by any means, but together enough to read a paper every day and follow what was going on. I even started to write a little again. It could have been another one of those turning points. If I'd had a break at *this* stage, I'm sure things would've worked out differently. But it never happened. The war ended and it started snowing. I saw out the rest of the winter at a night shelter in Hammersmith before going back to the Bullring, where I started drinking even more heavily than before.

I hadn't escaped. Deep down I hadn't really wanted to. I'd simply taken a couple of short breaths of a normal life before allowing the current to suck me back under again.

21.10

They drove for maybe ten miles with Jonquil holding the gun at Frank's head, screaming; Frank with his foot pressed to the floor, singing and shouting; Peter curled up in the back, shaking. Actually none of them had any idea how long this went on for. It could have been ten miles, it could have been a hundred miles, it could have been just one very long mile.

But eventually Jonquil lowered the gun, and started crying. Frank stopped singing. He kept his foot to the floor, though, and when he judged the time was right he put a hand on Jonquil's knee. Instinctively she tightened her grip on the gun and raised it again, but when she realised it was only Frank attempting in his oafish way to be kind, she went back to crying. The crying then descended into sobs, then into sniffs, before dying out altogether, leaving an uneasy calm.

Frank tried to keep his mind focused on his list of place-names, checking them off as the road signs flashed by, counting down the kilometres in the hope that this would make the time pass more quickly. In fact they were making good time as far as he could tell. The roads they were on, although not motorways (Frank had remembered you had to pay for the motorways in France, so he'd deliberately avoided them) and rarely more than one lane wide, were generally quite empty. Now and again they came up against a long line of cars behind a slow lorry or farm vehicle. But on these occasions Frank would simply offer a silent prayer, drop a gear and scream past the queue, blaring his horn as he went if they happened to be on a blind corner. Such manoeuvres didn't raise a squeak from either Jonquil or Peter.

As he drove he found his mind wandering. Under different circumstances, he thought to himself, this would be a very pretty drive indeed – especially seen, as now, in the glow of early evening. The countryside they were driving through wasn't radically different to that at home, give or take the odd enormous field of sunflowers which looked especially attractive at this time of day; it was just that there was *more* countryside here. It was a quantity, not a quality thing. There were longer drives, he noticed, between towns than you were used to on A-roads at home. It was as if the countryside here had just that little bit more room to stretch out and make itself comfortable. And then occasionally – not often; maybe two or three times in the whole journey – they would come upon a long, open, straight road, flanked on either side by two perfect rows of tall trees standing smartly to attention, and outside the trees shimmering golden fields as far as the eye could see – roads so French they could have been lifted directly from a tourist brochure. And at

275

these points, if it hadn't been for the ubiquitous red and yellow signs telling them how many McDonald's restaurants there were in the next town, Frank might truly have felt abroad.

All these signs for burgers were making him hungry – they hadn't eaten since Joyce had force fed them those sandwiches on the ferry, and how very long ago that seemed now – but he didn't want to waste time driving around towns looking for burger bars, which probably wouldn't do any veggie food anyway. If there had been service stations, or roadside caffs, he'd have stopped at one of those, but all he could see were vans selling chips. There were a lot of these: caravans, VW vans, all sorts of dodgy-looking vans with a few sad plastic chairs outside them and a large sign proclaiming FRITES! They didn't look very appetising.

So he ploughed on, not letting his gas foot rest for a moment. They reached the outskirts of Orléans shortly before nine without a further word being spoken between them. It was just about dark enough for headlights. Here the buildings reminded Frank of nothing more than Purley Way and the summer he had spent working for OFM there: huge warehouse stores selling furniture, electrical goods, mobile phones and more furniture, a whole planet of shops.

He decided that now was the time to enlist some help. 'I'm just going to head for the centre of town,' he announced. 'The station will be near the centre, don't you reckon Peter?'

'Yeah, guess so,' said Peter, who didn't have a clue.

'OK, we'll follow these signs for *centre-ville*.'

Orléans looked grimmer and wilder than Calais. Maybe it was because it was now past dusk and the town was bathed in a purplish glow, but this seemed like an exciting and dangerous place to be. Or maybe it was just that they knew they were driving around with a gun trying to find a dangerous man.

Frank was now driving at the other extreme: at a snail's pace, so they could get a good look at all the buildings as they went past, which infuriated other drivers, who would gesticulate wildly at Frank as they overtook him, and Frank would shrug his shoulders and mouth *anglais* back at them by way of explanation. After a short while they came to a set of traffic lights where *centre-ville* was signposted straight on and *la gare* was off to the right.

'What now?' said Frank.

'Straight on, I reckon,' said Peter. 'We don't want to go to *gare* do we. What's the point of that?'

'*Gare* means station, Peter.'

'It does?'

'Yes.'

'Oh well. Let's go right, then.'

'I think we should go straight on,' said Jonquil, opening her mouth for the first time in about two hours.

'But we want to head for the station,' said Frank. 'That's all we know, that avenue de Paris is near the station.'

'Yeah, but that's a fairly small road off to the right. I reckon it's just a short cut or something. We're less likely to get lost if we stick to the main roads, you know? And anyway stations are always in town centres, aren't they.'

'Are they?'

'Of course they are.' The lights changed. 'Come on, let's go straight on,' Jonquil repeated.

Frank turned right. They followed the small road down a gentle hill until it came out at a T-junction with a signpost for neither *centre-ville* nor *la gare*. Jonquil, somehow, managed not to say I told you so.

'Left,' she suggested.

'Right,' said Peter at the same time.

If he could have driven straight on, Frank would have done, but directly in front of them was what looked like the municipal swimming baths. So in the interests of preserving what remained of his tattered relationship, and because he felt it was probably correct, he turned left. A couple of turnings later and they emerged on a wide boulevard lined with flags, the flags of the EEC countries as far as Frank could make out, just as it became dark enough to trigger the street lights, which flashed on all around them like the bulbs of the paparazzi.

'This looks more like a ring road than anything else,' Frank muttered.

Ahead of them was a large roundabout with a newly illuminated fountain and more flags, this time arranged in a circle. Frank turned right here, back down towards what he imagined to be the centre of Orléans.

'There it is!' said Jonquil excitedly.

Frank nearly crashed the car. There indeed, on the right, nestling almost apologetically behind a large, glass-panelled office block, in which the flags and the fountain of the roundabout were mosaically reflected, was a squat, grey, concrete building with a load of wires and trains coming out of the back of it. Trains. If there were trains coming out of the back of it, it had to be a station.

'OK, there's the *gare*,' Frank said. 'Now all we need—'

Jonquil was looking to her left, however. 'No, you idiot. There's the place.'

They could easily have missed it, it was so obvious. Frank had been expecting a well-hidden, seedy dive, but the place Jonquil was pointing to was a large, brash nightclub, slap bang opposite the station. There was a vast cut-out of a black cat above the door, its eyes lit up, bulbs flickering to make it look like it was winking. LE CHAT NOIR was spelled out in foot-high flashing green neon letters.

'Well, something's gone right at least,' said Frank. It was on the other side of the road, so he executed a smart U-turn and pulled up in the gaping parking space right outside the venue. A grubby blue sign on the wall next to the club confirmed the road as avenue de Paris. He was tempted to thank the Lord for this piece of providence, but felt it would probably be pointed out to him that if the Lord really was with them perhaps this whole gun thing would never have happened in the first place. He cut off the engine and went to open the door.

'No, I think I ought to do this on my own,' said Peter. 'It might make them nervous, you know, if we all troop in there.'

This was absolutely fine with Frank. He pulled the door to again.

Then they sat in silence for a moment, waiting for something to happen.

'I, uh . . . I need the gun,' Peter pointed out.

'Oh yes. Yes, of course,' said Jonquil, becoming flustered. She paused briefly before handing over the weapon, handle first, as though she was passing the butter knife at a dinner party.

Peter took it and hid it away in one of his coat's many pockets. He climbed out of the car, shut the door and then, thinking of something else to say, knocked on Jonquil's window. Jonquil wound it down and Peter leaned in with one hand flat on the roof. Although he appeared to have sobered up, his breath still smelled of closing time.

'Maybe you'd better leave the engine running,' he said. 'You know, just in case.'

Whatever relief Frank and Jonquil might have felt at finding this place and finally getting the gun out of the car was neatly destroyed by this last casual remark. This wasn't over yet. It did occur to Jonquil that they might just bugger off at this point and leave Peter to it; they'd got him and his damn gun to where he needed to be, hadn't they. He could make his own way back from here, surely. But she didn't fancy her chances of convincing Frank of this and she couldn't be bothered trying.

So Frank switched the engine back on and they waited.

Peter took a deep breath and tried to muster up a purposeful march towards the club. Look hard, he told himself repeatedly. Look hard. That's the only way to deal with people like this; show fear and they won't respect you and then you'll be in trouble. You've got to look hard. Look hard.

Look fucking sober, at least.

Inside Le Chat Noir, the décor was as literal as it was on the outside. It revolved around black cats. Black cats everywhere, in a variety of different poses (the black cat with shades on, holding a pool cue was particularly popular). The look of the whole place was . . . well, it was black, and quite possibly it was meant to be feline as well. You could hardly see a damn thing. The only light was given off by the two giant video screens showing shaky images of people being burned at the stake and the strobe on the tiny, cramped dancefloor at the far end of the room, where a clutch of scantily clad – but scantily clad in black – girls were dancing to a song that sounded like it featured Dracula on lead vocals. Everyone wore black, even the young men posing around the bar were posing around the bar dressed in black. Everyone wore black, but their faces were all white. Not white as in Caucasian – although there wasn't of course a single ethnic face to be seen – but white as in *white*, as in the opposite of *black*. It was trying its hardest to be scary, this place, in fact it seemed to exist simply in order to be scary, but Peter felt strangely comforted as he breezed past the suits on the door without making eye contact. People who looked this self-consciously weird, who had to go to all this *effort* to be weird, didn't bother him; he'd have felt a lot more threatened if they'd been old geezers playing cards and staring into their pints and muttering. Feeling his way in the dark, he made a path for the bar, the other small oasis of light, near the dancefloor. He pushed his way past some of the posing young men on barstools and waved at the barman.

'*Oui monsieur?*' said the barman, having ambled over towards him extremely slowly.

'*Monsieur le Blanc!*' Peter shouted above the din of the music.

The barman laughed and started to walk away. Peter grabbed his arm. That's it; look *hard*.

'I've been sent by George Johnson in London ... England ... I'm here to see ...' Peter consulted his piece of paper; he'd been practising this name on the way down, '... Mister, *Monsieur*, Jean-Pierre le Blanc ... I have something for him.'

The barman's expression changed and he told Peter to wait. While he was gone Peter was left to gaze at the sparkling array of bottles behind the bar. He wondered if any other human being had ever needed a drink as much as he did now.

The barman returned and without a word led Peter over to a door by the dancefloor. He opened the door but didn't follow Peter through. When Peter turned back to face him, he just said, 'Up,' and indicated a staircase straight ahead.

When the door was shut it became quite dark, but at least, mercifully, the music was quieter. Peter spent a moment looking for a light switch and then gave up and groped for the stairs in the dark.

On his way up he reached into his coat and took out the gun. As well as practising le Blanc's name he'd also been thinking long and hard in the car about how he was going to enter this room. Everything depended on how he entered the room. He reached the top of the stairs and paused for breath, as much because he was simply unfit as because he was nervous. There was a door directly in front of him. Without giving doubts time to cross his mind, Peter kicked it open and leaped through, swinging the gun around in front of him. 'OK, which one of you is le Blanc?' he shouted.

He was met immediately by the three clicks of three cocked pistols which appeared inches away from his face. A smart, middle-aged man, also dressed head to toe in black, but somehow a different kind of black to the ice-people downstairs, approached him and said: 'I am Jean-Pierre le Blanc.'

'Uh . . . hello,' said Peter, unsure of what to do next. He seemed to have overestimated his element of surprise.

'I see you've brought my gun back,' said le Blanc.

'Uh . . . yeah.'

'Well. Are you going to give it to me or are you just going to wave it around in front of my face?'

'Uh . . . yeah,' said Peter again. He wasn't looking *quite* as hard as he'd hoped to at this stage.

Unable to see any other options, Peter handed over the gun. Le Blanc seized it and immediately turned it on Peter. He now had four guns inches away from his face. He wished he'd looked a little harder for other options.

'NOBODY POINTS A GUN AT ME IN MY OWN OFFICE!' le Blanc shouted. 'YOU . . . MOTHERFUCKER!' He pronounced it *mothère-fuckère*. His heavily accented voice sounded comical but there was an authentic menace behind what he was saying. He shouted a few more well-learned English insults and then drifted off into French, which Peter couldn't understand but which presumably meant something along the lines of don't ever point a gun at me again, you motherfucker.

Then, when he was finished shouting, le Blanc lowered the gun and began gazing at it fondly. He turned it over a few times in his hands and stroked the shaft. 'Still,' he said much more quietly, 'you brought me my gun back, eh?'

'Yeah, I did.' Peter nodded eagerly, pouncing on the first real sign that they might let him live.

'You know, this is my favourite gun.' Le Blanc was still staring at it fetishistically. 'It is beautiful, no, the way the front is tapered like this? And this little V-shape at the back . . .' He showed it for Peter to admire and indicated for his men to lower their less attractive weapons.

Peter exhaled and looked at the gun closely, making suitably admiring noises. He was starting to relax now. It was OK. Coming in with guns blazing had been a mistake, but a forgivable one. It was OK.

'They used to make these in France,' le Blanc went on. 'They used to be standard issue for the French army, but no more. These days the French army is run by pussy cats. All they teach you is how to cook and how to polish your shoes. They don't have weapons any more, it would offend the liberals.'

He moved away from under Peter's nose and began to pace around his office. It was a large room, most of which was taken up by a large boardroom table. There was a desk at one end and at the other a sofa, a couple of armchairs and a TV. The walls were covered with a delicate mix of posters advertising forthcoming events at the club and posters advertising the *Front National*. The thump thump thump of the music was audible through the floor.

Le Blanc was still concerned with his gun. 'So I had to buy this one from a man in Serbia. They still know how to run an army over there; they've still got a war to fight. It's worth nearly five hundred dollars on the black market. But . . .' Now he was bringing the gun to his lips, '. . . to me, it is much, much more.'

'Yeah, it's very beautiful,' said Peter. Then he coughed. Then he said: 'Mr Johnson said you might, uh, you might give me something for returning it to you safely.'

Le Blanc smiled at him, the smile of a kindly uncle or of a child-molester luring his victim. 'Are you a homosexual?' he said.

'I beg your pardon?'

'Mr Johnson told me he was sending a homosexual.'

'Oh, I see,' Peter started to explain. 'No, that was the other guy—'

'We like to identify homosexuals here,' le Blanc interrupted him. He took a pink triangle from a drawer in his desk and pinned it to Peter's coat.

Peter shrugged. If the French loony with the gun wanted him to be a poof, he could be a poof. 'So. Are you going to give me something?' he asked.

That smile again. 'Oh yes,' said le Blanc. 'With very great pleasure.'

And he raised the beautifully crafted Franco-Serbian pistol, pointed at Peter's head and pulled the trigger.

The empty chamber went click.

The silence, where there should have been the crack of a shot, was roaring and immense and echoed around the room.

'You are a very lucky homosexual,' le Blanc observed calmly. 'Mr Johnson told me he was returning this to me with the bullets.'

01.05

The bullets, fifteen of them, were actually in an old Marks and Spencer's bag in Candy's locker back at Stamford Street. The first thing she had done when George Johnson's men dropped her off (dropped quite literally; they had stopped the car a few yards up the road, kicked her out and screeched off again) had been to shakily empty the weapon and hide the ammunition. Things felt a whole lot safer once she knew the gun was empty.

Then she went to wash her face, and tend to her cuts and bruises as best she could. She washed the blood off her cheek and chin, where they had cut her, and kept dabbing at them until the flow was stemmed. She knew she had to be in some considerable pain, but she was unable to feel it through the blanket of shock. She tried to make herself feel it; she put her hands to her temples, closed her eyes and tried to *force* the pain out. Pain would be at least a gesture towards normality. But it wouldn't come. She ran some water through her hair and changed out of her torn and bloody top. When she was feeling as human as was likely under the circumstances, she went back to her room and lay down on her bed.

And burst out crying. She hated herself for doing so. She couldn't afford to cry now, she didn't have the time. She was in a jam: she had to keep a clear head and work out what she was going to do. She had to *think*; and you couldn't think and cry at the same time. So she fought back the tears. She rubbed at her eyes until they were scarlet and cotton-woolly and there was no room for the tears to escape, until it was a physical impossibility for her to cry any more. And she thought. She thought and thought and thought.

And then she thought of Peter.

Peter. Peter Peter . . . peterpeterpeterpeterpeter . . . She rolled the name exquisitely around her tongue.

Peter. It was brilliant. She couldn't envisage herself carrying the gun over to France, breaking away from the rest of the group and taking it down to this le Blanc. She simply didn't have it within her to do something like that. But, knowing what she knew about Peter Freeman, she *could* envisage forcing him to do it for her.

Suddenly awash with relief, she bounced up off the bed. She picked up the gun and took a nearly empty bottle of gin out of her locker and went to look for Peter. She wasn't sure which room was his, but it turned out to be fairly easy to identify: she simply headed for the room with the loudest, most elephantine snores emanating from it. It was the last room along the corridor. She pushed open the door gently and once she had made sure it really was Peter in this room, she sat down by his bed. Taking the gun in her left hand, she slowly stroked his cheek with it. It took a while to rouse him, but when his eyes finally opened, and then bulged as he realised he had a pistol in his face, she slapped a hand over his mouth to muffle the screams and said, 'Sshh!'

As he became accustomed to his situation, Peter's muffles subsided and sounded not unlike his snores. Only quieter.

Candy said: 'Now, if I take my hand away, are you going to make a sound?' She pressed the gun closer to his face.

Peter shook his head. She slowly took her hand away and he kept to his word.

'What are you going to do with that shooter?' he asked when he was able to speak.

'I'm going to give it to you.'

'No, I mean really.'

'Really,' she said, and she offered it to him.

He hesitated, wondering if this might be a trick, and then took it.

'Where did you get it?' he asked.

'It's not mine.

'Yeah . . .'

'It belongs to George Johnson.'

At the sound of the name Peter threw the gun down on to the bed, as though it had suddenly become white hot. *He'd been holding George Johnson's gun!* There were penalties for that, weren't there. Severe penalties. George Johnson didn't like nobody touching his shooter without permission.

Candy took a deep breath. 'He wants you to take this gun to France on the trip tomorrow, give the rest of the group the slip and then take it to this man at this address.' She gave Peter the piece of paper with le Blanc's details on it.

'Why me?' asked Peter. 'I mean, what's the point of that? He doesn't even know me.'

'Well . . . he asked me to do it. And now I'm asking you.'

'Why me?' Peter asked again.

'Because there's no way I can do it. I'm too . . . well, I can't do it, that's all.'

Peter examined the gun. 'Is it loaded?'

Candy didn't miss a beat. 'Yeah.'

He pointed it at her. 'So I could shoot you, yeah? And then I wouldn't have to do what you said.'

She shook her head. 'If you shoot me, you'll be arrested. And if you're arrested you won't be able to take the gun to France. And if you don't deliver this gun, Johnson'll come looking for you – in prison or on the outside, whatever. I've told him you'll be taking care of things on my behalf. It wouldn't be a great idea to let him down.'

'But now I've got the gun,' Peter said. 'I could make *you* take it.'

'But in order for me to take it, you'd have to give it to me. Then I could point it at you and we'd be back to square one.'

Peter's eyes glazed over as he tried to work through the logic of this.

'*And*,' said Candy, selecting the final ace from a well-stocked hand and preparing to play it, 'and I know about you and the telly.'

'What telly?' Peter pretended without much hope.

'The one downstairs. I know that it was you that nicked it. You sold it to Sparky at the market.'

'How . . . ?'

'I heard Riley talking about it. He saw it on Sparky's stall, Pete. You sold it to a guy five minutes walk away. I'm surprised no one else noticed it.'

Peter turned away. *Bollocks*.

'If you don't do this for me, not only will you have George Johnson on your back, but I'll tell Philip about you and the telly. He'll go loopy . . . You know how mad he got when it went missing.'

Flipping Philip or George Johnson: who was the scarier? Peter looked sadly at the gun. Only he, only *he* could be holding a loaded shooter and still be the one taking orders.

Candy opened her bottle and poured Peter a capful. She went through the arguments again for him a few more times and when she was convinced he had taken on board the gravity of the situation, she left him to it. Peter got out of bed and hid the gun in one of the pockets of his coat, which was draped over the back of his chair. He was already formulating his plan: he was going to finish off this gin Candy had left him (as though that made it all right! A little drop of gin in return for risking his life and getting involved with George Johnson. Fucking piss-taking, shirtlifting . . .), and then he was going to try and sleep so hard that when he woke up tomorrow it would all be a dream. And if that failed – if tomorrow really did barge uninvited into his life, and if it really did turn out to be as shit as he was expecting it to be – then he'd simply drink all day until he didn't give a toss any more. This was in fact Peter's plan for life in general, and he found it adapted pretty well to suit most circumstances.

Back in her own room, Candy fell into a sore and fitful sleep. She dreamed it was tomorrow evening already and she was safely home again.

21.30

Home again safely that evening, however, Candy found it still wasn't over. For a start she still had the bullets to get rid of. If she left them lying around sooner or later they'd be discovered, either by a cleaner or a thief. She opened the locker and emptied the small, incriminating pieces of metal into a polythene bag. She decided to wait until most people were asleep and then go for a little walk and drop the evidence in a bin somewhere. Somewhere a good long way away from the hostel. She wouldn't have to wait long; it was late already. It had been after nine o'clock when they got back to Stamford Street; Joyce wasn't the fastest driver in the world and they had got hopelessly lost trying to pick out a short cut through the tail end of the rush hour traffic. Even once she'd got rid of the bullets, though, it still wouldn't be over. It wouldn't be over until Frank and Jonquil and Peter were back and she knew the job was done and they were safe and, even more importantly, she knew they weren't so angry with her that they were going to report the matter to Philip and have her booked out. It wouldn't really be over until she had been back to BabyCakes on Saturday night and sung again and not been picked up by George Johnson.

She sent a prayer out to Frank and Jonquil. They'd be on their way home now, she imagined, feeling proud of themselves at how they'd handled the situation. Probably laughing about it already.

21.30

At half past nine their time, in fact, Frank and Jonquil were still sitting in their hire car outside Le Chat Noir, engine running, not knowing quite what to say to each other. What could they say? Their relationship had suddenly gone way beyond the point where things like previous experience or therapy or self-help books could be of much use. It inhabited a world all of its own now. They seemed to have moved straight from the getting-slightly-annoyed-with-each-other-first-thing-in-the-morning stage to the pointing-guns-at-each-other-while-driving-at-high-speeds stage in one giant leap, without stopping at any of the gentler, saner points in between.

What *were* you supposed to say to your partner in situations like this? Was there a chapter in *Men Are From Mars, Women Are From Venus* that covered it?

'We should talk,' Jonquil tried, after they had been sitting in silence for some time.

'Yeah . . . ? What about?'

'You know, this. Us.'

'What about us?'

'What we've just been through . . . things have changed.'

'Have they?'

'I don't know. I . . . I want to know if they have.'

In front of them was parked a yellow, German-registrated camper van with the words 'Destination Further' and some clouds painted on the bonnet. Pressed up against its windscreen, Jonquil could make out a battered, well-thumbed paperback, *Angst vorm Fliegen* by Erica Jong. She imagined this van packed with liberated, unshaven German women, driving around Europe, having impossible amounts of sex in between reading and discussing feminist literature. She was sorely, sorely tempted to leave Frank here and now, just get out of the car and walk away, to wait by that van until the Germans showed up and demand that they take her with them wherever they were going. Wherever *further* was.

'You want to talk about this now?' Frank asked.

'I don't know . . . I guess not.'

More silence.

Only interrupted by the sight of Peter tearing out of Le Chat Noir, his arms waving, his voice wailing blue murder.

Frank's heart froze. He revved up the engine and released the handbrake. Peter leaped theatrically into the back seat and screamed: 'FUCKING DRIVE!' Frank hit the gas and the car screeched away from the kerb. Peter had been followed out of the club by the two bouncers on the door and two of le Blanc's men from upstairs, any of whom could have caught him if they'd chosen to. Le Blanc's men were both armed. They could have shot out the wheels of the car as it drove away, but Peter wasn't important enough to risk drawing the attention of the police for. He was only an English homosexual.

Frank of course wasn't to know any of this so he drove like a lunatic anyway – he was getting pretty good at this. At the roundabout with the flags and the fountain he yanked the car round to the right. For all he knew there was an entire motorcade assembling behind them, every two-bit crook in the manor being roped in to help run them out of town. He glanced in the mirror. Nothing there. But that didn't mean they weren't being followed, simply that the motorcade was grouped just out of view.

'We should zig-zag,' said Jonquil as the smell of burning rubber reached her nostrils. 'Try and shake them off.'

'Good idea,' said Frank, hurtling into the next left. This took them down to a large square with an imposing green, bird-shat statue of a young woman on a horse – Joan of Arc quite possibly – surrounded by yet more flags.

'This square looks kind of pedestrianised,' Jonquil observed.

'Well, the pedestrians had better get out of the way, then,' said Frank, slowing down only marginally.

'And if it isn't pedestrianised, it's most definitely a roundabout.'

Frank looked over at her. 'So . . . ?'

'It's just that if it *is* a roundabout . . . we're going around it the wrong way.'

True. They were passing to the left of the statue, travelling clockwise. However, by the time Frank had worked out what she meant and worked out that she was in fact right, they were already – much to the amusement of the locals just beginning to assemble at the various café terraces – well round the roundabout.

And out on to the longest, most immaculately straight road either Frank or Jonquil had ever seen. It stretched out in front of them like a runway, lit up on either side by yellow streetlights, and seemed prepared to take them as far as they wanted to go. There was no other traffic around so Frank pounded his foot to the floor again and accelerated until the car shook. 'Not sure if they're keeping up with us,' said Peter, peering nervously out of the back window. They shot across an old lanterned stone bridge which rose to a V in the middle, at which point the car actually left the road for a couple of seconds before crashing back down again, as though it believed for a moment it was in San Francisco. Frank realised he had been seduced by the longness and straightness of this road into neglecting his zig-zagging, so at the end of the bridge he turned sharply left, tyres yelping on the tarmac, then shortly after this he turned right into a maze of side streets. And after that he turned this way and that as the fancy took him, always trying to cancel out a left with a right and vice-versa so they would keep going in vaguely the same direction. After about five more minutes of this, Jonquil stopped him.

'Slow down, Frank. I think we've lost them.'

Frank reacquainted himself with the brake pedal and slowed the car down to a crawl. He checked their surroundings, trying to work out where the hell they might be. Somewhere on the very outskirts of town unless they'd managed to drive around in a hideously large circle. He looked at Peter in the rear-view mirror.

'What in God's name was going on back there then?'

'He shot at me,' said Peter, still shaking.

'Who did?'

'The man ... Le Blanc. The one I gave the gun to.'

'Did he hit you? Are you hurt?'

Immediately, and shamefully, Frank's thoughts turned to his deposit. You weren't supposed to return hire cars with blood all over them, were you.

'No ... it was empty.'

'It was *empty*?' said Jonquil. They'd done all this under threat of an *empty* gun? 'Did you know that, Peter?'

'No!'

Frank pulled the car to a complete stop and turned round to face Peter. 'Did *he* know that?'

'Who, le Blanc? No ... I don't think so. I don't know.'

'But he still shot at you with your gun? The one you've been carrying round all day.'

'Yeah.'

'So you gave it to him.'

'Yeah.'

'So ... mission accomplished. We can all go home now, right?'

'Uh, yeah, I guess.'

They let this sink in. They could all go home now. Home ... Jonquil repeated the word to herself. Now it was within their grasp, the word had a strange, unfamiliar ring to it. She found it kept getting forced from her mind by the word *empty*.

As she murmured softly to herself, she found she was breaking into a yawn. At first she didn't understand it, why her face was creasing up like this, why her eyes were closing involuntarily, why a plunger seemed to be going down on her stomach. Then she remembered what it all meant: she was tired. Tired! Once she'd worked out what it was, it felt warm and comforting to be tired. Of course she was tired, she'd had a hell of a day. No, she wasn't just *tired*, you got tired from a day at work or a game of tennis; she was knackered. She was bushed. She was whacked, beat, pooped, fagged, fucked, all of these things, all wrapped up together. While the other two were still pondering the concept of home, still glancing occasionally out of the window to make sure they were truly alone, she began to rummage in her bag, checking she had the essentials. They were all here – hairbrush, mirror, tampons, book, even lipstick. She was sorted: home could wait.

'I think we should stop somewhere for the night,' she announced.

'I thought you wanted to get back,' Frank said.

'I did. That was a long time ago.' It seemed like a previous lifetime; a previous her. 'Now, it's late and we're exhausted and frightened, you know? And I think it would be much safer if we drove home sensibly tomorrow.' She pointed out a house a little further up the road they were on, which had the word CHAMBRES flashing in green neon in its window. 'I think we should stay there; it looks OK.'

'What if they're following us?'

'If they were following us I think we'd know about it,' said Jonquil. To make her point she cupped a hand to her ear and made a show of listening. There was nothing to be heard. They were in the quietest part of town on a quiet night.

'OK, what about the cost?'

'It doesn't look too expensive, that place. And don't tell me you haven't got your credit card with you.'

'And are we paying for him?' Frank indicated Peter with a disdainful jerk of the thumb.

'Well, I don't know . . .'

'Because he already owes me fifteen quid for that beer, remember.

Not to mention contributing towards the cost of hiring the car and the petrol . . .'

'Oh don't mind me. I'll just sleep in the car,' said Peter. 'I mean, what's the point of expensive hotels, eh? Perfectly good car.'

'Don't be silly, Peter. You can't spend all night in the car.'

'Slept in worse places,' said Peter, who had.

'Look, how's this – you still owe us for the beer and the petrol, but we'll pay for your room. OK?' Jonquil turned round to Peter, who nodded his agreement, and then she gave Frank a look which invited him to dare even think of arguing with her.

So that was that decided then. At long last, at exactly nine fifty-five in the evening, Jonquil – the senior member of staff on the trip – actually got her way on something. They parked the car in a secluded spot a few streets away – just in case – and got at a knockdown rate the last two rooms at the hotel, a single and a double, which allowed the owner to switch off his neon sign and go to bed himself. Although not before he'd reminded his guests, as he reminded all his English guests, that they were responsible – *personally* responsible, he liked to feel – for the death of the brave Maid.

'And therefore the entire tourist industry of this town, and consequently your livelihood,' Frank wanted to point out to him. 'Even though it happened five hundred years ago.' But he didn't say anything. It was too late to be arguing about this. Much, much too late. And anyway he needed the man to sell them some bread as it had become rapidly apparent, as the fear receded and the tiredness kicked in, that the three of them were starving. So he shrugged apologetically, in an attempt to convey the shame of a whole nation, and asked the man if he had a spare baguette. Shaking his head and tutting, the man sold them a hardening loaf for ten francs and they went up to bed.

Later that night, lying on the supposedly double bed, which in a very French way encouraged intimacy between the sleeping partners by practically forcing them to lie on top of each other, Jonquil watched Frank undress and tried to work out where the whole relationship thing stood now. They hadn't spoken – not *spoken* spoken – since Peter had brutally interrupted their halting discussion in the car park of Le Chat Noir, and Jonquil was desperate to know what Frank was thinking. Only a few hours ago she'd been pointing a gun, which they both believed to be loaded, at his head, and *she* hadn't known for sure whether or not she'd pull the trigger, so how could he? That *had* to have some kind of effect on his brain, on the way he thought of her. Didn't it? Some things you could sweep under the carpet, if you were the forgiving type. So you stayed out late and didn't phone . . . OK, just don't do it again. So you forgot my birthday/our anniversary/the amazing fuck we had last night . . . well, ho hum, we're all human. Even, *even* so you slept with someone else and now you want me back, you slimy toad . . . right, let's talk about it, sort it out, move on. *But not this*. Not the guns at head/driving at high speeds thing. This mattered. Whichever way you looked at, this mattered. Even if you were Mother Teresa (or *Saint* Joan of Arc, as all the signs around here reminded you proudly she was), you couldn't just forget this one. This mattered. She watched him hopping inelegantly from foot to foot as he pulled off his socks, unable to tell whether she found this endearing or pathetic; unable, in other words, to be sure that she still loved him.

The room was as cosy as the bed itself. The closeness of the four walls seemed to force you on to the bed; the bed then forced you on top of each other. The only other piece of furniture was a battered chest of drawers, on top of which stood a small black and white television. They had tried flicking around on it earlier on, to counter the awful absence of their conversation, but the only thing they could find was *The Thin Blue Line* dubbed into French, which was too surreal to contemplate. So they switched it off and munched their stale bread and sweaty cheese in silence. They considered opening one of their bottles of wine, but neither of them was really in the mood for drinking. A second door at the foot of the bed led into a cupboard-sized bathroom, where after they had eaten Jonquil enjoyed a long, steaming shower. Unprepared to be staying the night, she hadn't brought the wherewithal to wash herself properly, but just the feel of the hot water soaking her skin was wonderful after the day she'd had.

From the room next door there was audible and elephantine evidence (Frank recalled Candy's description of the sound from that morning and found it apt) that Peter was already fast asleep. Down to nothing but his boxer shorts, Frank climbed into bed next to Jonquil. She had put her T-shirt and knickers back on before re-emerging from the shower room. They didn't have their night clothes with them and the events of the day had reduced them to the status of platonic friends being forced to share a bed. With Jonquil lying on her back with her arms folded behind her neck, her preferred position for being deep in thought, there was only room for Frank to lie on his side, propped up on one elbow.

Say something, Jonquil thought as she turned her head to look Frank in the eye. Just say something, you bloody great oaf.

'Phew, what a day, eh?' he said eventually.

Jonquil stared at him. 'Is that the best you can manage?'

'What do you mean?'

'All the shit we've been through today, and all you can think of to say is *what a day*?'

Frank didn't know what to answer.

'It's left no lasting impression on you at all?' Jonquil went on.

'Well, yeah, it has actually.' He sounded nervous. Jonquil allowed her hopes to be raised just slightly. Maybe after all this had affected him. It would be difficult for him to find the words to express this, she had to remember. It was tougher for men. Even once he'd admitted to himself that he felt something, and then decided that he could bear to share his feelings, he still had to negotiate a way through the thick fog of male ego to find a *method* of communicating.

'I was just going to speak to you about it . . .' he began slowly.

'Yes . . . ?' Jonquil moved on to her side. Now they were lying facing each other, both propped up like a couple of Roman orgy-goers.

'Yeah,' said Frank. He reached out his free hand and began to stroke Jonquil's hair. 'I've been thinking about our . . . you know, our vow.'

'Our vow?' asked Jonquil.

Surely he wasn't going to suggest . . . ?

He was. 'Uh, yeah. You know. I was thinking we might, uh . . .'

Before he could finish the sentence, before he could blacken the air with the actual words, Jonquil leaped out of the bed. Unprepared, Frank rolled over into the middle. 'I don't believe it, Frank. You want to use what happened today as an excuse to try and *fuck* me?' She picked up her jeans and started pulling them on, tugging them on like she was taking part in a race.

'No! That's not true!' Frank shouted.

Jonquil paused mid-pull, only her right leg from the knee downwards had made it into the jeans so far. 'That isn't what you were going to suggest?'

'No . . . Well, yeah, but I wasn't going to put it like that.' (He'd been thinking the phrase *share a moment* might do the trick actually. But not fuck. Definitely not fuck.)

Jonquil resumed tugging. Frank carried on protesting.

'I just think . . . I just think we've, you know, crossed some sort of barrier here.'

'Too right we have,' said Jonquil, struggling with the zipper of her trousers.

'Look, this is only natural,' Frank tried. 'It's a reaction to stress and danger . . . OK, maybe I was wrong.'

Yeah, mate. Maybe you were.

Jonquil glared at him. He looked back at her pitifully. She sat down heavily on the bed, giving up on her jeans. Her hands had been too angry and fidgety to cope with the button, which had popped open as she tried to pull the zip up. She tried to carry on glaring, but she could feel it subconsciously being downgraded to a stare, and then finally to a look. A mere look, of pity, of disdain. Already she could feel the hate ebbing out of her. Why was she so hopeless at hating people? She saw his goofy, uncomprehending eyes pleading with her, the same dark brown eyes that had once drawn her in, and it was impossible to hate him.

And that, if she had to put a precise moment on it, is probably where it ended. When she realised she neither loved nor hated him, but merely felt a kind of sorry affection for him. Which was nothing, was it, *sorry affection*? You didn't kill and die for sorry affection. You didn't write songs about it or lie awake at night worrying about it. You couldn't be haunted by sorry affection. It was nothing. She ought to be crying, it struck her. She ought to be yelling and screaming and hitting him and biting him and calling him all the worst things she could think of. But she wasn't crying; she wasn't sure if she'd even know how any more.

She put a hand out and touched his arm. 'It's just that . . . this was one thing I really respected you for, you know?' she tried to explain. 'You had this thing that no one else I knew had, that most people would have found completely ridiculous, yet it was your principle and you stuck to it . . . and now it's gone.'

'I didn't really mean it,' said Frank, realising now that damage limitation was the order of the day. 'I'm glad you talked me out of it, made me see sense. It was just, like I say, the stress talking. I'd have only regretted it later.'

Jonquil turned to him and smiled. That really was it, then. *Smiling?* How could she possibly be smiling at a time like this? In a way it was a relief. If she didn't love him, there were so many things that didn't matter any more. If she didn't love him, for example, it didn't matter that he was insensitive; or that he was funny about working with her; or that often he seemed to forget that she was even there; or that he bit his fingernails, sometimes until they bled, and hogged the duvet and never cleaned out the bath. If she didn't love him, the fact that he had vowed not to have sex with her until they were married was simply of curiosity value, not something to lose sleep over in itself. Perhaps it didn't even matter that earlier this evening she had pointed a gun at his head and threatened to shoot. They were merely friends; the stakes had been lowered.

'Are you coming back to bed?' Frank asked, holding the covers open hopefully. He looked ludicrous, half-revealed in his skinny white body and his puffy, stripy boxer shorts.

Without answering, Jonquil slowly peeled off her jeans and climbed back in next to him. They lay for a while.

Then Frank said: 'You know, I'm glad we do this.'

'Do what?'

'Have these sensible discussions.'

Jonquil peered at him. The single ornamental table lamp in the room — on Frank's side of the bed; he'd made sure he got the side with the lamp (*but* . . . it didn't matter any more! She didn't love him!) — gave off a dull, pink glow through its moth-eaten shade, which made his profile look sinister. She didn't think there was anything remotely sensible about the discussion they'd just had. 'What do you mean?' she said.

'Well, you know, we could have had a big fight about all this, tantrums and fisticuffs. But we didn't. We had a solid, sensible discussion about it and now we're friends again.'

'Yeah,' said Jonquil, smiling some more.

They were friends again: friends.

They didn't discuss it, sensibly or otherwise, any further. They lay a while more without talking: a silence which might have been golden had it not been for the elephantine one's snoring next door. Then Frank reached over and switched off the light.

Frank immediately dropped off like a stone; inevitably it took Jonquil somewhat longer. She couldn't get comfortable in the small space allotted to her and she couldn't stand this long, tubular thing that was supposed to pass for a pillow. She couldn't pick it up when she was hot and bothered and beat it and turn it over to the cool, fresh side. It simply served to remind her she was a long way from home, in a place where even the little things were unfamiliar.

Eventually, beaten, she reached over Frank's head and switched the light back on again. Still he didn't stir. She picked up her book and turned it over a few times in her hands. She loved second-hand books; she loved trying to guess how many people had read them before her; the marks and creases on the pages seemed to tell a story as compelling as the words themselves. She had bought this book, she remembered, on her first date with Frank, at the book stall on the South Bank. And now, in the dusk of their relationship, she was finally getting round to starting it. She opened up the book and bent the front cover round behind the back. Smoothing down the first page of text, she began to read.

She read how the past was a foreign country. Apparently they did things differently there too.

Frank

I don't know what I'd do without her. Every so often, during torrid nights of dreaming, I catch glimpses of Jonquil-less worlds and they scare me to my bones. I wonder if these are the nights when she is unable to sleep, which she tells me happens quite frequently; the nights when she lies awake, her arms behind her head, and jealously wishes all sorts of evil and horrible things on my snoring, rested form. The nights she reads until four or five in the morning and then happily tells me the next day that the characters in her book mean more to her than I do.

Still, I am constantly cheered by our ability to talk to each other like sensible adults. These moods are never allowed to fester. They are dragged, naked and wriggling, out into the light where they quickly curl up and die. As long as we can continue to do this, continue to be brave and open and honest with each other, I don't think anything can touch us. We'll simply carry on, the relationship getting more and more solid. And I will never have to see those dark worlds for real . . .

23.59

Later, when she judged the coast to be clear, Candy took her plastic bag of bullets outside. Most of the other residents had drunk themselves into a stupor; the few that remained awake were in the wet room, bawling and barking at the television. The two night workers were fast asleep in the staff room. Candy crept out of the front door looking as suspicious as it was humanly possible to look while carrying a half-empty Marks and Spencer's bag.

In the yard outside the hostel, she noticed firstly that the minibus was still parked there, then that light was on inside it, and finally that Joyce was sitting with her head slumped over the steering wheel. Forgetting for a moment that she was supposed to be creeping away unnoticed, Candy went over and knocked on the window of the passenger door. Joyce leaped out of her skin, turned round and shrieked 'Candy!' in a voice of recognition, partly embarrassed at being caught being so morose like this, partly relieved that it was only Candy and not a mugger or a rapist knocking at her door.

Candy opened the door. 'What are you still doing here?'

'Just thinking,' said Joyce in a voice which tried to imply that it was perfectly normal for her to be sitting alone in this bus, just thinking, almost three hours after they'd got back to London. The juggling balls were sitting on top of the dashboard like three bright clowns' noses, which suggested that Joyce had been helping herself think by juggling. Something clearly wasn't right.

'What are you thinking about?' said Candy, climbing in and sitting next to her.

'Oh, you know. Today. How it went.'

'I thought it was a lovely day,' said Candy. 'It was really kind of you all to take us. I'm sorry it got . . . so messed up. But I had a good time, Dougal had a good time . . .'

'Dougal had a terrible time. Didn't you see his face when he came back from the supermarket without that pâté he'd been told to buy? He looked like he'd be traumatised for life.'

'OK . . . Well, I still had a good time . . . And *Mikey*: Mikey had a *fantastic* time.'

'Yes . . . I feel so silly for breaking down like that and shouting at him . . . I wonder if I'm really cut out for this job.'

'Of course you are,' said Candy uncomfortably – wasn't *she* supposed to be the fucked-up one? Wasn't Joyce supposed to be looking after *her*?

'It's just . . . I shouldn't have allowed him to get to me like that.'

Candy didn't know what to say, so she said: 'Why do you do this job? If you don't mind me asking.'

Joyce looked up. 'Why?'

'Yeah.'

'I don't know . . .' *Beth*, she was thinking. Beth Beth Beth Beth. But she couldn't have begun to explain it. 'I just wanted to do something to help people, I suppose.'

'Hmm . . .' Candy thought about this. 'Sounds kind of vague. You should ask Philip that question. He has the perfect answer.'

'He does?'

'Yeah. I asked him once, while he was booking out a friend of mine for, I don't know, looking at him in a funny way or something. I said, why on earth do you do this job? Do you actually enjoy doing stuff like this? And you know what he said. He said, because they pay me twenty thousand flipping pounds a year to do it, that's why, which is probably more than you'll earn in your entire life.'

'I don't get paid twenty thousand,' Joyce said.

'Yeah, same principle though.'

'And this helped you, did it?'

'Let me know where I stood.'

Joyce smiled. The kind of smile you smile when you've just stopped crying; when you've realised how foolish you were to cry in the first place.

'Do you fancy going for a drink?' Candy said suddenly. 'I still owe you one from the boat.'

'What . . . now?' said Joyce, looking at her watch. 'It's nearly midnight.'

'We're in the city that never sleeps,' said Candy with a twinkle.

'Well OK . . . if you think you know somewhere . . . what have you got in your bag?'

The twinkle disappeared. 'Oh nothing. Just . . . just some rubbish I'm getting rid of. Come on, start her up, let's hit the town.'

'Where are we going?'

'I know a tasteful little place in Soho. You'll love it, believe me.'

Tonight. Candy had realised she had to go back to BabyCakes tonight. To show that she wasn't afraid to do so. Once she had been back, she felt, *then* the nightmare would be over.

Joyce started up the engine and pulled away, still unsure if she really wanted to do this. It was late and she had work again the next day. On the other hand, she was churned up inside and it would be good to talk to someone.

Candy was ideal company. She chattered away and kept Joyce entertained while they drove. She described the events of the day, leaving out, obviously, the stuff Joyce didn't need to know about, and made them both laugh. She made Joyce see that it wasn't such a big deal after all. Mikey certainly wouldn't bear a grudge; he probably wouldn't even remember it in the morning. Inevitably they got lost on the way, but Joyce coped with it calmly, unlike earlier on that evening when traffic, short cuts and roads in general had all seemed like particularly cruel works of the devil.

By the time they reached the West End Joyce had even been persuaded to agree that it had, indeed, been a lovely day.

'Oh yes, I remember,' she said, reversing effortlessly into the last free space in Soho Square. 'While I was sitting feeling sorry for myself, I worked out Tom Riley's riddle.'

'Yeah?'

'You know, the one about the man going towards a field, knowing he's going to die.'

'I remember,' said Candy.

Joyce shut off the engine and looked at Candy, willing her to work it out for herself.

'Well?' said Candy, who couldn't see the point of working things out when there were people around to tell you.

'He's doing a parachute jump!' said Joyce. 'And his parachute hasn't opened, so he's going towards the field, vertically, and when he gets there he knows he's going to die. Easy!'

'Oh right,' said Candy, nodding. 'So Riley's the man, yeah?'

Joyce didn't understand. 'What do you mean?'

'Well he had that parachute accident, didn't he, when he was in the army.'

'Did he?'

'Yeah. I've heard him talking about it. Him and this other guy, a friend of his, they were on a training exercise when their parachutes got tangled up and Riley was really badly injured and his friend was killed.'

Joyce looked astonished. 'Really? I never knew that. Isn't that awful? That I could work with him for so long and not know that?'

'Don't think he likes to talk about it much. I reckon that's what fucked him up, though.'

'You think so?'

'Oh yeah,' said Candy cheerily, opening the door of the bus. 'I mean, *some*thing had to fuck him up, didn't it. Otherwise no one would pay Philip twenty grand to look after him.'

They walked slowly up to BabyCakes. It didn't feel like the early hours of a Thursday morning; more like a Sunday afternoon. You could hardly move for the bustle of people down Old Compton Street. Every single one of the pavement tables was taken by people drinking coffee and eating cake. Cake, at this time of night. Joyce, however, was too preoccupied with thinking about Riley. She felt guilty for having dismissed him all along as a drunken, belligerent idiot, without pausing for a second to consider *why* he might be like this. Was she cut out for this job? Was she really? She picked her way through the crowds without taking in that they were there. At the door of BabyCakes Candy brushed away enquiries about her bruises and breezed them both in without paying.

Inside, all Joyce's empathetic thoughts about Riley were driven away instantly by the campness of the place she now found herself in and the sheer, relentless strangeness of the other people in it.

Beaming proudly, Candy showed her to an empty table and ordered up a couple of sea breezes. Joyce was wide-eyed and lost; she had to be led by the hand to the table.

'So what do you think?' Candy asked.

It was a stupid question. Joyce had no frame of reference within which to form an opinion. She shrugged her shoulders. 'I have no idea what I think,' she said.

'Thank you for coming with me,' Candy said seriously. 'I needed to come here . . . I can't explain why, but I did.'

'Thank you too,' said Joyce. 'I needed the company.'

They held hands across the table, the two people who needed each other.

And Joyce did very well. Considering she didn't exactly have extensive experience of walking on the wild side, she coped admirably. Her eyebrows didn't truly hit the ceiling until about twenty minutes after they had got there, when the lights went down and Dolly strode on to the stage in her formidable evening wear for the second half of the cabaret and bellowed into the microphone in her sharp, sarcastic voice: 'Welcome back, fistfuckers!' *Then* Joyce let out a little shriek and turned to Candy and breathed, 'Oh my lord!'

Candy giggled hysterically. She felt right at home.

Riley

We were clinging to each other, Irene, as we fell. Clinging and screaming . . .

Usually the worst part of an exercise jump like this is the flight: three hours of flying at two hundred feet in a hot, airless, semi-lit Hercules crammed full of sixty other greening Paras is enough to loosen the hardest stomach. And once one bloke lets fly, it starts off a chain reaction. Soon all you can see is helmets buried in puke bags, all you can hear above the engines is sloshing and groaning. So we were all pretty relieved when we felt the plane pull up to eight hundred, signalling that we were about to jump. We finished the final safety checks and the side doors of the plane were opened up. The red for ready light came on. We lined ourselves up in two rows, bumping into each other with our bergens as we did so. Always at this point I'd be desperate to get out of the plane, desperate to leave the close, sicky atmosphere of the Hercules and feel the cold rush of the wind on my face. I'd ignore the banter and the come-ons going on around me and fix on that red light, willing it go green, *willing* it to go green ...

Green. The first man in each stick got a tap on the shoulder and we started tumbling out, using both sides of the plane alternately. Andy and I saw we were partnered as we shuffled up the line, his stick jumping just ahead of mine. I think he may have given me a wink, I wasn't really looking at him, only out of the corner of my eye. I was staring at that green light, psyching myself up – go, go, go! Green, green, green! I made the front of the line, got a hearty slap from the despatcher and leaped into the void, embracing the air as I jumped.

It was obvious immediately that there'd been a cock-up: Andy and I had gone at exactly the same time. The slipstream pulled us both underneath the belly of the Hercules. I could see him coming flying towards me, both of us shouting what the fuck ... So as soon as I was clear of the plane I pulled my chute open. Far too early – this was supposed to be a low-open descent, practising for that magical day when we'd be called upon to drop undetected deep into enemy territory and fight our own secret war. But fuck it, there'd been a cock-up, it was only an exercise, safety was the main consideration. I reckoned that if I could get my chute open before Andy and me collided, either he could pin me and we could both fall with my chute, or it would give him plenty of time to pull well clear of me before he opened up his own. So I pulled the handle and waited for the comforting jerk as the canopy inflated. It never came. The lines flew out of my pack and extended fully, but the bastard never inflated. The slider had got jammed at the top of the lines and the fucking canopy was just hanging there uselessly like a limp fart. I looked up at it in disgust. This was the first time this had ever happened to me, but it was a fairly common occurrence. We'd been told about it in training. I knew enough about it to know there was no way back. The only thing to do was to cut away the main canopy and use the reserve chute. The act of cutting away automatically triggered the reserve and I got a tiny, brief moment of relief as I felt it flutter out above me. Then I remembered Andy. During all of this – a few seconds at most – I'd forgotten all about Andy and that he was flying towards me and the importance of not getting our chutes entwined. As my reserve flew out above me, however, I suddenly noticed the bastard was practically on top of me. His face was right in front of mine, as though he was asking me outside, and his eyes were blank with terror. He was close enough that I could see how scared he was (and he was fucking scared). He'd also activated his chute. I looked up, over my shoulder. He'd also activated his *reserve* chute: his main had failed too. Like me, he'd been so overcome by calm, reasoned panic at the failure of his main chute that he'd forgotten to check if it was safe to cut away, and now our two reserves were wrapping themselves around each other like a couple of teenagers at a school disco.

I'm embarrassed to admit that at this point I started looking for alternatives. You've seen that James Bond film where he falls out of a plane, has a couple of fights, snogs the girl and nicks a chute off the baddie before hitting the ground, right? Well, I was thinking of something along those lines. There were sixty other men in the sky. One of them had to be able to help us out. Andy, however, the more experienced jumper, knew the game was up. And I knew it too as soon as I looked back into his eyes.

And we *clung* as we fell. Andy grabbed my elbow so hard I could feel the bone squeezing.

Basically one of three things happened. Apart from the Lottery-like coincidence of both our main chutes failing, one of three things had led this to being the tragedy it was. The two sticks were supposed to go out one second apart, one second between each man, to avoid just this happening. It's a simple and natural thing, you get into a rhythm as you shuffle forward – go, go, go. It's the second between the gos, that's the second which guarantees you your own pocket of personal air space. It can't be more than a second because you've got to get sixty men out over the same drop zone. But a second's long enough.

Me and Andy, though, we went out at exactly the same time, which put us on a collision course the whole way down. So: *either* the despatchers lost their rhythm, lost their synch, put us both out together; *or* Andy jumped too late, had some split-second hesitation (on something like his two hundredth jump) as he stood in the door.

Or I jumped too early. It was like a road accident; there had to be a victim and a perpetrator. Even if we were both at fault, one of us had to be more at fault than the other. One of us was a stupid berk, and the other was merely the innocent victim of a stupid berk, about to pay for it with his life.

Of course the immediate assumption is that it was me; I was to blame. Fair enough. I can understand that. If you're looking for the berk in any given situation, you often don't need to look any further than me. And I hold my hands up: I honestly couldn't tell you exactly what happened. It all went by in a blur, like the rushing of the wind in our ears as we fell. It could easily have been my fault. After all, Andy was the more experienced jumper.

But maybe, just maybe, it wasn't me. Maybe it was Andy who went early, maybe he *knew* that this was his fault and that explains what he did.

What he did was this: about two hundred feet from the ground, with the earth speeding towards us, he suddenly flips himself underneath me and puts his hands around my neck, holding on just as tight as before. We've fallen the whole way horizontally, head to head. Now he's underneath me, gazing up into my eyes with . . . whatever it was, I've never seen that look on anyone before or since. Horror . . . Pity . . . I don't know – the look a man gives you when you're both just about to smash into the ground at eighty miles an hour. When you suddenly realise you're going to die in about two seconds' time and you're trying to work out what you're going to think about for the last two seconds of your short and sorry-arse life. We've all got to go sometime, was what I ended up thinking. We've all got to go sometime. Then I remembered Gibbsy and his stupid pranks and what me and Andy had said to each other on Longdon: life's too short to worry, Riley. And that was the thought in my head as we hit the ground. Life's too short. Too bloody short by half. When we landed Andy was killed instantly, but his shattered bones provided me, just, with enough cushion to survive.

Survive and fall in love with you, Irene, and lose you and find you and lose you again to your cancer, and to end up here in the house next to yours in St Omer, watching your friend Natalie as she sleeps, thinking of you. I've Andy to thank for this. I don't ever forget it.

You see, I have to hold on to this notion that Andy acted out of guilt, because otherwise what does that leave me with? If it was *my* fault we jumped at the same time, that means Andy gave me his life to save me from my own stupidity. How could I possibly carry on if I thought that was the case? Because I can't escape the fact that it could have been me that saved him. Either one of us could have slipped underneath to save the other's life and *it could have been me*. I'm ashamed that I never had the presence of mind to do it first. I'm ashamed to admit that we could have fallen all the way from fucking Jupiter and it would never have occurred to me to do that.

The other thing I managed to do during our time-frozen plunge was, amazingly, to find the whole thing a giggle. It was funny. I have this on good authority. Steele told me later, when they finally broke me and Andy apart, I had a bloody great big grin all over my face. I suppose I was laughing at how stupid the situation was – how me and Andy could survive a whole war together and then go down to a freak accident like this. But also I think I was laughing because I thought it was the macho, Para thing to do. I tried to see the funny side because I wanted to save face, probably because I was *embarrassed* at having fucked up in the first place. Can you believe that? When they picked me up off the burst body of my dead friend, *I tried to make a joke out of it.*

Private Steele was the first one to reach me. 'Fucking hell, Riley,' he goes, 'are you OK?'

For a moment I couldn't think of anything clever to reply to this. At first I thought of saying that it was just our way of getting out of the tab ahead. This was the start of an extended exercise, several days living on the land. Our back-breaking bergens, which we'd jettisoned just before impact, contained our provisions, stoves, bivvy bags and what have you. A few hundred yards away they were dropping in radios, machine-gun tripods, ammo – and we were going to have to lug this gear, at speed, to the first rendezvous five miles from the drop zone. So I was going to say, yeah, me and Andy couldn't face another cold, wet tab in the dark. Fancied a warm night in a hospital bed instead.

Then I had a better idea. I remembered the trainasium at Brize Norton. I remembered McKenzie, the hard bastard who used to take us on it, and I remembered his catch phrase. It seemed the perfect thing to say in my situation – casual, funny and appropriate. It's a much-admired quality in the Paras, a sharp sense of humour; you don't last long without one.

So I turn my broken head up towards Private Steele, taking in his shocked, concerned expression, knowing he's going to appreciate the joke, and I tell him – and I swear on my mother's life this is the truth – I say with a big, broad grin all over my stupid face: 'Yeah, mate. Don't worry about falling off – the ground will always stop you.'

Acknowledgments

Special thanks to Michelle Shocked for allowing me to quote from her song. Thanks also to the following for permission to quote from copyright material: 'Goodnight Irene' written by Huddie Ledbetter and Alan Lomax © 1936 (renewed 1964) and 1950 Ludlow Music Inc., New York, USA. Assigned to TRO Essex Music Ltd, London, SW10 0SZ. International Copyright Secured. All rights reserved. Used by permission; 'If You Go Away (Ne Me Quitte Pas)' words and music by Jacques Brel, English lyric by Rod McKuen © 1975 Warner/Chappell Music Ltd, London W6 8BS. Reproduced by permission of International Music Publications Ltd, UK. While every effort has been made to contact copyright-holders, if an acknowledgment has been overlooked please contact the publishers.

Two sources were particularly helpful on 3 Para's escapades in the Malvinas: *Green-Eyed Boys* by Christian Jennings and Adrian Weale and *Excursion to Hell* by Vincent Bramley, both of which provided me with exciting new words for my vocabulary.

Finally, thanks once again to Sarah, Dinah and all at Sceptre, without whom etc.